SHOOT THE MOON

First Edition
First Printing, 2018

Book design by Sarah Winkler
Cover design by Sarah Winkler
Cover images by Ostill/iStockphoto; marcduf/iStockphoto

Flux, an imprint of North Star Editions, Inc.

Library of Congress Cataloging-in-Publication Data (Pending)
978-1-63583-014-9

Flux
North Star Editions, Inc.
2297 Waters Drive
Mendota Heights, MN 55120
www.fluxnow.com

Printed in the United States of America

To Jeff: the Walter to my Paige; the Dice to my Billie; the Ozone to my Kelly; the Papa Justify to my . . .

You get the picture.

SHOOT THE MOON

KATE WATSON

Mendota Heights, Minnesota

CHAPTER ONE

Tate Bertram was an addict.

At least he'd told the room as much twenty minutes ago. His sponsor, Nia, had nudged him for the tenth time in an hour. She was always encouraging him to "share" and "be vulnerable" and a bunch of other things he didn't particularly care about. Because, as much as he had no problem saying it to appease Nia or his dad, Tate was *not* an addict.

Over the last few months, he'd heard everyone in the room go on and on about chasing that high, about what had happened the last time they felt the grooves of a chip beneath their thumbnail or how they'd lost everything the last time they'd walked into a casino. Tate wasn't like them. He wasn't filled with these pitiful regrets, because he wasn't an addict.

But if he was, this whole meeting would be one big, fat trigger.

He put a hand in the pocket of his charcoal pea coat, pushing past the thirty-day chip Nia had given him earlier to get to the small deck of cards he always kept with him. The feeling of the cards—worn well beyond any practical use—calmed him. He purposefully avoided looking at Nia. She had a shrewdness that came not only from her extensive gambling history but also from her being a detective with Chicago's Bureau of Organized Crime. If anyone could pick up on his tells, she was the one.

Fortunately, her phone vibrated before that could happen. She quickly silenced it, but Tate knew something must be going on for her to have her phone on at all. That was a major faux pas at GA, and Nia was nothing if not dedicated to the program.

He watched her face out of the corner of his eye. It was so slight, her reaction to whatever had appeared on her screen. Most people would altogether miss the slight tensing around her brown eyes when she blinked. If she'd been on her guard, she never would have let that slip. But, then, she'd been out of the game for too long.

"Something wrong, Detective Tafolo?" Tate muttered to her while a sketchy old guy with more ear hair than head hair rambled on about dog racing at the front of the room.

Nia snapped to attention, her poker face in perfect form. "Nothing. Why do you ask?"

"Your phone is on, which was my first clue—and it was your work phone, which already makes it painfully dull. But my second clue was that you did the thing with your eyes, you know, where you blink a bit too hard? Gives you away every time."

She didn't do the thing with her eyes now. "Tate," she said, her voice low, "one of these days, you'll realize that you can't get better until you stop treating every interaction like it's a play in some long con—"

"I'm not a grifter."

"And I'm not your mark. I'm your sponsor."

"Yeah, yeah. And you're a great sponsor. Dogged. Relentless. Determined. Synonyms." He stretched his arms out, then clasped his hands behind his head with a rakish grin. "But that doesn't mean I'm wrong."

He got no response, which was all the response he needed. When Nia slipped out of the room a few minutes later, he wasn't surprised. After another ten minutes of studiously not paying attention to the meeting, though, Tate felt listless. Nia still wasn't back, and keeping her on her toes was the only real point in coming. Without her there, monitoring his every move? Bo-ring. He didn't think he could take another minute of people bemoaning their addiction, whining about how gambling had ruined them when they so obviously—so desperately—missed it.

His hand found its way back to his pocket, his thumb running over the tattered cards.

Screw this.

He stood and looked around the room. Faces turned to his expectantly, and Tate realized there was a break in speakers. They thought he was going back up, didn't they? They wanted more from the guy who'd been impaled on a curtain rod trying to escape a debt (details Nia had as much as blackmailed him into sharing). Hell, maybe he should show them the scar that had turned his six-pack into seven.

Now *that* would be fun. And because this was an open meeting, Nia wasn't the only girl here tonight. In fact, there was one with smoky eyes he definitely wouldn't mind comparing scars with if he could make it till the end of the meeting.

But then he'd have to stay till the end of the meeting . . .

Nah.

"Well," he said to everyone and no one, "this was real."

He walked out of the room.

Whispers and a few grumbles scored his departure. He smiled, even as he realized he wasn't getting that girl's number now. *You win some, you lose some,* he thought as he waited for the elevator. He took it to the ground floor, ignoring the vast and disapproving sanctuary on his way out of the famed Chicago Temple building.

In the bustling, brisk evening air, he breathed a little easier. He ran a hand through his blond hair and buttoned up his pea coat while he walked. The smell of exhaust and humanity filled his lungs. People crowded the downtown streets, heading to and from restaurants and shops and plays. Skyscrapers towered over him. Theater lights winked at him. Beautiful girls smiled at him.

This was more like it.

On his way to the subway station, a flashing sign in a convenience store window caught his eye. The Powerball was up to $564 million, and the meeting had left him impulsive, itching for something. He hadn't played poker for thirty days . . . thirty painfully dull days. But did Nia believe that he didn't have a problem? Of course not. And that was nothing compared with his family. He could go a lifetime without even saying the word "poker" and his family wouldn't believe him.

He needed a scratch-off.

A bell announced his entry into the store. He never got the lottery tickets right away—it felt obsessive to care that much about something as stupid as scratching silver flecks off a piece of paper. Instead, he wandered the few small aisles, walking past pockets of teenagers and the odd patron until he reached the drink machines. As he poured himself a Slurpee, he looked up in time to see a sloppy, box-faced man in a winter hat eyeing the vodka in the refrigerator from beneath his heavy brow. The man looked left and right, then slid a bottle into an inner pocket of his oversized jacket.

He looked familiar. The old dog-racing-obsessed guy from GA, maybe? No, even hunched down, this guy was bigger than the bald, squirrely dude from the meeting. Besides, the man in front of him was also already drunk, something no one from GA could have managed in the five minutes since Tate had left the meeting.

Not that he cared. He jammed a straw in his drink and went over to the counter, where he dropped a ten-dollar bill to pay.

"Will that be all?" the clerk asked.

Tate spotted the drunk trying—and failing—to make his way to the door inconspicuously. *Dude.* Something like pity rooted in his chest. Gesturing to the clerk to keep the change, Tate took two steps toward the door and pushed it open. When the bell dinged, he kept the door cracked open with his foot. Then he swiveled his head back to the clerk, and told her, "Actually, I'll take a Powerball ticket, too—quick pick. And a couple of Triple Plays."

The clerk didn't bother asking for I.D., sparing Tate the trouble of pulling it out of his pocket. He had only his fake I.D. on him, but even without it, he was almost twenty, which was old enough to buy a lottery ticket. And he'd lived enough to make him look older, anyway. The clerk turned her back to Tate, who caught the drunk guy's attention and nodded toward the door. Tate opened the door wider to let the middle-aged man duck under his arm unnoticed. When the clerk faced Tate, she was none the wiser. Tate took his foot from the doorjamb and grabbed the tickets and his change. Then he headed out into the night with his Slurpee and lottery tickets.

Where he promptly bumped in to Finley Price.

"Fin?" he asked at the same time that she said, "Tate?"

He slipped the tickets into his back pocket while the girl's deep brown eyes crossed to look at a spot of Mountain Dew slush on her nose. "Did you just spill Slurpee on my face?"

"It's your fault for being so short," he said, chuckling as she swiped a finger across her nose and sniffed at it.

"Oh hush, you giant Ken Doll." She took the Slurpee from his hand and took a long drink. "You're lucky it's Mountain Dew."

He grinned at her. It had been months since he'd seen Fin, and she was prettier than ever. "Lucky? What were you going to do if it was fruit punch?"

She cocked her head at him, her long black waves tumbling to the side of her face. "Duh. I'd give you the beats."

"Very threatening," he assured her, taking back his Slurpee. "So what are you doing in Downtown on a Thursday night, anyway? Don't you have school tomorrow?"

She pointed at a group of high schoolers inside the convenience store. The two girls from her group giggled when Tate looked at them. "Theater outing for extra credit, but tomorrow is the start of spring break."

"You running the theater department yet?"

A flush rose to her naturally tan cheeks. Her theater talent was as much nurture as nature. She was the daughter of a famous actor and had been practically raised on a soundstage. After her dad died and her mom went off the deep end a few years ago, Fin and her brother had moved in with Tate's family. In the last year, she'd come into her own. Found herself. And now she was a director with Chicago's most prestigious youth theater company.

"I'm not running anything," she said.

"That's not what my mom says."

She lifted her eyes to his. "You've been talking to your mom?"

He swept a lock of hair from her face, tucking it behind her ear. His fingers warmed where they touched her cheek, and he let his hand linger there. "Of course I'm talking to her. I'm not a monster; I'm in college."

He could see Finley's B.S. meter flashing. "Yeah, so is your brother, but that doesn't keep him from coming home."

Tate dropped his hand, balling it into a fist against his leg. "Oliver is a freshman—"

"Cut the crap, Tate. You haven't been home since Christmas, and I know you haven't spoken to your dad or Ollie in that entire time."

"Ah, Oliver. How is my insufferable little brother, anyway? Still saving the world, whether it wants it or not?"

Her gaze flitted past him. "He's good, just really busy. He's taking a ton of credits and heading up a volunteer group on campus and planning another trip to Guatemala this summer to build an orphanage, so . . ."

He studied her face. "So all that time being a do-gooder means he doesn't have much time for you anymore."

She swatted his chest a bit too hard to be playful. "Stop trying to read me. You know I'll tell you anything you want to know."

"But where's the fun in that?"

"Tate—"

"Okay. Why are you still dating him when he puts everything else in his life ahead of you?"

She drew a big breath and exhaled. Tate hadn't realized how cold it was until he saw a hint of purple in her pursed lips. "I'm not."

With that, she took three steps to the door of the convenience store, opened it, and said something to the group inside. Her friends waved at her, and Tate noticed one of the guys frown. He bit back a grin.

"What's the deal?" Tate asked Finley.

"You're taking me home."

Suck it, Oliver.

Finley linked her arm in his, as she'd done countless times in the years since she'd lived with his family. She was two years younger than him and had, up until last year, been painfully shy and walled off, a consequence of living with an alcoholic mother. Tate had never let Finley's walls get in the way, though. He'd flirted, flattered, and teased her to such an absurd degree she couldn't take him seriously. Which meant in a world where everything scared her, he never had. If they weren't best friends like she and Oliver were, it was still something. It still mattered.

One night last year, though, something had changed—*she'd* changed—and they'd shared a moment. He wondered if she was thinking about it right now.

As they approached a construction project up ahead, they walked beneath a temporary sidewalk parapet. On the ground a few yards away, Tate spotted the same man from a few minutes ago: he was slumped against the wall of a building, his bottle already half empty. The sight made the tickets in Tate's pocket feel like lead. He didn't care that he'd helped the man shoplift—he didn't even care that the guy was a good four sheets to the wind—but with Finley on his arm, he hated that he'd bought those stupid scratch-offs.

"Hold up," he told Fin, putting a hand in his back pocket. He'd stashed the tickets there with a twenty he kept on hand for cabs. He pulled the stack out, deftly slipping the tickets into the middle of the twenty, and dropped it in the man's lap.

The man opened the bill and glanced up. The scaffolding above them obscured his features, but the ambient light was enough to reflect his eyes when they met Tate's. The man visibly started. So, Tate wasn't imagining it—the man recognized him, too, though it didn't matter. They weren't exactly in a place to debate whether they knew each other from the rehab or the not-so-anonymous meetings their families forced them to attend.

"Good luck, buddy," Tate said, and kept walking.

"That was nice of you," Finley said. "Was it for my benefit?"

He chuckled. "Wow, getting a little full of yourself, aren't you? First, you have decidedly not been pining for me, what with you being hotter than ever. And now, to accuse me of trying to impress you? Can't a guy just do something nice for someone?"

"A *guy* can . . ."

"You wound me," he said, putting his hand strategically over his right side.

Finley placed a gentle hand over his. She remembered where his scar was. "How . . . how are you? Have you had any problems since—"

The concern in her voice struck something deep inside of him. "None at all, Fin. I'm fine."

She was still looking at his side, concern tightening her eyes. She had sacrificed to take care of him, spent long hours waiting on him and doting on him and teasing him exactly when he'd needed it most. He didn't take that lightly.

Of course, once he'd started recuperating, Oliver had scheduled his intervention. Finley had sat by Tate for hours, holding his hand, while his family . . . intervened.

So even though it pained him to say it, he did for her: "I'm sorry about you and Oliver."

"Thanks," she said, her voice not shaking as he'd thought it would. "He's still my best friend, and we've agreed to a completely drama-free breakup, for your parents' sake as much as our own. "

Finley was shivering when they reached the station, so Tate had her huddle close while they waited for the Red Line.

"It's friggin' April. Why is it still so cold?"

"Come here, you little baby," he said, wrapping his coat around her and resting his chin on her head. "When did you get so soft?"

She pinched his abs. "When did you, Stay Puft?"

He squeezed her side, and she squealed. "Do you really want to do this right now?" He tickled her again. "I own you, munchkin."

"Stop!" Her already high voice was practically squeaking. "Tate, I will murder you in your own bed!"

A dozen horrified faces glared at them. Tate stopped tickling but didn't drop his hands from her waist.

"How dare you make a joke like that," an older woman said, eyeing Finley's dark features suspiciously.

Finley's cheeks burned, but that didn't stop her from scowling at Tate and muttering, "It wasn't a joke. It was a promise."

"It's true," Tate told the woman with a wink. "She's a killer in the sack."

Finley gasped, and Tate wrapped her more tightly in his jacket. She buried her face in his chest, laughing uncontrollably while the woman grumbled.

When they boarded, the woman was nowhere to be seen, no doubt having chosen a car devoid of teenage hooligans. They dropped to a bench, and Finley's chuckle faded into a sigh.

"You thinking about that woman racially profiling you?" he asked. "Half Brazilian, half Irish, all trouble?"

Her eyebrows raised, as if she was surprised by his observation. "Uh, no, actually. This isn't my first rodeo."

"Wait, there's a rodeo?"

She elbowed his side. "I've missed you, Tate. I wish you'd come home."

He took her hands and warmed them between his. "Maybe I will."

CHAPTER TWO

It was barely 10:30 p.m. when they reached Mansfield Square. Tate and Fin walked the quiet sidewalk, and everything looked so peaceful, particularly compared with the action he'd find when he got to Zach's apartment. Running an illegal card room out of his friend's place may not have been Tate's most relaxing idea ever, but it paid the bills. Besides, he liked watching rich kids do stupid things with their money.

Well, *other* rich kids . . .

He made a mental note to text Karla. She could handle things without him, but she was also pretty sure that one of their dealers was skimming. He'd promised to keep an extra eye on things tonight, so he had to get back soon.

But not before saying goodnight.

They reached the stairs, and he walked Fin up to the front door. "Well, this is where I stop."

"Aren't you going to come inside?" Fin asked.

"First date and you're already inviting me in? I like your style."

"You're incorrigible."

He bumped her arm with his. "You like it."

"And you still didn't answer my question. Are you coming home or not?"

"When did you get so tenacious?"

"Can you stop messing around and just talk to me?" Her dark eyes bore into him, reading him in a way only one other girl ever had. He wasn't thinking about her tonight, though. Fin was enough.

Tate ran a hand through his blond hair before returning it to his pocket. "Come on, Fin. Oliver's convinced everyone I'm an irredeemable mess. My parents are disappointed in me, to put it mildly, and ever since I got out of rehab, my dad insists that I go to Gambler's Anonymous meetings, which sort of takes the 'anonymous' out of the equation. You're the only good thing about home these days. You're one of the only points of light in my otherwise dreary world. Is that what you want to hear?"

She grabbed his coat pocket, and for a moment, he was worried she'd reach in and feel the deck of cards—two worlds he definitely didn't want colliding. Instead, she tugged on the jacket. "Enough of the meaningless flattery, okay? I know why you do it, but I'm too old for it now. It . . . does things to my head."

He raised an eyebrow. "Does it?"

She was too flushed from the cold for her embarrassment to register, but he could feel it roll off her in waves. Adorable waves. "Oh, like you didn't know. What tween girl hasn't had a crush on her best friend's hot older brother?"

"Hot? And we've escalated from head games to a crush? Tell me more."

"I said 'tween girl.' Not anymore, obviously."

"Except for the things I do to your head." He grabbed the hand that was still holding on to his pocket. It was freezing, and he wanted to warm it. Wanted to warm up her nose and cheeks and—

"Grabbing my hand isn't exactly helping," she said.

He threaded his fingers through hers. "What if it isn't meaningless? The flattery and flirtation?"

She wrinkled her nose. "Don't do this, Tate."

"I know you remember last year," he pressed. "After the play."

Her eyes narrowed. Oh, yes. She remembered, all right. "You were drunk."

"You've seen me drunk. I was barely buzzed."

"I thought you were joking."

"You know me better than that, Fin."

"Why didn't you ever mention it again?"

"You were sixteen, and I was in college. I didn't want to make you uncomfortable."

"You're still in college, and I'm only seventeen now."

"Eighteen in June . . ."

She pulled her hand free and locked her eyes on his. "What are you doing here? Are you trying to get back at Oliver, or are you just playing around with me? Either way, I thought I mattered more to you than that."

He'd begun to forget the cold entirely, but now it swirled around him, biting his skin beneath his clothes. What *was* he doing? Was this about Oliver? Was it about how antsy he'd been after the meeting?

Or was this a continuation of that night last year? When she'd thought he'd needed her and had come running, ignoring everyone else, even Oliver. When he'd whispered into her ear . . .

"Last year, that night, I meant every word. When I said that you're the type of girl who could save a guy, I was talking about me."

She hugged a hand across her chest, grabbing her shoulder. Clutching her scars—both the literal and figurative ones. "That's not how it works, Tate. You can't wait for someone else to save you—"

"If it's you, I can."

Her breath hitched, and his own started coming more quickly. He put a hand under her chin and tilted her face up toward his. He came closer. Her breath puffed between them.

"Don't do this if you don't mean it," she whispered, even as her eyes closed.

"I mean it." He leaned down.

The door flew open.

"That's long enough, you—" His dad stopped, sputtering. "Tate? What are you doing home? Finley?"

Finley had rocked backward, so Tate leaned close again and brushed a finger softly against the corner of her eye. "There, got it," he said, before looking at his dad. "She had an eyelash in her eye. I was getting it out."

She smiled coyly at him before sneaking beneath his dad's arm and walking into the warm house. Tate stayed outside, jamming his hands in his pockets. "Ran into Fin downtown after my meeting. Thought I'd bring her home."

His dad's brow crinkled, his disapproval obvious. "Don't you have class tomorrow? Shouldn't you be getting home?"

Tate gave him a wry smile. "I thought this *was* home."

"You know that's not what I meant," his dad said, running a hand through hair that had grown more salt than pepper of late. "I'm glad to see you—"

"But I have class tomorrow. And heaven forbid this be the quarter that I finally bring home a GPA that doesn't start with four."

His dad frowned.

Tate shook his head. "It's okay." He looked past his dad down the long hallway to the kitchen, where Fin was. "I was making sure Fin got home safely."

"I would think her date could have done that, but I appreciate that you were watching out for her."

Date? Finley had been on a date? Oh, this more than made up for the awkwardness of talking to his dad.

He squeezed his dad's shoulder. "Well, Pops, give my best to Finley and Mom. I need to get back home if I'm going to make it to Advanced Pet Costuming tomorrow morning. We're making curtain dresses for schnauzers. As if they have the waist for them!"

He was already walking down the stairs when his dad's words stopped him. "Why don't you come back home tomorrow after class? Your mother and Finley miss you." He cleared his throat. "I miss you, son."

The words gripped his chest. He turned his head back around. "Thanks, Dad. I'll see if I can make it."

In the cab on the way to his apartment, Tate shot a quick text off to Karla before texting Finley about her date.

I wasn't on a date! There were seven of us!

It's cool. It explains why that kid in 7-11 wanted to shoot me with mind bullets.

Laugh it up, pal.

Oh, I am.

Are you coming home this weekend?

He smiled. Only if you promise we can finish that conversation my dad so rudely interrupted.

Three little dots appeared on his phone. Then disappeared. Then appeared again. Only if you stay the weekend.

First you invite me in, then you ask me to stay the weekend? Sold.

I'm ignoring the first part and only saying GOOD to the second part. See you tomorrow. :-)

When the cab pulled up to Hyde Park Luxury Apartments, Tate handed the driver a couple of bills before stepping out into the chilly air. A few moments later, he was passing through the glass door and into the building. The front desk attendant, a tall, skinny law student, greeted him with a smile.

"Mr. Bertram. Good to see you."

"You too, Johnny."

"Big study group tonight," Johnny said as Tate put an elbow on the spacious desk.

"The bigger the better. Did anyone look lost?"

"Nah. A couple kids looked like freshmen who'd wandered into advanced physics by mistake, though."

Tate grimaced. "I'll have to loosen them up. Freshmen are only okay if they're hungry to prove they're smarter than everyone."

Johnny snorted. "Good luck with that."

Tate and Johnny slapped hands, and Johnny pocketed the bills Tate had slipped him. "Let me know if anyone shows up who isn't in my class, will you?"

"Always," Johnny said. "Have a good night, Mr. Bertram."

Tate took the elevator to the sixth floor and headed down the hallway to his friend's apartment. He looked up at the small camera he'd installed months earlier. A moment later, his security guy, whom Tate called Danno, was opening the door. He was still wearing his campus security uniform, something Tate had repeatedly told him he didn't need to do. But the burly kid insisted it made him look more official. Who was Tate to argue?

The sound of someone playing with chips was the first thing Tate heard as he hung up his jacket in the entry closet. He breathed in deeply, as if he could absorb that sound. He was smiling as he walked into the living room, where two tables of eight were playing poker. TVs were set up in opposite corners of the large room, a baseball game on one screen and a basketball game on the other. There was little conversation—the sound of someone calling, one of the players flirting with the dealer on break, the hum of a game—but it was music to his ears.

He'd promised Nia and his parents that he'd stop playing poker, and he had. He'd promised his dad that he'd pay him back for taking care of his gambling debt last year, and he had. That was why he'd started the card room in the first place. He kept it going now because it was a way to make money. A job, something his dad had always said he needed. And if being here was a little like a contact high, even better. Instead of making him itch with the desire to play, it soothed him, at least partly because he was so much better than the competition. He liked to win, not to embarrass fools.

Karla was running chips. She'd been his brush for two months, and she'd taken to the job well. She had a knack for appeasing players and balancing tables, not to mention her exactness with the money. When she and Tate made eye contact, she flicked her hazel eyes toward the dealer she thought was skimming. Tate nodded and walked over to the table.

The dealer, Cat, had been working there for only a few weeks. She was beautiful, like his other dealers, if too blonde for his tastes. He studied her table. Three players were still in the game—Charlie Brown, Smokey the Bear, and Miami Jill. Aliases were mandatory, even though every player had to be vouched for personally by a dealer, Karla, or Tate. A lot of players knew each other from campus, but while they were here, they stuck to their nicknames. Extra security in case someone managed to sneak a recording device past the security guard.

Poker was a simple game: to win, a player needed to make the best five-card hand possible using a combination of the two hole cards he or she had been dealt and the five board cards that had been dealt faceup on the table.

It was fun watching amateurs try to complicate things.

With the king on the board and a pair of kings in the hole, Charlie Brown had a set. It was a good hand, but even if the guy'd been sitting on Four Horseman and his competition had rags, he wouldn't last. His eyes were all over the board, over his competition, over his own cards. He was going to fold at the last minute as he always did.

The flop—the first three board cards—sat faceup on the table, and Cat was dealing the fourth card now. The turn gave Smokey a full house. A monster hand. The odds of Miami getting the five of spades she needed for a straight flush were . . . he did the math in

his head . . . two percent, give or take. Nothing. The smart move
was to fold.

Yet Miami was betting. He watched her throw her chips into the
pot, then watched Charlie Brown fold. No surprise. After a small hes-
itation, Smokey called, matching Miami's raise. She rerose, pushing
a small stack of chips into the middle of the table, drawing Smokey
out. He called again.

The girl was playing him like a pro, despite her mediocre hand.
He'd seen her play enough over the last few weeks to know that she
was never this aggressive unless she had an unbeatable hand—the
absolute nuts.

Which she didn't.

Yet when Cat flipped over the fifth and final board card, there
it was.

The five of spades.

Tate pulled Karla into the kitchen.

"What's the story?" she asked quietly.

"How's Miami been playing lately?"

Karla flipped through a notebook while Tate kept an eye on the
tables. "Good. She must be playing online at night, or something,
because she's getting better. She's had a couple of monster nights."

"Who's she been up against? Anyone good?"

Karla paused. "Yeah. Donkey. Ash. And you can see she's already
up on Smokey."

"They're cheating."

"What? Who?"

"Miami and Cat. Smokey had the nuts on the turn, and Miami
reraised on him before beating him on the river with a backdoor
steel wheel."

Karla whistled. "That's badass, but that doesn't mean she's in
on anything."

"It does when Cat's culling. She dealt from the bottom."

"Are you serious?" Karla swore. "I brought her in. This is my fault."

"It's not your fault. It's Cat's fault. She's the one screwing us over. Unless you're telling me you're in on it with her?"

She rolled her eyes. "Of course not. I make as much in three nights here as I did in a month catering. I'm not stupid enough to jeopardize this." She chewed on her lower lip. "What do we do?"

"When are the dealers switching?"

"Five minutes."

"Miami's cashing out now. I'm about to deliver her some urgent news."

"Okay. What do you want me to do?"

"Grab Danno and get Cat the hell away from my game."

CHAPTER THREE

Two minutes later, Miami Jill was cashing out in a rush while Cat flashed her anxious looks. Tate followed the first girl from the apartment, grabbing an apple on his way out. Miami was pacing during the elevator ride downstairs, texting furiously. Tate started on his apple.

When they reached the lobby and stepped out of the elevator, the girl's phone chimed. A moment later, she spun on Tate. "What the hell, man? Why'd you pull me from the game? You said my roommate was in the ER, but she just sent me a bunch of pics from a party off campus! What are you playing at?"

Tate held a finger up, taking another bite while he watched the numbers above the opposite elevator tick down. "I'm sorry, but this is one of the best apples I've had in a long time. What kind is it, do you think? Gala? Ambrosia, maybe?" A moment later, the doors opened, and Danno escorted Cat out.

Cat and Miami reddened and avoided looking at each other. "What's going on here?" Cat asked, rotten with guilt.

"You're done, both of you," Tate said, examining the apple for his next bite. "And in about five minutes, your pictures will be up on every poker forum in the city."

"What?"

"You're bluffing. You wouldn't!"

"Haven't you heard my reputation by now? They say I never

bluff. Do you really want to test that?" He bit into the apple again, the crunch magnified by the lobby's marble floors. "And before you get any vindictive ideas, if either of you breathe a word of this game or this apartment, I release tapes of you two playing to the police, blurring out the other faces to protect the innocent, of course." Cat looked as if she wanted to claw his eyes out. "Miami, you're lucky I'm not taking everything you made tonight." Then, to Cat, he said, "Of course, everything you made tonight is mine. I'm sure you can understand."

Cat's voice rose. "You're being a fool. I *made you money.*"

"No, you stole money from our customers. And, if I'm not mistaken, me."

"No, Tate, listen: I gave them good cards, which drove up bets, which means the rake was that much higher every time! I was helping you!"

"You were helping your accomplice," he said. Miami looked away. "And you're both out." He walked over to Johnny, who was already rounding the desk. "It turns out these two were enrolled in the wrong class."

"Got it," Johnny said.

Tate looked at Danno. "Remind me to ask Karla to stock more of these apples. They're spectacular." Danno nodded, standing at attention. Tate cocked his head. "Go, Danno. Earn your keep, for Pete's sake."

Danno grabbed Cat's arm and escorted her toward the door, while Johnny ushered Miami out.

"You're going to regret this," Cat hissed, the words echoing through the lobby.

"Of course!" Tate snapped his fingers. "It's Honeycrisp. I should have known. The best apples are always Honeycrisp." He took one final, juicy bite. Then he tossed the core into the garbage and went back upstairs.

He hated using the "z" word, but the fact was, Tate felt like a zombie. With Cat gone, they'd been down a dealer, so Tate had stepped in to help all night. He'd finished his homework after everyone left at dawn. He'd even managed to fit in a workout, though it hardly deserved the name. In all his years of jumping rope, he'd never had so much trouble with his double-unders. And now, he was almost falling asleep in class? Pathetic.

On his walk across campus, Tate pulled up Twitter and went to the official University of Chicago account. He scrolled through to find the first tweet of the day. With a yawn, he replied, "Sucks abt study hall closure 4 the wknd."

There. The game was canceled until he could find a new dealer and a new announcement system. He'd had to kick only one other person out in the last three months, but then, as now, it meant changing his system. The venue was fixed—mostly—but everything else had to change, in case Cat or Miami got any funny ideas.

He dialed Zach Yates. His friend answered on the fifth ring, sounding rough and groggy. "Tate? What time is it there?"

"Noon. What time is it there?"

"Too early, bruh."

Tate shook his head. "Hawaii has ruined you, Yates."

"You know I hate it when you call me that, *Bertram*."

"Yes, Zachary, I do. But Yates sounds so much more like Tate."

"Egomaniac."

"Jealousy doesn't suit you, my man," Tate said over his friend's grumbling. "So I need to give you a heads-up about an issue with a dealer." He described the previous night's drama.

When Tate finished, Yates said, "Okay, I'll see about using the penthouse for a few weeks. My parents are in Paris for like the whole month, so they won't know, let alone care."

"Cool. Thanks, man. Catch some gnarly waves for me."

"I will," Yates said. "Enjoy Philosophy of Pretentious Douchebaggery. Bruh."

Tate chuckled. "I'm too embarrassed to talk to you. Call me when you're back in town."

"Will do. See you, buddy."

After making a few quick calls to Karla, Johnny, and Danno, Tate went to his next class.

A few hours later, the card room had already been moved up to the penthouse. His friend's parents used the apartment only when they were taking in a show or spending an evening in the city, but the place was big. In fact, it was big enough that Tate could easily run a couple of extra tables for a few weeks while he waited for Cat to try (and fail) to exact whatever ill-conceived revenge she and Miami could plan.

Still, he wasn't running any games for a few nights, just in case. With his day and night suddenly free, he was faced with hours and hours of mind-numbing free time. He pulled out his phone and shot off a text, tapping on the case while he waited for a reply. When his phone buzzed a minute later, Tate grinned like a Cheshire cat.

He swung by the apartment and filled a bag with clothes for the weekend.

He and Finley had unfinished business.

When he got to his parents' place late that afternoon, Fin was nowhere to be seen, despite the fact that they'd been texting not twenty minutes earlier. He searched the fourth floor for her, but she wasn't in her room, the gym, or the theater room. She wasn't on the roof deck, either. As he went back downstairs, he paused on the second-floor landing. The door to his mom's room was cracked open, and the TV was on.

Maybe Fin was in his mom's room. His mom would want to see him anyway.

He held his hand over the knob, thinking about how much worse her fibromyalgia symptoms had been over the last nine months. She always seemed to be in agony when he talked to her, even if she tried to hide it. She'd looked so drawn at Christmas. She'd been so worried about him . . .

He shouldn't be here.

He was halfway out the front door when the back door opened from the garage. "Do you think you'll be going out with that boy again anytime soon?" Tate's father was saying.

"Oh, hey, did you hear someone won the Powerball?" Fin said, her voice carrying down the hall. "And, yes, that was me changing the subject."

Tate's dad laughed. "You're being evasive."

"And you're acting like a nosy matchmaker," she said. The smell of Thai food wafted to Tate, and his stomach growled happily. "Chen is nice, but he's not—"

"Oliver?"

"My type," Finley said over the sound of rustling bags and clanking utensils. "And I thought we all agreed not to talk about this at home." Her tone was affectionate, teasing. She was so different from the girl who'd still squeaked when spoken to only a year ago.

"I know, I know. But you can't blame me for hoping."

"We'll figure it out or we won't. It won't change anything around here, I promise."

His dad cleared his throat. "And Tate?"

Fin's tone was careful. "What about him?" she asked. She was thinking about their near-kiss outside. She had to be.

"He's really coming home this weekend? How did you manage it?"

Her words were warm. "I invited him."

"Thank you, you angel girl," his dad said, voice cracking. "Thank you for bringing him home."

A moment-long-enough-for-a-hug later, he heard Finley say, "In fact, I'm going to call Tate. I thought he'd be here by now."

On cue, Tate opened and closed the front door loudly enough to announce himself. He hung up his coat and called out, "Do I smell Thai food?"

When he reached the kitchen, they were both smiling, though Finley's smile was a lot more interesting.

His dad patted Tate on the back before draping his suit jacket across a bar stool. "Good to see you again, son. I got your favorite."

"You know my favorite?"

"Number twelve, no bean sprouts, extra sauce," his dad said, handing him a container that smelled like heaven wrapped in bliss.

Tate grabbed the container, then bopped Finley's head with it. "Aw, Fin, you remembered?" She shrugged. "We'd all be lost without you, wouldn't we?"

"Utterly," she said, sitting on a bar stool and digging into her food. Tate sat beside her.

"You two eat," Tate's dad said. "I'm going to go upstairs and get your mother. She'll be so excited to see you."

The pit of his stomach hit the floor.

"She's not disappointed in you," Fin said. "You mentioned last night that you thought she was. Your mom's doing okay, and she loves you."

Tate got up and grabbed a soda from the fridge, getting an extra for Finley. He put the drinks in front of them and sat back down. His hand reached for his pocket when he realized he wasn't wearing his jacket. "What could I possibly do to disappoint anyone, right?"

"Stop it. I'm serious. She's worried about you because she doesn't see you often, but she's not disappointed. She talks about you all the time. Something funny will happen, and she imagines what you'd say, or she sees something and asks me to remind her to tell you."

He pushed his meal away. "And yet her fibromyalgia is the worst it's ever been."

"She's also the oldest she's ever been, and this winter has been longer and more brutal than usual, which you know makes her symptoms worse. Tate, you're reading into things. She's going to be thrilled to see you."

He managed a smile. "Of course she is."

True to Fin's word, his mom was ecstatic to see him. They ate around the island, elbows on the white granite, laughing and smiling. Finley reminded his mom about all of the stories she'd wanted to tell Tate, and he reacted exactly as he knew she'd hoped.

At one point, Fin's hand squeezed his beneath the counter. He didn't let go. Instead, he traced patterns on her palm, tickling her soft skin until he felt goose bumps spread up her arm.

"Isn't it great to have Tate home?" his mom asked Finley after dinner. Fin nodded, a pink tinge to her cheeks, and his mother turned her gaze back to him. "With Juliette away at boarding school, you and Oliver so busy in college, and Finley's internship at Mansfield Theater, the house feels a bit lonely sometimes." His mom patted his arm before the guilt could settle. "Fortunately, your aunt Nora's campaign has her in town for the next couple of weeks before she goes back on the trail."

At the mention of Nora, Finley's hand tightened. His aunt had always been beyond hard on Finley, probably because Finley's mom and Nora had been rivals for the same man in college: Finley's dad. Or it could simply be the fact that Nora had a vicious streak wider than Lake Michigan. It was part of what made her such an exceptional lawyer and could make her such an effective state attorney general. It was also likely to keep her from getting the job.

But, apart from the occasional text or phone call to pester him about his future, she'd always been good to him and better to his siblings. Too bad the same couldn't be said of Finley.

"How's the campaign going?" Tate asked.

"Oh, as well as we could expect," his dad said, his mouth twisting unpleasantly. "You know she's running against Connor Wolf, of course." The name made Tate sit up taller, steering his thoughts to another Wolf altogether. He forced the image from his mind so he could listen to his dad. "He isn't making it easy for her, but he can hardly tarnish his brother-in-law's widow outright. They're keeping it all very civil. Unfortunately, Nora's not a very sympathetic character. People don't know how to classify a woman who married a wealthy, older man and never had kids. Her success makes it even harder. Successful women scare people."

Finley coughed, no doubt to cover a snort.

Tate's dad picked up on this. "Yes, well, Nora's scary enough on her own, I'll grant you that. No doubt you've seen the way the media is capturing her. Always with that cold sneer while Wolf oozes charm in every picture. He knows how to turn it on for the cameras, all right."

"It helps that he and Cynthia are so heavily involved in the community," his mom said. "You know, Cynthia's always been perfectly lovely to me, yet there's something . . . off about her. Like her eyes are cold even when she's being warm."

"Mariah," Tate's dad said in a voice that wasn't quite chastening. But kind of was. "Maybe this isn't a conversation to have in front of the kids."

"Pfft," Tate's mom said. "If we can acknowledge my own sister's flaws in front of them, we can certainly do the same for Cynthia Wolf. I tell you, there's something off about her."

"Well, she and Connor have been through a lot over the years," his dad said. "And Connor's always had a stiff upper lip—"

"Yeah, I've heard that's his poker tell," Tate quipped, not sure if he was being self-deprecating or self-immolating. "Wonder if his gambling will keep him out of office."

"Connor's gambling earnings have been scrutinized carefully for years; he reports them accurately to the IRS and even donates portions of them to charity," his dad said. "I'm not saying there's a right way to gamble—"

"But if there were, Connor Wolf would have it right," Tate said, putting both thumbs up. His dad frowned.

"Don't the Wolfs have a daughter?" Finley asked, in an obvious effort to change the subject. Too bad it was the wrong subject.

"They do," his dad said. "Alexandra. She's Nora's niece through marriage."

Tate felt a flutter in his stomach, which he promptly tamped down. *Grow a pair,* he told himself.

"Well, that's enough politics for me for one night," his mom said, standing with a grimace. "Finley, do you mind helping me upstairs?"

Tate rose. "Mom, let me help."

She waved a hand. "No, no, I just need someone to steady me, not carry me. You and your father catch up."

Ah ha.

She kissed Tate on the head before walking out of the room with Finley. He didn't have the heart to watch her pained steps.

"So what did you want to talk to me about, Dad?" Tate asked, grabbing an empty container and throwing it into the garbage.

His dad held both hands up. "Not everything is part of a conspiracy, Tate. Your mother acted on her own accord. But I'm glad that we have a minute to talk," he said, grabbing some utensils and walking around the island. "We've missed you, son. Why don't you stay the weekend? You could even come to Mass with us Sunday."

"It isn't Easter or Christmas, is it?"

His dad gave him a tired laugh, but didn't press the issue, thankfully. His family had never been religious. At least not until Tate's accident and "miraculous recovery" (which wasn't the least bit miraculous). Since then, his dad had found God in his heart again.

Now if he could just find forgiveness in there.

"I haven't had the chance to tell you how proud I am of you."

Tate kept his expression calm, but he couldn't keep his chest from swelling. "Proud?"

"Yes." His dad smiled, opening the dishwasher and loading it. Tate had forgotten what his dad's smile looked like. "After I paid off your gambling debts last year, you promised to pay me back." His smile faded. "I didn't believe you, son."

Tate's chest deflated.

Emotion shone in his dad's eyes. If Tate didn't have such an exceptional poker face, his dad's earnest gaze would have finished him. "When I got your final check last month, that was one of the proudest moments of my life, yet I've never felt so ashamed. *I doubted my own son.*" He paused, and a tear spilled down his cheek. "I've become painfully aware of my failings as a father in the last year. I hope you'll forgive me."

Tate walked around the island and gave his dad a tight hug. "Thanks, Dad." The words were so empty, so meaningless. Still, he injected them with emotion. "That means a lot."

CHAPTER FOUR

Ten minutes later, Tate escaped his dad's regret and affection to find Finley. He felt antsy. Charged up.

He wanted those lottery tickets back.

He took the stairs two at a time the whole way up to the fourth floor, where he knew she'd be waiting. Once upstairs, he strode into the home theater, weaving around sectionals and beanbag chairs to where Finley was curled up on the couch, watching an old Samurai movie.

He stopped in front of her, holding out his hand, keeping his breathing steady, despite the stairs.

"What's going on?" she asked, looking at his hand and blinking too fast.

"Do you trust me?"

"*Aladdin*, Disney, 1992," she blurted.

"I'm not playing your movie game right now, Fin. I'm not playing at all."

"Oh."

With a deep breath, she put her hand in his, and he pulled her up. Wordlessly, he led her upstairs to the roof deck, where the air was crisp and the sun was setting. Once at the high wall overlooking their street, he turned to face her, standing close. The sound of her breath catching drew him closer.

She laid a hand on his chest. "I'm not sure how smart this is." Her voice was soft, unsteady.

He cupped her face in his hands, his eyes bouncing back and forth between hers. The current running through his veins needed an outlet. *This* outlet. This girl. "Give me one reason—apart from our ages. I'm not going to do anything stupid, Fin."

"Oliver."

"A reason I care about."

She stepped back, a frown on her face. "Don't say that. I know things are . . . tense between the two of you, but don't stop caring about him because you're angry."

He wanted to punch the wall. Or Oliver's face. How had his brother managed to ruin his night when he wasn't even here?

No. No, he wasn't going to let that happen. He was going to ruin Oliver's night, whether his brother knew it or not. He was going to break that fool's heart.

Tate pulled his expression into a frown. "You're right, Fin. It isn't Oliver's fault."

She leaned forward. "He thought he was helping, Tate. You know that, right? After the . . . accident, you seemed, I don't know, manic. Out of control. Oliver researched for days on end. He wanted to help so badly. He honestly thought rehab was for the best."

This definitely wasn't going the way he wanted it to. Somewhere on the street below, a car door opened and closed. Refusing to close the door on this moment, Tate slowed his breathing. His pulse calmed with it. "I don't agree with what he did, but I know he wanted to help." That much, at least, was true, and the lift of Fin's eyebrows told him she bought it. Good. He returned a hand to her cheek, stroking it with his thumb. "I don't mean to change the subject, but can we change the subject? I'm working on all of this. I really am. But it doesn't mean I like talking about it to a girl I would very much like to kiss."

Finley's cheek went hot beneath his hand. He loved how she unwittingly telegraphed her every emotion. "You can't blame me for being cautious."

That almost hurt. "You're right, I can't. I know I haven't given you reason to trust me—"

"What? No, that's not what I meant. I trust you." If anything, her cheeks were hotter. "But I don't know if I can trust . . . this."

"This?"

She looked down. "Tate, come on. The last thing I need is to jump into something with *another* Bertram, especially if it's not going to last."

He leaned back to see her better. She was still hurting from Oliver. That was clear as a bottle of Cristal. But she was wary, too, and he was losing her.

He didn't want to lose her. Not just because he was angry at Oliver or because the conversation with his dad had been a kick to the nads. Not even because he was exhausted from a late night watching amateurs embarrass themselves in a game he loved as much as he loved breathing.

He cared about Finley—and always had. Tate didn't need to be saved from anything, but if anyone could make him want to be, she could. That had to count for something.

"Fin, this can work," he said. "We've known each other our whole lives, and we're good for each other. If we go down this road, I don't know exactly what happens next. But I want to find out."

She peeked through her eyelashes. "You sound like you're begging. The Tate Bertram I know doesn't beg."

She was coming back to him, and the knowledge had him smiling. "Then allow me to introduce you to another side of myself." He cupped her cheeks, and her eyes danced. "One I think you'll like very, very much."

"Oh, will I?" she asked, rocking toward him.

"I guarantee it."

The heat from her face spread into his arm and chest. He leaned down and guided her face toward his. She stood on her tiptoes, and he couldn't help but smile when their lips met. Stroking her hair, he kissed her softly, still smiling.

"Are you laughing at me?" she said, her mouth on his.

"You're too damn short."

She backed up just enough to laugh. But when their lips touched again, the levity was gone. The moment became supercharged.

As they kissed, the energy coursing through his body calmed, even as his pulse raced. It was strange how he could feel so content and so amped up at the same time. This was what he'd needed. The electricity still animating him sparked where he touched Finley's lips, her neck, her back. A current seemed to run from her fingertips back into him, where her thumb was running over the scar on his side.

"I could get used to this," he said when they broke apart. She was breathing heavily, and the sound was intoxicating.

She touched her lips, smiling. "I've wanted to do that since I was thirteen."

"*I've* wanted to do that since you were thirteen."

"Ew!" She laughed. "Perv. And liar." She poked his abs. "Lying perv."

He chuckled. "Okay, you should really stop calling me a perv now, little girl."

She swatted him with her hand, which he caught. He tugged her to his chest, wrapping his arms around her. "This feels good, Fin."

Her enormous eyes blinked up at him. "Yeah?"

He leaned down to kiss her nose. "Yeah." And then he moved to her lips. Which was when the door to the deck opened.

His dad's hand was on the doorknob, his eyes flying over the roof deck. He looked as if he was about to yell when he saw Tate.

He stopped himself when he saw Finley.

"Hey there, Dad," Tate said, masking his annoyance even as Finley broke apart from him. "Didn't expect to see you here."

With his gaze darting between Finley and Tate, his dad looked like a powder keg ready to blow. His eyebrows pulled together. "Is this why you really came home this weekend? To . . . make a move on Finley? Was this all some ploy to break your brother's heart?"

"Right, Dad, because of course I could never want something that's actually good for me, could I? I have to have some ulterior motive? What happened to our conversation twenty minutes ago when you finally admitted that you're proud of me?"

Instead of inspiring the shame Tate intended, his words turned his dad from atomic to nuclear. "I spoke too soon."

Tate recoiled, as if he was hurt. "How could you say that?" he asked, even as a suspicion wormed its way into his head. After the moment they'd had downstairs, for his dad to be this unapologetically angry—

"I just got off the phone with Bruce Yates."

Oh, shittlesticks.

"He'd like to know why there's currently an illegal card room in his penthouse when his son is studying marine life in Hawaii." His dad's fury crumbled just enough to reveal the overwhelming disappointment fueling his nuclear core. "And I would, too."

A surge of adrenaline kicked Tate's instincts into high alert. He shifted ever so slightly, mentally cataloguing the nearest exit, the deck chairs and table in his way, the size of his . . .

Dad.

This was his dad, not some security guard or bouncer. *This isn't like that night in Hammond with that high roller's bodyguard. Are you really going to sweep your dad's legs, slide over the table, and run for the exit?*

The idea had its merits.

"I paid you back, like you wanted."

"Not like I wanted," his dad roared. "I wanted you to get a job! I wanted you to work for something for once in your entire life—"

"For once? Dad, I was in student government every year of high school! Model UN! Captain of the debate team! I've had a 4.0 since I was in diapers, and have you ever told me you were proud of me for that?"

"I thought you were competitive. I thought you wanted to be the best in every class because you *cared* about being the best. But it's always come so easily for you." His dad shook his head. "Maybe too easily."

"What's that supposed to mean?"

"You've cheated and lied your way through too much for me to simply believe you've earned those grades."

"I'm on a full ride scholarship!"

"Which you could have cheated your way into."

His ears were ringing. He clenched his fists, realizing for the first time that Finley's hand was no longer in his. The hurt that absence caused was a drop in too large a bucket. The emotions bubbling up inside him were so strong, so furious, so all-consuming . . .

He turned them off.

"I'm sorry you're disappointed. I'll move everything from Yates's apartment—"

His dad's laugh was toxic. "You think they left it there? It's gone, Tate. All of it."

His blood turned to ice. "What do you mean, it's gone? Like they threw it in the dumpster?"

"They turned it over to the police. They aren't going to press charges, because they know their son is involved somehow, but it's gone. The cash box and safe, too."

The floor seemed to drop out from under him. He was going to be sick. He was going to throw up all over his dad's Italian loafers. All that money. He'd plussed a couple of regulars only two nights ago. There'd been a few more players than usual, and more cash was going out than normal, so they'd agreed to get the money he owed them next time, because they knew he was good for it. He was supposed to be good for it.

And he had been. Every penny he'd made had been in that safe. Tens of thousands of dollars.

Gone.

"That despair you're trying not to show," his dad said in a voice that bit like frost. "That is the reason I can't help you out of this. You need to experience the consequences of your actions, son. I love you too much to bail you out again."

He'd forgotten his dad was an expert at reading people, too. Tate wiped his expression clean. It was time to shut it down. Time to move on.

With a half smile, Tate patted his dad's shoulder. He walked over to Finley, who was hugging her body. She looked so small; her pained expression was heartbreaking.

"I'm sorry, Fin."

"This isn't okay, Tate."

"I know," he said, his throat and chest feeling hot. He wished he could reach out to her, but he knew what a violation that would be. She looked as if she was trying to protect herself from him. He cleared his throat. "I really am sorry."

"Me too." With a sniff, she rubbed her nose. "Ca . . . can I help?"

"You're not saying—"

"No." Her expression was almost flat enough to mask the hurt in her eyes. "You gotta sort some crap out, Tate. But . . . I'm always here for you. Don't forget that."

She threw her arms around him and hugged him tightly before he kissed her cheek and whispered good-bye.

"Don't bother walking with me, Dad," Tate said, not looking back as he left the roof deck. "I know the way out."

Six minutes later, Tate was walking down the stairs with his bag and a few things from his room—and more from Oliver's—that he could pawn for a few hundred bucks. With what he had left in his own bank account, that would take care of some of the money he'd plussed. Enough to pay back one of the three players. He just didn't know which one.

Most of his regulars were college students, but a few he'd known from his "old life." He knew what all three were capable of, but he'd never had reason to be wary of them. Until now.

He rounded the second floor without stopping to see his mom. He needed to leave. To move. To not see the lines and wrinkles of her face and know how many of those he'd caused.

When he reached the front door to leave, Aunt Nora was standing in his dad's office. In her tailored red dress suit and perfectly styled bob, she looked every inch the politician.

"Tate? What are you doing home?"

"Not staying." He shouldered his bag and turned the doorknob. She followed him, stopping at the door as he walked down the stairs to the sidewalk.

"You know, you haven't been answering my texts."

He turned around. "Nope. I haven't."

"I could really use another intern—someone I trust, not another ambitious brat looking to pad his résumé, actual politics be damned."

Tate shifted from foot to foot. "Making calls to supporters and bringing you green tea doesn't require a particularly trustworthy candidate, Aunt Nora."

"No, but that isn't all I'd ask of someone I trust."

Standing around like this was agonizing. There was too much to do. "You may want to talk to my dad before offering me a position of 'trust.' I think he'll have some choice words to say on the matter."

"Tate. Do you really think that your gambling worries me in the slightest? You knew my husband. You know me."

"Playing the stock market and going on gambling cruises isn't quite the same as high stakes poker. And you're a respected lawyer—"

"I'm talking about risk taking. Isn't that exactly what gambling is? Seeking that thrill? Taking risks and seeing them pay off?"

She made it sound like flipping a coin. "Policing the gaming industry is one of your talking points. How could having me on your team possibly help?"

"Security companies hire ex-thieves to test systems. The FBI uses reformed criminals to catch other criminals. Tech companies use hackers—"

"This isn't as persuasive as you think it is."

She sighed. "Think about it, Tate. I need people I trust, and I trust you."

"Fine. I'll let you know."

CHAPTER FIVE

Call Karla. Find out debt to Grizzly, Shakes, and Dolly. Swing by apartment. Junk-punch Johnny. Check account balance. Try not to piss pants. Sell plasma. Sell kidney.

What the hell was he going to do?

Using a pass from Oliver's bedroom, Tate took the bus to Yates's apartment, saving him the cost of cab fare. Dolly would be reasonable. He could tell her what happened, get the money to her in a week's time, and they'd be square. But Between Grizzly and Shakes, he was stuck. They both had tempers and went on tilt with little provocation. Not getting their money more than qualified.

Why had he ever plussed them? That was one of his first rules when he and Yates had started the games after Christmas. It had been so straightforward those first few nights: close (rich) friends only, play with cash, no rake. But then they invited a few people from class. And after a couple of weeks, they had enough for two full tables of eager donks who thought they were in *Ocean's Eleven* and were prepared to drop real money to make that happen. Monetizing had seemed the next logical step.

Like a fool, Yates had let him do whatever he wanted. The guy had trusted that Tate knew what he was doing, as if the scar in his side wasn't proof otherwise.

Now here Tate was, sitting on a grimy bus seat, staring at his feet on the sticky gray floor, debating selling bodily fluids to get out of debt.

Maybe his dad was right. Maybe he *should* have taken a real job. He was so stupid. So reckless and stupid.

Before he knew it, Tate's hand had slipped into his jacket pocket, curling around the cards. His thumb stroked the worn edges, calming him. Focusing him.

When the bus reached his stop, Tate exited. A dozen or so people were waiting to get on after him, and a few jostled him in their haste to get on. For a moment, he felt like a kid taking the train to Aunt Nora's place in Lincoln Park for the first time. Confused. Lost. Overwhelmed. He wouldn't mind thirteen-year-old Tate's problems right now.

Stop it, he told himself. Who was he kidding? Life at thirteen had sucked. He wouldn't go back to pubescence for anything. Pre-orthodontia, pre-growth spurt, pre-abs. Not on his life.

Yet here he was, feeling sorry for himself again. Wishing for a girl he couldn't (or shouldn't) have, again. Wishing for a win . . .

What he wouldn't give for a win.

His breathing was shaky when he walked into Hyde Park Luxury Apartments. His plan to assault Johnny was thwarted by the very non-Johnny-like figure sitting behind the front desk.

Tate affected a slight Swedish accent. "Are you new?" he asked the guard, who looked like he more than dabbled in MMA.

The guard eyed him carefully. "Yes. And you are . . ."

"Jens Eriksson, up on seven." The guard instantly started looking him up in the system. "I travel a lot for work—in fact, I'm on my way out tonight for a shoot in Minsk—but it's good to meet you."

The guard glanced back and forth between Tate and the image on the screen. Tate leaned against the desk, smiling with pursed lips the way Jens always did. The new guard nodded. "Have a good night, Mr. Eriksson."

Feeling a little better that he'd successfully passed for a male model, Tate took the elevator upstairs.

Time to pilfer the crap out of Yates's apartment.

"Zachary Yates, you feckless, spineless loser," Tate said conversationally on his friend's voice mail as he shoved crystal goblets and sterling silver candlesticks into his suitcase. "A little heads-up about your parents being back in town would have been appreciated. The police have confiscated our entire operation, and I've been banned from the building, or at least I will be once the new guard realizes I'm not Jens."

He stuffed an expensive-looking wall clock in next. "So just wanted to say that I'm emptying out the apartment and selling everything to cover the plus I never should have given, but I still blame you because *YOU TOLD ME YOUR PARENTS WERE IN FRANCE.*" He took a slow breath. "Anyway, if I'm not around when you call, it's because your parents didn't love you enough to decorate the apartment with actual luxury items and the pawn shop couldn't give me any money for it, so Shakes and Grizzly had to carve out my organs and sell them on the black market to settle the debt." When he reached the kitchen, he threw in the $1,300 commercial-grade Vitamix blender. He grabbed the rest of the Honeycrisp apples for good measure. "Anywhoo, call me when you're back in town so I can punch you in the throat." He turned off the light and closed the door. "We'll grab Gino's. Later, pal."

With a suitcase and shoulder bag each weighing Tate down with every step, he was hardly inconspicuous on the way down to the lobby. But he had a good cover in Jens. Tate made a point of talking to him in the gym whenever the guy was in town for this very reason: in case things went south. They were both good-looking guys with excellent bone structure and a fanaticism for exercise.

Besides, all blonds looked alike.

He was counting on that fact when he stepped out of the elevator and saw two uniforms talking to the guard at the front desk.

Tate's pulse hammered in his throat.

He took out his phone and started speaking French into it: the words to the nursery rhyme *Frère Jacques*, to be precise. He marched through the suddenly too-long lobby as if he owned the place, alternately scowling and reciting the nursery rhyme angrily. When he got closer to the front desk, he pretended to listen to the call.

"The Yateses don't want to press charges, but the last guard lost his job for not paying attention. You keep an eye out for anything suspicious and you call us, all right?" one of the officers was telling the new guard as she pulled up something on her phone.

"Of course," the new guard said. He looked as if he wanted to salute.

"Good. Now the locksmith is coming tomorrow, but if this kid tries to get in, call us immediately." She showed the guard her phone, and Tate caught a glimpse of blond hair and a face too handsome for prison.

"Got it. Apartment 611. Tate Bertram." Then he caught Tate walking past. "Everything okay, Mr. Eriksson?"

"My ex," he said, covering the speaker in a way that obscured part of his face. "Some people cannot take no for an answer. *À bientôt.*" He gave a finger wave and walked through the sliding glass doors.

"Wait, Mr. Eriksson!" the guard said.

Tate forced himself not to run. He turned his head around partway, just enough to show his profile, but not enough for the officers still huddled around the desk to get a good look at him. Distracted, but not evasive. "Hmm?"

"Did you want me to call you a cab?"

Tate forced an easy laugh. "No, thank you. What good are exes for if not for rides to the airport? See you in a few weeks."

A hundred yards from the building, Tate slumped against a wall. His hands were shaking.

He pulled out his phone, bracing himself before listening to the voice mails that had amassed over the last hour. Word had spread fast. He had messages from Karla, a few regulars, and the people he now owed money to. He mentally tallied up what he'd taken from Oliver and the apartment. If he could sell it on Craigslist, he'd have enough. But he didn't have time for anything but a pawnshop, and they would rip him off.

Unless he took the money, hit a game at the Horseshoe, and made enough to pay them all off tonight.

He just needed to win.

Holy hell, did he ever need a win.

With fingers numb from the chill, he started texting.

Hey, you up?

Ten seconds passed. Twenty.

His phone buzzed and he jerked it up to his face.

Yes. What's up?

Nothing.

Tate, I know you didn't text your sponsor at 10:16 p.m. for a booty call because we both know I could beat your pretty face ugly.

Silly Nia. You know all I really want from you is your gracious, sparkling conversation.

What are you doing? Are you gambling or thinking about it?

He huffed. Why had he texted her, anyway? Why wasn't he on his way to the Horseshoe right now? For the last thirty-four days, he'd managed not to gamble once, despite running a friggin' card room for a living. And what had that done for him?

Tate answer me. I want to know you're OK. I'm at my nephew's birthday party but I can come get you. Where are you? Can you make it home?

Home. Perfect excuse for texting. **I'm okay. I went to my parents' house tonight. Just set me off a bit, but I'm cool now. I'm at a friend's place. No cards in sight.**

Her response was filled with reminders, things he'd told her in moments of weakness, moments in which her interrogation techniques had become so irritating he'd told her whatever she wanted to get her off his back. But he thanked her, because it was his fault for bothering her in the first place.

Thanks for trusting me, Tate. I hope you know I'm always here.

Does this mean I get some of your grandma's coconut caramel dumplings?

Make it to the next meeting, and I'll bring the faikakai. Night, Tate.

See? He wasn't an addict. An addict would've been halfway to a casino by now. But Tate was here. He was in control. And he needed a place to sleep.

He slept on Karla's couch that night and laid low the next day, making a couple of quick sales online through a campus yard sale page. But even combined with what was left of his account balance, he was still two grand short and needed to pay up, fast. Shakes, in particular, was getting persistent. As the day wore on, that persistence started to sound a lot like threats.

"Tate, I'm getting worried, man. Don't make me come after you."

"Have you been hit by a car, or something? If you don't pay up, you will be."

"I'm gonna pull out your teeth with pliers if I don't have my money tonight."

And Tate's personal favorite:

"Listen, I'm not tryin' to scare you off, but I will literally rip off your head and take a dump down your throat if I don't hear from you in an hour."

He played that message out loud for Karla while she was getting ready for a date. "I wish he'd tell me how he really feels, you know?"

She smiled, accidentally smearing her lipstick. "Have you considered maybe paying him first?"

"And miss his tempered, reasoned messages? Never."

"That's a dangerous game you're playing." She examined herself in the mirror, turning to see how the gorgeous cocktail dress hugged her curves.

"You're stunning."

"You're sweet," she said. "Thanks." She grabbed her clutch and twirled her keys around by her Puerto Rican flag key chain. "You know you can stay as long as you need, right? My roommates both practically live with their boyfriends, so neither of them will mind."

"Aw, you care about me." He kissed her cheek and got the door for her. "Knock 'em dead, tiger."

Once Karla left, Tate sat on the ratty couch and buried his head in his hands. He'd call Shakes in a minute and pray that Grizzly and Dolly weren't equally unhinged.

Not pray . . . wager. The smart money was on paying Shakes first. This was just good business . . . born of bad business. He curled his hands around his hair and tugged, giving himself ten more seconds of not coping. Five more seconds.

His phone buzzed.

It was a text from his aunt: **Time to grow up, Tate. Call me.**

He cleared the message and called Shakes.

"Tate, just in time—"

"Shakes? Shakes, are you there?" Tate said over him. "I can't hear you, but if you can hear me, meet me at the Sugar Shack on 26th in thirty."

Click.

A half hour later, Tate was sitting at a table on the sidewalk in front of the bustling Sugar Shack with a caramel apple sundae. He flirted with a couple of UC Delta Gammas at the table next to him until Shakes showed up a few minutes later.

"Shakes, my good man. You have got to try this sundae. I know everyone talks about the funnel cake sundae, but the sweet caramel combined with the tartness of the apple . . . mmm. It's like a dance for your taste buds."

Shakes sat, scratching a patchy goatee. "Why am I here, Tate?"

Um. Tate scooped up an apple, swiping it around in the caramel. He brought it slowly up to his mouth. "What do you think?"

"Do you expect me to say sorry? How did I know you weren't planning to stiff me and run, you know? It wasn't personal. I just wanted to get paid."

"You made that abundantly clear."

"Exactly. I made money, and I made *you* money. Let's leave it at that."

What? Tate put another bite in his mouth. After a few lazy chews, he said, "So we're square?"

"We're square," Shakes said. "Call me if you pick up the games again."

"Will do," Tate said as Shakes got up. "And seriously, do yourself a favor and get the sundae. You won't be sorry."

He watched the man's retreating form, taking bite after bemused bite. When he was done, he tossed his bowl and started walking down the sidewalk. He called the next name on his list. "Grizzly, how are you?"

"Better now that you paid. I didn't recognize the courier, but you should be glad he showed up when he did."

Huh. "Please don't tell me you doubted me. We hit a small speed bump. Nothing I couldn't handle."

"So you're starting up again?"

"Maybe. Not until the heat dies down, though. I'll be in touch."

The conversation with Dolly was much the same. After he hung up with her, he pulled up his aunt's text again.

Time to grow up, Tate. Call me.

He called.

CHAPTER SIX

Aunt Nora's house hadn't changed much in seven years. At thirteen, Tate had spent the summer there while his parents and siblings toured the Eastern Seaboard. As much as he'd wanted to see the Smithsonian museums and go to Ellis Island, he'd stayed back for an academic camp on the Loyola campus that he was even more excited about.

Being in the house took him right back to that summer. The place was more than a hundred years old but had been renovated only a year or two before Tate's stay. The light ash wood flooring, white carpets, walls, and blinds contrasted too starkly with the heavy black couches and accents. Instead of classic or comfortable, it felt sterile and ambitious.

A little like Aunt Nora.

Regardless, Tate was in no position to turn his nose up at a free place to stay, one of the conditions he'd given his aunt when he accepted the barely paid internship. She didn't balk at the proposition, just gave him a spare key and told him to start on Monday.

Walking up the stairs, he caught a hint of lavender from a candle or room scent. It was a nice touch. Humanizing. On the second floor, he went down the hallway to where the spare rooms were, and he caught an undertone of something else . . . vanilla, maybe.

You've gotta be kidding.

Instead of opening the door to the room he'd used all those years ago—the one on the right at the end of hall—he turned left and knocked.

Several heartbeats later, the door opened and there she was.

Alex Wolf.

A slash of eyebrows framed her big, dark brown eyes, and a rosebud mouth bloomed beneath a strong nose. With light olive skin and long black hair, she was a veritable Snow White, and she smelled faintly of vanilla. Just as she had at thirteen, when she'd spent almost every day that summer at his aunt's house.

He'd seen her a hundred times since then, but Tate still had to keep himself from flexing his abs. While she had already been beautiful at thirteen, he had been cute and distinctly pudgy. He'd never been self-conscious about it until she'd looked down at his stomach and poked it, calling him "Doughnut Boy" and telling him to take up a sport. Or five. She'd scoffed when he said he preferred science to soccer, and she'd groaned when she found out he'd never smoked, shoplifted, or cut school. Like ever.

In truth, Tate had doubted Alex knew as much and had done as much as she claimed. Yet as the day had neared an end, he'd found himself wondering if he was really as pathetic as she'd said he was.

He'd also found himself thinking she was the most beautiful girl he'd ever seen.

He still did.

But he wasn't thirteen anymore—he had abs she could wash a shirt on, a jaw that could cut diamonds, and a past that even he knew better than to be proud of. He could handle Alex Wolf.

She quickly smothered her surprise, replacing it with an air of intimidation that couldn't quite work on him anymore.

"Good to see you, Alex."

She folded her arms, looking strong and fierce and perfectly feminine. The corners of her dark eyes wrinkled in a calculated smile.

"So you're the other intern," she said, looking him over.

"Other? You can't mean—"

"I'm supporting my aunt instead of my bastard of a father? *Bet on it.*"

The emphasis she placed on those words made him groan. "Why, Alex Wolf, have you been keeping an eye on me?"

"We share an aunt. Don't let it get to your head."

"Whatever you have to tell yourself."

"I don't have to tell myself anything. Word is you've been running bad."

"The deck was stacked against me."

"No, you just went on tilt."

"Least I'm not a donk."

"Only a donk would say that."

"Says the nit."

She scoffed. "Quit with the foreplay—you suck at it."

He let that one go.

"So what are you doing here?" he asked. He looked past her into the spare bedroom across from his. It was decorated in the same white that dominated the house, but with ivory accents rather than black. The effect was both soft and inaccessible. Look, but don't touch.

"Tate," she said slowly, "think about it. I can't exactly live at home after telling my dad I don't support his beliefs or campaign."

"How does your mom feel about it?" he asked.

Her eyes lost focus for a split second. "She's too busy sitting on hospital boards and throwing charity functions to notice much of what I do." She looked at him. "When it comes to parental concern, I'm always running bad."

He debated drawing her out more, but the Alex he knew didn't do warm and fuzzy conversations. Instead, she planted intriguing bits of information like land mines. He'd stepped in one that summer, his very first night at his aunt's. Alex had been peering out the window, absentmindedly shuffling a deck of cards while she waited for her parents. And waited. He'd seen her watery eyes in the reflection of the glass, and like a fool, he'd asked her about it.

He knew better than to ask about it now.

"So we're both living here for, what, the duration of the campaign?" he asked.

"You're living here, too?"

He kicked the suitcase at his feet. "Didn't see this, did you?"

She glared. "Oh, go to your room."

He blew her a kiss, deposited his suitcase in his room, and closed the door behind him.

♠

The next day after class, Tate took an easy train ride to the Loop, where Nora had rented campaign headquarters space in the same building as The Law Offices of Bertram, Mallis, and Associates. He wondered what his dad thought about his involvement with Nora's campaign. He'd warned her against the idea, no doubt. If his dad suspected Nora had paid the plus to Shakes and the others, the man would go on tilt in a big way.

Not that Tate was planning to tell. And he felt certain Nora wouldn't, either. After all, when she'd arrived home yesterday evening, she hadn't so much as hinted at the fact. She'd just told him it was about time he started taking some initiative.

As if running a card room hadn't taken initiative.

Alex had been a delight at dinner last night, taking an interest in everything Nora said and responding with a kindness he was sure she reserved for people she wanted to impress. And, boy, did she want to impress Nora. The only thing that could compete with her regard for her aunt was her total disregard for Tate. She'd ignored him most of the night, something she reserved for people she *wished* she didn't care about.

Tate walked through the main doors to the ground floor office where Nora's campaign was headquartered. Beyond the glass walls, he saw that Alex was already there. Nodding and taking notes, she was talking to a short man Tate recognized as Nora's campaign manager. Unfortunately, Tate's brother was there, too. He was standing outside the glass office doors with his hands in the pockets of his navy jacket, looking as if he was waiting for someone to call his parents.

"Are you lost, little boy?" Tate asked, pulling open the door and striding past Oliver.

"Can we talk?" Oliver said over the general office buzz.

Tate spotted a side office with the lights out and pulled Oliver into it with him. Closing the door and flicking the light switch on, he said, "How did you even know I was here?"

"Aunt Nora told Mom and Dad."

"And you're here why, exactly? You want tips for staging an intervention?"

"Nah, I came to borrow your 'Abs of Steel' workout video," Oliver deadpanned. "Listen, I heard what happened the other night, and I just wanted to check in. I was worried about you."

"You sure sabotage my life a lot for someone worried about me."

"If you're talking about Finley—"

Tate smiled, leaning back against an empty desk. "You heard about that, huh?"

Oliver's nostrils flared. "I heard you were trying to be the rebound guy and she shut you down."

"Really? Was that before or after we kissed?"

Oliver's eyes bugged out and he clenched his hands into fists— trembling, angry fists. Was his little brother going to punch him? He was half excitement, half amusement just thinking about it. "Dad must have left that part out," Oliver said through clenched teeth.

"Wait, Dad told you? Not Fin? Ooh, that has to hurt," he said, twisting the knife. Oliver looked physically pained, and the sight warmed Tate's heart. He was about to go into detail when the image of Finley clutching her shoulder on the roof came to mind, her big eyes rounded with pain. As much as he wanted to stomp on Oliver's every last hope, he wouldn't use Finley to do it. He couldn't even bring himself to text her a real apology.

"Let me be clear," Tate said begrudgingly. "The only reason I'm not with Fin right now is because I know she's too good for me. I'm backing off because it's the right thing to do, not because I don't care about her. Too bad you can't say the same thing."

"What's that supposed to mean?"

Tate shook his head, looking around the bare office. "Do you love her?"

"More than anything."

"Then why do you treat her like she's a puppy?"

"What? I do not!"

"You expect her to sit and stay and beg on your command."

"Don't criticize me for my relationship with her. You *lied* to her about being in recovery—"

"I'm not an addict."

"—and about *running an illegal card room*."

"I didn't lie, kiddo, I withheld things from her. Meanwhile, you made her promises you weren't willing to keep. You think that's better?"

Oliver didn't answer. He scratched his head, tousling his floppy brown hair. He looked so young. If Alex had ever gotten her claws into him, she'd have eaten him alive.

"I'm trying. I don't know how to balance being in college with—"

Tate made a sound like a buzzer. "Meh. Wrong answer."

"You're such a dick," Oliver whispered. "I came here to see if you needed anything, but I was obviously wrong to come at all."

"Winner winner," Tate said. "Between your intervention, rehab, GA, and now this cute little brotherly chat that's making me late for my first day of work, I've had quite enough help from you, Ollie. You need to leave."

Oliver frowned. "I do love you, Tate, and all I want is to help. I hope someday you'll be able to see that."

Tate gave a sharp laugh. "Your concern is touching. Now if you don't mind, I have work to do."

Oliver's head hung low as he left the office. Tate took a moment to unclench his jaw before walking over to Alex, who was still taking notes.

When she saw him, she said, "Tate, this is Oscar Solano, Nora's campaign manager. Oscar, this is Tate Bertram, Nora's nephew."

In gray slacks, and wearing a shirt and tie, Oscar carried an aura of total competence. "Great." He shook Tate's hand. "Thanks for joining the team. Alex, could you show Tate around and give him his first assignment? I'll come around later to make sure you're adjusting all right."

"Lucky you, getting to take me on a private tour," Tate told Alex after Oscar walked away.

"I'm the volunteer coordinator, so I'm just doing my job," she said, a flush of pride blooming on her cheeks. It was impressive that Alex was already managing such a large function, but it wasn't surprising. After their summer together, Aunt Nora had made a point of updating Tate on Alex's doings, and he'd faced her in debate a handful of times in high school. She was an overachiever by nature. "What was that back there in the office?" she asked. "Was that your little brother?"

"Yes."

"Did he come to play Candyland?"

"No, he came to warn me of the error of my ways."

"You mean the gambling?"

"It's always about the gambling with them."

"Ouch. I hope your parents never find out I'm the one who taught you to play cards."

He shook his head. "Let's move along with the tour, shall we? I assume I should keep my tray table in the upright and locked position?"

But Alex wasn't moving yet. She tapped her fingernails on the back of her tablet. "I get the feeling you don't like talking about this? Does it *wound* you?"

"Look at you, casually dropping mention of my impalement like you don't actually care."

"Don't let it get to your head, sweetie. Remember that shared aunt of ours?" She started walking, taking bigger steps than her black pencil skirt should have allowed. "You know, the way I heard it, you almost died." He didn't answer. "Seriously?"

"Define 'almost died.' I was bleeding out when my roommate found me, I got a dangerous infection, and the rod nicked my intestines. Without modern medicine, yeah, I would have died. But without modern medicine, people could die from sinus infections. So." He shrugged.

She exhaled slowly, as if blowing through a straw. "I think I see why they're all so intent on babysitting you."

"And by 'they,' do you mean you? You're showing your hand, Alex. Remember what happened last time you did that?"

"No, but then again, I'm not the one who spent an entire summer trying to master every card game in the world just to win a kiss," she said.

"Right," he said. "You're just the one who set the stakes."

"That summer's over, Tate. Try to keep up," she said before starting the tour. In an efficient voice, she told him about the myriad different volunteer jobs on the campaign—scheduling, research, policy, fund-raising, field and advance teams, community outreach and constituent liaisons, and more. She showed him to the different stations, smiling and waving to other volunteers and workers.

"How are you so familiar with all this? Were you helping your dad before jumping ship?"

Her hackles seemed to rise. "No, I'm a political science major. And I hardly jumped ship. I joined Nora's campaign a few months ago, and this opportunity means a lot to me. Now did you still want to play twenty questions, or are you ready to work?"

"Seeing as I still have eighteen questions left, obviously I want to finish playing."

She ignored this. "You're in for a real treat today, sweetie." She showed him to a small cubicle with a phone and a computer. "You're starting on the field team."

It shouldn't have come as a surprise to him that the field team was a suck-fest. The team was responsible for contacting registered voters to inform them about Nora's campaign, encourage them to vote for her, and occasionally listen to them scream about why she was the spawn of the devil.

When he got back to Nora's that night, Tate was wound up. After a long day of getting yelled at, he was coiled like a spring. He needed release or he'd scatter into a million pieces.

Upstairs, he changed into shorts and gym shoes. He grabbed his speed rope and a mat and went downstairs to the back patio, the same place he'd started jumping rope nearly seven years ago. At least now he didn't have to hide it from Alex.

The night air was cool enough to send a wave of goose bumps over him. He kicked away a stray nail, no doubt from the neighbor's house, which was being extensively remodeled. He unrolled the mat, glanced at his feet, and started jumping.

Tate loved jumping rope. He had started it the summer he met Alex. As much as Finley had always tried to talk him into running, he'd never been able to get into it. But jumping rope was different.

He shut his mind off and let the endorphins rush through him, washing away the day's frustrations. His breathing came heavily, but steadily, sharpening his mind like a razor. He ran through mental notes for an exam tomorrow before turning his thoughts to a linguistics paper due next week. Then he thought about the ethics lecture his professor had given earlier, and St. Thomas Aquinas's views on temperance in relation to the moral common good, and Tate's argument that—

"Do you know how long you've been out here?"

The rope slapped the back of his hamstrings. "Ouch." The world came back into view around him, and he saw Alex, arms folded, wearing an oversized t-shirt and a frown. "Huh? I don't know. Twenty minutes?"

"It's been over an hour. You worried about your figure?"

He feigned a laugh to hide his surprise. An hour? Really? He normally felt dead on his feet after thirty minutes, but he could have gone on forever. His muscles ached and his lungs burned, but his thoughts felt clear. He tossed down his speed rope. "Not as much as you, obviously," he told Alex. She scoffed. He grabbed his water bottle from a nearby table and guzzled it before getting down on the mat to stretch his hamstrings.

"You do that a lot."

"What, work out?"

"No, throw yourself into things, like this. I can't imagine losing track of time exercising. I count down the minutes every day during Pilates. I hate working out."

"I like it."

"You don't just like it, though, you lose yourself in it. You do the same thing when you're studying."

"We've lived in the same house for twenty-four hours. How do you know what I'm like when I'm studying?"

"In the library on campus. I was sitting a couple of tables away from you once last year. After, I don't know, an hour, you put your laptop and books in your bag, but you kept all the research books out and started looking through them. You just kept opening one after the other. It's like you went down this research hole and didn't want to come back out until you knew everything you could about that subject. I bet that's not the first time, either, is it?" When he didn't deny it, she said, "Why do you do that?"

"Why do you care?"

She pulled her shoulders back. "Don't confuse curiosity with caring, Sprinkles."

He switched to stretch his other leg. Sweat dripped from his forehead and the tip of his nose in a steady stream. "You say all this like you don't exercise and study religiously every day."

"I do it because I have to. It's what people do. You have to exercise and study to have the kind of life I want to have."

"That's no different than me."

"Yes, it is. I do it out of a sense of, of . . ."

"Duty?"

"Close enough. But you do it out of—"

"Inclination."

"Again, not the word I'd have chosen, but yes."

Tate stood and leaned against a column, stretching out his calves. "You know, Immanuel Kant believed that doing something out of duty is a moral act, while doing something out of inclination isn't."

"Explain."

"Imagine if you hated dirty things and every time you saw litter, you picked it up and threw it away. Most people would say that you were doing a good thing, a *moral* thing, because you were helping the environment. But Kant would say you were just following your natural inclinations, so there's nothing moral about it." He stretched out his other leg.

"So Kant would say I'm more impressive than you are for exercising and studying out of duty, while your actions are less impressive because you enjoy them?"

"Exactly."

"That's crap."

He grabbed a towel and wiped the sweat from his face. "Thoughtful counterpoint."

"No, I mean it. It's crap. What's so impressive about me doing things just because everyone tells me I should?"

"Health and knowledge are inherently valuable—"

Her brow wrinkled in anger. "So what? That doesn't make doing something out of love any less worthy than doing something out of duty. If anything, wouldn't the fact that your natural inclinations drive you to do things that have inherent value mean that you're naturally a better person?"

"But I can't control my nature, just my actions."

"And you choose to do things that have value when I'm pretty sure you'd rather be gambling."

He smiled. "Aw, Alex. Are you trying to convince me that I'm a good person worth loving, no matter what Kant says?"

"Are you serious right now?"

"Are you?" he asked. In the few minutes since he'd finished working out, his lungs had started to feel raw and his legs like jelly.

"Am I what?"

"Are you defending me to myself?"

"No, I'm having a pointless philosophical debate with you."

He got up and took two steps toward her. "I don't believe it. You have a kind heart whether you want to admit it or not, Alex Wolf."

"You're delusional, Tate Bertram," she said before turning around and going back inside the house.

He gathered his things and had a long drink of water in the kitchen. When he made his way upstairs, Alex's door was closed and her light was off. "Try not to dream about me, Alex," he called through her door.

"Try not to die in your sleep, Tate," she said back.

"Try to shut the hell up!" Nora yelled from the opposite end of the hall.

Tate went to bed smiling.

CHAPTER SEVEN

On Thursday evening, Tate pulled off his headset, tugged on his earlobe (as if to shake the scream out), and stretched like a cat. Then he hopped up and walked to a white board, where a grid pattern was set up, with outcomes along the x-axis and names of volunteers along the y. He'd set up the board on his first day working with the field team and had added to it throughout the week.

Tate studied the boxes. "Hey, Ruby," he said to another volunteer, "how were we qualifying 'she should be making sandwiches, not laws' again? Ah, yes, 'women belong in the home-slash-kitchen.'" Tate added a tick to one of the boxes.

"And why aren't we classifying all those under misogyny again?" Ruby asked from her cubicle.

"Besides losing half of our board? I don't know, fun?" Tate said, looking to a tall, perpetually pissy volunteer. "What do you think, Glasses?"

The guy shook his head. "There's nothing *fun* about misogyny."

"Not with that attitude, there's not."

Ruby snickered, making her freckles dance on her pale, round cheeks. "Only you could turn getting yelled at by stodgy old men into a game."

"Hey, hey, hey. Don't sell yourself short, kid. One day, with a great deal of practice and dedication, this could be you."

"I should be so lucky."

He looked at the board, and then the clock, which had just ticked past eight o'clock. Glasses packed up his things and was already heading out. "Doesn't matter, anyway," Tate said. "It's closing time, and you won. What do you want tomorrow?" She gave Tate her coffee order and they said good night.

Tate slipped on his jacket and was walking out when he saw Alex up ahead in the lobby talking on her phone. When Tate exited the office, Alex stabbed the END CALL button with a curse.

"Everything okay?" he asked.

"Just peachy." She jammed her phone into her jacket pocket. "You on your way home? I'll take you, assuming you don't mind a slight detour."

"Um, sure. After you," he said, holding the lobby door for her. He followed her out into a light drizzle, popped his umbrella, and held it over them. "So, that call seems to have gone well. What's going on?"

"Do you want to know how smart I am? I moved out of my parents' house two months ago, but I didn't bring enough clothes. Lots of sweaters, but nothing for warm weather." She sped up, her strides matching the frantic outpouring of words, almost outpacing him and the umbrella. "I don't want to go out and buy anything when I have a perfectly good wardrobe at home and my parents have basically cut me off financially. But I don't want to go home and risk seeing my dad by myself, because he might get mad, and he and I haven't really spoken since I left. I need a buffer."

He caught up. "Alex, are you trying to ask me something?"

She side-eyed him. "Don't get so excited."

"Not excited. Just doing the math. Whoever you were speaking to on the phone obviously refused to go home with you, and based on your little rant a moment ago, you still need to go home but you don't want to do it alone, particularly when you have such a fine specimen of manhood and chivalry here before you. Sound about right?" She didn't answer. "So why aren't you asking your boyfriend or one of your friends?"

"Are you trying to find out if I have a boyfriend?"

"Please. Give me a little credit."

She rolled her eyes. "Whatever." Rain pattered lightly on her face. Tate adjusted the umbrella over her. "My friends aren't exactly the kind you call in your hour of need, and my boyfriend worships my dad. He thinks I'm a fool for choosing Nora's campaign over my dad's, which has made me question our whole relationship. So, yes, I need someone to come help me pick up my crap. And yes, it would be convenient if it were you, seeing as you're the only person I know without a horse in the race."

"I don't bet on horses."

"Tate," she said.

"Are you asking me to help, Alex?"

"Obviously. I just said that."

Obviously she hadn't, but he dropped it. Alex was adversarial by nature, at least with him, and it made his life easier to not get worked up by it. "If you're sure you don't want a friend with you, then yes, I can help."

She guided him quickly toward her car, which was parked in the covered garage adjacent to the building. He shook out his umbrella before sliding into the passenger seat of her slick white Audi A4. "We're friends, aren't we?" she said as she pulled out.

"Excuse me?"

"You said you'd help if I don't want a friend with me," she said with a slight tremble in her voice. "Aren't we friends?"

He studied her profile, the set of her lips. "You're yanking my chain."

"Oh, undoubtedly. We barely know each other."

The memory of her lips on his came to mind. "I wouldn't say that."

"Knowing someone at thirteen hardly qualifies you as knowing them at twenty, so don't even."

He settled into his seat and watched the traffic around them. "Can I tell you what I think your problem is with me?" She arched an eyebrow at him expectantly. "You've never forgiven me for beating you at hearts."

Her laugh was the sound of icicles shattering on the ground. "You didn't beat me, you tricked me."

"I didn't trick you. I shot the moon, a rule you taught me about, mind you."

"It's an absurd rule: *try* to get the worst possible hand, and if it somehow works, everyone else loses? You took a gamble that miraculously paid off."

He hated how Alex, of all people, was reducing a game of skill down to dumb luck. "It wasn't a gamble, it was strategy. I set that last hand up meticulously so that when I dropped the queen of spades, the game would be over."

"You couldn't have known you'd have the queen of spades, Tate! It wasn't even a bluff, it was dumb luck—"

"No, I had a contingency plan. If you'd have had the queen of spades, I knew I'd—"

"I get it," she snapped. "Congratulations. You purposefully tanked a hand and won the game because of it. Do you think I still care? Do you think I've harbored resentment about a card game for *seven years* just because you clearly can't stop fantasizing about it? Maybe if you'd learned to move on, your family wouldn't have sent you to rehab."

From the corner of his eye, he saw the wipers swish across the windshield. "Do you feel better about yourself?"

A muscle beneath her eye tensed. "What are you talking about?"

"Putting me down. Do you feel better now by comparison? Or do you even know that you do it?"

Lights from a passing car illuminated her beautiful, imperious face. "Whatever. I don't even know why I asked for your help."

Neither did he.

A short forty-minute nap later, Tate was waking up in Alex's rounded driveway in the über-rich suburb of Wilmette, Illinois. Tate's family was wealthy, but the Wolfs' craftsman-style estate home achieved an almost unbelievable level of opulence. Tate and Alex walked through the enormous front door and into the elegant foyer, their steps echoing on the cold marble floor. She dragged him past a library, guest suites, multiple pristine sitting rooms, and what he could only imagine was a climate-controlled room for all of their gems.

He snorted at the thought.

"Don't act like you're not rich," she said as she pulled him up a spiral staircase.

"Wouldn't dream of it."

Upstairs was more of the same—cold statues, lifeless paintings, and empty rooms. The house resembled nothing more than a mausoleum—with less life and fewer personal touches. A nice haunting would have cheered the place right up.

"What's that room?" Tate asked, pointing to a closed door with a faded lace V on it.

"That's Vivienne's room." Her tone was as sweet as arsenic.

"Who?"

"The other baby. You know, the one that died at birth before they adopted me from Bulgaria. They named her after my mom's middle name. Door's locked, so don't bother trying to go in. Only my mom has the key."

"Have you ever gone in?" Tate asked.

"Of course I have. I stole the key from her jewelry box when I was ten. Everything looks like it's right where they left it the day they went to the hospital."

"That sounds ... creepy."

"Creepy as hell," she said, the crack in her voice hinting at emotions neither of them was going to touch.

When they got to Alex's room, Tate hoped, for her sake, that it would be different than everything else he'd seen. It wasn't. From the antique bed frame and matching furniture to the pale pink walls and lace curtains, the room would have been better suited for a dollhouse. There were no posters, no shoes on the floor, no jewelry scattered across the gold leaf vanity. The paintings looked expensive, understated, and as if a museum curator had chosen them rather than a living, breathing girl.

Alex was right that they didn't know each other well. He didn't know her favorite color or her golf handicap. He couldn't say what songs she belted out in her car when she was alone. He didn't know what she thought about at night when she couldn't sleep.

But it was abundantly clear her parents knew even less. Because this room didn't represent the bold, strong, cunning Alex he knew. Instead, it was as if her parents had found a pattern called "Ideal Young Woman's Bedroom" and had installed it without modification or an attempt at personalization.

In fact ...

He walked across the soft white carpet to a framed magazine article. The title read, "Every Girl's Dream Room," and the picture ... the picture was of Alex's room.

Her parents hadn't found a pattern, they'd *made* the pattern.

"Wo-o-o-ow," he said, drawing the word out under his breath.

"Notice the date on the article?"

"Yeah, uh ... wait, this was last month?"

She nodded. "When I moved out, I left my room a mess. Clothes everywhere, my bed unmade, my dressers and closet wide open. It was like a tornado had touched down in here. It was the first time in my life this room wasn't perfectly pristine. It felt so good."

She looked around her room, her hands clasped in front of her. It was a neutral gesture, but the skin was puckering around her hands where she was clutching them too tightly. "My mom didn't talk to me for over a month. Then a few weeks ago, a copy of *Dolce Vita* magazine appeared in the mail at Aunt Nora's addressed to me. You can imagine my surprise when I flipped through to find my bedroom featured in one of the most exclusive magazines in the country."

"That is seriously messed up."

She was staring at the article. "When I called her, she acted like I'd never left, like I was just living with roommates. She went on and on about the photo shoot and the article, not asking me a single question, not yelling at me or saying how disappointed she was. She may as well have been talking to herself."

"I'm sorry, Alex."

"It's stupid." She shook her head. "It's going to take a few minutes for me to pack, so feel free to wander or pilfer some gold candle-sticks, or something. And if you, uh, see my dad, run the other way."

"Your dad's home?"

"I saw his keys hanging up in the foyer, so . . ."

He wanted to ask why her dad hadn't come to see her yet, why she hadn't gone to see him. But Alex kept her eyes low and away from him, making it obvious that she wasn't interested in conversation.

"Got it," he said. "I'll send up a flare if I get lost."

The first thing Tate did was break into the "other baby's" room. He opened the door and flicked the light switch, but nothing hap-pened. The hall light showed a lamp on an end table. He pulled the string, and it bathed the room in a light too dull to be soft. If he hadn't deadened that part of him years earlier, this room would have been disturbing.

Everything was white, but not the pure, too bright white of Nora's house. Twenty years had faded the curtains, carpet, and wallpaper. A canopy hung open above the crib, revealing bedding that was undisturbed. The lamp showed a layer of dust over the rails, sheet, and canopy. When was the last time anyone had been in here?

He turned around to the cushy glider. It looked less dusty than the rest of the room. Tate sat on it, and it rocked back before pushing him forward again. He set his feet down, halting the movement. In front of the chair, a yellow-haired porcelain doll lay facedown in a basket atop a tufted storage ottoman. It stood out in the perfectly preserved room. He could imagine Alex's mom coming into the room and clutching that doll to her chest while she rocked and mourned her loss. It was odd that she wouldn't have put it back with more care.

Tate picked up the doll and stared into its dead green eyes. This is how Alex's parents must have imagined Vivienne before they lost her. No doubt the loss would never go away, but this curly, blonde, Little Bo Peep knockoff had nothing on Alex.

Tate laid the doll faceup in the basket. He tugged the lamp string, killing the lights before he walked out. The light from the hall struck the carpet at such an angle that Tate could see the outline of a large shoe on the soft fibers. A man's shoe. Several inches away was another shoeprint. And another. The prints marched a sad circle around the room. How often did Mr. Wolf's grief bring him here?

Unbidden, a memory hit Tate of being in the hospital after surgery. He had come to briefly. His throat was dry and parched, and the lights in the room were like pins stabbing his eyes. But he heard his dad pacing, heard the sound of heavy, worried steps falling in a practiced rhythm. Tate fell back out of consciousness, and it was hours before he awoke again. When he did, he pried his eyes open and saw his dad by his bedside, softly crying and praying into his clasped hands. "Please, let me keep my son. Please."

Tate shook off the memory, pulled his eyes from Connor Wolf's shoe prints, and walked out of the room. He closed the door more tightly than necessary. If the rest of the house was a mausoleum, this nursery was the tomb. He should have left it to the dead.

A few minutes and two hallways later, Tate heard the distinct, sharp sound of a basketball being dribbled. So that's where Alex's dad was hiding. Tate knew he should steer clear; Alex had flat out asked him to. But no one had ever accused him of being compliant. Especially not Alex.

He followed the sound until he came upon a half-sized indoor basketball court.

Fit, handsome, and still dressed from a day of campaigning, Alex's dad was dribbling the ball with his sleeves rolled up. He handled the ball with some skill, dribbling it several more times before picking it up and taking a jump shot from fifteen feet. He sank it easily. When the ball bounced back to him, he stepped back a foot and shot again with the same result. He did this two more times until he was at the three-point line. He shot, and the ball hit the rim, bounced into the air, and missed the net.

"There was a time when I got nothing but net eight times out of ten on that shot," Mr. Wolf said, beads of sweat lining his dark blond hair.

"That makes one of us," Tate replied, walking onto the court. He held his hands out, and Mr. Wolf tossed him the ball. Tate dribbled with less skill than the older man, but when he shot from the free-throw line, the ball swished through the net.

It bounced back to Mr. Wolf, who walked over to where Tate was standing and shot from the same spot. He made it. Tate grabbed the ball and tossed it back to Mr. Wolf.

"I thought I heard Alex come in, but it's a nice surprise to find you here, too, Tate," Mr. Wolf said. "I haven't seen you much since Robert's funeral. How have you been?"

Tate let out a low laugh. "That's a very complicated question."

"Isn't it always?" Mr. Wolf said, shooting again. "I heard you had some trouble with gambling a while back." He didn't look at Tate for a response. "It's a tough line to walk between winning and losing. Both can draw you in for different reasons."

"When you're winning, you feel invincible," Tate said, parroting what he'd heard people say in GA.

Mr. Wolf nodded. "And when you're losing, you keep thinking, 'But this next hand could be the one.'"

"The sting of running bad stays with you a lot longer than the high of running good."

"You have that right, son." He shot again, and the ball bounced off the backboard and into Tate's hands. "Some of my friends run a friendly game the second Wednesday of every month. All above-board, of course. You're welcome to call my assistant anytime if you'd like to come."

"That's very kind of you, Mr. Wolf."

He smiled, the same charming smile he always seemed to have for the press. "Please, call me Connor. We're practically family."

Tate held a finger out and spun the ball as fast as he could on it. It spun for a few seconds before wobbling off. He tried again. "But I also work for the enemy. Are you sure you want to be too friendly with me?"

"Nora, the enemy?" Mr. Wolf barked a laugh. "Hardly. I can't imagine a better scenario for the people of Illinois. Either way, they'll get an exceptional, dedicated attorney general."

"I admire how polite you've both kept your campaigns. You've managed to stick to the issues rather than sinking to name-calling. It's almost enough to restore my faith in politicians."

This earned him another laugh. "That's an oddly pessimistic view coming from a political intern."

"Believe me, I'm strictly there in a nephew capacity. I'm as apolitical as a University of Chicago philosophy major with law school aspirations can get."

Mr. Wolf looked at him. "I forgot how much I like you, Tate. If you ever want a job, call me. In fact, after the campaign, regardless of the outcome, call me. I'm not looking to poach you, but if I can ever help you out, it would be my pleasure."

"Thank you, sir. I appreciate that."

"And . . . how is Alex?"

"All indications point to her being fine. She's a real asset for Nora. You have every reason to be proud." He watched Mr. Wolf closely, a deep, concerned crease forming between the man's eyebrows. A crease Tate had seen before.

At Uncle Robert's funeral almost four years ago, Alex had walked up to the casket alone to say her good-byes. Her parents were in the receiving line with Aunt Nora and either hadn't noticed her slip away or hadn't cared. When a sob escaped her, though, Mr. Wolf stepped out of the line and put an arm around Alex. For a minute, maybe two, he whispered in her ear while she quietly wept. It had seemed so sweet, such a tender moment between a father and daughter. But when Alex and her father finally turned around, the tears and emotion had been wiped clean from her face. Tate had seen marble statues give more away than Alex in that moment.

Later, when the viewing was over and the casket was closed, Alex had started walking over to Aunt Nora when her father's hand fell on her shoulder, stopping her and returning her to her place. Meanwhile, Mr. Wolf had that same concerned crease between his brows. And it looked just as real then as it did now.

"I'm happy to hear that. And I *am* proud," Mr. Wolf said. "I've always encouraged her to assert her independence. When she was young, I tried to force it, in fact." Mr. Wolf paused, looking down at his feet. Tate kept spinning the ball. "My own father was hard on me, but it made me stronger and turned me into the man I am today.

I resented him at the time, but I forgot that, even as I did the same very thing to Alex. I never wanted to keep any advantage from her. I'm afraid that all I did, though, was create distance between us and make her think I don't care." He shook his head. "I don't know if I'll ever forgive myself for pushing her away."

The ball was still up on Tate's finger. "I'm sorry."

Mr. Wolf grabbed the ball, and his blue eyes held Tate's. "Keep an eye on her for me, will you?"

"I will."

"Good man." He dropped the ball at center court and clapped Tate's shoulder. "Now our cook makes a key lime pie that is out of this world. Come on downstairs and have a piece with me while you wait for Alex."

CHAPTER EIGHT

Weaving through the Wolf estate, Tate amended his earlier opinion. The place wasn't just a mausoleum; it was also a fancy, convoluted laboratory. A place where rats were sent through mazes and subjected to psychological experiments while scientists observed their response times and reactions.

A gilded cage.

As Tate leaned against a quartz countertop eating a piece of key lime pie across from Mr. Wolf, he had to wonder what the man was playing at. What could he possibly want from Tate? Even living at her house, Tate wasn't privy to anything important in Nora's campaign.

If Tate didn't know better, he'd have thought all Mr. Wolf really wanted in life was to eat pie and swap bad beat stories from past games as if they were old friends. "I have another one. You won't believe it," he told Tate. "One night at the Majestic early on in my poker days, I was with a few players, one of whom raised pretty aggressively pre-flop. I was holding a five, six clubs, so I stayed in, just in case. Miraculously, the flop came three, four, seven rainbow."

"You flopped the nut straight," Tate said, gripping his fork.

Mr. Wolf nodded. "So one player checked, and I led out with a bet nearly half the size of the pot. The aggressive guy next to me went all-in. I'd been playing long enough to know he was bluffing. So the action folded around back to me, and by this time, all I wanted to do was shut the guy up. I've learned to keep these comments to myself since then, but at the time, I couldn't stop myself. I said, 'I guess this is where the guy with the nut hand calls.' I turned over my hand and pushed my chips in.

"Now, of course, the aggro was bluffing. He flipped over a Royal Couple. But you won't guess what happens next."

"No. Don't tell me—"

Mr. Wolf slapped his knee, laughing. "Yes! Five on the turn. Six on the river."

Tate laughed hard. "You split the pot with that aggrodonk!"

"You want to talk about pain? I had a 99.09% chance of winning when the money went in."

"The poker gods didn't want you getting cocky," Tate said, chuckling. He stabbed his fork into the pie, taking two huge bites in succession.

Alex walked in on them still laughing.

"What's this?" she asked, her face blank except for the slight pull of her eyebrows. Confusion? Anger? Hope?

"Just catching up with Nora's nephew," her dad said with a smile, pushing his plate toward the sink. "He's a delightful young man. Bring him by anytime . . . anytime you feel like coming home, of course. I wouldn't want to tell you what to do."

Alex's expression fell. It had been hope, Tate realized with a pang.

"Alex, do you mind if we get back soon? I have an 8:00 a.m. class," Tate said. She nodded. Tate set his plate and fork next to Connor's before grabbing Alex's bags. He turned to Mr. Wolf. "I'm sorry to eat and run, but it's been good catching up."

"Remember," Mr. Wolf said, walking them out through the labyrinth-like mansion, "the second Wednesday of the month. I'd love to see you there."

Tate uncurled a fist he hadn't known he was making and shook Mr. Wolf's hand at the front door. "Thanks again, sir."

Mr. Wolf and Alex shared an awkward hug as Tate went to the car. He popped the trunk and lifted the first suitcase, but his muscles trembled as he loaded it into the car. He hadn't lifted this morning, but his arms and pecs felt weak, as if they could give out at any moment. By the time he climbed into the passenger seat, the shaking had extended to his whole body. Tate shoved his hands beneath his legs to stop their trembling.

"What is wrong with you?" Alex asked when she got in. "Are you on something?"

"No," he said. His skin felt too tight for his body, as if it was squeezing him. Suffocating him. "It's nothing. Just feeling light-headed."

"Are you diabetic? Or having an allergic reaction? You don't look good."

"No." The car was closing in on him now. The air was getting thin. "Could you stop at a gas station? I need to run in and grab something for my head."

"Yeah, of course."

A couple of minutes later, Alex was pulling into a station. "Do you want me to get it for you?"

"No, I got it," he said, already opening his door before the car was in park. He ran into the convenience store and straight to the checkout counter.

"What can I get you?" the cashier asked.

Tate took out his wallet. All he had was a fifty. He dropped the bill on the counter, his hands shaking too hard to give it to the cashier. "Ten Money Play scratch-offs."

Tate shifted from side to side on the balls of his feet, waiting.

When the cashier held out the tickets, Tate snatched them and darted for the automotive aisle. He bent down and used his thumbnail to start scratching the first ticket. Just the first. That's all he would do. He went as slowly as he could, scratching the first little circle of colorful UV ink. A fist seemed to clench around his lungs, and the anticipation was building.

Slow, he told himself. *Slow*.

The first number appeared, and it was as if floodgates had opened. His hand flew across the card as fast as it could. It took only a few seconds to finish, but he was panting. And excited. And . . .

Just one more.

In less than a minute, he'd scratched off all ten cards, and his thumbnail was coated with a rainbow of flecks. He'd won a hundred dollars. He'd won! Of course he had. He could win at anything. His heart skipping, he clenched the deck of cards in his pocket triumphantly. A wild grin made its way onto his face.

Holding the winning ticket, he went back up to the cashier. "I'll take twenty more Money Games."

Two minutes later, he was back in the automotive aisle frantically scratching ticket after ticket.

Loser.

Loser.

Loser.

They were all losers.

Just like Tate.

He grabbed the back of his head, crouching down like an abused dog. He was so stupid. So, so stupid. What was he doing here, hunched over in a convenience store with a hundred and fifty bucks in lottery tickets like some pathetic, desperate . . . addict.

He slapped his palm on the ground. *No. That's not me.*

Drawing in a shaky breath, Tate gathered up the losing tickets. He made himself walk slowly into the bathroom and calmly toss the losing tickets into the garbage bin. After a few more breaths, he looked at himself in the mirror. Other than his eyes being a little red, he looked fine. Alex wouldn't suspect a thing.

There's nothing to suspect. You bought a few lottery tickets, and you didn't spend a cent that wasn't yours. It's not a big deal.

Right. That was right. It wasn't a big deal. This wasn't the end of the world. But there was a time when a hundred and fifty bucks could have multiplied into a thousand after even a friendly night of poker with Yates and their buddies.

How was this better? How the hell was he standing in a gas station bathroom with scratch-off UV ink beneath his nails when he could be—

Knock, knock, knock.

"Tate?" Alex's voice said through the bathroom door. "Tate, you alive in there?"

Dammit. Control yourself.

"Yeah, one sec." He flushed the toilet, then turned on the water, splashing some on his face for good measure. When he came out of the bathroom, Alex was biting her thumbnail. She dropped her hand and stood pin straight.

"Are you okay? You've been gone for like ten minutes."

"I'm fine."

"I thought you'd passed out or something. You look peaked."

"Peaked? Really, Grandma?"

"Shut up. I'm serious."

"Why don't we continue this conversation in the car instead of at the bathroom door?"

She looked around, noticing someone waiting behind her for the bathroom. "Fine. Come on."

He steered her past the automotive section, in case he'd forgotten any tickets. At the exit, he held the door open for her, noticing the scratch-off flecks caked under his thumbnail. He tucked his thumb before she could see it.

When they got into the car, he'd already removed the evidence.

They hadn't even left the parking lot when she demanded to know what had happened.

"It's nothing, I swear," he said. "The pie didn't sit well with me. I just felt dizzy and thought I was going to throw up, okay?"

"So why didn't you say that?"

"This may come as a surprise to you, but most guys don't like talking about bouts of gastrointestinal distress with beautiful girls."

She didn't answer at first. Then she chuckled. "Point taken."

"Which point? The one about you being beautiful? Is that what you're taking away from all this?"

"Obviously," she said.

"I should have expected that." He reclined his seat and put his hands behind his head. He watched as the lights from passing cars illuminated her face. He was already feeling better, feeling the frenetic energy leave his body, just as he'd left his temporary lapse of judgment on the aisle of that convenience store. He focused on Alex. "How was being at home?"

"Crappy."

He let the word linger in the air until it was practically decaying. Eventually, Alex's hands tightened around the steering wheel and she cleared her throat. "You know what the worst part is? My mom *knew* I was coming home tonight. She knew it, and she told me 'it wouldn't be right' to pull herself away from the Hearsts' fund-raising gala, as if yet another overpriced plate of rubber chicken is more important than seeing me."

"That's pitiful."

"Excuse me?"

"Not you, her. She doesn't realize that she's losing you, and one day, I bet it'll eat her alive."

"It won't," Alex said, her voice sounding scratchy. "She doesn't *care* that she's losing me. And I'm officially done with this conversation."

"Alex—"

"I'm done, Tate."

He popped his seat upright and snatched a quarter from Alex's coin tray, finger-walking it across the back of his knuckles. "I have a better idea. I'll flip you for it."

She gave him a suspicious glance. "Flip me for what?"

"For a question. Heads, I get to ask you something. Tails, you get to ask me something."

She pulled her shoulders back, sitting up straighter. "Okay."

He flipped the coin, catching it and plopping it on the top of his hand. "Heads."

She rolled her eyes. "Of course." Around the steering wheel, she ran her thumbnail over the jagged nail on her ring finger. "What do you want to know?"

"Why do you think your mom doesn't care that she's losing you?"

"Ask something else."

"That isn't what we agreed. I won the coin flip, I pick the question. Or do we need to talk about the consequences of reneging?"

"No, I'll play your stupid little game." Alex paused, taking a deep breath. "When I was eleven, she gave me The Talk. After she explained all about puberty and sex, she said there was one thing I absolutely had to remember: love was for fools. That's a direct quote. She said practical considerations like security and compatibility were more important than such a worthless emotion could ever be, because emotions and attraction would fade. She talked about animals in the wild, hormones, pheromones. She reduced love to mindless lust, and she told me she would be ashamed if her daughter ever succumbed to it. *Ashamed.*

"That night before bed when she said she loved me, what was I supposed to think? How was I supposed to believe her, when she thinks the very concept of love is a lie? I sometimes wonder if the problem is that she didn't actually give birth to me, you know? Like maybe her maternal instincts never kicked in because she never went through pregnancy and childbirth."

They both knew it had nothing to do with that. Or at least Tate did. His parents loved Finley at least as much as the rest of the family. Unfortunately for Alex, Mrs. Wolf was a crappy human being. That's all there was to it. He debated saying this, but Alex's eyes already looked dewy.

"What about your dad?" he asked.

She looked at the coin in his hand. "You flipping me for that, Sprinkles?"

He flipped it. "Heads."

The words rushed out of her. "I've never been enough for him. No matter what I do, he's never approved, and that only makes me work harder to get him to care." Now that, Tate understood. "I think he knows that, and he uses it against me."

"In what way?"

"I don't know how to put my finger on it. He has a way of finding a person's weaknesses and crafting whole scenarios to exploit them. Like how he said he didn't mean to tell me what to do? It was so . . ."

"Passive aggressive? Backhanded?"

"Manipulative," she said. "Speaking of which, did he actually invite you to his poker game?" Tate nodded. "What a bastard. He *knows* you went to rehab. I was there when Aunt Nora told him. He was messing with you. I guarantee it."

The memory of his trembling hands scratching tickets assaulted him. "Don't worry about it."

"Good. Now flip that coin again," she said.

He flipped it. It was heads, again. "Tails."

"Finally," she said. "I need something horrific and blackmail-worthy after my overshare. So . . . give me something horrific and blackmail-worthy."

He put his hands behind his head. "Let's see. I was caught making out with my brother's ex on the same night that my dad found out I was running a card room, and he cut me off and kicked me out—"

"Why'd you make out with your brother's ex? Do you like her?"

"Are you asking me to flip the coin again?"

She narrowed her eyes.

"Fine," he said. Thinking of Fin made him smile, if a little sadly. "Yeah, I like her. She's probably the best person I've ever known and way too accepting of me, honestly, even when she has no reason to be. Last year, she broke up with her boyfriend, Harlan, because he made her choose between helping me recuperate and going to New York with him."

"She made the right call, but only because if he really cared about her, he'd have taken her to Paris."

"Nice. That's very kind of you, Alex." She shrugged, but he could tell she was waiting for more. "There was also the matter of him cheating on her," Tate said. "But he blamed her for it, said that if she'd chosen him over me and my family, it never would have happened." Alex shook her head. "I probably should feel guilty for that, but I don't. Without her, I'd have had a way harder time recovering after the accident and surgery. And I never could have made it through the intervention. She held my hand the whole time. She's the kind of person a guy would spend a lifetime trying to be worthy of."

Her words carried an edge. "That's what you want? Someone you're always trying to prove yourself to?"

"It's not what *she* would want."

Alex frowned. "Do you mean as opposed to me?"

He smiled. "No, Narcissus. I meant me."

"You really want to be with her, don't you?" Her lips pursed tightly while his smile broadened.

"It doesn't matter what I want," he said provokingly. "I respect her too much to drag her down with me."

She groaned. "You sound like a romance novel."

"Why? Because I care about someone more than—"

"If you don't shut up about this girl, I'm going to unbuckle your seatbelt and throw you out of the car."

He laughed. "You know, my buddy Yuri told me that there's a verb in Russian that means 'to throw someone from a moving car.'"

"Good," she said, "I'll have my lawyer use it in my defense to save time. Or I could just throw you out the window and plead to defenestration."

"What?" he said, sitting up. "Defenestration?"

"Yes! How do you not know that word, School Boy? It's delicious—it literally means to throw someone out a window."

"Man, and I thought Russian was so much cooler than English."

"Nope."

"Unless we're talking about Teddy KGB. That accent . . ."

"You're such a cliché!" Her laugh sounded a little punch-drunk. "Of course you would make a *Rounders* reference."

"'Pay that myan his myoney,'" Tate quoted in an over-the-top accent.

Alex broke into a fit of laughter. When she snorted mid-laugh, they both laughed harder.

Watching her shake and giggle beside him, a feeling washed over Tate, pulling on him like a tide.

Alex was going to be trouble.

CHAPTER NINE

The following morning found Tate and Alex eating breakfast at the same time. With Nora in Springfield, they were louder and more casual than normal. She teased him about philosophy, saying things like "Newsflash: If a tree falls in the forest and no one hears it, the animals and bugs it falls on are still dead, and you are still insufferable."

"Wow. Clever," he said. "You should come guest lecture some time."

"Maybe I will," she said, reaching for the last piece of bacon. He grabbed it first, shoving it in his mouth before she could stop him. She pointed at him. "I know where you live."

"That would be a lot more threatening if you didn't have schmutz on your chin," he said, dipping his finger in the cream cheese and wiping it on her face.

"Very mature," she said, grabbing a napkin.

"Did I say your chin?" He leaned across the table again and smeared cream cheese on her cheek. She gasped and tried to grab his finger. "I meant your cheek."

"Tate!" She wiped the cream cheese from her cheek and threw the napkin at him. "This is your last day on earth."

"My last day? Are you driving us to school, or something?"

"Did you make a joke about my driving because I'm a woman? You sexist dink."

They both got up and made their way to the door, where they grabbed their bags and Alex, her keys.

"Considering you threatened to defenestrate me—"

"I was demonstrating my superior command of language."

"—I'd say being called an unsafe driver is an accurate, if grossly understated, representation."

"Unless you're looking to be defenestrated, you need to shut your pretty mouth and get in the car."

When Tate arrived at campaign headquarters later that day, Oscar pulled him aside.

"Alex has been telling me good things about your work with the field team, so I was wondering if you'd be interested in a position of a little higher responsibility."

Alex had complimented him to Oscar? "Sure, I'm interested."

"Great," Oscar said. "One of our key opportunities is with outreach across racial and ethnic boundaries. Nora's platform should be appealing to immigrants, for example, particularly considering the work she and your father have done to expand the civil liberties of undocumented immigrants. You interned with your father during Juana's case, and I think that'll be invaluable for this outreach. You start today."

Oscar gave him a few more instructions, including introducing him to other liaisons both in person and by phone, as some of them worked out of Springfield.

A few hours later, Tate was already at work doing something he actually enjoyed: research. Before doing outreach, he needed to find local minority community leaders he could contact about how

Nora's candidacy would support them and the members of their community. After creating his list, he highlighted one name in a big, bold stroke: Juana.

Juana Valdez had been an undocumented immigrant living in Albany Park. Nine months pregnant, she was going into labor when a police officer stopped her for rolling through a stop sign. She tried to explain, but when labor pains made it virtually impossible to get out of the car, the officer claimed she was resisting arrest and denied her access to a hospital. She delivered in a holding cell, handcuffed to a bench, and the ambulance didn't arrive until after she delivered. Unfortunately, the cord was wrapped around her son's neck and he didn't get enough oxygen during the delivery. At the hospital, although they managed to stabilize him, they discovered he had brain damage as a result.

Tate had joined his dad and his legal team as an intern when his dad appealed the case to the Illinois Supreme Court. They were gone for nearly a month prepping, going over notes, and doing interviews. Ironically, being an intern had given Tate glimpses of compassion he hadn't seen from his dogged, driven father since he was a child.

Nora and Tate's dad were equal partners in their firm, so while she had been involved in the case, she had stayed behind to manage the office while Tate's dad and some junior partners worked on the appeal. Few people could speak about the case or Nora's involvement as well as Tate could.

When the phone rang, Tate cleared his throat.

"*Bueno*," a female voice said.

"*Buenas tardes*," he said. "*Se encuentra Juana Valdez?*"

"*Quién habla?*"

"Tate Bertram."

"Tate?" the woman repeated. "This is Juana!" she said in an excited voice. Her accent was milder than it had been even a year ago, probably a result of doing so many interviews in the months following the state Supreme Court decision.

She had been awarded an enormous settlement that would provide the best care and best possible life for her and her son. It wasn't justice—nothing could undo what had been done—but it was something. Tate asked about how she and her son, Mateo, were doing. She told him about the excellent doctors, their beautiful house, her new car. She was sponsoring her parents, providing an education for her nephews and niece, and she'd finished her GED. She had made donations to local charities and had become an important member of her community. She couldn't believe her blessings.

His nose tickled as he listened to her. After all that had happened to her, she had every right to be jaded and bitter—Tate still was. But her joy was infectious.

When Tate explained why he was calling, Juana wanted to help. She remembered talking to Nora, remembered thinking what a proud, strong woman she was. Juana offered to talk to local leaders in the schools and churches, and anything else Tate might want.

They ended the call with a plan to speak again soon. Tate put down his headset feeling better than he had in . . . he didn't know how long. Talking to Juana was like pressing a reset button on his soul. He pulled out his cell phone and, before he could talk himself out of it, texted his dad.

I talked to Juana today. She and Mateo are both doing great—still in Albany Park. Thought you'd want to know.

He wanted to say more, wanted to say that he was proud of the work his dad had done for Juana, but Tate wasn't that big a person. He was proud of his dad for helping Juana. He was. But it hurt that the man reserved such sympathy and concern for his clients when he had so little for his own son.

Tate went back to researching, but several minutes later, he heard an angry voice punctuate the low hum of conversation.

Tate stood in his cubicle, looking over the five-foot walls to see Oscar talking to his dad.

"Why would you authorize this?"

"We didn't authorize anything; we allowed an intern autonomy to reach influential citizens—"

"You tell Nora that Juana is off-limits."

Anger built in Tate's chest. He walked out of the cubicle and over to where Oscar was trying to steer his dad into an office. When Tate joined them, his dad was all tight lips and clenched jaw.

"Good afternoon, Dad. Pleasure to see you. Why don't we take your inappropriate tone off the floor," Tate said, leading his dad into Oscar's office. When Oscar closed the door, Tate folded his arms. "Why are you so angry that Juana asked to help?"

His dad tugged on his cuffs. "I couldn't believe it when Nora told me she still wanted you as an intern. After all the ways you've proven you're not responsible enough, it boggled my mind. Now I get it. I told her not to solicit Juana's help, but if a plucky intern who knows her personally does it . . ." He held up his hands. "They manipulated you into calling Juana. That's the whole reason Nora offered you a position on her staff."

Tate breathed in and out slowly, refusing to let the rage in his gut boil over. "I chose to call Juana because I care about her and thought she could recommend some influential leaders in Albany Park. Again, I didn't ask for her help. She offered."

"Of course she offered; she's a good, kindhearted person who feels like she owes us everything. Taking her up on her offer was exploitative."

"No, it was allowing her greater involvement in something she feels passionately about. You don't get to make decisions for her, Dad."

"Is that what you think this is about? Me making decisions for you?" his dad asked.

Tate actually chuckled. "Oh, Dad. Thank you for reminding me not to extend another olive branch. I thought you'd want to know Juana is happy and moving forward with her life. I'm sorry you're disappointed that she won't stay in the protective bubble you tried to make for her." He grabbed his dad's shoulder. "And yes, we're speaking about me now, too. And Finley, come to think of it. Maybe even Mom."

Over the sound of his dad's furious protests, Tate strode out of the small office. Rather than return to his cubicle, though, he left the headquarters and then the building altogether.

If he smoked, now would be the time to pull out cigarette upon cigarette. Instead, he walked up the sidewalk, ducking into the first alley he saw. Halfway down the alley, he stopped, clenched his fists, and roared. He picked up a piece of rotting wood and whacked it against a dumpster until it broke into a thousand splinters. He tossed it down, heaving. A black cat jumped out from behind the dumpster, darting down the alley. When the creature was out of sight, he kicked the dumpster.

"You feeling better? Working out your daddy issues?"

"Sort of." He kicked it again. "What are you doing here?"

Alex's heels echoed off the buildings as she approached him. "Wanted to see if you knew where the dumpster was." She pointed. "Looks like you found it."

"Ha."

"Come on. Coffee. I'm buying."

He clenched and unclenched his hands. "No, I'm too keyed up already. I need to calm down."

"So, what, a drink?"

"I can't. I have a huge exam tomorrow. Besides, drinking, uh, leads to impulse control issues for me. Not the best choice for someone who tends toward the self-destructive."

"I didn't think about that."

He waved her off. "You were being nice."

She paused, looking distinctly uncomfortable, and in the back of his mind, he knew why. She'd been more open with him lately, more real, something he knew had happened precious little in her life. If her concern had been an act, she'd have known exactly how to go through the motions. But this was real. Alex had never been taught how to do real. And here he was, shooting her down.

He rolled his neck around and shook his shoulders out, letting the tension ease out of his body. "How about a milkshake?"

"Are you ten years old?"

He groaned. "Please don't tell me you're too fancy for a milkshake. That will ruin every fantasy thirteen-year-old Tate had about you."

She grabbed his arm, leading him from the alley with a sniff. "I knew you'd been fantasizing about me all this time."

"Yes, fantasizing about you drinking a milkshake. Of course, I also fantasize about milkshakes drinking milkshakes, so it's not as flattering as you're imagining."

"Whatever you have to tell yourself, Tate. Whatever you have to tell yourself."

CHAPTER TEN

A few nights later, Tate and Alex were sitting at Nora's table with a bowl of popcorn between them and their homework in front of them. The late hour was making them silly, and they kept knocking their feet and legs into each other beneath the table.

"Stop kicking me," Tate said, deleting a typo.

"You kicked me," she said, throwing a piece of popcorn at him. It landed in his hair. He pulled it out, popped it into his mouth, and kept typing.

"I'm bored," she said a few minutes later, slamming a book shut.

"Call your boyfriend," he said.

"Shut up," she said. "You know I haven't talked to him in weeks." He didn't know that, but the fact that she thought he *should* know it was interesting. "Why don't you call Finley?" She said the name as if it belonged in a diaper.

"You're cute when you're jealous," he said, still typing.

"You think *I'm* jealous? You're the one who mentioned my boyfriend," she said, even as the back door opened and Nora walked in.

Tate glanced up. His aunt looked exhausted. "Long day?" he asked.

"Long week," she said, kicking off her heels and joining them at the table. "And I think I just drove over a nail pulling into the garage. If the neighbors don't finish that damn remodel soon, I'm going to sue."

"Do you want me to take your car into the shop, Aunt Nora?" Alex asked.

"I'll have my assistant call someone." Nora sighed and rubbed Alex's back. "But thank you, Alex. I read your political science paper in the hotel last night, by the way. Beautifully written. And such a clever argument. I can see why your professor shared it with the class. Very well done, dear," she said with a proud smile.

"Thanks, Aunt Nora." Tate was sure Alex's cheeks must have hurt from trying so hard not to beam. "But you seem stressed. Are you okay?" Alex asked. "Can I do anything?"

"No, it's just the usual in politics: attack ads have started."

Alex frowned. "What? No. My dad promised he wouldn't—"

"Oh, they're not coming from your dad's campaign. They're from a PAC. The governor is proposing a state-owned casino. It'll include changing video gambling throughout the state and at horse tracks. There's a question over the legality of it, yet Connor says he'll do everything he can to support it."

"My dad and the governor have become pretty close friends over the last year," Alex said, "so that's not a big surprise."

"No, the big surprise is who the governor wants to run it: Michael Landolfo," Nora said.

Tate let out a long, ominous whistle.

"Isn't he on the liquor control board?" Alex asked, looking from Tate to Nora. "I thought I saw something about him wanting to change liquor licensing for restaurants."

"He's rumored to have serious mob connections," Tate said.

"What? No," Alex said. Her voice sounded pinched. "My dad would never knowingly associate with the mob. Landolfo must be clean."

"Maybe," Tate said before looking at Nora. "But what does he know about running a casino?"

Nora shook her head. "Damned if I can tell. I've been on the phone with the Illinois Gaming Association, gambling regulators, and addiction recovery groups for days, hearing their concerns over the proposal. I'm already getting smeared in the media. They're saying I want to enforce puritanical standards on the citizens of Illinois that rival Prohibition. They may as well have shown me painting a scarlet 'A' on someone's dress."

"Or a 'G,' as it were," Tate said.

"Should I not talk about it in front of you?" Nora asked, grabbing a single piece of popcorn and studying it.

"Video gambling and horse tracks aren't my speed. You're fine."

She nodded. "How's the interning? What does Oscar have you working on?"

"Constituent liaising." Tate eyed his aunt. "Didn't my dad call you?"

She pinched the bridge of her nose. "Juana. That's right. He asked me to call her and tell her that we don't want to 'make her relive the horror and heartache she's already experienced.'"

"Did you?" Tate asked.

"Of course not. Juana reached out to me early in the campaign offering her support, but your dad talked me out of accepting it. Now that she's involving herself, though, who am I to stop her?"

"You know, maybe we should consider featuring her in some ads," Alex said. "We could drum up a lot of sympathy and support—"

"I don't know," Tate said. "That feels like it's crossing the line. If Juana wants to help, it needs to be on her terms, not ours."

Nora sighed, rising from the table. "I agree. It would help, but I wouldn't feel right about it unless it's her idea. Anyway, I have another full day of accusations and attacks to look forward to. I'll see you both at HQ tomorrow." She kissed the top of Alex's head before going upstairs.

After Nora was gone, Tate couldn't ignore the slump to Alex's shoulders. "It was a good idea, having Juana in an ad," he told her.

"You have a strategic mind."

Her eyes narrowed to pinpoints. "Don't patronize me."

"I wasn't trying to."

"No, you were trying to soften the blow to my ego. I don't need you, of all people, to protect me," she snapped. "I suggested something and it got shut down. End of story."

Stupid Tate. She wasn't looking at him, so he took the opportunity to study her. *Stupid Tate.* Her hunched shoulders weren't the sign of a wounded animal but one waiting to attack. He should have known better. "You're right. I'm sorry."

"And now you're telling me whatever I want to hear." She stood and marched the popcorn bowl over to the sink. "I'm a big girl, and, between the two of us, who has an impeccable track record for decision making? That's right, me. This doesn't change anything."

"Alex, do you want to talk about what's really bothering you?"

"Landolfo can't be shady, Tate."

"He is, Alex. I'm not saying your dad—"

"Of course he's not. Just because my dad knows someone who allegedly has mob connections, that doesn't mean he's involved. Besides, we live in Chicago. Everyone knows someone with mob connections, whether they realize it or not."

"True."

"And there could be a hundred different reasons for him to support this casino proposal."

"Right. Casino taxes go to building schools and roads."

"Exactly. It makes good business sense for the state. And my dad is the most disciplined person I know. He's always in complete control of any situation, so the idea that other people may not be is so foreign to him. I bet when you guys were talking the other night, he didn't even think about what he was doing. He was just talking to another poker enthusiast. That doesn't make him a bad person."

Tate nodded for Alex's sake.

"Stop pandering and just listen to me, okay? My dad isn't stupid. He's brilliant and the hardest worker I know, and . . . and he likes you! He texted me after we were there and told me to bring you over again soon. My dad is a good guy, Tate."

"Alex—"

"If you really get to know him, you'll see. He's a good guy."

"Why does it matter if he and I like each other?"

She shook her head. "No. It doesn't. That's not what I'm trying to say."

Tate stood and walked around the table to her. "Can I tell you what I think?" he said, standing close enough to count her eyelashes. "I think I drive you absolutely wild, and you don't know what do with it."

"That's absurd." She sounded almost breathless.

"You had your life perfectly planned out, perfectly under control. Then I came around, and ever since, you're having to reconcile these two sides of yourself: the dutiful daughter and the girl who actually wants something for the first time in her life."

Her eyes fell to his mouth, making his stomach clench as it always did right before he dropped a winning hand. "Something?" she asked.

"Me."

"You're delusional," she said, but a small smile was flirting with the corner of her mouth.

He brought a hand to her face, and her eyes looked as if they wanted to close. Leaning in, he took a strand of hair that had fallen forward. His fingers trailed across her cheek as he tucked the strand behind her ear and whispered. "You're not denying it."

It was the wrong move. Alex's eyes snapped open and she knocked his hand away, pulling the hair back out. "You're wrong. And don't do that. I hate having my hair behind my ears."

The tension between them evaporated, but a smile stretched across Tate's face as he backed up. "I know. That's why I did it."

She looked heavenward and inhaled deeply, as if exasperated. Or as if the space between them was finally enough for her to breathe. "You did not. That's your signature move, and when I didn't melt into a puddle at your very touch, you changed your story."

"That's true, too," he said.

"You're agreeing with everything I say again. Stop it."

He grabbed his things and headed for the stairs. "Good night, Alex."

The following evening, Tate pulled off his headset and placed it next to his office phone. He tapped out a few notes from the conversation, before pulling up tomorrow's calendar and adding a few more items to the list. Since talking with Juana, he'd been more and more invested in his aunt's campaign, almost as if he had purpose.

It was overrated.

His phone buzzed—Finley sending a GIF of a cat popping out of a shoe. He smiled before a sour feeling bubbled in his chest. He cleared the message, pushed his chair away from the desk, and looked at the time. It was nearly nine o'clock. He still had homework to do, and he should probably fit sleep into his schedule at some point. And how was it already mid-May? He had less than a month left in the quarter, and he was seriously considering taking a break during the summer, even if he was still playing catch-up from the time he missed last year. Just the thought of all that time wasted in rehab made his lip curl. He hadn't bought a lottery ticket in days, maybe even a week. How many "addicts" could say that?

Nia had texted him to invite him to meetings. He'd been able to tell her—honestly—that he was simply too busy. As busy as he was, though, it was nothing compared with Alex; on top of everything else, she was helping organize a bipartisan charity function for her dad and Nora.

Alex's desire to prove herself to her dad eclipsed even her desire for Nora's approval. The girl was burning the candle at both ends, and the wax was piling up. Tate rubbed his eyes and looked through the now darkened offices to see Alex scowling at her computer.

He made his way to her office to hear her cursing with the fluency of a seasoned trucker.

"You're still here?" she asked when he opened her door.

"I was finishing up with a community center manager in Albany Park." He leaned against the door frame. "What has you so upset?"

"The charity insisted on a theme Nora, Oscar, and I hate, and they refuse to work with us on it." She rubbed her temples. "But if we back out, they'll say Nora's coldhearted, hates the poor, hates kids, killed JFK, blah blah blah." She shook her head. "This sucks."

"What's the theme? Is it really so bad?"

"They swore me to confidentiality." She sighed. "And, no, most people won't mind."

"But..."

She pushed her chair out and slammed her laptop closed. "But I have a job to do, okay? It's not up to me."

He blinked a slow, tired blink, lacking the energy to figure out if she was still mad about their fight the other night or this charity theme or something else entirely. "This is fun and all, but—"

"Oh, don't walk away mad," she said. "Just wait." She grabbed her things and walked out with him. A glance at her pursed lips showed that she was feeling pissy, not penitent. He held the door and followed her out into the smoggy night air.

"I have a twelve-page paper to finish by tomorrow morning. So unless we can keep it civil, I'm not really in the mood for"—he moved a hand back and forth between them—"this."

"Relax, Drama Queen," she said, turning for the parking garage.

"Alex . . ."

"Don't get your panties in a twist."

He turned around, walking in the opposite direction.

The click of her heels stopped. "Wait! You're seriously taking the L instead of driving home with me?"

He waved.

"Fine!" she called out. "Be that way."

The L train took twice as long as driving, but it had two advantages: it salvaged his pride and gave him time to work on his paper.

When he got home, Alex was sitting on his bed, arms folded, spitting fire.

"Fancy meeting you here," he said, dropping his bag on the small desk in one corner of the room before rolling his head back and forth. "Can I take a rain check on the angry make-out session? I'm wiped."

"You are an insufferable jackass."

"I've been called worse." He peeled off his shirt and threw it in the hamper. He didn't have to flex to make his abs visible, but he did anyway.

Force of habit.

As he tugged a pajama shirt over his head, he caught her looking at his scar. It was probably a trick of the light, but her eyes looked damp.

He pulled the shirt down the rest of the way and started unbuttoning his pants. "Are you staying for the whole show, or . . ."

She growled, jumped up, and slammed the door behind her.

He yelled after her, "Rain check!"

CHAPTER ELEVEN

Alex shot him frosty looks all the next day, looks he successfully ignored in favor of work. Juana had plans to meet with some business owners in Albany Park in the next few days, so Tate had been coordinating with another volunteer rather than getting sucked into Hurricane Alex.

But that evening when only a handful of employees and volunteers were left in the office, Tate heard a throat clear behind him. He glanced back to see Alex.

"I thought you might need a ride home tonight," she said, not quite meeting his eye.

"You thought I might need a *ride*? That's all you have to say?"

Her lip curled. "You know, you're right. I came over here to tell you to go to hell." She turned on her heel and stormed away.

A roar of thunder shook the building, and Tate realized too late that it was raining. And he had forgotten his umbrella. And it was a quarter of a mile to the train station.

You didn't think that little plan through, did you?

He jumped up and followed at a run. "Alex! Wait, I was kidding. Of course I'd love a ride home. Thanks for offering!" He caught up and put a hand on her lean shoulder. "I was kidding, Alex. Hold on."

She shrugged him off, and he heard a sniff. Was she . . . was she *crying*?

Don't ask. She will carve you open.

"Are you crying?"

Her head whipped around, and she was completely dry-eyed. Of course. She smacked his chest with the back of her hand. "Are you serious? You think I was *crying?* About *you?*" She practically cackled. "Tate, I didn't cry at my uncle's funeral," she said, which he knew was a lie, no matter how much her dad had tried to force the emotion out of her. "I didn't cry when I broke my arm in Cabo last year. I didn't cry when Bethany Taylor and her middle school minions followed me around school for a week straight after finding out I was adopted to ask me what the orphanage was like, as if I can remember being three months old, and 'how much I cost,' and why my parents didn't want 'their own kids,' and—"

His disgust was too much to hide. "What horrible human beings," he said.

"Yeah, I know. They sucked. And if they couldn't make me cry, you sure as hell can't."

She shoved the door open to the outside and popped open her umbrella. He followed closely behind her. Hard rain struck them from all directions.

"I get it, okay? Those vile little douchebaguettes couldn't bring you down. Nothing can," he said, because he knew it was what she wanted to hear, even if it wasn't true. Lightning flashed in the sky, reflecting off the slick streets, and the rain only seemed to come harder. He had to yell to be heard. "I didn't think you were upset over me, but I know you have a lot going on. I just wanted to make sure you were all right."

They reached the garage in record time, where Alex shook out her umbrella a little higher and closer to his face than was strictly necessary.

"Next time you want to make sure I'm all right, just ask." She unlocked the car and they both got in.

"I will," he said seriously. "Alex, are you all right?"

The frantic swishing of the wipers was all he heard for a moment. Then: "I need another favor," Alex said, not answering the question.

"Okay."

"My mother wants to go to brunch Sunday. I don't want to go."

"So, what, you want me to call her and turn her down?"

A wicked smile played across her lips. "She would lose her mind. That would make her badgering me this week all worth it."

"All week, huh?" Her recent attitude was making more sense.

"Yes. All. Effing. Week. So I need you to come with me to brunch. It's a Sunday, and I know you don't have anything else going on, because you haven't been answering your friends' texts and you seem to have screwed over every member of your family."

"When you put it so nicely, how could I refuse?"

She stole a glance at him. "Is that—will you come?"

He held back his annoyance. "I'm a guy. I'll do anything for a free meal."

"Good." She exhaled loudly, and he could almost detect a *thank you* in that breath.

"So what's my cover?"

"What do you mean?"

"I mean, what do you want her to think—that you broke up with your boyfriend, or something?" he asked, aware he was fishing. "Why would I, of all people, be joining you for brunch with your mom?"

If he didn't know better, he'd think she shrank. "We're friends, obviously. Friends go to brunch with each other's families."

"Are we?" he asked.

"Huh?"

"Are we friends, Alex?"

She kept her eyes on the rain-splattered windshield and her hands at ten and two, as if her diligent obedience to the rules of the road would protect her from this conversation. "Sure. Why are you being so weird? I just need you there so she'll have to put on her entertaining face, okay?"

"No problem," he said.

He watched her from the corner of his eye the rest of the way to Nora's. She'd downplayed everything—her anxiety about seeing her mom, why she was inviting Tate, their relationship—but it all so obviously mattered. Could she recognize her lie?

He'd known she was starting to care about him, but he hadn't known he had the power to hurt her.

He had no idea what to do with that.

On Sunday, Alex picked out Tate's shirt and tie. And jacket. And shoes. It was a miracle she'd let him pick out his own slacks.

It was a shame she hadn't picked out his underwear.

"How do you still not know how to do your hair? It's been seven years, Bertram. Look in a damn magazine already," she said, fixing his hair in his bathroom.

"You know it looks exactly the same as it did when I finished, right?" he asked, looking at her in the mirror. "I think you're looking for excuses to get your hands on me."

"Shut up. I'm concentrating," she said, screwing up her face. She moved a single tuft of hair a sixteenth of an inch. "There. Perfect." She turned him by his shoulders to face her. In her heels, she was nearly as tall as he was. "Now if you mess that up, I will hurt you." She looked at her reflection, wiping her lipstick line. She'd curled her hair, and the effect made her look deceptively innocent. Like a doll in a horror movie . . . or in her dead sister's room at home. "Are you ready to go?"

"You tell me," he said, holding out his hands.

"Good enough, GQ. Let's get this over with."

On the drive to the restaurant, Tate admired Alex. Her pale pink dress and white blazer made her dark eyes and hair all the more striking. "You look beautiful, by the way."

"She's going to complain about something. I've gotten too much sun. I look tired. I should get highlights. My hair is too long and the weight of it is giving me premature wrinkles."

"She's clearly a woman of substance."

Alex's brow wrinkled. Prematurely. "She's not all bad. She spends dozens of hours every week volunteering and heading up charities. She's on the board of Mercy Hospital, and that takes up a lot of her time. She wishes she could see me more, but her schedule really doesn't make it easy."

"For someone who's essentially left them, you spend a lot of time defending your parents. I'm not criticizing, just pointing it out."

She honked at someone who cut her off. "It's not like I don't love them just because I don't support my dad politically."

"Believe me, I know where you're coming from." He swiped a hand over his slacks. "So what can I expect from your mom today? She's not going to hit on me when you go to the bathroom, is she?"

"Gross."

"I notice you didn't deny the possibility."

She exhaled noisily. "I hate you sometimes."

"But you love me always."

Twenty minutes later, they left the car at valet parking and walked into the sophisticated restaurant just past the lobby of one of Chicago's most upscale hotels. It was one he'd been to with his family on occasion—the social graces such a place required were second nature to him. But over the last couple of years, these situations had grown tiresome. The people here wanted to be seen. In the places he preferred, the people had the opposite desire.

Ultimately, the motivations of both groups were identical: they were self-serving and built on lies. The difference was that here, everyone pretended to believe everyone else. In casinos and card rooms, no one did. But Tate was versatile, and he could wear one set of lies as easily as another. And apparently he was wearing this set well enough to attract the eyes of a handful of women, who smiled at him appreciatively.

"Knock it off," Alex hissed.

"Just getting in the mood in case your mom gets frisky," he said beneath his breath.

The host showed them the table and pulled out Alex's chair for her. She smiled tightly at her mother. Tate hadn't seen Mrs. Wolf in a few years, but she looked as beautiful as ever. Better, even. Parts of her body had somehow managed to defy the gravity to which they'd previously succumbed.

"Mrs. Wolf, thank you for allowing me to come to brunch today. Pleasure to see you," he said.

"Tate Bertram, how nice to see you again." Mrs. Wolf smiled prettily. "But, please, call me Cynthia." Blonde highlights masked her naturally red hair, makeup covered her smattering of freckles, and her blue eyes sparkled under eyelashes that were just long enough to look stunning, but real, when they most certainly were not. The same applied to nearly every part of her body. She was an exceptional knockoff of a real woman.

It wasn't her fault he could see through her so easily, though. He doubted anyone else in the room could tell. But Tate could always spot a cheat.

They exchanged niceties, and she asked after his family. He pretended to really care as he told her about Oliver and his volunteering, Juliette and her swanky boarding school, his dad's job. Only when he spoke about his mom did he feel any emotion other than apathy or anger.

"It's hard for her," he said. "A lot harder than she lets on."

"I'm so sorry to hear that," Mrs. Wolf said. "Mercy Hospital has some excellent pain management specialists. Please give her my number. I'll make sure she gets the best possible help." It was a kind, if pointless, offer. Tate's mom was already seeing the best specialists in the state, none of whom were at Mercy Hospital. Maybe Mrs. Wolf simply didn't know.

Maybe not.

"I'll talk to her," he said, smiling as if her words had touched some deep part in his soul. "Thank you, Cynthia."

Alex pinched his leg beneath the table.

Brunch was outstanding—from the cheese and charcuterie plate to the smoked salmon and egg scramble. And Mrs. Wolf and her conversation were all kinds of polite. She listened interestedly as Alex talked about school and work, and Tate was quick to add his praise for Alex's influence and leadership. Mrs. Wolf squeezed her daughter's hand, beaming.

He could almost wonder if he was judging the older woman too harshly. Sure, he'd seen Barbie dolls with less plastic, but her attention to Alex seemed sincere and loving. It would be so easy to think that years of gambling dens had hardened him into seeing liars and cheats everywhere.

Except, she hadn't made the time to see her daughter last month when Alex went home to pick up her things. And Alex kept tensing under the table and carefully holding her breath when her mom spoke.

More than anything, though, he remembered Cynthia's neglect. Night after night all those years ago, Cynthia would show up late to pick Alex up from Nora's, when she picked her up at all. Alex had pretended not to be hurt, had lied that she wanted to stay, but Tate had learned more than how to play cards that summer. After the first few nights of being humiliated at each new card game Alex introduced him to, he'd begun studying. He'd spent hundreds of hours learning different games, like hearts, gin rummy, and poker, until he was dreaming in clubs and spades, hearts and diamonds.

After he learned the ins and outs of each game, he moved on to the psychology of tells, studying micro-expressions and even facial action coding systems.

But even if he hadn't studied so much, the memory of Alex shaking with sobs in their aunt and uncle's arms was burned into his brain. The sound had been so foreign, it had drawn Tate to peek into his aunt and uncle's room, even though he knew he shouldn't. But he could hardly believe anything in the world could make Alex Wolf cry.

"Why don't they love me?"

Uncle Robert and Aunt Nora both made shushing noises. "Oh, Alexandra, of course they love you," Aunt Nora said.

"Then why aren't they here? Why are their parties more important than me? Is it because I was adopted?"

Her sorrow shattered everything Tate thought he knew about the girl. Uncle Robert clicked his tongue. "Don't be silly. They love you. It doesn't matter how you were born. Your parents chose you."

"Only because Vivienne died. If she'd lived, they never would have adopted me. They'd have the baby they wanted."

Uncle Robert started talking, saying something about his sister, but Aunt Nora cut him off. "You are a strong, accomplished girl, and they know that. The way they are has nothing to do with you, but them. Your parents' choices are their own. You will never change them, just like you can't let this change you."

Alex hiccupped. "I just want them to love me."

"*We* love you."

He could still remember the way her sobs tore through the air. The echoes of her sorrow were trapped in his mind, even now. Yet here was Cynthia, cooing over Alex as if she was the one who'd wiped away the girl's tears and smoothed her hair, as if she was the one who'd assured Alex of her love.

Obviously, Tate wasn't the only one who could wear a pair of lies.

He was filled with a desire—a need—to know what was really

happening here, but too much was going on beneath the surface. If Cynthia and Alex were going to put their cards on the table, they had to think they were alone. So when brunch was being cleared, Tate excused himself to use the restroom. He left the table and ducked around the corner, where he stopped still within earshot. In case a server or hostess walked by, he leaned against the wall with his phone up to his face.

"It looks like you two have gotten to know each other well," Mrs. Wolf said.

"We're friends," Alex said. He wished he could see her body language.

"And does your friend know what you're doing? Do you?"

"Everything's under control, Mom. Us being friends is hardly a problem."

Her mother's voice was cool. "You aren't taking him to the charity event. This isn't up for discussion."

Nearby, dishes clinked in the kitchen. "Speaking of the event, what were you thinking? Are you trying to make Dad look—"

"Shut your mouth," her mother said, the words slicing the air like a knife. "You have no right to speculate or to pass judgment. You know nothing about the sacrifices we've made for this family."

Alex's voice dropped so low, Tate strained to hear it. "I've heard about your *sacrifices* for years, Mother, yet it feels like the only thing you've ever sacrificed is *me*. I have every right to say these things."

There was a pause, during which time Tate was worried one of them had left the table. He snuck his phone around the corner, using the surface like a mirror to see if he was missing anything. He wasn't. Mrs. Wolf was taking a drink from her teacup. She set it down.

"You're trying so hard to prove how strong you are, yet you're too naive to realize it isn't strength motivating you, it's emotion," her mother said calmly. "And nothing makes one weaker than emotion. It's coarse and ugly, and I didn't raise you to be ugly." There was something so sinister in her words. Maybe it was how she was able to sound so sweet as she said them. Or maybe it was the fact that only a sociopath could actually believe, let alone say, such things. He could as easily imagine her dismantling a corpse as sipping her tea. "Emotions are a lie, darling. They cloud your judgment and make you stupid and sloppy. We've taught you better than that. If you can be reasonable and careful, you'll find that with great risk comes the possibility of great reward."

As if a switch had been flicked, Alex's tone went from seething to dispassionate. The shift was jarring. "Only the possibility?"

"Of course. Your little experiment with Nora could either launch a powerful career for you or see you fail spectacularly. If the latter is the case, you'll be more reliant than ever on the connections your father and I can make for you, though I have no doubt you'll be relying on them, anyway, unless you can clear your head of all your foolish romantic notions."

Tate checked his watch. He wished he could wait another few minutes, figure out what they were talking about, but he was pushing it on the bathroom break. He stowed his phone and rounded the corner. Mrs. Wolf and Alex both smiled at him, however falsely.

Tate took his seat and said the first thing that came to his mind. "You know, you two have the same smile. It's beautiful."

Color rose to Alex's cheeks—he couldn't tell if it was from flattery or frustration. But there was no questioning the look on Mrs. Wolf's face.

"That's a sweet—if silly—thing to say. You know Alex was adopted."

Only his practiced poker face kept him from recoiling. To throw away the compliment—a true one at that—so she could remind him that Alex wasn't her biological daughter? It was as if she was slapping Alex's face in front of him and just expected him to watch.

"That only makes it more special," Tate said.

"Thanks," Alex said. "I can't imagine a nicer compliment."

"It was very kind of you to say," Mrs. Wolf said. "I simply don't wish to give off the wrong impression or try to erase her history. I'm proud of Alex's heritage."

"And I'm sure you couldn't be prouder of the woman she's become," Tate said, smiling at Alex rather than Mrs. Wolf. In that instant, Alex's eyes were so deep and vulnerable, it almost hurt to look at her. She dropped her gaze.

Mrs. Wolf took another sip of tea. "I'm sure no mother could be prouder."

CHAPTER TWELVE

A lex didn't speak to him the entire way home. She turned on the music in her car and let it fill every inch of the quiet. Just thinking of her mom sent a bitter, icy feeling over him. She was an exceptional actress—he saw where Alex got it from—and utterly mercenary. The things she'd said to her daughter had carried a ruthless subtext that he couldn't begin to grasp. But he knew Alex had felt every word to her core.

At Nora's, she dropped him off.

"You're not coming in?" he asked.

She shook her head, staring through the windshield. "I need to go . . . somewhere. Anywhere. I'll see you tomorrow."

He closed his door behind him and watched until she turned off Nora's street.

What was he supposed to do now?

Brunch had been so charged, the interplay of subtle yet powerful emotions exhilarating. Watching Alex and her mother carry on whole conversations with single, loaded words. The subtext. The feints. The deceit.

Hunger hit him like a wrecking ball, a craving so intense, he felt that he was starving. His body practically throbbed with the need for action. For excitement.

You should exercise, a voice inside his mind said, sounding more like Nia than anything.

I worked out this morning.

Study, then, the voice said.

I finished my homework last night, and finals are still a few weeks out.

He felt his thumbnail scratching the palm of his other hand. Maybe he should get some scratch-offs . . .

What for? So you can drop another few hundred bucks and have nothing to show for it? The system is rigged.

His protests dried up, and in their place were images of all the places he could go, all the games he could play. He could imagine himself at a table, surrounded by opponents, assessing their weaknesses and styles of play. Different hands flashed before his eyes, and he calculated the odds of a win with each one, imagining playing out endless scenarios. So many ways to win. So many people to beat.

A car backfired nearby, sounding for all the world like a gunshot. Rather than jump, Tate went further down the rabbit hole. In his years of gambling, he'd been in a handful of games where trouble started, but only one with a gun. A guy across the table from him had pulled it out after a bad hand and shot at the ceiling before turning it on each of the players. Fortunately, the security guards stopped the guy before things escalated. Maybe that should have scared him, but instead, it gave Tate a rush that he couldn't explain. He'd always loved winning, and he was so good at poker that half the time, it felt effortless. But in that moment, he'd felt the thrill of real risk. And when everything turned out to be fine, it was as if he'd won a hand against fate.

He could go so easily. To a casino or a card room or a game some kids were hosting on campus. In thirty minutes, he could have cards in hand and a stack of chips in front of him, if he wanted.

And boy, how he wanted.

He knew the exact sound the table made when the dealer knocked it before play. He could hear the clacking of chips, the soft sound of cards slipping against each other, the attempts of his opponents to regulate their breathing. He yearned to feel chips in his hand, to feel their heft and the ridges beneath his finger. He longed for the stiffness of green felt under his forearms.

And the smell. It was intoxicating him without him even being there. That scent of a fresh deck of cards mingled with cigar smoke and alcohol and the hint of rubber from the felt table. The want of that particular blend of smells carved a hole in his chest.

He could have all of that in thirty minutes. Thirty short minutes, but the wait, the anticipation, would make them the longest minutes of his life.

Now.

He had to go right now.

He had to he had to hehadtohehadtohehadto.

Someone slammed into him from behind, yanking Tate from his reverie and causing him to stumble to catch himself. He caught a glimpse of dark hair and broad, hunched shoulders, but the sounds of cars honking turned his head back. The sounds and sights were disorienting, and he was having a hard time processing it all. People were yelling. A lot of people. And there was that damn car honking again. Honking, honking, honking.

In a blink, awareness crashed into him. He was standing in the middle of a street. A busy, crowded street. Cars were stopped on either side, one of them only a foot or two from taking out his legs.

He gaped at the car.

He could have been hit.

I could have been hit.

So why didn't he care?

The senseless cacophony continued to assemble itself, and Tate could make out individual voices now.

"Get out of the street, you psycho!"

"Are you trying to get yourself killed?"

"Hey, buddy, are you okay?"

He blinked rapidly, looking from side to side, taking in the sidewalk, road signs, his cross streets.

He had been walking. Not just walking, but he'd gone a quarter of a mile from Nora's front steps, and he knew exactly where his body had been leading him.

He was almost to the train station, on his way to find some action. He hadn't even known he was moving. He had crossed two streets and wandered into the middle of a huge intersection. Those cars could have so easily hit him—shattered his kneecaps—yet what he wanted more than anything was to keep going.

Even now, shaking as he dropped to the steps in front of Saint Clement Parish, he wasn't scared for what could have happened. He was shaking like a junkie in withdrawal, as violent as if his body needed a cigarette or a drink. Or heroin.

What was wrong with him?

Regaining his thoughts required a Herculean effort, especially in the shadow of the pale gray stone parish. He felt naked and exposed. The windows from the old church's towers stared down at him like disapproving eyes. If the church was peering into his soul, it wouldn't like what it saw. He wanted to walk away, but he didn't trust himself to move, didn't trust where his feet would take him. Where Tate *wanted* his feet to take him . . .

Stop it!

He clutched his head as his thoughts turned inward. Images swirled around in his mind of the people he would never want to see in his world, people he didn't want to disappoint again.

Finley's was near the top of that list, but he'd already disappointed her. She was too accepting, cared too unconditionally, even if she disapproved of his gambling, even if he'd been ignoring her since their kiss. She would help him without question. He could go to her right now. He could sneak into her room and take the emergency money she kept in her vintage film reel case. And when she found out, she'd be mad, but it wouldn't change anything for her. She'd love him and try to help him and he would just do it again.

The thought of Alex was worse. Depressing. Confusing. She would care if he gambled, wouldn't she? Since he was thirteen, he'd never wanted so badly to win someone's . . . not approval, exactly. Affection? Or concern? Whatever it was, he'd never wanted it from anyone as much as he did from her. He needed her to care and to be devastated and angry and to tell him how stupid he was. If she didn't, he would spiral. He couldn't imagine where he'd end up.

He couldn't bring himself to picture his mom. She would hold him and tell him how much she loved him, but she would internalize all that pain and get weaker and sicker. He could barely live with himself just thinking about her.

He grabbed his head more tightly. This wasn't working. This only made him want to escape worse.

Another face came to mind. He dialed, and Nia answered on the third ring.

"Where are you? Are you okay?" she asked.

"I don't know. I mean, I know where I am, I just don't really like it. I haven't gambled."

"Good. Run away now, Tate. Turn around and go home. Better yet, tell me where you are, and I'll come get you."

Huddling up against the stone wall that lined the steps, he cleared his throat. "You don't need to come get me. I just need to talk."

"Tate, tell me where you are. Now."

He told her.

Nia forced him to stay on the phone with her the whole drive over. She worked in Bridgeport, so even with her police powers, it was still almost twenty minutes before she arrived. She stayed on the phone the whole time, pressuring him into talking about everything he could think of. Work, school, Alex. How he had left things with his family. He'd never admit it to her, but the talking helped.

Finally, she rolled up in a black Ford Explorer, her department car. She got out of the SUV and came around to meet him, wearing a gray pantsuit.

Tate held his hands out to her, wrists up. "Cuff me. I'm yours."

She pulled him up and led him to her SUV. "Come on. We're getting doughnuts."

Tate couldn't get over the fact that he was sitting with a cop eating doughnuts. And he told her that. Repeatedly.

Nia yawned. "Are you done?"

"Well, with you sucking joy like it's a Boston cream . . ." He blew a raspberry, then frowned. "Fine. Yes, I'm done. Thank you for coming."

"I'm really glad you called me. That took a lot of willpower. Believe me, I know."

"Yeah, yeah." Now that the moment had passed, he felt silly about what had happened, but even more annoyed. He'd overreacted because he'd found a car two feet away from his knees. That was it. "Are you going to lecture me about my compulsive tendencies, about how I'm throwing myself into work or school or my abs to fill the void?"

"No, because those are healthy alternatives, as you well know."

"Then what will you lecture me about? How I need to get back into the program? How I need to take this all more seriously?"

"Yes. That, and Alex Wolf."

Tate dusted his hands off, leaving a puff of powder in the air. A few specks dotted Nia's bronze skin. She grabbed a napkin and brushed them off. "What about her?" Tate asked.

"You need to be careful with her. She could be dangerous to you," Nia said, crinkling up the napkin like a stress ball.

"Because of her dad?"

She tossed the napkin into the trash behind their table. "What do you mean?"

"The casino proposal and Michael Landolfo? I can only assume—"

"Don't. That's no concern of yours," she said sharply. "You're pursuing Alex because she represents all the risk and thrill you love about poker. You're trying to read her, best her, even as you think she's doing the same with you."

"She is."

"Then she sucks and you should move on. You don't need someone like her, as much as you want her. Of everything in the world you need, a relationship that full of tension, stress, and drama could lead you down a very dark road."

He wasn't sure whether to nod or shake his head. Of course he knew this. Hadn't he thought the same thing an hour ago, that if she didn't care, he'd lose all control? But that was then, in a moment of weakness. He was annoyed that she'd just left like that, and he'd found himself bored. Nothing more. If anything, the distraction of being around Alex for the last several weeks had done more to keep him from wanting to gamble than endless GA meetings could. If Alex was any danger to him, it wasn't in the way Nia thought. It was in a way he liked. A lot.

"Are you listening?" Nia asked.

"Yeah, I'm listening. But I know all this. Risk and reward, highs and lows, yeah, yeah."

Nia leaned in. "Tate, do you even know how lucky you are? How worse things would have been for you if you weren't a rich white boy with a connected family who loves you enough not only to stage an intervention but also to put you in rehab and find you a kick-ass sponsor? Most addicts can't dream of the privilege you take for granted every day." Tate dipped a finger in the powder at the bottom of the doughnut box and brought it to his mouth. "You have to take this more seriously. You called me because you needed me. You wandered off looking for action without meaning to, and when I found you, you were still shaking. Don't think I didn't see it," she told him, before he could argue. "I left work to help you. I've left family to help you. I've taken calls at all hours of the night, and you don't even care. If you aren't going to listen, then you're going to find yourself in the middle of a dark alley somewhere, down another ten grand you're not good for, getting your teeth kicked in. Or worse." She reached across the table and slapped his side over his scar. "You got lucky, fool. Don't tempt fate again."

"You're right," he lied. "I need to be careful."

"Not just careful. Tate, you need to admit that you need help and start accepting it. Come to a meeting with me tonight."

"I can't. I have other plans."

Nia rose, dropping her napkin on the table between them. "I hope this isn't it."

"What do you mean?"

"I hope this isn't the moment you look back on three months or three years down the road when you find yourself desperate and hurt and alone and think, 'I wish I would have accepted her help.' But, Tate, I swear to you: it'll come. You think things are under control because it's been a couple of months since you last gambled. But that's you trying to prove something to me or yourself or your brother, maybe. You're not doing it because you actually think it's the right thing to do. And unless you do *that*, unless you start taking this more seriously and admit you're an addict, that moment will come, and it will ruin you. It almost ruined me, and I'm a hell of a lot tougher than you, Frat Boy."

"Hey," he said, grabbing her arm. She stopped, looking down at him. "I'm offended you think I would ever be in a frat."

She was too used to him to get worked up by the comment, but her disappointment loomed when she shook off his arm. "And I'm offended you don't take anything I say seriously. See you around."

He considered going after her and apologizing, but to what end? He was in control again, and he didn't see the point in lying to her when she was already too wary to believe him. With a sigh, he picked up the last old-fashioned sour cream and took a bite.

CHAPTER THIRTEEN

Nia may have considered them healthy alternatives, but Tate's devotion to his work-slash-school-slash-exercise regimen was taking its toll. School was something he'd always cared about, despite thirteen-year-old Alex's best efforts to persuade him otherwise. Yet working late night after late night had come to mean that he was keeping even later nights to finish his homework. He was used to this with the card room, but that had buzzed with an energy that could keep him going for days on end. Without it . . . well, it was a good thing he was dropping his course load when summer quarter hit at the end of June. Hopefully that would help him accommodate the extra work Nora would need.

Work? Extra work? That's what we're thinking about now? Get ahold of yourself.

His lip curled. He was no Peter Pan, resisting adulthood at all costs, but he'd never thought he'd become such a friggin' grown-up so early. A lifetime of board meetings and briefcases flashed before his eyes, making him yawn.

"You look like you could use a nap," a girl's voice said. Tate spun around to see Ruby, the girl he'd volunteered with on the field team. "Or a cup of coffee."

"It's nine-thirty. What are you still doing here so late?"

She pulled up the rolling chair from the cubicle next to him and sat. "I was doing outreach and got caught up in a conversation with some old lady from Irving Park, Misha Starkovich. She was talking all kinds of nonsense, like a conspiracy nut."

"Irving Park is right next to one of my neighborhoods. What's going on?"

"I'm still not sure. The woman spoke pretty broken English, but it was something to the effect of how we needed to help them with the other one because he's stealing from them."

"The 'other one'? Any idea who she was talking about?" he asked. She shook her head. "What made her start talking about this guy? Was she ranting about it when you called, or did you bring up something that set her off?"

Her eyebrows pinched together. "No, she was normal at first. It wasn't until I told her why I was calling that she went off the rails."

"What did you tell her?"

"My normal spiel: that I was calling to talk about the upcoming vote, to help her register, and about Mrs. Mallis."

Tate didn't sit up straighter, though he wanted to. "So you mentioned Nora specifically, that she was running for state attorney general?"

"I finished my whole introduction about her running against Wolf, and that's part of it. So yeah."

"And she said she needed your help with the other one . . ."

She was nodding. "Who's stealing from them, yeah. But then she started talking about machines and money, maybe? That's pretty much all I could get from her."

Tate made a show of scratching his head. "Wow. That's just . . . weird."

She threw her hands up. "I know, right? For a minute, I expected her to tell me the machines were rising up and it was getting all *Terminator* up on Pulaski Road." Tate laughed. "But maybe Nora has a doppelgänger who's wreaking havoc in Irving Park."

"I could see that."

"Of course, Mrs. Starkovich's granddaughter took the phone from her and told me not to listen to her 'crazy babushka,' so I'm not sure why I'm telling you about it."

"Because I love a good story, and you live to please me," he said. She rolled her eyes. "Did you and the granddaughter at least have a good laugh about it?"

"Hardly," Ruby said, pushing her rolling chair back. "She seemed pissed and hung up the phone before I could say almost anything. She must be sick of the old lady's shenanigans."

Ruby stood up to leave, and Tate threw his arms out for a stretch. "Out of curiosity, what does Babushka do for a living?"

"She runs Misha's Restaurant over on Pulaski. I'm betting her kids will be taking that over sooner rather than later."

"No kidding. I owe you a coffee tomorrow for the entertainment."

"You got my order," she said, pointing finger guns at him. "It was good chatting. Misogyny isn't the same without you."

He barked a laugh. "Of all the things that have been said about me, this is the one I want on my tombstone."

She grinned. "See you tomorrow."

Once Ruby was out of sight, Tate let himself react. She had no idea what she'd just told him, but he thought he did. And he was freaking out.

He flipped through stacks of paper on his desk, then on the desks near him. When he couldn't find what he needed, he got into his computer, searching through *Chicago Tribune* and *Daily Herald* articles for any mention of . . .

Bam.

The casino proposal.

He looked through the talking points, but nothing jumped out at him. He went to the governor's website, looking for the link that would explain the proposal in more depth. But there was no depth. Just the bare bones of the idea that the news had reported.

But there was something there. He knew it.

He called Oscar. When the man picked up, Tate relayed the conversation, including his own suspicions at the end. Oscar was on the campaign trail with Nora, visiting towns and cities throughout Illinois for town hall meetings and rallies.

Oscar sounded wary. "I agree that it's suspicious, but your aunt is in a sticky situation, being up against her brother-in-law. You know how ugly this could get if she and Connor let this become a mudslinging contest, and who do you think the public will back in a battle between a rich, childless widow and a successful, charming family man? They'll be calling her the Black Widow before you know it. She can't win like that."

Tate played with the office phone cord, wrapping it around his finger. He knew Oscar was right, but he also suspected that if Alex weren't a factor, Nora wouldn't be so quick to pull punches.

"I get what you're saying, but if Connor really does have mob ties, this goes way beyond public opinion of Nora. It puts the entire state in jeopardy," Tate insisted. He pulled the cord off his finger, stretching it taut before letting it bounce back. "Come on, Oscar. You know I'm right."

The phone muffled, and then Oscar spoke again in a hushed voice. "Fine. You can investigate this, but for now, it stays between us. And if you talk to anyone in the course of your research, do not tell them who you are."

"I'll let you know what I find out."

Several days later, Tate was exactly where he'd started: nowhere. He'd researched the proposal but only found more vague language and uncertain promises. When he called the governor's office to see if they had more information, he'd been drilled with questions about his identity and why he wanted the information.

Okay, maybe he hadn't been drilled, exactly, but Oscar had him a bit spooked.

Or maybe he was still just itching for some action, looking to make things riskier.

Alex hadn't said more than a handful of words to him since brunch last week, and he didn't know how to take that. She was still around work and the house a lot, which made him wonder what the story was with her boyfriend. She was never with the guy. They had to have broken up, right? Or maybe he was just hoping.

Who even knew anymore?

What he did know was that it was Memorial Day, and instead of spending it with his family or on the lake with friends, he was meeting Juana and a community leader in Albany Park to strategize.

So naturally he ran into Alex on his way downstairs. Wearing a navy and white striped dress, she looked adorably nautical. She was smiling that radiant smile she held back and used like a weapon. He didn't need that smile right now.

"Hey, where are you off to so early?" she asked. Before he could answer, she said, "I was going to ask if you wanted to come to my grandmother's garden party with me this afternoon."

He walked down another few steps, so they were almost level with each other. "I'm meeting a friend, but text me the when and the where, okay? I might be able to make it work."

Two quick blinks gave her away. "A friend? Anyone I know?"

"You haven't met, nope." He walked down the rest of the stairs.

"Is it Finley?" she asked. "Because you should bring her! I'd love to meet her."

He turned and walked backward to the door. "Good-bye, Alex. I'll see you later."

"Later later or today later?"

He just waved.

Tate got off the train in Albany Park, where Juana was waiting with her son, Mateo. Short and curvy, Juana was smiling and bouncing the now four-year-old boy on her hip. Mateo was holding a long wave of Juana's hair in front of his face and peering at Tate through it. Tate smiled and gave them both hugs.

"The little dude is getting so big. Want me to carry him?" he asked.

Mateo gripped more tightly to Juana. She smoothed his shock of dark waves. "He won't let that happen," she said with a smile, leading him through the dirty station. "He didn't let my boyfriend hold him for weeks."

"Weeks? Now you've given me a challenge," Tate said, attempting a quick game of peekaboo with Mateo as they walked. He wasn't interested. "Teo," he said, "you'll see. *Tio Tate* will be your favorite by lunchtime."

Being in Albany Park was relaxing to Tate. He'd had reason to come here a handful of times over the last couple of years (some of them even legal), and he liked how unpretentious it was. Despite recent attempts at gentrification, it was still one of the most diverse neighborhoods in the city, and its colorful personality extended beyond the people to the buildings and even the sidewalk and wall art. Whereas residents of his aunt's neighborhood would turn their noses up at it and call it graffiti, here it was viewed as a thing of beauty. In some ways, with its old brick buildings lining the sidewalks in place of strip malls, it looked like so many Main Street USAs. Except that half the barbecue joints were Korean.

Together, Tate, Juana, and Mateo walked down Seoul Drive to the Albany Village Community Center.

After the meeting with Juana's friend, Mateo was restless, and they were all hungry.

"Why don't I buy us lunch?" Tate said, as if he was really just craving pierogies and not itching to find out what Misha Starkovich really knew.

"Lead the way," Juana said.

The restaurant was a couple of streets down, so as they walked, Juana told him about Mateo's challenges from his birth complications. The boy had a few visible symptoms—he had a bigger forehead and his eyes were different sizes—but the majority of his problems were developmental. He couldn't speak yet and had impulse control problems, among other things. Tate saw the impulse control firsthand, but it didn't bother him. Mateo was a cool kid.

"I like your sunglasses," Tate said, looking past Juana to the little boy in her overburdened arm. Juana had explained that Mateo had to wear them due to his light sensitivity. "I bet the girls love them on you, huh? Maybe I need to get a pair like that."

Mateo smiled and gestured for Tate's glasses. "Whoa, you think I'm just going to give you these? I got these at a gas station for eight ninety-nine. I don't know if I can afford to lose them."

Mateo held out his hand, grunting. "Okay," Tate said, "but I need yours. How am I going to get a girlfriend otherwise?"

Mateo's laugh was breathy, barely vocalized. Tate counted to three and tried to switch sunglasses. But Mateo grabbed Tate's and kept his own, too. He put both pairs on his face and clapped, giggling.

Tate shook his head, but he couldn't keep the grin from his face. "That's cold, dude."

"You are really good with him," Juana said when they stopped at an intersection.

"I know what it's like to be judged by people who don't know what they're talking about. Mateo gets me."

Juana's eyes watered, and Tate put a hand on her shoulder. Then Mateo put his hand on Tate's.

Tate's eyebrows shot up. "Come here, pal," he said, reaching for the little boy. When Mateo reached back, Tate's eyes watered, too.

They arrived at Misha's Restaurant only a minute or two after Mateo let Tate hold him, but by the time they got there, Tate had a newfound respect for Juana's biceps. He told her as much.

She laughed. "Men do not know how to carry kids. It isn't the size of the arm, it's the size of the hip," she said, patting hers.

He didn't know if it was the accent or the hips or both, but it was sexy. He told her that, too.

"Oh, stop," she said, walking through the door that he held open for her.

The smell of potato pancakes filled his nose, and he was suddenly starving. The restaurant was run-down, as the best restaurants so often were. Cracked tile, off-balance tables, rickety chairs. Ukrainian folk music played in the background, and a couple of handfuls of customers sat eating. The setup of the restaurant was odd, though, with all the tables and bar on one side of the restaurant and a blank wall on the other.

Tate walked up to the counter where a teenage girl was working the till. He rested Mateo on the counter and gave the girl his most devastating smile. Rather than blush, she narrowed her eyes.

"I'd like to speak with the owner, Mrs. Starkovich. Is she in?"

The girl shouted in what Tate assumed was Ukrainian loud enough to be heard past the door that separated the clanging kitchen from the dining room. A moment later, a voice shouted back.

"She's not in," the girl said.

"Is she going to be coming in later? I can wait or come back," he said.

"No. She won't. I don't know when she'll be here."

"Later in the week, maybe?"

The girl's eyes turned to flint. "Like I said, I don't know when she'll be here." She yelled in Ukrainian again, and a moment later, three men came through the kitchen door. Two looked like they were cooks, but one looked like security. He was as tall as Tate and twice as wide, and the state of his bulbous nose made it clear that the man had seen his share of fights.

All of his plans, his promises to Oscar to keep a low profile, flew out the window. Although his face was neutral, inside, Tate smiled. A grim, ugly thing. "You don't know or you don't want to say?"

The muscle started toward Tate, whose breathing quickened with excitement.

"What do you want with Mrs. Starkovich?" the sinister-looking man asked, only feet away from Tate.

Tate was leaning toward the man when he felt a pair of small arms tighten around him. Then a hand gripped his shoulder.

"I am so sorry," a woman's voice said behind him. No, not just a woman, Juana.

Holy hell. Juana was with him. *Mateo* was with him.

What was he doing?

Tate forced his eyes open as wide open as possible, pulling Mateo closer to him. "I . . . I'm so sorry. I think there's been a misunderstanding."

"What do you want with Mrs. Starkovich?" the muscle repeated in an accent that was more menace than anything.

Juana's hand gripped Tate's shoulder hard. "I'm a . . . a student . . . at NEIU?" he said. "In, uh, business management? I'm supposed to interview at least five business owners from different"—he cleared his throat—"countries? It's for my class—Immigration and Industry?"

The muscle looked back at the teenage girl, who shrugged. To Tate, he said, "And why did you pick Mrs. Starkovich?"

"Uh . . . Yelp? My girlfriend wanted to try the borscht." He put an arm around Juana, clutching Mateo with his other arm.

The guy eyed Tate like he was a bug. "Go find someone else. Misha Starkovich doesn't do interviews."

Tate gave him an anxious nod while the men went back to the kitchen. He was about to say something to Juana when the kitchen door swung open, and Tate saw the face of a man looking back at him. A face he recognized, just as he had the last time he'd seen it.

It was the man from the convenience store.

The man he'd given his lottery ticket to.

A chill ran over Tate, covering his whole body with goose bumps. It was just a coincidence—it had to be. After all, he was in a Ukrainian restaurant, and the man was obviously Eastern European. Maybe even Ukrainian, for all Tate knew. It wasn't a stretch to assume that the man had friends in the area. It didn't need to be a big deal that he just happened to be in this restaurant at the exact same time Tate showed up . . .

"We need to go, Juana," he muttered.

"Es obvio, idiota."

With his arm still around her shoulder, Tate turned them around and walked them out the door.

CHAPTER FOURTEEN

Once they were out of view of the restaurant, Juana wrenched Mateo from Tate's arms.

"What were you doing in there, huh?" she asked, spitting fire. "Were you trying to pick a fight with that man while you were holding *my son?*"

Tate swallowed a hot lump in his throat. "No, I had it under control."

Her hand cracked across his face. All the nerves in his cheek seemed to go numb and start on fire at the same time. "Never again, Tate," she said, pointing in his face. "You do not get to play macho little games like that around me or my son again."

He expected her to storm off, but she didn't. Instead, the force of her gaze made him drop his.

"You're right, Juana," he said, her words striking him far more than fear or pain could. "I'm sorry. I thought I knew what I was doing, but I shouldn't have put you at risk like that." He put a hand on a whimpering Mateo's back, but the little boy shoved his arm off.

He wished he'd been slapped again. He deserved to be.

Juana was still breathing hard. "Do you want my help with your aunt's campaign still, or no?"

"You would still help?"

"Yes, because I believe in her and because I know that even though you're a fool, you have a good heart."

He rubbed the back of his neck. "Thanks, Juana."

She sniffed and nodded. "Okay, but we do this my way, not yours."

"Of course. Of course," he repeated. "I really am sorry, Juana. And thanks."

She rolled her eyes. *"Ya basta,"* she said. Enough. *"*Now *vámonos.* We'll eat somewhere else and then walk you back to the station. *"*

When Juana and Mateo left him forty-five minutes later, Tate felt disgusted with himself. Mateo hadn't looked at him even once at lunch, and while Juana had still been conversational, her warmth had cooled. How could he have been so reckless with them?

And why did that make him feel like doing something even worse?

He checked his phone and saw several missed messages, one from Alex. She'd sent him the location of her grandparents' garden party with a message that read, "Please don't leave me alone with those monsters. Come!"

The rage and contempt burned away as a sense of dark purpose filled him.

His fingers flew across the screen: *I'll be there.*

At three o'clock, Tate waltzed around the back of the Wolfs' estate. Alex had failed to mention that her grandparents' party was being held at her parents' house. She'd probably assumed he wouldn't want to go if he knew where it was.

Nothing could be further from the truth.

Dressed in baby blue pants, a pale pink shirt, and loafers (no socks), he was every rich douchebag from an eighties movie. Or from most college campuses. He smiled and made eyes at the western-outfitted servers, while inside, all he wanted to do was drive a car through the whole stupid thing.

The Wolfs had spared no expense on their red, white, and blue celebration. The heavens seemed to smile down on them, granting their party the first cloudless day in weeks. Their impressive grounds overlooked the lake, and farther across the yard, Tate saw steps that must have led down to it. Geometric topiaries lined the immaculate main lawn, where small, artfully decorated round tables were set up with crudité centerpieces.

Off to one side, a platform had been erected and a band was playing. He'd expected a quartet, but the Wolfs were trying to show how down-to-earth they were, that they could connect with the common folk . . . whom they were paying to serve them. Indeed, they had spent a lot of money making sure this expensive charade made them look down-home.

A down-home garden party with truffled asparagus crostini. Nailed it.

As he sauntered around the grounds, he kept an eye out for Alex or her parents. There were maybe a few dozen people here, not counting the photographers Connor had let sneak in. It shouldn't have been hard to find any of the Wolfs, and as much as he loved to make a show, he was getting bored mingling. The atmosphere, for all its beauty, felt too uninspired and manufactured. The people equally so.

In fact, everything the Wolfs touched had that same aura of falseness to it, as if their charmed, golden lives were gilded with nothing more than spray paint. With any luck, he'd be able to scratch the surface and expose the cheap tin beneath.

A server came around with champagne flutes on a platter, and Tate reached for one.

"Pleasure to serve you, Mr. Bertram," the server said sarcastically.

"Do I—" He broke into a smile and raised his glass. "Karla, what are you doing here?"

His former brush gave him an arch expression. "Ridin' horses and wrastlin' . . . I don't know, is it cows? These outfits are ridiculous. I can't believe you didn't notice me."

"I was too busy making sure everyone noticed *me*."

"Sounds about right."

He smiled. "So you're back to catering, huh?"

"Making money off of douches playing poker couldn't last forever."

He held a hand over his heart. "Now you're just being mean. You know that's my entire ten-year plan."

"Oh, I know, Playboy." She looked past him. "Anyway, I need to get back to work. If I'm caught mingling with the guests, there goes my paycheck."

"It was good seeing you, Karla." He snapped his fingers. "Oh, and do me a favor?"

Her eyes narrowed. "What?"

"My aunt is running for office against Mr. Wolf. If you hear anything interesting, let me know, will you? I'll make it worth your while."

"Sure. But you should know, I would have done it for free. Before you mentioned payment, that is."

"How do you know your payment isn't my glorious body?"

"No thanks. All you blonds look alike."

"That's my line!" he said as she walked away, obviously swaying her hips for his benefit.

Tate watched in satisfaction, just about to bring the flute to his mouth when a voice stopped him.

"I thought you weren't drinking," Alex said from nearby. "You said it makes you self-destructive."

He turned to see her approaching, her forehead creased in concern beneath her wide-brim straw hat. He should never have told her about the drinking. "And I thought this was your grandparents' party." He tipped his head back and poured the champagne down his throat.

He grimaced.

"Sparkling cider," she said with a nasty smirk. "My grandmother is twelve years sober and refuses to supply alcohol at her parties. Says she doesn't want to contribute to anyone else's demise." She took his empty flute, dropped it on a passing server's platter, and linked her arm in his.

"Well, that sucks," he muttered.

"Tell me about it."

The guests were among the rich and powerful of Chicago, many of whom Tate had met at functions of his father's. He asked Alex if Michael Landolfo would be there—the man the governor was recommending to run the city's casino if the plan moved forward.

"Why do you want to know?" she asked in the buffet line.

He helped himself to a crab-stuffed chicken breast. "What do you want to hear? That I'm a curious college student? That I'm thinking of pursuing gaming law? That I'm interested in liquor licensing as a future profession?"

Her fingers tightened around the tongs in her hand. When she spoke, it was in a hushed, angry tone. "Are you trying to get yourself—"

"Killed? Please say killed," he said.

"—thrown out," she continued between her teeth. "And keep your voice down."

"Oh, well, that's far less exciting. But I've been tossed out of worse."

"Shut up. And play nice," she hissed, storming off with her plate.

Tate put a few more things on his plate and followed her to her table, where her parents and grandparents were sitting.

He set down his plate.

"That spot is reserved for—" Cynthia Wolf began.

Alex cut her off. "I told you, it's not." She looked up at Tate with warning in her eyes. "Please, have a seat." She ducked her head and whispered, "And don't screw up."

"If you're sure I'm not intruding," he said, sitting beside Alex before they could answer. "It's a pleasure to see you again, Connor and Cynthia."

Connor welcomed him and introduced him to his in-laws, Alex's grandparents. He smiled and they indulged in a moment of small talk before Cynthia's father asked Connor about his campaign.

"No politics," Cynthia said, before her husband could answer.

"Oh, Cindy, just let the boy talk," Cynthia's mother said.

Connor smiled and put an arm around his wife's shoulders. "No, no, she's right." He kissed her cheek, and, while Cynthia smiled prettily, Tate didn't miss the fact that her head was tilted away from Connor's. The man kept his arm around her, rubbing circles on her shoulder with his thumb.

Another guest came over to say hello to the hosts. After thanking Cynthia's parents, the woman turned to Connor. "Look at you, still doting on your blushing bride after all these years."

Connor looked at his wife earnestly. "She's the love of my life."

Cynthia put a hand on his cheek and kissed him quickly on the mouth. Connor looked disappointed when she separated. "That's sweet, dear," Cynthia said softly.

The other guest put her hand over her heart. "Absolutely precious," she said before leaving.

Cynthia's mother looked at Alex. "That's what you need to hold out for. A man who'll take care of you and stay by your side no matter what, like your father."

"Don't worry, Mother," Cynthia said. "I've taught Alex exactly what to prioritize in a relationship." She looked at her daughter, her sea blue eyes cold enough to freeze hell over. "Right, dear?"

Next to him, Alex was stiff. She sat there as if she was carrying a stack of books on her head and would get slapped with a ruler if a single one fell down. "Of course, Mom," she said. Tate reached a hand under the table and squeezed hers, but she brushed it away and put on a determined smile. "The organza chair covers are lovely, by the way," Alex said. "The entire party is."

"Thank you, dear," Cynthia said before drawing Alex's attention to the centerpieces.

Tate leaned back in his chair and tipped the contents of his glass down his throat as if taking a shot. His nerves were humming with a need to act out. But he let the restlessness grow, biding its time, waiting for the right moment, when Cynthia would stop going on about the garden topiaries and what a surprise the lavender in the lemonade was . . .

Screw it.

"I was surprised by the choice of beverages, too, Cynthia," he interrupted. "Between you and me, that lavender lemonade isn't cutting it."

Alex's grandmother gasped, Cynthia glowered, and Alex stamped on his foot beneath the table. Tate didn't care. He looked at Connor, who put down his glass slowly. Tate kept talking. "But I'm even more surprised to hear about your support of the governor's gaming proposal, Connor. Michael Landolfo's an interesting recommendation to head it, isn't he?"

It was a testament to Connor's self-possession that he could radiate such intense displeasure while nodding pensively.

"Well, Tate, Michael has an MBA from Stanford and a law degree from Yale. He also has over a decade's worth of experience in civil service as the executive director of the Liquor Control Commission."

Tate huffed, ignoring Alex's nails digging into his thigh. "You don't find it odd that someone with such impressive credentials— someone who could easily be making double or triple in the private sector—would work for the government?"

Connor smiled and rested his clasped hands on the table. "Some of us believe that there are more important things than money, Tate."

"Clearly," Tate said, gesturing to his surroundings.

Connor chuckled. At some point, the band had started playing "Bye, Bye Miss American Pie." "I'm very blessed in my success, as are your parents. And your aunt, if you recall. I've found that many successful people develop a desire to give back to their communities. After all, money can't buy everything."

"If that's the case, then why do you gamble?"

The man's teeth glinted as his smile grew into something with bite. "To win," he said. But of course he couldn't leave it at that; he really *was* a politician. "To learn more about the human condition, to assess strengths and weaknesses and reactions, to learn everything I can about someone so that I know if he has the better hand or if he's bluffing—"

"Haven't you heard my reputation, Mr. Wolf?"

"In fact, I have. Apparently you never bluff. Which makes you a mouse."

Tate could have rolled his eyes at the reference. It was one thing to study Phil Hellmuth's poker animals. It was another to cite them in casual conversation to feel cool. "And I suppose that makes you—"

"An eagle." Connor's lips stretched into a tight, vicious smile. "And that's how I know you'll never win."

"You're wrong about that."

"Stop it," Alex hissed.

"Is this the kind of trash you let into your parties, Cynthia?" Alex's grandmother asked. The woman was shaking with rage and, quite probably, the desire for a stiff drink.

Cynthia's Botox didn't allow for a reaction. She sat there perfectly composed, like a good Stepford Wife. "Mother, have some compassion. The boy is in Gambler's Anonymous—"

"Keeping tabs on me, Cynthia? You should know: you're not my type." Tate's leg ached where Alex's fingernails were making their mark. He looked at Connor. "I'm not wrong about Landolfo, am I?"

Connor sat back in his chair. "Tate, you should know better than to listen to rumors. How stupid would I have to be to get in bed with the mob? I could *buy* the mob."

There. There it was. Something in Cynthia's plastic face moved, an involuntary response that not even Botox could prevent.

Tate had him. He didn't know how yet, but he had him.

"But Connor, don't you remember? Money can't buy everything."

He stood, dropped his napkin like a mic, and strolled away.

CHAPTER FIFTEEN

On the ride home, Tate felt like some kind of Greek god—all powerful and clever and riding a chariot across the sky. So when his phone rang a few minutes after he got into the backseat of the driver's car, he answered with a smile.

"Hello, darling. It's been ages."

Alex screamed obscenities in his ear.

"Alex, Alex, slow down. I'm missing at least half of the f-bombs you're launching at me."

"I invited you as my guest! I wanted you there, Tate, and you just threw it in my face! How could you say those things to my dad? Why would you do that to me?"

His chariot crashed into the sun. "Come on, Alex, don't act like you don't know what he's doing. Your dad's shady."

"Don't say that." Her words punched through the phone. "He's not perfect, but he's not suicidal. He would never jeopardize everything he has, never risk hurting his family—"

"Then why are you supporting Nora's campaign instead of his? And don't tell me it's about the politics, because I don't believe that for a second."

There was a long pause during which he heard only her unsteady breath. "I was just doing what he told me to do."

"What do you mean?"

"My whole life, he's always pushed me to be better, to 'act like a Wolf.' No crying, no losing control—ever. He'd never help me with projects or talk to my teachers when there was a problem, because 'Wolfs solve their own problems' and 'create their own opportunities.' I believe in Aunt Nora, so I took his advice."

She sounded equal parts defensive and uncertain. The memory of Alex crying on Aunt Nora's shoulder, begging for her parents to love her, struck him again. He leaned his head against the car window. "You just want him to notice you."

"No, it's not that—"

"He notices you, Alex," Tate said, hating his own kindness.

"Wha . . . what do you mean?"

Tate watched his breath fog up a small patch of the window as cars blurred past. "When we went over to get your things, he told me that he's always pushed you because he wants to give you every advantage in life but that he realizes now it was a mistake. He said that he's never forgiven himself for hurting you."

He wished he could see her right now, wished he could interpret her choppy breathing. "Did he say anything else?"

"Like what?"

"That he's, I don't know, proud of me? That he loved me?"

Tate thought hard. "Probably. I don't remember."

"You'd remember, Tate, because you read people so well." Her voice quivered. "If he'd said he loved me, you'd have known he was lying."

"Alex—"

Click.

Dammit. Dammit. Dammit.

Only the entry light was on when he got home. Nora was gone till the end of the week, and he doubted he'd see Alex tonight. She was probably doing damage control with her parents, though if she were smart, she'd stop trying to change them. They weren't just crappy parents, they were crappy people. Alex deserved better. And when he exposed her dad, she'd finally realize that and cut ties with her parents once and for all.

Tate kicked off his shoes at the entry and flipped on a light when he heard a floorboard creak upstairs.

"Alex?" he called out. "I thought you'd be staying with your parents on the Hellmouth tonight. How did you beat me here?"

There was no answer, but he heard another creak, followed by footfalls too heavy to be muffled.

It wasn't Alex.

"Alex?" he called again, even as he grabbed a fire poker from the living room. "Want to get takeout while I pee? I'm friggin' starved. And I think that lavender lemonade is finally catching up with me."

He opened the bathroom door, flipped on the fan, and closed the door from the outside. If he was smart, the intruder upstairs would try to make his escape now. With only two exits—one of them blocked by Tate—there was only one direction to go. Tate just hoped there was no one else in the house.

He crept carefully on his bare feet from room to room, crouching low to peer around walls and doors for the intruder. Adrenaline was pumping fast through his body, enlivening his limbs until he was buzzing with excitement. He listened closely for any sound, and as he neared the kitchen—where the only other exit was—he heard it. The sound of pants rubbing together as the intruder tried to rush.

Tate sprung into action, sprinting for the back door. He held the fire poker high, ready to strike. When he rounded the wall to the kitchen, a picture frame exploded against the wall next to his head.

Tate flinched as glass shards sliced into his skin. But he kept running. He caught a glimpse as a black hat and dark jacket disappeared through the back door.

Tate whirled past the counter, grabbing a mason jar and dumping the water and fresh flowers from it, even as he propelled himself out the back door. The intruder was running hard and had almost made it to the sidewalk. Tate threw the jar as hard as he could and watched with satisfaction as it smashed into the man's head, bouncing off and crashing onto the ground below.

Tate jumped down the stairs to chase after the man, who was wobbling and unsteady, but before Tate had gone more than a few yards, something drove into his bare foot.

A nail.

Tate dropped to the ground, screaming in frustration. He cursed at the man's retreating form. Then he pulled out his phone and dialed 911.

"What were you thinking, going after him like that?" Nia asked as a paramedic cleaned his foot in the back of the ambulance. She'd arrived only a few minutes after the police and ambulance had, standing beside the interviewing detective and taking notes. She hadn't said anything, but her rotten disapproval filled the air.

Tate shrugged off the blanket the paramedic had draped over his shoulders. He wasn't in shock, he was pissed. Why had he taken his shoes off? He knew better! The neighbors were still remodeling, and he'd found a half-dozen nails outside while jumping rope at night over the last several weeks. If Nora didn't care so much about her precious white floors, this night would have ended very differently.

"Tate, are you listening to me? Why did you go after him? Why didn't you call 911 the second you heard someone in the house?"

Another paramedic with a flashlight mounted on his hat was looking at the slivers of glass embedded in Tate's face. Tate tried to look around the man. "Why are you here, Nia? I though you worked Organized Crime, not break-ins. Or do I need to report you for stalking?" He knew he was dancing on the line, if he hadn't already set fire to it and peed on the ashes. But he didn't care.

She looked as if she wanted to punch him in the face. "Nora Mallis isn't a typical victim of a B & E—she's running for public office."

"Still not sure how that applies to you, and last I checked, you work the day shift. I get the feeling you're here in a personal capacity more than a professional one."

"You're pretty stupid for a schoolboy," she said, not denying anything. "The officers on the scene reported that nothing seems to have been disturbed. Obviously once your aunt and Ms. Wolf arrive, they'll be able to tell us for sure. But if nothing is missing, that's suspicious."

"Not if I scared him off before he could take anything."

She looked at her notepad. "Yeah, you fake crapping your pants must have been so terrifying that he completely missed the jewelry and electronics on his way out."

The paramedic's tweezers tugged a bit hard on a piece of glass in his face. Tate flinched.

"Okay," Nia snapped, "stop being such a spoiled prince and let us take you to the hospital already."

"Not a chance in hell." His dad was still his emergency contact. He wasn't risking that call for anything.

Nia saw through him. "You have to know your aunt will call your parents, if she hasn't already. He's going to find out."

The paramedic pulled out another piece of glass, then dabbed the wound with an alcohol wipe. Tate winced. "As always, Nia, your assistance is as appreciated as a flaming pile of—"

"Tate!"

It was Alex's voice, followed by the sound of a car door slamming. With the paramedic digging in his face, Tate could hardly watch her approach. But the worry in her voice made his stomach flip.

She burst onto the scene looking like a nautical avenging

goddess, the interviewing detective behind her. "Are you okay?" Alex demanded.

"I'm fine, dear. How was your day?" An alcohol swab stung him, and he hissed, ruining the moment. Or not. The concern on Alex's face put a cheeky grin on his.

"Buddy, you need to hold still," the paramedic told him.

Nia sighed from behind them as Alex put a hand on Tate's leg.

"I got a call from the police saying there was a break-in and asking me to come find out if anything is missing, and now I come to find you bleeding in the back of an ambulance. What happened?"

Tate filled her in.

"There was someone here when you got home? How long do you think they'd been here?" she asked, looking between Tate, Nia, and the other detective. The paramedics finished bandaging and cleaning Tate's wounds and excused themselves.

"We can't know for certain," Nia said, "but based on the fact that nothing appears to be missing or disturbed, it either wasn't long or the man wasn't here to take something—"

"But to leave something," Tate said, acting as if he'd made the connection an hour ago instead of a second ago.

Horror registered on Alex's face. "Like what, a bug? A camera? *A bomb?*"

The other detective shook his head. "We have no reason to suspect anything violent, but we've had a bomb-sniffing dog comb through the house just in case. We have teams coming to sweep the house for listening devices any minute. We'll need you both to stay elsewhere tonight while we sweep and process the house. But Ms. Wolf, we really need you to go upstairs and see if anything is missing."

Alex was frowning, staring at Tate's bandaged foot. "Sorry, what?"

Nia studied Alex. "What are you thinking right now, Ms. Wolf?"

"I'm thinking how stupid Tate is." She rubbed her temples and stood.

"Easy," Tate said.

"Why did you have to pick a fight with my dad, Tate? Why couldn't you just have played nice for once?"

He knew what she was really saying: if he hadn't argued with her parents, they would still be at the party, and he never would have been hurt. She was more concerned than she knew how to admit.

"Tate has a knack for being a fool at even the best of times. What did he and your dad fight over? The shrimp cocktail?" Nia forced a laugh, as if this was all just her chewing the fat rather than digging for information without putting Alex on the defensive.

"If only." Alex sniffed. "No, it was politics. And the lack of actual cocktails, for that matter. I'll be right back," she said, following the other detective into the house.

After they left, Nia rubbed both hands over her face. "You argued with Connor Wolf tonight? And you didn't think that would be relevant when the detective asked if you knew of anyone who may wish you harm?"

"Oh, come on. You really think Wolf would have someone plant a bug here just because I called him on the Landolfo connection?"

"You accused him of having mob ties?" She released a long, slow breath, then turned and paced a circle into the pavement. The fury rolling off her made the night air boil.

"I'm right, aren't I?"

She brought a fist up to her face, but it wasn't a threatening gesture. She looked as if she was struggling to keep her cool, which he found overdramatic, to say the least. He'd confronted Wolf tonight, and now he had confirmation that the man was crooked. How was that a bad thing? Why couldn't she just acknowledge that he was right? "I can't believe I forgot you're only nineteen. You are a reckless, self-destructive child."

"And you're not denying anything, Nia. Or do you even know?

Am I out-sleuthing you, Detective Tafolo? Is that what's really pissing you off?"

She strode up to him so fast, if he'd been anyone else, he'd have leaned back. Instead, he let her get uncomfortably close to his face. "Say you were right, Tate? What do you think happens to people who accuse powerful men of having mob ties, *especially* when they're right?"

Tate felt his heart speed up. If Nia knew it was excitement, not fear, kicking his pulse in gear, she'd flip. *He* should have been flipping. "Come on. You think Wolf would send someone to hurt me when I live in a house with his sister-in-law and daughter?"

"I'm not saying anything, Tate. I'm asking you to care about your own wellbeing. But if you can't do that, then at least care enough about your aunt and friend to *think a little*!"

He leaned back on his elbows. "I don't think this is connected to Wolf. And if it is, the guy he sent better not quit his day job. He ran when I got home, Nia. Clearly he wasn't sent to bust my kneecaps . . ." Tate trailed off, something tickling at his memory. He thought hard, trying to remember what it was his brain wanted him to remember . . . it was so close . . .

She sat down beside him in the back of the ambulance, and the fierceness in her voice belied the casual gesture. "Honestly, we don't know why someone was in the house. But if you suspect Wolf has mob ties, and you're on his bad side, don't think for a second that something so mundane as family would stop him from bugging you or looking through your laptop or copying a notebook, at the very least." She stared hard. "Tate, you've been, what, two, maybe three months without a bet? And you feel like you're on top of the world, don't you? Like you're totally in control, like you could start up again and quit anytime you wanted? Bullshit. You haven't gambled, not because you're strong, but because you're terrified of how weak you really are."

"Weak? Nia, I ran a friggin' card room out of my buddy's apartment for months and I never gambled."

"Leaving aside the contact high you got from watching those losers, I don't think you're addicted to poker, you're addicted to winning at poker. Beating some sucker frat boys who couldn't tell their own nuts from a nut hand is about as appealing to you as sitting on a knife."

Tate widened his eyes. "That's a lot of visceral imagery, Detective. You doing okay?"

"Your little mob theory? Leave it alone, Tate," she said, her voice low and looming in the quiet night air. "Quit while you're still ahead, and while the people you care about are, too."

"Nia—"

"Leave it alone."

CHAPTER SIXTEEN

When Tate finally spoke to Nora, the first thing she asked was where he was staying that night.

"Gee, I'm fine, Aunt Nora. Just a few dozen flesh wounds and possible tetanus from the rusty nail I stepped on chasing down an intruder. How are you?"

"I know you're all right; I already got the report from the detective. I'm very relieved," she said, underselling it a smidge. "The detective said they're processing the house, so I can book you a hotel room—"

"Don't bother. I have a place to stay." He stuffed his clothes into a bag and grabbed everything he'd need for school.

"That's good. Oscar tells me you've been pushing yourself hard, so if you need to give yourself a day off after your disturbing night, you should do it. Or two, if that's what you need."

"Aw, keep up the mushy stuff and you'll become a real boy any day, Aunt Nora," he said, zipping his suitcase.

She cleared her throat. "I'm glad you're okay, Tate."

"Thanks, Aunt Nora. I'll see you when you get back."

Tate limped downstairs and opened the front door to find an officer waiting with Alex.

"Waiting for a cab?" he asked. She nodded. "Hotel or home?"

"Home? I can't go home after the disaster you left. The fact that

I didn't quit Nora's campaign the second you left as much as told my parents that I support your mob theories." Her fine features looked as if they'd been preserved in ice. Only her tone gave away how fired up she was. "Honestly, what were you thinking, Tate? I needed you today! You know how much my parents' approval means to me; why couldn't you just be there for me, already? Why did you have to ruin everything?"

Tate's hand was in his pocket, stroking the worn deck of cards as he watched Alex work herself up. Her anger was masking feelings too deeply rooted for her to even name. On any other night, he'd have engaged with her. He'd have drawn her out until she was one step closer to realizing the truth. But he was still furious about the way this day had unraveled. His triumph of knowing Connor was compromised was tarnished by everything that had happened with Juana, the intruder, and Nia.

"Why am I even bothering with you?" Alex was saying. "You are completely self-sabotaging! You're your own worst enemy, and the more I—"

"Alex." He grabbed her shoulders, even as a part of him told him not to, screamed that this was a bad idea.

"What?" she fumed.

"Shut up." He put a hand in her hair, pulled her close, and kissed her.

Almost kissed her, anyway.

She pushed him away just before their lips touched. "What do you think you're doing? Do you think this is some sexy angry hookup you see in movies? I'm pissed, Tate. Trust me, nothing about this situation is hot."

Tate ran a hand through his hair and backed up against the railing. *Stupid, stupid move.* Her rejection was no less than he should have expected, yet it drained him of the fumes he was running on. "I just wanted you to stop talking. Seemed like the easiest way."

"Take a cold shower."

Their cabs arrived a frosty few minutes later. The officer didn't look either of them in the eye as he escorted them to their vehicles, and Tate didn't bother saying good-bye to Alex.

He needed to sleep.

The sound of the driver clearing his throat woke Tate. He rubbed his eyes and looked around to where a stumpy brick residence hall looked like it was trying to give the world's most awkward hug.

Riviera Hall.

Tate paid the driver and limped out with his bags. When he passed a skinny kid walking down the stairs with his bike, Tate lifted the guy's ID card, scanned it to get into the building, and dropped it on the ground. Holding the door open, he called out.

"Hey, buddy, I think you dropped something."

He didn't wait for the kid to turn around. He was already hanging a left and heading into the house, keeping an eye on the RA at the front desk. Tate crouched, as if to tie his shoe, then pulled up the number for the Riv on his phone and dialed. When the RA turned his attention to the phone, Tate slipped past the front desk.

He made his way upstairs and down a hall. The place was run-down by both age and generations of obnoxious college students who thought a motto like "Let It All Hang Out" was somehow quaint and free-spirited instead of an invitation for dudes to streak during intramural disc golf. The place was practically dead; the residents were probably all outside cooking s'mores and kicking around a hacky sack.

But, of course, the one resident he wanted gone was in his room, studying at his tiny, dumpy desk, when Tate broke in.

"Hey—what—*Tate?*"

Tate dropped his bags and swung the door shut with his leg.

"Hi, honey. I'm home."

Oliver didn't give Tate the warm reception he was owed. And when Tate explained why he was there, Oliver grew more upset.

"You confronted an intruder, there's a chance the guy was sent after you specifically, and you came *here*?" Oliver ran his hand through his shaggy brown hair. "I guess that explains the limp. And why you look like a failed *Hellraiser* experiment."

"And they say you're just a pretty face." Tate shoved Oliver's things from his tiny, ratty bed and slumped down on it. "Don't worry, it's only for tonight. I need to give the occupant of my apartment twenty-four hours notice to leave before I can move in."

"It's fine. I'm just glad you're safe," Oliver said, before frowning. "Wait, you have an apartment? So you were living at Yates's place—"

"Rent free, so I could make money by subletting my apartment, yes. And I've continued that clever trick since moving to Aunt Nora's. And, no, Dad doesn't know what I'm doing. And I'm sure he doesn't realize that he paid the rent a year in advance on the apartment, or else I'd have been kicked out months ago." Oliver shook his head, and Tate chuckled. "Come on, man. I've been gambling since I was thirteen. I ran an illegal card room for months. I get into fights with people. I've won—and lost—more money in a single night than you've ever seen in your life. And I know more than one guy who calls himself Gator. I'm not a good guy, Ollie. Is this news to you?"

Oliver slammed his books shut, making the desk rattle precariously. "I'm so sick of this tough guy routine, Tate. I grew up with you! I know you better than probably anyone alive. You're not a bad guy! You're doing all of this because somewhere, deep down, you *hate* yourself. You have to prove that you're better than everyone else, that you're this brilliant mastermind who can beat anyone at anything, when the one person you're really trying to beat is yourself."

Tate yawned, nodding and making a "keep going" gesture with

his finger. "I'm listening, really, and this is all good stuff. But I've had a pretty long day, so I'm going to just lie here on your bed and keep listening. With my eyes closed." He punched Oliver's pillow into a comfortable shape and put his head down. Another yawn. "I'm really interested in how you feel, though, so please don't stop on my account."

Before he could hear the rest of Oliver's lecture, Tate was out.

Tate awoke the next morning to an empty room and a missed text from Karla:

Kept an ear out all night, but nothing to report. Sorry.

Tate cursed and got out of bed, looking down when he stepped on . . . a note. The little bugger left a note.

Tate—I hate this distance between us. I know you blame me for everything that happened last year, and from your perspective, I can understand. But please, for once, try to see it from my perspective: my older brother—my hero—almost died. And the way you were acting made me think you weren't willing to do anything to keep something worse from happening. I didn't know what else to do. I thought you were going to get yourself killed, and I did the only thing I could—

He crumpled up the note. "Bo-ring," he said. He debated throwing it away but settled on stuffing it into his pocket. He had enough decency not to throw the note away in Oliver's own trash.

The next day after class, Tate took the bus out to Irving Park. He didn't have a working theory yet, but he did have a pretty reliable gut. After what happened yesterday, his gut was crying foul.

He went to a nearly empty Polish restaurant and sat in a corner ordering Dr Peppers and doing his homework. The place was sketchy, at best, with foreign heavy metal blaring over the jukebox and pictures of scantily clad Polish stars in the bathrooms. The walls were covered with sheet metal and posters from Eastern European movies . . . all except one, which looked as if it had just been painted. No pictures hung there, although there were tables pushed up against it. Strange.

Tate tottered up to the bar, favoring his injured foot. He waved to the bartender, who hadn't served another customer in the hour since Tate arrived.

"Out of curiosity, did you guys recently redecorate?"

The bartender stared at him. "What?"

"Weird question, right? My girlfriend talked me into taking this interior decorating class with her because, well, she clearly hates me. Yet now, it's like the class has worked its way into my brain and I find myself noticing the stupidest things. Anyway, I can't help but notice the wall across from here doesn't match the rest of the room, so I'm just wondering if you guys redecorated."

"Guy." The bartender slowly leaned in. "I don't know if you're stupid or suicidal, but you don't go around asking questions like that around here, okay?"

Tate rocked back on his heels. "Okay, so not a fan of interior design, then. Got it. I'm just gonna—" He hobbled back to his table, grabbed his things, and vanished through the door.

When he was out of view, he pulled out his phone to see the next location on his list. Yup, there was definitely something going on here.

CHAPTER SEVENTEEN

The rest of the week gave Tate more of the same—school, then hunting out new restaurants for homework and recon. He'd called Oscar about his hunch, and, although Oscar wasn't convinced, he agreed that there was something worth looking into.

"You should know," Oscar had said, "Juana has asked to work with someone else, so we moved Ruby over from Field to free you up for your new role as tracker."

"Tracker?" he asked, not wanting to think about Juana's request. About how stupid he'd been.

"Yes, it's what we call campaign spies."

Tate smiled. "Perfect. I'll keep you posted."

By Friday, he was moved into his one-bedroom apartment just a half mile off campus. Before Tate had sublet the place, it had been nice—granite, tile, stainless steel. The occupant hadn't been happy to get kicked out on such short notice, but considering none of their arrangement was aboveboard, it appeared trashing the place was her formal complaint. Doors were missing from cupboards, more than a few tiles were cracked, the bathroom had an unexplainable, ineradicable funk, and smears that looked suspiciously like blood decorated the walls.

He'd seen worse. But he wasn't going through with a black light anytime soon.

His dad had rented the apartment for him after he started going to GA at Christmas. Tate had only agreed to go to shut Oliver up, as he'd been acting more superior and infuriating than ever during the break. But his dad had seemed happy, and Tate was forty-five minutes closer to campus.

The one thing he and his dad had always agreed on was school. For a long time, it had been the only thing his dad cared about. If Tate was doing well, he could go out whenever he wanted, few (if any) questions asked. And Tate did well, always. Even thirteen-year-old Alex hadn't been able to stamp that out. He liked school, liked the challenge, the competition, the fact that there was always something more to master.

Kind of like poker.

Holy hell, did he miss playing poker.

He put his hand in his pants pocket, feeling the cards while he watched the time tick down on the microwave. He had five minutes to eat before he had to leave for a meeting with Oscar. The bipartisan charity event was tomorrow night, so Alex would be in rare form.

The microwave beeped, and he pulled out last night's leftovers. With his fork, he grabbed a steaming pierogi and blew on it. He took a careful bite, letting more steam waft from his mouth before chewing and swallowing. It didn't go down well. He'd have to cross Karczma off his list if their food couldn't make for good leftovers. Although, hopefully, he'd get answers soon so he could stop stalking every dive restaurant in Irving Park.

He'd need to branch out to new neighborhoods soon. Oscar was still insistent that Tate's new role remain a secret until they had something concrete to work with. That meant he had a lot of ground to cover before the election in November.

After a few more unappetizing bites, Tate dumped the food into the garbage. He walked to the other side of his studio apartment and cracked a window. Didn't want to stink the place up. Then he flipped the window lock so it couldn't be opened any farther without breaking. Not that that would stop someone motivated. He held a hand over his scar.

No one was chasing him. Why would they?

Still, when he got downstairs, he looked in every direction for the man he'd seen at Misha's Restaurant on Monday, or anyone else, for that matter. On his way to HQ, although he didn't see anything suspicious, he couldn't shake the feeling that someone was watching.

Tate had been in Oscar's office a handful of times, though he'd never paid much attention to the decor. Along with his degrees and an inspirational poster on the wall, there was a large family picture behind Oscar's desk of him and his family dressed up in front of an uncomfortably bright white church. Tate avoided looking at it as he updated Oscar on everything he'd observed. The church was almost blinding.

"I have a theory now."

"I'm listening," Oscar said.

"It has something to do with video gambling. You know how I mentioned the weird blank walls? I noticed some discolored patches of carpet in a couple of places, too. I think someone either outright took the gambling machines or strong-armed the owners into giving them up. And it's mostly Eastern European joints—Ukrainian, Polish, Serbian. A few Korean bars and a Lebanese restaurant too. But no chains or well-known establishments."

Oscar sat with one ankle across his knee, tapping a pen against his black leather shoe. "Okay, but what does that have to do with Connor?"

"I don't know," Tate admitted. "I think it's more to do with Landolfo, actually. He's running the casino if the proposal goes through, and they want to change the gaming laws, right? I've been reading up on how video gambling has hurt casino revenues—what if Landolfo's connections are trying to take care of the problem on their own to make sure the new casino is a success?"

Oscar shook his head. "Doesn't matter."

"What do you mean, 'doesn't matter?'"

"I mean that this is less than nothing. The most you have is a bunch of skittish restaurant employees in Irving Park, one who complained that someone you think *might* be Connor is to blame. But that woman's own family implied she has dementia, and her employees say she doesn't come in to work anymore. In other words, you have some weird events that may or may not be related, especially not to Connor."

"But the machines—"

"You *think* there are some missing machines. Even if there are, it could have been done by any number of gangs on the North Side, of which there is no shortage. Or the restaurants could have had some complaints or violated state liquor laws—"

"What?" Tate sat up.

"You know what I mean: serving to minors, over-serving someone already drunk, intoxicated employees—"

"I know what violations are. I don't understand why that would impact the machines."

"Because . . ." Oscar's eyes widened, as if he'd just discovered the formula for cold fusion. "I can't believe I didn't consider this. Video gaming is only allowed in establishments with valid liquor licenses."

"And Landolfo's the head of the liquor board. This explains why the bars have been empty, why the employees have all been on edge."

Oscar's mouth pulled into a tight line. "It's a tenuous connection, and you'll have a tough time tying Landolfo to any wrongdoing, let alone Connor. If he's involved here, it'll be nearly impossible to prove."

Tate leaned back in his chair, arms up on the sides of it. "That's what a tracker does, isn't it?"

Oscar laughed. "Hardly. Trackers follow around opposing candidates to catch them saying something incriminating that they can release to the media."

"Yeah, I don't think I'm low profile enough to get away with that."

"Not even a little," Oscar agreed. "Anyway, if you want to stay on this, do it. I need to go help your aunt with an upcoming interview. Want to sit in on the prep? Alex will be there, too."

"Why not?"

Oscar rose from his chair, exiting his office in short, strong steps. Tate followed languidly. Oscar stopped at Alex's office, and a minute later, the three were waiting at Nora's door while she finished up a call. Alex was carrying a steaming cup of tea, something he'd never seen her do before.

When the door opened, Nora was scowling. "Finally, people with IQs higher than a teaspoon's," she said, marching back to her desk.

"I heard your last call didn't go so well," Alex said, placing the tea in front of Nora, who sighed.

"And you even remembered that I like lemon? Thank you, dear. I don't know what I'd do without you," Nora said, squeezing Alex's hand affectionately. When Alex sat down, she had a pink tinge to her cheeks.

"Suck-up," Tate muttered to her as he took the chair next to her. She ignored him. "Wait, I stop an intruder from pillaging your home while Alex brings you a cup of Cubby Wubby Womb Room Tea, and *she* gets the thank you?"

"Yes. Nice facial," Nora said, eyeing the tiny cuts on his face that had yet to fully heal.

Tate grinned. "How I've missed your sparkling wit."

She turned to Oscar. "Why did you want Alex and Tate here?"

"I thought it would be nice to have a few more perspectives on how you come across in interviews."

"I know how I come across."

"Rhymes with witch?" Tate said.

"Funny," she said, her drawn eyebrows telling Tate that it bothered her more than she wanted to say.

He glanced at Alex, who was shaking her head. "You don't come across like that, Aunt Nora. You're a role model. Once voters get to know the real you—"

"Don't listen to her. Okay, what have you got?" Tate asked, tugging Oscar's list of questions from his hand. He scanned them. "Ms. Mallis, how do you respond to Connor Wolf's accusations that, if elected, you'll prioritize your puritanical beliefs over your responsibility to uphold the law?"

She practically jumped from her chair. "First—"

Tate held a hand up. "It's too late, you're done."

"Excuse me?"

"You're done." He stood his phone up on the desk, centering it on Nora, and pressed RECORD, all the while talking. "Your body language showed that you're already on the defensive. You just told viewers everything they needed to know about you without saying a word."

"But I—"

"Ms. Mallis," he continued, talking over her. "Why do you hate America?"

Her nostrils flared. "Excuse me?"

"Last year, your firm helped an illegal immigrant in a case that ultimately led to a police officer being fired and facing civil charges. If elected, how many more police officers do you hope to fire?"

Clenched jaw. "I would never—"

"Will you target other public safety officers?"

Mouth pulled into a grimace. "That isn't even part of—"

"What about the rumors that you look down on mothers and women who don't work?"

Forceful exhale. "That's absurd."

"And how do you answer—"

Her hand pounded the desk. "Enough! I get the point."

Tate gave the questions back to Oscar, who rolled and clutched them. On Tate's other side, Alex's foot was jiggling. "If you get the point, why didn't you control yourself?" Tate asked.

"It's not that easy for me," She said in a pinched voice.

"This isn't a courtroom where the wilder your expressions, the more strongly it'll impress the jury. Your expressions are everything. You need to look humble, thoughtful, and passionate."

"You don't think I look passionate enough?"

"You look angry. Bitter. Maybe even mean. People don't vote for any of those things."

She rocked back from her desk. "So let me guess what my body language is saying." She put up her hand, holding a finger up for each new point. "I'll force my beliefs on anyone and everyone if I'm in office. I'd rather take down a cop than an illegal. I think gambling turns people into losers. Mothers are a drain on the economy and, probably, lesser beings. Am I missing anything?"

Alex cleared her throat. "No one thinks those things about you."

"According to Tate, my body language would suggest otherwise."

Alex cast a quick glance at Tate. "I agree that body language is important, but I don't think it's as dire as Tate is saying. What I'd recommend is softer expressions. More subtle emotion. It's okay to be upset about a misleading question, but you need to look like it's beneath you, like it isn't worth your time, but that you care about voters enough to respect any question someone would ask you," she said. "So if someone asks you why you chose an immigrant over a police officer, what do you *want* the person to leave thinking?"

"That I value all human life and expect our government to do the same." Her eyebrows pulled up, and her features shifted as concern bloomed on her face. "That we have a dedicated, humane police force, and the people of Chicago can't allow one bad apple to spoil the bunch, but if it does, we'll stand for justice. I want people to know that immigrants matter, and that we can work together to find a better solution to the problem of illegal immigration, but that the cost of that solution should never be the inhumane treatment of a person or a child."

"And what does inhumane treatment look like?" Oscar asked.

Nora's eyes tightened with emotion. "It looks like a woman hand-cuffed to a bench in a holding cell, screaming and writhing with con-tractions. It looks like a newborn baby suffocating and struggling for life because someone put his own prejudice above not only protocol, but human decency." Her voice trembled with conviction. "We are the greatest nation in the world, and with every law we uphold, we have the chance to do so with great respect to human life. If our laws ever come at the expense of supporting life, liberty, and the pursuit of happiness of any person, our legal system allows us the chance to reconsider. Isn't that wonderful?"

Oscar smiled at Tate. "Did you get that?"

He stopped recording. "Got it. I'll send it to all of you," he said before pressing play for Nora.

When the video was done, Nora said, "Okay. So how do I keep doing that?"

"Prepare," Oscar said. "Practice answering the questions over and over again."

"I can say the prettiest damn words in the world, Oscar, but that won't change my subconscious reactions."

"Practice when you're already angry, then," Oscar said. "And make yourself answer the most misleading questions until you can stay calm."

"And say them in front of a mirror," Alex said. "Practice while you watch yourself."

She shook her head. "You think I haven't tried all of that?"

"Answer the question you *want* them to ask—" Alex started.

"And record yourself like Tate did," Oscar said. "Watch for things that trigger your emotions."

"Expect triggers," Alex added.

The set of Nora's jaw and the wideness in her eyes betrayed both frustration and fear. She was getting lost in their sea of advice.

"Watch horror movies," Tate said.

All eyes turned on him. He kept his breathing controlled, not letting this be anything other than advice he was giving his boss. "Horror movies are all about manipulating your emotions, trying to elicit a primal response that you can't control. Force yourself to watch them until you can stop flinching, until you can keep your heart from racing and your breath from catching. Then when you can disassociate from those reactions, start controlling them. Smile when you want to scream. Laugh when you want to cry. At the most inappropriate moments, when every instinct tells you to be horrified, *be stronger*. Keep it up until you can convince yourself that a huge, hairy spider is the cutest thing you've ever seen. Once you can do that, this'll be easy."

Tate didn't care what Oscar and Alex were thinking just then. He didn't. So he didn't bother looking at Alex to see her reaction. It didn't matter if she was horrified or bored by what he'd said, by his advice. It didn't.

Nora was staring at him. "That is the most disturbing thing I've ever heard."

"There's the aunt I know and love."

He kicked his legs up on her desk. She looked at his feet as if they were covered in dog feces. But she didn't ask him to move them, and he didn't offer. "You can do all of this, though, and it won't change anything if you can't fix your main problem."

"My main problem? Do enlighten me."

"You just don't seem very nice."

Before Nora could stab him with her letter opener, Alex leaned forward. Her black hair hung between them like a curtain. "What Tate's *trying* to say is that if you focus on showing that you're approachable during your answers, your reactions will follow."

Oscar nodded. "Being a successful woman makes this battle harder—no question. But it is possible to show voters that you're both committed and compassionate."

Nora put her arms up on the armrests of her chair. She usually radiated power, but now, something was missing. "That's a kind way to put it, but Tate's right." She looked at him appraisingly. "I'll try your little trick. If it worked for a degenerate like you, it's worth a shot." Then she reached across the desk and shoved his feet off.

His feet dropped to the ground, and he used the momentum to spring up, hiding how much it hurt his injured foot. "You know, instead of horror movies, maybe you should watch clips of kids on your lawn—"

"Shut up, Tate. And get the hell out of my office."

CHAPTER EIGHTEEN

Alex pushed Tate from Nora's office, leaving a wincing Oscar and a puce-faced Nora. Alex's office was across the room from Nora's and a fraction of the size, but equally stark. Tate doubted that was a coincidence. He let Alex push him into the small room and then watched, amused, as she closed the door and rounded her desk, putting herself in the position of power.

"Why, Tate?" she asked. "Why are you so hell-bent on ruining every relationship with everyone who cares about you?"

"I just told her the truth, Alex. She needed to hear it."

Alex's expression was pained. "Not like that. That was too harsh. You could have driven the same point home in a way that let her keep her dignity."

"Oscar brought us both in there for a reason. My guess is he needed me to be blunt and hoped you'd soften the blow. Either way, we helped her today. And you saw her face—her dignity is intact."

Alex placed a hand on her desk, sweeping aside the hair that fell in her face. "That's what she wants you to think."

"Why do you say that?" he asked. "Why do you think she wants me to think she's okay?" He took a step toward Alex's side of the desk.

"Because you're a hard person to be vulnerable around."

She wasn't talking about Nora, she was talking about herself, and by the way she stood pin straight as he took another step toward her, her subconscious mind knew it. "No, I'm not."

She eyed him warily. "Fine. You're a dangerous person to be vulnerable around, then."

"Not for Nora, I'm not." They were face-to-face now. Her eyes were right at the level of his lips, but Tate saw her look lower—to his jaw, his neck, then back up to his eyes. "You don't need to be afraid of me, Alex."

Her scoff was all show. "I'm not afraid of you, Sprinkles. I own you."

"Protesting a bit much, aren't you? Don't make me quote Shakespeare."

A flush crept up her cheeks. "Everything is a game to you."

"No, it isn't," he said, dropping his voice. "Sure, we play our little games. We tease and snap at each other because we like it. Because we're good at it. But this? This isn't a game. I'm not going to hurt you, Alex."

Her eyes were like dark pools, seductive and inviting. He wanted to dive in and lose himself there. He wanted her to want him to.

He reached a hand out, grabbing hers. Tugging her closer. Her skin was the softest thing he'd ever touched. "Why are you fighting this? Is it because of your boyfriend?"

She was looking down at their hands. "Why is everyone but me so obsessed with him?"

"Because he's your boyfriend." He ran a finger down her cheek, and her eyes fluttered closed.

She shifted closer, breathing slowly, almost as if she was breathing him in. "Last I checked, boyfriends were supposed to do things like call or come over or not sleep with other girls."

Tate brought his lips to her temple. "That's a good point."

"Mmm-hmm." She rocked forward on her toes.

He let his fingers study the angles and curves of her face.

A moment later, her hands were on his stomach, her thumbs running over the muscles beneath his shirt. "I don't trust you," she said. "That's why I'm fighting this."

He kissed her cheek, right next to her ear. "Trust is overrated."

She sniffed a laugh, but pressed her face against his mouth. "Hardly words to live by."

"What don't you trust?"

She took a moment to respond, her husky breathing making his heart race. "Your motives. You could be doing this to get back at my dad. Or me."

He chuckled. "Yes, thirteen-year-old Alex has a lot to answer for."

"Every Alex does."

He pulled back to study her, but an approaching figure caught his eye through the mostly shuttered blinds over Alex's window.

"To be continued," he said, stepping back.

The set of Alex's eyes looked . . . regretful. Or wary. "To be continued." When Oscar knocked on the door, Alex called to come in. "Uh, Tate, you sent us that recording of Nora, right? Maybe we can go over it Monday?"

"Sure," he said, and Oscar added his assent.

"Good. See you tomorrow night at the event. Right?" she asked Tate.

He stopped at the door. "Wouldn't miss it."

It was perversely satisfying to get ready in a mirror cracked from where a fist had rammed into it (especially when the fist wasn't his). Tate's wrists flicked one end through the other, expertly tying the bow tie that completed his tuxedo. When he was finished, he smoothed his hair and cocked an eyebrow at his reflection. The barely healed cuts on his face were the perfect complement.

He had twenty minutes until the car would pick him up for the charity event. It was taking place in one of Chicago's finest hotels, and some of Chicago's finest (wealthiest) citizens would be there. The engraved invitation hung on his stainless steel refrigerator, partially covering the message his previous tenant had scratched into the metal; only the F— and —OU were still visible.

The invitation called it a Roaring Twenties Charity Fund-Raiser, with little period touches designed to heighten the anticipation. There was a quarter note to denote jazz, a blind tiger to represent a speakeasy, and a pair of lips blowing on dice, among other things. As usual, there'd be a fancy prize for whoever guessed the theme during the cocktail hour, and as usual, the money would be better spent toward actually helping people. The charity hosting the event was famous for attracting the city's elite, as well as for not donating nearly enough of their proceeds to actual charity. But if Nora had backed out on principle, the press would have eaten her alive, posting headlines like "Candidate Mallis's Barren Home and Heart," or something equally vicious.

Tate looked at the (remarkably untouched) wall clock. Nineteen minutes before his cab arrived. Nineteen minutes.

He was so bored.

He pulled out the deck of cards from his pants pocket and sat at his little kitchen table. He wouldn't be able to take the cards with him—bulging Tuxedo pockets weren't exactly his style. He was cutting the deck when Oliver's note flew out from the middle. Tate stopped and picked it up, catching on one line:

my older brother—my hero—almost died

He crumpled the note and threw it behind him before picking up the cards and recutting. He shuffled, letting the sound of the cards swishing against each other calm him. Closing his eyes, he cut and shuffled and cut and shuffled and cut and shuffled . . .

The ring of his phone surprised him, and the cards flew into the air like confetti from a canon. He cursed and punched the ANSWER button.

"Hello?"

"Mr. Bertram? This is your driver. I'm waiting outside your building."

What?

"Thanks, I, uh—" He looked at the cards scattered all over his table and floor, and the urge to touch them, to take them with him, made his palms sweat with need. "I'm just getting dressed. I'll be right out."

He dropped the phone and fell to the floor, scooping up the cards too fast. His haste affected his coordination, and as he added a new card to the pile, two more jumped from his hands. He roared, slapping the tile and dropping them all.

"Stop it," he told himself sharply, flexing his hands in and out. "Stop it stop it stop it stop it stop it." He closed his eyes and breathed as slowly and deeply as he could, holding his breath for ten seconds, then exhaling for ten seconds. His hands were balled into fists so tight they ached.

His phone rang again. The driver. With a longing look, Tate left the cards and strode from his apartment.

He was barely in control when he got to the hotel. There was a red carpet entrance for people who wanted to make sure the world knew how generous and beautiful they were. Naturally, he walked down it. He smiled and winked for the cameras like he was Jay Friggin' Gatsby. He reveled in the spotlight, in the eyes all turned on him.

The Wolfs would follow soon, but it would be down a trail he'd already blazed the hell out of. His parents, on the other hand, would avoid it. His dad was quietly generous, a fact Tate had discovered when he'd gone through his dad's office last spring looking for credit card numbers. He'd seen a ledger with a list of charities, as well as private individuals, to whom his dad anonymously donated tens of thousands of dollars annually.

It had almost caused Tate enough guilt to keep him from using those same credit card numbers on that online poker site. In the end, what had turned Tate away from online poker wasn't remorse but rage. He'd discovered that he hadn't been playing against five separate players online, but five different aliases for the person who hosted the website.

Talk about the house always winning.

Thinking about it now made Tate's teeth clench so hard he worried a tooth would crack.

Get yourself together, man. What is wrong with you?

A pretty hostess in a short dress and pillbox hat with a cigar box around her waist ushered him in. Thinking of cigars made him think of that smell . . . that particular blend he could only equate with a card room, with poker, with winning.

His cards were at home, so he couldn't reach for them, couldn't wind down. He needed a distraction. He needed . . . he needed . . .

A drink.

This time, he had the good sense to look at the server before taking a glass. It wasn't Karla, fortunately. Unfortunately, his parents had just entered the ballroom. His mom was smiling at the glitz and glamour. Tate's hand hesitated on the stem of the champagne glass.

He downed the drink.

He put the glass on the tray just in time—his parents spotted him and were already approaching, with his mom appearing in rare health. He'd have taken another drink if it had just meant pissing off his dad, but it would also disappoint his mom, and the stress would cause a fibro-flare. He couldn't handle that on his conscience.

"Sweetie!" his mom said, breaking away from his dad when another guest stopped him. She wrapped her arms around Tate, and her smell was achingly familiar. "Don't you look dashing? I hope you're not planning to break too many hearts tonight."

"I could say the same of you, Mom. Look at you, killin' the flapper style. You look great."

She wrinkled her nose and patted his cheek. "The more you lie, the more I love you," she teased, but the words struck a nerve. Even knowing it was a joke, he couldn't tell if there was a deeper meaning. And if so, he couldn't begin to tell if it was good or not.

"I love you, too, Mom," he said, grabbing her hand. "Save a dance for me tonight, will you?"

"Do you think swing dancing is part of the secret theme? I guessed that it would be . . ." She shook her head, looking away from him.

"What did you guess it was, Mom?"

She fiddled with her long string of pearls. "Something mob related."

Tate could have kicked himself. "It's a casino night, isn't it? I'm so stupid." How had he missed the clues? Nora and Oscar had hated it because of the casino proposal. Alex had hated it because of what it would do to him.

He needed to leave.

He wanted to stay.

"I'm so sorry, sweetie. Why don't we go? We could head up to the restaurant on the top floor and get milkshakes like we used to do when you were younger and—"

Tate put a hand on his mom's arm. "Mom, it's fine. *I'm* fine. I haven't played poker in months. I hardly even think about it anymore."

Concern wrinkled her brow. "Are you sure?"

"I'm positive. We're going to have a great time tonight, and if you play your cards right, I'll even sneak you a milkshake later. How about that?"

She smiled, her worry clearing. "I love you more than anything. Don't you ever forget it."

"I'm rubber, you're glue," he said, taking her arm and escorting her back to his dad, who said good-bye to the man he was conversing with and turned to them.

"Son," he said.

"Father."

His mom linked an arm through his dad's and then through Tate's. "That'll be enough, boys. We're here to have a good time. Try to remember that."

Tate had no problem remembering that he was here to have a good time. The problem was not succumbing to it. After cocktails and appetizers, the head of the charity—one Cynthia Wolf—announced the night's theme and the three winners who guessed it. When his mom's name was called, she gave the room a tight smile.

Casino Night.

He considered not taking it personally—chances were that the board of the charity had settled on the theme months ago—but he didn't believe it. Connor and Cynthia would stoop to any level to get what they wanted or to eliminate what they didn't. And when it came to Tate, they didn't.

All night, he'd been keeping an eye out for Alex. He'd caught glimpses of a sheet of black hair and a gold sequin flapper dress, but he couldn't get close enough to talk to her. There were too many people: people who wanted to talk about his parents or Nora's campaign or his stint in rehab.

He left every interaction feeling drained, as if the life was slowly being sucked out of him. Everything about the night made him crave a win. He wanted to best every useless tool in the room, beat them so hard they'd grind their faces in the dirt to hide their shame. So when Alex finally came his way, he was in the mood for action, not banter.

He took her hand and tugged her toward a small corridor he'd spotted earlier. She gave him a curious look but followed him through the crowds. After a moment, he glanced back to see her hiding a smile.

"What do you think you're doing?" she asked as he leaned her against the wall. She kept her hand in his, playing with his fingers.

"I think you can guess," he said, pressing close.

"Seriously? With all of Chicago's elites just around the corner? Our parents?"

"Right, because you're just dying to spend time with your parents right now."

Her gaze sharpened. "I've been with my mom all day. She showed up out of nowhere this morning and insisted on taking me dress shopping—because heaven forbid I wear the dress I picked out on my own. After that, she took me to a salon so we could get our hair and makeup done before we put the finishing touches on this sham of an event. You wouldn't believe the lectures I've had today."

"Forget all of that. Forget her. You've done an outstanding job, Alex," he said, running a finger over her collarbone. "Now's your chance to enjoy the fruits of your labors."

"Oh, I always enjoy myself, Tate. You should know that about me by now," she said, her tone too hard and biting for the moment. But he was done reading into things. They'd been playing this same game for months, and the moves had become so predictable, he knew her cards before she even threw them down. It was time for something new.

He pulled her close, speaking softly in her ear. "Then why don't we enjoy ourselves together?" he said. He felt her shiver at his touch, and he smiled as he moved his lips across her jaw line. Before he could kiss her again, she pulled back enough to catch his eye.

"Think about what you do next, Tate. You can't come back from this." She sounded cold, ruthless even, but the flush in her cheeks told a different story. Alex wanted this, even if she couldn't admit it. She was a mess of contradictions, and that should have turned him off.

It didn't.

In a flash, he was pulling her close and his mouth was on hers, hot and needy. Alex was matching him, kissing with an urgency he hadn't expected but that made him want more. More, more, more. With every kiss, he felt the stakes were raising. He was throwing chips into a pot that was going to make or break him. And the way Alex was kissing him back felt like she was planning to steal that pot. He didn't care. He put one hand in her hair and another on the small of her back, wanting this to last forever.

It didn't.

When she pushed him away after a few short minutes, he felt anxious. Utterly unfulfilled. "Come on," he said, kissing her neck. "Let's get out of here."

"Get out of here? The night has barely started."

"This night is my personal hell," he said, running a hand through his hair. She tsked and smoothed it back down. The feel of her hands made him wild. "Come on, Alex. You know how hard this is for me."

She bit her lip to hide her frown, and in doing so, her sharp edges seemed to soften. "I know. I was so mad about the theme. I begged them to change it. Nora did, too. But it's not actually a political event, and Mom said the board suggested the idea, so she had to go along with it. We made sure there were no poker tables, at least. That's something, right? You know I didn't want this."

"I know." Tate rubbed his face, then dropped his hand and kissed her nose. "You're adorable when you're upset. It means a lot to me."

She backed up, and something in her glance changed. Or maybe it was something in him, because she was eyeing him as if he was a feral animal. "What's going on with you? You're off."

"I'm just wired. It's been a long week, but I can promise you the next three hours will feel longer."

"Be careful, okay? Don't do anything stupid."

"Your concern is heartwarming."

"I'm serious," she said. "Watch out for yourself."

"Won't you be watching out for me?" he asked, leaning back into her.

"Not even a little," she said before putting her teeth around his earlobe. "My parents are here. You're on your own."

CHAPTER NINETEEN

After Alex touched up her lipstick and wiped some from Tate's mouth, they returned to the party. The casino tables were up, and a big band was playing on a stage in one corner of the room. Tate stopped, but Alex gestured across a row of roulette tables.

"Over there—it's Nora and your parents. You should go say hi," she said, veering in the other direction.

He grabbed her arm, a sign of panic that he couldn't keep down. "Where are you going?"

He may as well have asked her the winning hand in blackjack. "I'm going back to my family, obviously. What did you think? That I was going to stay here with you all night?"

"Come on," he said. "Just for another few minutes. I need to work my way up to my father's level of disappointment." He smiled so she'd think he wasn't serious.

But Alex's tone turned waspish. "And here I thought you'd want to see your little girlfriend."

"My what?" Tate looked around, trying to understand what Alex was talking about, when he saw her.

Finley. She was standing to the side, watching the room while Tate's dad and Nora were in a heated discussion about something. The girl looked beautiful, too clean and pure for her surroundings. Sure, this was a charity event, but the scent of desperation clung to the place like cheap cologne. People were laughing too loudly, staring too intently, cursing too seriously for this to be all fun and games. This was as real as any high stakes game to these people. They weren't here to donate; they were here to fill the same void as any junkie, yet their despair didn't carry a label like "addict" on it, so they could stand there, sanctimonious and superior, and judge everyone else who wasn't them. They were pathetic.

All of them except Finley.

He beamed. He could have stopped himself, but he didn't. It would piss off Alex more.

"I'll talk to you later," he said, not glancing back.

Her mumbled curse words joined the background noise as Tate made a beeline for Fin. When she saw him, her eyes sparkled.

"Hey there, hep cat," she said.

"Whoa, look who read up on her twenties slang," he said. He was debating going in for a hug when he heard the clearing of a self-righteous throat meant to stop him in his tracks. It had the opposite effect.

Tate wrapped his arms a bit too tenderly around Finley, regretting how good it felt even as he gave his brother a wolfish grin. "Great to see you, Ollie," he said. Then, more quietly: "You too, Fin."

She squeezed him tight, then pulled back. Oliver stepped beside her. And grabbed her hand.

Finley's reaction was mixed—her slow blink showed annoyance clear as day—but the way she shifted ever so slightly toward Oliver told Tate everything he needed to know.

He grabbed a fruit kebob from a tray. "So how long have you guys been back together?" he asked before sliding the kebob into his mouth.

Fin's eyebrows pulled together. "Nothing is official—"

"A couple of weeks," Oliver said at the same time.

"We've been hanging out again for a couple of weeks," she clarified, looking pointedly at Oliver.

"But this is a date," Tate said, surprised by the sting of it. He'd imagined her missing him, not making up with his brother.

With a glance at Oliver, she nodded. "I texted you a handful of times. I figured when you didn't answer that you didn't really care—"

"Of course I don't care," he said, using the toothpick from the kebob to pick at his teeth. "Why would I?"

Her cheeks turned a deep red, but she didn't drop her gaze. "I just didn't want you to . . . you know what, never mind."

He tsked. "Aw, were you worried about hurting me? Did you imagine I'd been thinking about you this whole time? That is . . . *precious*." The hurt on her face should have shamed him. Instead it fueled him like green wood on a fire. "Listen, Fin, we had fun, but I never took your little crush seriously. How could I? You're practically a kid."

Oliver's whole body tensed while Finley's shook. She put a hand on her boyfriend and glared at Tate. "I hope *this*—what you're doing now—is worth what you're risking." Fin turned, pulling Oliver with her.

The fruit in Tate's mouth turned to ash.

Nothing a few drinks couldn't fix.

It had been only twenty minutes since he'd seen Alex—fifteen since his encounter with Fin—but it felt like hours. He'd stopped by the bar for a quick pick-me-up, but all that small talk made him want to cry with boredom. Or, better yet, ditch these pathetic fools and their silly little games to hit up a real one. Because playing roulette or baccarat was about as tempting as stale beer to a wine aficionado. It wasn't *gambling* he craved right now, it was poker. The psyche of it. The thrill of anticipation that ran down his spine as he waited for an opponent to reveal a hand. The skill that went into knowing not only the odds of any particular hand, but also the tells of the players around him. He missed the sweet taste of winning, not because his hand was better than everyone else's, but because his mind was.

The people who threw around the term "gambling addict" were the same ones who thought it was about money. But Connor Wolf was right: it wasn't about the money—it was never about the money.

It was about the win. The win that proved once and for all that you were the best. The king. The absolute nuts.

And if he did nothing else tonight, he'd prove that to Alex.

Her gold dress shimmered through the crowd. Nearby, a woman took a sip of a drink before putting it down on a small table behind her. Tate grabbed the drink, drained it, and set it down on a server's tray without breaking stride. When he reached Alex, he felt keyed up but unstoppable, the same way he always did right before sitting at a poker table.

Tate put a hand on her elbow, ignoring whomever she was with. But Alex pulled her arm from his grasp when she looked at him.

"Walk away," she whispered through gritted teeth.

Movement caught his eye. A guy maybe a couple of years older than Tate was standing on Alex's other side, looking as if he belonged on a yacht or atop a horse or playing cricket at the country club.

He looked like every rich douchebag who'd wandered into Tate's card room. And lost.

"Tate, what a surprise to see you," Cynthia Wolf said across from him. Her Botox didn't let her look annoyed, yet she managed to look exultant. Like a loan shark who'd collected a large vig. "I don't believe you've met Brooks, have you?"

Alex froze in place.

Her mom continued. "Brooks, this is Tate Bertram. Tate, this is Brooks Sinclair, of the Sinclair Hotels, of course. But around our home, he's simply Alex's boyfriend."

Tate wanted to break the boy's hand. Instead, he shook it and pasted a look of pleasant disinterest on his face. "Good to meet you, Brock, er, Brooks, was it?"

Brooks gave him a bored smile. "Yeah, you too." He draped his arm across Alex's shoulders. "Alex told me about you. You're the guy who's so obsessed with poker, right?"

"I'm not surprised she told you all about me. But you may want to be worried that she's never mentioned you."

Alex glared, but Brooks waved his hand. Either he wasn't bright enough to catch the insult or he didn't care enough. "I'm not worried."

Cynthia laughed. "Of course you shouldn't be worried," Cynthia said, but she was looking at Tate. "You were looking at engagement rings last weekend."

Tate had to shut down all feeling before he became a whole host of tells. He'd known Alex to play games, lie, keep secrets, but he'd thought they were small things. Bluffs and feints.

But this . . .

"With Alex working so much, I'm surprised you've had the time," he said. "Even tonight, I know for a fact she's been keeping busy."

"Considering she's been staying with Brooks since the break-in at Nora's, I'd say they've found plenty of time," Cynthia said, the slight curl of her lips conveying more than enough meaning.

Tate's thoughts turned to a hand he'd played a couple of years ago. After the cards had been dealt, he'd carried pocket aces. The monster of all monster hands. If the game had ended right then, Tate would've had the absolute nuts. His initial bet was confident without being aggressive, enough to keep some of the tighter players in the game for a bit longer. He'd been playing with a couple of people he knew and a couple he didn't, including a tourist from South Dakota. Dakota had only played a few hands, and he was a typical newb. Happy, eager, and with only the most basic grasp of hold 'em rules, like flushes beating straights. But he was on vacation on a riverboat casino for the first time in his life, and he'd come to have fun, he'd told them.

The flop came K-3-A, rainbow. Dakota called, as did a few others. With trip aces, Tate raised.

Then another three on the turn. Aces full of threes? Tate's odds of winning were ridiculous. Ninety-seven percent, give or take. The others folded. Tate raised, Dakota called, and Tate reraised. Dakota hesitated before shrugging and calling again. Tate didn't smirk, didn't react at all. But Dakota was way, way up a creek without a paddle.

Until the river. The dealer flipped over the final card: another three.

With a whoop, Dakota dropped his cards, showing a two-three. He had four of a kind.

Quad threes to beat an aces-over-threes full house.

Dakota gave the table a sheepish smile, gathered his chips, and cashed out, whistling Kenny Rogers.

It was about as bad a beat as they come.

Watching Brooks kiss Alex's cheek—such a casual, intimate gesture—was almost that bad.

But what Brooks couldn't see, what Alex's father was too busy schmoozing to see, and what her mother callously ignored, was the anguish caged behind Alex's eyes. They were cats, these people, and Alex was their mouse. They'd caught her, but she hated them for it.

While Tate congratulated Alex on her happiness, Connor joined them.

"Tate. You're like a bad penny. Not that you'd be able to hold on to it."

"And I thought I was worthless in your eyes, Connor," Tate said as if sincerely flattered. "Thank you."

Alex slipped out from under Brooks's arm and dug her fingernails into Tate's arm. "I need to go check in with Aunt Nora. Tate, why don't you come with me?"

She dragged Tate away before he could say anything else. Once they were out of sight, she pushed him into the same lonely corridor they'd visited earlier.

"Wanting seconds already, huh? I like your style, Wolf."

"Shut up, Tate" she snapped. "Just shut up."

"Is someone regretting her life choices?"

"That's the first sane thing you've said all night."

"What are you doing with him, Alex?"

Her mouth dropped. Actually fell open. "*Him?* You think what I'm regretting is Brooks? Tate, look at yourself: you're ridiculous! You pick fights with people out of boredom. You're pathologically incapable of making the smart choice—"

"You didn't mind an hour ago." He put a hand on her hip to keep from smashing his fist through a wall. "Admit it, Alex. You can't stand that you're with that tool when you really want to be with me."

She backed away, and her laughter chilled the air. "You're a loser who flunked rehab. I could never be with someone like you."

Tate didn't let the hurt register. "You're lying to yourself, and we both know it. Do you honestly think they know you? Your parents or your cheating jackass boyfriend? They only see who they want to see—the dutiful daughter, the future Stepford Wife."

"You act like I didn't abandon my father's campaign for Nora's. How is that dutiful?"

"Next time, steal a car or light your house on fire. You think you rebelled, but you're missing the fact that your *parents don't care.*"

Alex recoiled as if he'd hit her. With a snarl, she pushed him. "You don't know what the hell you're talking about." She shoved him again, harder. "Now get out of my way."

All night. Tate waited all night to corner Alex, to force her to talk to him again, to admit that she was lying, that she cared more than she wanted to admit. He tried to dance with her, to follow her to the bathroom. When his mom tried to catch his eye across the ballroom, he ignored her in pursuit of Alex. He walked the long way around to keep out of his mom's line of sight after that, not that it mattered. He saw his dad walking her out only a few minutes after he blew her off.

He should have felt guiltier than he did. But in between each new, throbbing disappointment, he took a drink. Unfortunately, the bartender cut him off before he was good and truly drunk; Tate was acting too manic. He knew it, and he refused to stop himself

Why couldn't Alex see what was going on? Why couldn't she see that these people didn't care about her?

Tate's presence hadn't bothered Brooks at all, which meant the guy didn't care enough for Alex to get bothered. Connor had disappeared at the first sign of someone more important. He was too busy greasing palms to pay his daughter even the slightest bit of attention.

Meanwhile, Cynthia watched Tate like a hawk, but he could see the reason in her eyes as clearly as if it were written there: she wasn't watching Tate because she cared about Alex, but because she worried that Alex cared about Tate.

Which she did.

Why wouldn't she admit it?

Why wouldn't she admit it?

"Why won't you admit it?"

"Leave me alone," Alex demanded when he stopped her outside of the bathroom, "or I'm calling security."

Tate stormed from the hotel and went straight to the train station, with a stop at an ATM. While he waited for his money, he texted a handful of his old contacts. Within five minutes, he had what he was looking for.

Twenty-five minutes after that, Tate was waiting at a back door in a dank, skinny alley in Armour Square. When a beefy security guard answered, he gave Tate a pat down before letting him inside.

The smell was the first thing that hit him. That heady mixture of cigar smoke, alcohol, and sweat, with a hint of felt from the tables. He even caught a whiff of a new deck being opened. He breathed it all in and held it, letting the smell and flavor of the place linger inside of him.

"Hey, James Bond, you playin', or what?" the brush asked.

"I'm playing." Tate smiled. "It's just good to be home."

CHAPTER TWENTY

He should have worried when the dealers switched early, especially when the replacement turned out to be Cat. The last thing he needed tonight was to see his former dealer. But she looked only too happy to see him.

"Long time," he said.

"Water under the bridge." She flipped her too-blonde hair. "Without the experience I got working for you, I'd never have landed this gig. Besides, these guys tip better than your little college boys. So really, I should be thanking you." She smiled.

The smile should have warned him.

Two hours of the smile definitely should have.

After the first run of good hands, Tate thought the gambling gods were simply smiling on him. A run of good luck was as likely as a run of bad luck—of which he'd had plenty of late—so at first, he didn't think anything of it. But as the chips added up and Tate's not-quite-drunkenness started to fade, he realized he'd had an unlikely number of face cards over the night. And they were still coming.

He should have cashed out when Cat took her break. If he'd been thinking, he would've realized she wasn't going to the restroom or getting a drink. She was talking to security, telling them how he'd had the King of Spades on five of his last eight hands.

He should've run the second that beefy security guard started for the table. He should've run faster when the guy brought reinforcements. He should have stayed down when the first fist drove into his gut. But Tate was pathologically incapable of making the smart choice.

"Seriously, guy, is that all you got?" He wheezed, clutching his stomach in the light drizzle. With his other hand, he pushed himself up from the dirty alley ground. The wet grit cut into his palm; he wiped it on his tuxedo pants right before the next hit.

In anticipation, he exhaled fast, at the same time flexing his abs and core and doubling over just before it landed. He'd taken enough body shots to know how to absorb the punch, but still, it hurt like a mother. Yet a surge of adrenaline overtook him when the next hit came, and the pain got momentarily lost in a sea of hyperawareness. The sounds of the city's ever-present traffic. The scent of garbage and urine and rain hanging heavy on the predawn air. The flickering light at the end of the alley. The pitted acne scars on the guard's face. Each sense and cell and nerve ending in his body felt more alive than ever.

Which wasn't great for getting punched in the face.

He saw the fist coming in time to duck and take it on his forehead instead of his nose. The pain blasted through his head, causing sparks to explode in his vision. He stumbled back several feet before falling into a puddle of oil and rain. After some dazed blinks and a shake of his head, Tate got to his knees, then came to a stand. Everything ached. His head was pounding.

He was gloriously alive.

"You had enough, Hot Shot?" the guard asked, flexing his hand. That last hit had to have bruised his knuckles. His two compatriots looked on with bored expressions, their presence required only to convince Tate not to do something stupid, like run or fight back.

Tate embraced the pain. "Did you hear me say 'when'?"

"You too stupid to know what's good for you?"

"Maybe I just like the feel of your hands," he said with a wink.

The guy's lip curled, and he took three heavy steps toward Tate.

He grabbed the back of Tate's collar, and Tate braced himself for impact, glad when the guard went for a body shot again. Winded and aching, Tate braced himself for the next hit. And braced . . .

The guard dropped him, and Tate saw the men backing up right before a police siren blared in his ears. The sound magnified the effects of the recent head punch, making Tate wince.

A voice he knew only too well yelled, "Back away and put your hands up!"

A moment later, Nia and her partner were slapping handcuffs on Tate's assailants. "Get in the car, dumbass," she told Tate.

For the first time that night, he did the smart thing.

Tate watched from the back of Nia's SUV as she and her partner instructed a group of uniforms. The guards were already sitting in the backs of squad cars. Tate had no intention of filing charges, but they'd be charged along with everyone who'd played or assisted with the operation, all of whom were sitting in the backs of squad cars of their very own.

When Cat was brought out in handcuffs, Tate knocked on the window. She looked up and glared past the tint at him. He kissed the glass.

A moment later, Nia's hand slapped the window. Tate squelched the urge to flinch.

"You can stop making out with my car now," Nia said, loud enough to be heard by everyone. She rounded the SUV and climbed into the driver's seat before slamming her door. "Why am I not surprised?"

"Because you're stalking me, I assume." He leaned back into the black bench, and the throbbing in his head joined the nauseous ache in his stomach and side. He squeezed his eyes shut.

"Stalking you? Tate, *I'm working.* We got an anonymous tip and came to bust up the game. What the hell were you doing here?" The anger in Nia's voice made him wish he'd been knocked out.

He rubbed his temples. "What do you think, Nia? I was gambling. I won a lot of money. A dealer I used to know set me up, and I got a beating for it. I make bad life choices. Is that what you want to hear?"

"No, what I want to hear is how you ended up in a card game run *by the Outfit?*"

That got his attention. "The Outfit?"

"The Southside crew. What were you thinking, going to a mob game when you already suspect Wolf has a target on your back?"

"Do you think he sent me here? Is that what you're getting at?"

"You tell me. Of all the card games in the city, how'd you find out about this one?"

He pulled out his phone. "I just texted some old contacts. I got four locations in a matter of a few minutes, so I'm not sure how he could be behind this."

She took his phone without asking and scrolled through the texts. Maybe a few too many texts, based on her judgmental eyebrows. She handed it back to him. "Three of these are suspected mob joints."

"What?"

"He's on to you. I'm guessing he's dug pretty far back into your life to find anyone connected to you who's willing to help him out. It's not like your old buddies are rollin' in it. Telling you about a game is a pretty easy payday."

He groaned. "I should have run the second I saw Cat there."

"No! You should have called me and never gambled in the first place. What do you think the point of a sponsor is?"

"You dropped me, remember?" Not that he'd have called her, anyway.

"Of course I didn't drop you; I was trying to scare you. I wanted you to realize that this life will be the death of you if you're not careful. And tonight, it almost was!"

He leaned back into the seat. "They weren't going to kill me. Come on."

"Maybe, maybe not. But you have to stop this. You have to stop letting your addiction control your life."

"And I'm officially bored."

Nia shook her head. Her partner got into the vehicle a moment later. Nia looked at Tate in the rearview mirror. She looked livid, except for the worry wrinkling her eyes. "If you're sure you don't want to press charges, we'll drop you off at your apartment."

"I don't want to press charges."

"Good thing you weren't caught inside, or we'd have to take you in," her partner said, his words dripping with sarcasm.

"Nope," Tate told him. "Like I said, I was just walking by when those three jumped me."

"You sure got lucky we came when we did," the guy continued.

"I'm always lucky."

♠

When they reached Tate's apartment, Nia insisted on walking him to his door.

"Thank you for the lovely evening," Tate said, as if he wasn't utterly spent.

"Drop the act, Tate," she told him. "Do you see how serious this situation is getting?"

He didn't want to answer, even though they both knew what the answer was. "Yeah."

"Doesn't it concern you how hard it was for you to admit that? Do you think tonight was just a coincidence? Do you think your old dealer really just set you up on her own?"

"I don't know. Maybe."

"I don't think she did, and I'm terrified something's going to happen to you. Please, Tate: you need to back off."

"I'm not going to back off."

"Then promise me—*promise me*—you'll call me if you get into trouble. And let me post some uniforms outside."

He was too tired to fight and too sore to think. Pain kept crashing into him like waves, and he wanted to fall into it and let it drown him. "Do whatever you want, Nia. I need to put a steak on my face and go to bed."

"You're not putting up a fight? You *must* be beat."

"Ha. Clever," he said.

A hint of a smile crossed her face and faded just as quickly. She grabbed his shoulder. "Be careful, Tate."

He entered his darkened apartment and closed the door, resting his head against the wood. He didn't move, didn't think, barely even breathed. He couldn't remember a time he'd felt more tired. He wanted to stop. He just wanted everything to stop so he could rest for a night. A day. A year. Yet a jumble of self-destructive emotions taunted him.

You're a loser who flunked rehab.

You're a loser.

A loser.

He'd lost tonight. His family, Alex, the game. How could he have let himself get set up? By Cat, of all people? Or was it really Connor?

He yelled and slammed his hand into the door again and again, until he heard a low chuckle from behind him.

He whipped around to see the silhouette of a man sitting by the window, the city lights the only thing illuminating his shadowed figure.

"Are you done yet?" the man asked. "We need to talk."

CHAPTER TWENTY-ONE

Tate went still, despite the adrenaline spike that intensified his every pain. "Who are you, and what do you want?"

The man leaned forward and flicked on the lamp. Recognition crept up Tate's spine in a thrill of nerves and terror. He saw a middle-aged man with a boxy face, broad shoulders, and short, dark hair, but this time, he knew exactly where he'd seen him. Something about this night—the combination of losing money and being riddled with pain—brought it sharply into focus.

It was the man from the convenience store.

The man from Misha's.

The man who, just last year, had come to Tate's apartment when he was drunk and down a terrifying amount of money to the Uzhhorod Bratva. Tate had been so preoccupied after yet another bad night at the tables that he hadn't realized he had company until he was halfway to his bedroom.

"We came to talk," a voice had said. Tate had whirled around to see the city lights from the window illuminating the figures of two beefy men sitting at the kitchen table.

He knew exactly why they were there, and it wasn't to talk. Instinct took over. The men were closer to the front door than he was, which left him . . . the window. Tate was already sprinting for it when he heard the scrape of chairs across the tile as the men jumped up from the table.

His head was pounding from the alcohol and his heart from adrenaline as he dove through the open window out to the fire escape.

"Wait!" one of the men yelled.

Tate ignored the voice. Climbing the ladder would take too long, yet the only option was down. He looked over the railing to the full dumpster several yards below. Drawing in a sharp, deep breath, he jumped.

For a split second, he was free. But before he could even exhale, a metal curtain rod tore through him. It felt like lava was erupting from him, scorching his side and melting his body from the inside. This was pain like nothing he'd ever known. It took every ounce of effort not to scream, but buried beneath bags of garbage as he was, he could see the men who'd come to collect his considerable debt. One of them peered over the railing of the fire escape as Tate panted through gritted teeth and nearly bled out in the dumpster.

And here that same man was now, sitting in an armchair in Tate's apartment.

How could Tate have missed the connection? The man was considerably thinner now, and he looked as if he'd aged ten years since Tate last saw him, yet he still reeked of danger. Hot fury bubbled in Tate's gut. He wanted to rush the man, attack him, throw him out the window. But he had every reason to assume the man had a gun.

"Sit down," the man said in his accented voice. Tate kept standing. "Fine. I thought you'd be exhausted after the beating you took earlier, but suit yourself."

"How did you know about earlier?"

"Apart from the bruises covering your face? You know how to take a punch. I'll give you that."

Warning bells sounded in Tate's head. Had he been in the alley? How could Tate have missed him?

"You've been following me," Tate said. "When the police picked me up, you knew I'd be stuck with them for a while. You took advantage of the situation to beat me home." It was strange to hear himself sounding so calm, when he was about to face so much violence. There was no other reason for the man to be here now. "I saw you at Misha's Restaurant. And the convenience store . . . hell, were you working for Wolf then? Does the Bratva know you switched mob affiliations like that?"

The man pounded the arm of the chair. "I *do not* work for Wolf. I don't work for anyone anymore."

"You can just stop working for the Russian Mafia?" The man didn't answer. Tate breathed heavily and leaned back against the kitchen counter. "So you're, what, a contractor? Who hired you? What do you want? Are you here to finish the job those bastards in the alley started?"

A smile spread slowly across the man's face. "I'm not here to hurt you."

Tate pinched the bridge of his nose. He just wanted answers. "Okay, this mysterious assailant routine is fun and all, but if you came to beat me up, just do it now. Send me to the hospital, please. A couple days in a coma would do wonders for my nerves."

"Would you like to know why I am here, or would you like to keep talking?" the man asked. His Russian accent was mild, but he had a way of making everything sound gravely formal. Final. Tate drew a weary breath and gestured for the man to continue. "My name is Sascha Lunov, and until a few months ago, I was dead broke. Now I am just dying."

The air conditioning unit clicked on, and the blast of cold air gave Tate goose bumps. "You're dying, but you're not broke. Okay. So what happened a few months ago?"

"I found out I had leukemia and that I need a bone marrow transplant, but the hospital refused to put me on a donor list because I'm an alcoholic."

"They can just keep you off a list like that?"

He shrugged. "Over a little boy who needs a transplant or a mother with three kids? Who would prioritize me over them? I wouldn't."

"What about your family? None of them are a match?"

Sascha's face clouded. "None so far."

"Chatty one, aren't you?" Tate said after a pause. "Tell me about the 'not broke' part."

"I won the Powerball."

Tate's spine straightened. The traffic noise outside faded into nothingness. "You won the Powerball?"

"Yes. And I won it with your ticket."

Tate's chest and lungs swelled with excitement. Did this—was this—was he—

"I'm not leaving you the money. You'd just throw it away at the tables."

He wouldn't let himself deflate visibly, not even in his state of exhaustion. But he wouldn't keep the bitterness from his tone, either. "So you came to, what, thank me? Warn me away from my sinful ways, 'from one addict to another'?"

"I came to help. In fact, I've been helping for months."

"How do you figure?"

"In the convenience store months ago, I recognized you. I couldn't understand why you would choose to help me, considering that we met under unfavorable circumstances," Sascha said, understating the fact just a touch. "I was in your debt in a way I have rarely felt before." Sascha explained his shock when he realized that the Powerball ticket was a winner, and he said the first thing he'd done was pay someone to track down Tate. When Sascha had learned about Tate's card room, as well as the plus he owed, Sascha had paid it.

Sascha had paid it. Not Nora.

"I've tried keeping an eye out for you these last few months, but you don't make it easy."

"What do you mean? Have you been following me?"

"Only once. I saw you walking into the middle of a busy street and stopped you from getting hit. You were oblivious to everything around you. I thought you were high, and I almost stopped helping you right then. But I still owed you. I had to settle my debt."

The words matched the man's proud demeanor, but Tate sensed Sascha's motivations were murkier than he was letting on. Still, Tate remembered that day, after brunch with Alex and her mom. He'd been out of his mind until he'd felt that shoulder smack into him, pushing him away from the car that had almost taken out his knees.

"What about this morning? When I was getting beat up in that alley?"

"Who do you think called in the anonymous tip to the police?" Sascha said, giving him a hard look. "You seem determined to destroy yourself, but if you change your mind, I'm here to help." Sascha stood, taking a card from his pocket and taking the few steps to the kitchen. "Take this. Call me if you ever need me."

"For what, cab fare? Why should I call you?"

Sascha brushed his thick hands over his slacks. The man was no taller than Tate, and his illness had made him gaunt, despite his large shoulders. Yet he projected intimidation. "You should call me because you are a very stupid young man, and I am not." Tate bristled. A mean smile stretched across Sascha's square face. "You find the word insulting, don't you? You think you're smarter than everyone around you, which is why the description is so appropriate. Stupidity is a deliberate, informed choice to act in one's own worst interests.

When confronted with two choices, which do you make? The most reckless one. What could be more stupid than that?"

Tate was shaking his head, not at the description, but at Sascha's utter certainty. And maybe a little at the description. "You don't know what you're talking about."

"When I showed up in your apartment last year, we weren't planning to hurt you."

Tate looked at him from where he was leaning against the counter. Or from where the counter was propping him up, more accurately. He was too bone-weary to move. "Why else would you have been there? You worked for the mob. Probably still do. Organized crime syndicates are famous for the efficacy of their collection agencies."

"The key word there is 'collection.' I was no enforcer. I was an accountant at one of the clubs. Why would I have someone break your knee or your neck when I want money from you?" Sascha asked. "We were there to let you work off your debt as a prop player."

Tate focused on breathing in and out of his mouth slowly, or else he was going to start breaking his furniture. A proposition player? They were there to ask him to fill a seat, to *keep games going* in their club? If he'd have stayed still for two seconds . . . if he'd just listened! The last year—rehab, GA meetings, everything with his family and all of his friends—it all amounted to *nothing*. To stupidity.

He forced himself to speak, but despite his best efforts, he couldn't keep his voice steady. "Why would you have done that? Why didn't you tell me then?"

"We tried. You jumped out a window," Sascha said, walking to the door. Tate caught a glimpse of the back of the man's head, and something else clicked into place.

"You were at my aunt's house!" Tate said, pushing himself from the counter. "You broke in! What were you doing? Were you trying to stop someone or trying to find something?"

Sascha's thick brows drew tightly together. "I was looking for something that belonged to me. None of you were ever in danger."

"You threw a frame at my head!"

"And you threw a jar at mine. The difference was that I missed." Sascha put a hand on the doorknob and started turning.

"Wait!" Tate cried. "Is that really all you're going to tell me?"

"For now, yes. Be careful, Tate. You can't imagine what you're getting yourself into." The door opened and closed behind him, and Tate leaned back against the counter, massaging his temples.

What was he supposed to do now?

Bright light stabbed Tate's eyes. He threw an arm up in front of his face to shield them. Where was he? He peeked to see the sun beaming through a window. *His* window. He'd fallen asleep on his couch last night. That explained the kink in his neck. The pain in every other part of his body, though, had nothing to do with his sleeping arrangement. He carefully pulled himself up and into the kitchen, where he shook four ibuprofen tablets from a bottle and swallowed them without water.

Hazy memories of last night—this morning?—shook around in his head, making it throb even harder. The party, the game, the conversations with Nia and Sascha. The game.

He'd played last night, and beating aside, he felt fine. Nia had made it sound as if the world would collapse all around him if he ever played again, that his defenses would crumble and that he'd spiral out of control.

But the worst hadn't happened. If anything, he'd felt a release. He felt more normal today than he had yesterday, when he'd felt so anxious and manic. No, he'd played poker last night, and he felt perfectly normal.

He looked at the clock and saw that it was just past noon, and it was Saturday. He could sleep off the worst of his bruises, do a little homework, and still make a card game tonight. He'd play a small game, five- to ten-dollar blinds, and he'd cash out at 2:00 a.m. so he wouldn't get carried away.

No problem.

As the painkillers started kicking in, he smiled.

Everything was coming up Bertram.

On Monday, Tate strolled into the office early with coffee, doughnuts, and a smile for everyone. He whistled when he walked by Alex's office, unfazed by her angry glare. He'd had a good night. A great night, actually. He'd decided to slum it after hearing about a game over at Psi U. Most of the frat boys could hardly tell an ace from their armpits, but one of them had been kicked out of a casino last month for counting cards. The guy knew what he was doing, which made beating him so much more enjoyable.

It was only a couple hundred bucks he'd won, but Tate couldn't remember the last time he felt better.

"You look like crap," Ruby said when he put the doughnuts and coffee down near her desk.

"Fell down a flight of stairs," he said, handing her a cup.

She took a slow sip before thanking him. "Juana says hi, by the way."

"No, she doesn't."

"Uh, yes she does," Ruby said, giving him a strange look. "Why wouldn't she? Did you hit on her?"

Tate shook his head. "Just teasing. How are things?"

"Things are going really well with her. She's done an amazing job rallying the community leaders on the North Side. Let's hope next week's poll numbers reflect that."

Tate gave Ruby a smile. "I'm sure they will. You're the right person to be working with her."

She flushed. "Thanks, Tate."

He left Ruby's desk on the same high that had carried him through last night. When he bumped into Oscar a couple of hours later, he was still smiling.

"How are the preparations going for the debate this week?" Tate asked.

"As good as we can hope. You'll be there Sunday for final prep, right?" Tate nodded. "Good. Your aunt will never admit it, but your help means a lot to her. You know she spent all weekend watching horror movies on your recommendation? And I can't believe I'm saying this, but I think it might be helping her disassociate from her emotions a little."

"I'm hurt that you doubted me, Oscar, but I'm glad it's working."

Oscar squinted at him. "What's going on with you? That sounded almost sincere."

"Almost sincere is exactly what I was shooting for." He grinned. "Ruby mentioned polls—how are things looking there?"

Oscar dropped his voice. "They'll be better if you can get me something actionable on Wolf."

"I'll do my best."

CHAPTER TWENTY-TWO

Unfortunately, Tate's best wasn't good enough. Late Friday morning, after a slow night at the tables and an even slower week all around Irving Park and into Avondale, he took his jump rope up to the roof of his apartment building, where a makeshift gym had been set up. Day after day, he'd sat studying in little bars or restaurants all along the North Side with nothing more to show for it. The nervous faces had turned resigned, and the bare walls had been decorated, and Tate was no closer to uncovering a smoking gun. He'd considered calling Sascha, just to see how far the man's offer for help actually extended. But somehow, Tate doubted that finding dirt on a crooked would-be politician was what the man had in mind.

So Tate had been working out his frustrations at the poker table.

Each night, he'd stuck religiously to his rules: five/ten blinds, out by 2:00 a.m. It was already getting dull, but he needed to keep to the rules for now, at any rate. There was only a week left in the quarter, and no way was he going to jeopardize his grades. He'd worked too long and too hard. It had nothing to do with his dad, either. If anything, the idea of coming home with a subpar grade report was tempting. But all that would do is make his dad think he'd *stopped* cheating.

No, Tate wasn't going to give him the satisfaction of thinking he was right, and he wasn't going to let his dad taint another thing he cared about.

Tate closed his eyes and skipped, pushing his anger away so that he could be hypnotized by the sound of the rope slicing through the air and slapping the ground below him. When his muscles screamed in protest and sweat poured down his body, he stopped, tossing the rope and dropping to the ground to do crunches. Pushups. Triceps dips. More and more.

Ninety minutes later, an exhausted Tate made his way downstairs to his apartment, thinking about how Nia was wrong about him. He'd been back to playing poker for a week now, and he was still studying and working out as much as ever. If he'd been throwing himself into those things only to distract himself from his need to play poker, wouldn't he have stopped?

Though, in fairness, he hadn't bought any scratch-offs in a week, either . . .

He filled up a glass from the sink and drank. It didn't matter what Nia thought, only what he felt. Which was amazing.

A few hours later, Tate was leaving his ethics class when he saw Oliver twenty feet away, frowning at his phone. Their paths would cross in just moments, and Tate had every intention of letting those paths cross quietly. But at the last second, Oliver looked up and started.

"Tate, what are you doing here?"

Annoyance buzzed around his head like a fly. "Really? I go to school here."

A muscle in Oliver's jaw tensed. "You know what? Never mind. Good seeing you, bro," he said before looking back down at his phone, frowning again.

Tate tried to look at the screen, but the sun's reflection made it impossible to see anything except Oliver's pitiful face. "What's going on with you?" Tate asked.

Oliver glanced back up in surprise. "Oh, I, uh, screwed up."

It was the last thing Tate expected to hear. He wanted to hear more. "What do you mean?"

Oliver glanced up, and his eyes were as vulnerable as his words were wary. "Like you care."

Something about the way Oliver's hair fell in his eyes made him look eight years old, and a memory flashed in Tate's mind. They had been playing Frisbee outside, and Tate had kept throwing the Frisbee too high, not to be a jerk, but because he sucked at Frisbee. But as he kept throwing, Ollie got more and more upset, and Tate realized his brother thought he was doing it on purpose. So he laughed rather than let Ollie know he was actually trying, and his brother gave him an angry scowl. The next time Tate threw the disc, it soared perfectly to where Ollie's hands should have been. But, anticipating another high throw, his brother had leapt too high into the air. The Frisbee crashed into his face, giving him a bloody nose.

When Tate had run over to check on his brother, Ollie—with his messy light brown hair in his eye—said that exact same thing: "Like you care."

So maybe it was the memory of a time when he and Ollie had liked each other, or maybe it was sympathy for whatever was making his brother look so pathetic, but Tate found himself saying the last words he'd expected to say.

"Of course I care. I'm your brother."

It wasn't quite what nine-year-old Tate had said all those years ago. Nine-year-old Tate had added "I love you" at the end. But it was enough. After carefully studying Tate's face, Oliver nodded.

Tate slapped his back. "Come on. Lunch is on me."

There was something both familiar and foreign about sitting across a table from his little brother, eating pizza. He let muscle memory take over.

"So, you ready to talk?" Tate asked after they'd both eaten a few slices.

Oliver rubbed the back of his hand across his forehead. "I'll give you one guess."

"Finley," Tate answered, expecting the name to burn his tongue. "What else?"

Their last encounter weighed heavily on his mind. What he'd said to her, how he'd acted . . . it was as close to shame as Tate would let himself feel. He pushed past the inky, cloying feeling. "I don't get it. You two looked cozy enough last weekend. What went wrong?"

"You," Oliver said bitterly. "How could you say that stuff to her, man? Why did you treat her like that? She's one of the only people in the world who accepts you as you are and loves you anyway."

Tate glanced out the window, not actually looking at anything. "Is this really about me?"

Oliver tore his crust into tiny pieces. "No. You were a jerk, but I got overprotective, and she didn't like it. I just . . . I love her, and there you were, being the worst, and I just got so *jealous.*"

He would have laughed, if he didn't feel so hollow. He leaned forward. "Oliver, Fin had a crush on me. She loves you. But you have to stop getting in your own way. You can't protect her from every-thing—not even from me. And you can't expect someone like her to just sit around and wait while you traipse around the world looking for ways to save it from itself." At Oliver's frown, Tate continued. "Listen, I get it. You're trying to be this noble white knight for the downtrodden of the world, and that's fine. Fin certainly won't fault you for it, and she won't ever tell you to stop—"

"But she just broke up with me out of nowhere, Tate! If she was feeling excluded or left behind, or whatever, why couldn't she have said something to me before?"

"Ollie, why would she do that? You put everything before her. How do you think that made her feel? Besides, Harlan Crawford—her first real boyfriend—tried to change her and make every decision for her. There's no way she was going to do the same thing to you.

Should she have told you how she felt? Sure. But she's not perfect, and for years, she had every reason to fear telling people how she felt. What did her mom do when Fin said she missed her dad?" Oliver winced, no doubt remembering the bruises on Finley's face, how her jaw was wired shut when she first moved in with their family. It was an impossible image to shake. "And what happened when she stood her ground with Harlan? The guy cheated on her and broke her heart. So can you blame her for being reluctant to let that happen again?"

"You're right." Oliver's mouth pulled to the side. He started picking his cuticles. If Alex had been here, she'd have slapped his hands to make him stop.

Where had that come from?

"What do I do?" Oliver's eyes were puddles of sadness.

"You figure out what your priorities are, and you figure out where she ranks. If she's not pretty damn near the top of your list, you walk away. You're not doing her any favors if you pull her in just to push her away again."

Oliver blinked fast, as if he was already putting his list together. "Yeah. Yeah, I think you're right."

He leaned back in his chair. "I'm absurdly smart. Don't act surprised."

"Says the guy who thought Michael Jackson was the first man on the moon."

"I was eight and he invented the Moonwalk. What else was I supposed to think?" Tate argued. Oliver laughed. "Besides, you thought chocolate milk came from brown cows."

"Only because you told me that, you turd!"

"I didn't think you'd actually believe me."

"I always believed you. I thought you were the smartest person alive." Oliver grabbed his straw from his drink and started tightly winding both ends. He held it out to Tate to flick.

Tate did, and it popped loudly.

"I know what Dad said isn't true," Oliver said. "I know you've never cheated for a grade."

Tate looked at the discarded straw on the table, at the rip in its middle. "How can you be so sure?"

"Because I grew up across the hall from you. I can't tell you the number of times I walked by your room in the middle of the night and peeked in to find you studying. Or doing crunches." Oliver half smiled. "You *like* school. You like knowing things other people don't, being smarter than other people. I don't know if that's for your own sake or because it was the one way to get Dad's attention when we were growing up. Either way, I know you've earned every grade. I'm sorry he said that."

It was hard keeping the emotion off his face, making sure that Oliver didn't see too much. His nose started to tingle, and he opened his mouth to respond. But Oliver said one more thing.

"When did we lose you, Tate? Was it the intervention? Or before?"

The tingle stopped abruptly, and Tate's emotions dried up faster than a drip of water on a hot skillet. The memories of last summer were still too raw: the hole in his side throbbing while Finley held his hand and cried; his parents and Oliver telling him for hours how they were scared for him, how his gambling was hurting them, as if it had caused them problems for years instead of weeks. His parents hadn't even known about Tate's gambling before that stupid dumpster.

His mom had been so weak, had been riddled with pain, yet she'd stayed up all night to drive with him to rehab.

Tate blinked, clearing his head. He grabbed his wallet and dropped a generous tip on the table. "It was good seeing you, Ollie. Good luck with Fin," he said, surprised by his own sincerity.

"Tate, hold on," Oliver said, standing. "I just want my brother back—"

"That's the thing, Ollie: I didn't leave. You kicked me out."

Oliver didn't try to stop him from leaving. He didn't know if he was relieved or upset by the fact.

That night at the tables, Tate was stacking and racking, a nice change from the rest of the week. But beyond getting hit by the deck—beyond all those monster hands—he had a read on his opponents unlike anything he could remember. Every player's tell was so clear, their cards may as well have been transparent.

And if he found a game with bigger blinds, if he closed the card room down, stumbling into his apartment with the sun instead of leaving at two, so what? He didn't have class the next day, and he wasn't hurting anybody.

He was running good, and he needed to make the most of it. No one could run good forever.

CHAPTER TWENTY-THREE

Tate awoke to an angry buzzing beside his ear. He blinked eyes that felt caked in sand. Squinting at his phone, he picked it up and put it on speaker, holding it a few inches from his face on the pillow.

"Hello?"

"WHERE ARE YOU?" Alex demanded.

Tate grimaced, pushing the phone farther from his throbbing head. "Home," he said, looking around quickly to confirm it was true. He cleared his throat, which felt raw. "Why do you care? It's Sunday."

"Exactly why I'm calling, Einstein. Do you have any idea where you're supposed to be right now?"

"Please tell me I'm not missing your grandmother's sobriety brunch."

"Where were you last night?"

He pushed himself up, rubbing his eyes. "Do you really want to know?"

She laughed under her breath. "Looks like recovery's going well, huh?"

His thoughts were too hazy for a witty comeback. He squeezed his temples "Obviously I'm missing something, so why don't you save us both the lecture and tell me how I've wronged you this time."

Her tone almost froze the connection. "Do you even remember

leaving work Friday night? You promised you'd help Nora prep for the debate, which starts in less than two hours. We've been drilling her all day *without you*, even though she explicitly asked for your help. *You promised,* Tate. She's going to need you today more than ever. I can't believe you'd let her down like this."

"Alex—"

"Save it. I hope you'll at least have enough respect for her to show up."

Click.

Forty-five minutes later, a showered and somewhat less hungover Tate arrived at the auditorium where the debate would soon take place. Anger with himself boiled beneath his skin, but he wouldn't let it show. He couldn't.

Still, how could he have let this happen?

It didn't matter, he told himself. It had happened. What mattered was what he did now.

He found Alex, who looked stupidly hot in a black pencil skirt and white blouse. She had glasses on, and behind the rims was an expression that could turn a man to stone.

Tate was just tired enough and his head just fuzzy enough that he didn't feel like arguing. "I'm sorry, Alex. I don't have an excuse."

"What are you playing at?" she snapped.

He held out his hands, palms up, as if to show he wasn't hiding anything. "I'm just being honest. I screwed up. I should have been here for Nora, and I wasn't. I'm sorry. I'll apologize to her as soon as I can find her."

Alex clutched her phone, and Tate saw, for the first time, an enormous diamond ring on her left hand. The sight was like getting stabbed again, but he was bleeding internally instead of bleeding out.

Could she see how badly this affected him? He looked in her

eyes, expecting to see that same perverse pleasure she always seemed to feel when she tortured him. But instead, she looked as if she was torturing only herself. He studied her more carefully. Her makeup was perfectly applied; she didn't have a hair out of place. She was a study in poise. Yet it was almost as if there were fractures too fine for the eye to see, just beneath the surface of her pristine, porcelain face. One strong wind could push her over, and she'd shatter into a million perfect pieces.

"Are you okay?" he asked.

"What are you talking about? I'm fine."

He softened his voice. "I know the last couple of weeks have been . . . weird between us, but I'm here if you want to talk."

"Right, because the last time we talked—"

"Alex," he interrupted. "I'm recovering from a hangover, so I'm just off enough not to have an agenda, okay? I'm trying to be your friend."

With Alex, it was impossible for him not to have *some* agenda. But it was mostly true, and judging by the way her grip let up on her phone, she knew that. She looked past Tate, and there was something almost haunted about her gaze.

"Do you ever feel like it's all too much? Like if one more person tries to cram you into their mold, you're going to lose your shape altogether?" she asked, not waiting for an answer. She shook her head. "Forget I said anything. I'm just tired. I don't mean it."

"I know that's not true," he said. Even in his haze, he could recognize it: she was off today. Distinctly off. It wasn't just her anger at him for disappointing Nora. Was it the ring on her finger? "When are you going to start standing up for yourself? I know, I know: you left your dad's campaign for Nora's. But taking a stand isn't the same thing. They're still walking over you just as much as they always have. Your mom won't be happy until you're her dutiful, pliable little clone. She wants a prize pony, not a daughter. And your boyfriend"—he wouldn't say fiancé—"wants someone to show off on his yacht."

"And my dad?"

"For you to be useful to him, maybe. I . . . I don't know."

"He wants me to go away. He wishes his precious Vivienne had never died and that I had never been born."

"No. That isn't true."

"Of course it is. You don't have to pretend otherwise. You're the one who told me he doesn't care about me, remember?"

"That's not what I—"

"For that matter," she said, "what do you want, Tate? Everyone wants something from me. So what is it?"

Her tone was short, accusatory, but her dark eyes burrowed into him, worming their way past his bravado into the soft recesses of his heart. Honesty spilled out of him, making his throat itch. "To matter to you."

Her mouth fell open. "No." She backed up, shaking her head. "Don't say that. Don't put that on me. After everything that's happened, after everything we've said and done . . . how could you still say that?"

He put on his most disinterested face and rolled his eyes, not wanting her to know how badly her words hurt, how they gnawed a hole in his chest. What was he thinking, admitting that to her, being so reckless with his heart? "Alex, I'm playing. What I really want is for you to be just happy enough that you lay off me at work. You're cramping my style with the ladies."

She looked at him askance, as if she couldn't quite trust what he'd said. "Are you sure?"

He gave her a tired look. "Do you really think after everything that's happened between us, all I really want is for us to become besties and braid each other's hair at night? Do your thing and let me do mine," he said, stifling a (fake) yawn.

It was the right touch. "I'm tired, Tate." She looked past him, her eyes glossy. "I think what I want more than anything is to just . . .

leave. To move to a different state, change my name, maybe. Put all of this behind me."

"I'd rob your parents blind first. Starting over takes capital."

"Good point. I'll do a smash-and-grab job later. Don't rat me out, okay?" she winked.

He smiled, glad she was being normal—actually, nicer than normal. Weirdly nice, in fact. "I make no promises, Wolf. You're on your own, remember?"

"I couldn't forget it if I tried."

An hour later, Tate had apologized to a frosty Nora and the debate was starting. He couldn't shake the way that she'd looked at him, a mix of disappointment and self-doubt that peeked out of the corners of her eyes. She'd needed him, and he'd failed her.

He'd make it up to her next time. There was nothing he could do about it now. The moderator was introducing the candidates, and Tate found himself wandering. Nothing new was going to happen tonight; Nora and Connor would both twist questions in a way that let them rehash the same talking points they'd been spouting off the entire campaign, while simultaneously trying to prove the other's ineptitude.

Tate walked around behind the scenes of the auditorium, where several small hallways intersected in a backstage maze worthy of *This Is Spinal Tap.* Nora's and Connor's voices were amplified well enough to be heard in every square inch of the place, fortunately, but that didn't help him find his way out of a hallway that looked suspiciously familiar.

What's the trick to leaving a maze? Always turn left?

He came to another small hallway and tried to remember which way he'd come. To the left, he caught a glimpse of a woman with honey blonde hair, an expensive dress suit, and an uncharacteristically nervous look on her artificially youthful face. Cynthia Wolf.

He followed her down the cramped corridor and then another. Something about the look on her face made him curious. And with no new dirt to dig up on Connor, Cynthia was his next best bet. The second hallway led to the back of the stage (success!), but Cynthia was nowhere to be seen among the curtains and interns. He turned back around and noticed a room at the opposite end of the hallway. A light was on. He walked toward it, opening the door to a small break room and acting surprised when he saw Cynthia. She was gnawing on a fingernail.

She dropped her hand when she saw him, and the slightest tinge of pink colored her cheeks. "Mr. Bertram," she said.

He nodded at her, looking around the room. He spotted a water dispenser and filled a paper cup. "Mrs. Wolf. How are you?" She didn't answer. A quick glance showed her staring at her phone. Clutching it a bit too tightly, as her daughter did when she was upset. He cleared his throat. "Mrs. Wolf, is everything okay?"

She blinked twice and looked up at him. "Are you still here? Doesn't your aunt need you for . . . something?"

Tate took a long, slow drink of his water and placed it on the linoleum counter. "You don't like me, do you?"

"Why would I have any opinion of you, Mr. Bertram? I'm not in the habit of thinking of the children my daughter plays with."

"So you're saying Alex can come over and play tomorrow? Gee, thanks, Mrs. Wolf."

She took a deliberate breath. "Did I say play? I meant *toy*."

The word pierced his thoughts like a needle. "Is that what you think she's been doing with me?"

"That's what I *know*. I never wanted her to get attached to the wrong sort of boy, so I gave her the tools to protect her heart. I didn't want her to care too much about someone who would leave her or use her."

"Why do you think someone would do that to her?"

"Because that's what men do," Mrs. Wolf said, as if they were discussing the weather. "Tate, you should understand, I don't care about you. I don't say that with any sort of malice. I simply mean that I can't find the energy or interest to think about you if you aren't in my immediate view. You have no lasting place in my daughter's life. Therefore, you have no lasting place in my thoughts. You are a sad, empty shell of a man, and I know that you would use my daughter to fill that void until you moved on to something else, if she were to allow it. I taught her never to allow it."

"You talk about her like she's some kind of robot that you've programmed."

"If she was a robot, she would be the kind to rise up and enslave her makers." The woman's words sent a chill down Tate's spine. She was talking about her own *daughter*. What was wrong with her?

His anger smoldered like hot coals. "Cynthia, do you even care about her? Do you think Brooks *cares* about her?"

Cynthia gave him a rare smile, and he wondered if the effort would make her face pop. "It appears I've misspoken. You have feelings for my daughter, don't you?"

He wiped his face of emotion. "She's a friend. And she deserves better than you and her father have ever given her."

"You know nothing of her father," Cynthia said, and this time, her words had some bite to them. Wolf was a sensitive subject for both of the women in his life.

"And you know nothing of your own daughter; you just ignore everything about her you don't like. You've spent a lot of money trying to convince people otherwise, but you're an ugly person, Cynthia, and you're going to lose her. In five years, when Connor leaves you for a younger, newer model, you're going to beg Alex to care about you so you don't have to wallow in misery in whatever condo your lawyers can get you in the divorce. Then you'll finally see yourself for the terrible mother and human being you really are."

Something pathetic flashed across Cynthia's face—something like fear. But rather than cow her, it brought out her claws. "You think *Connor* would leave *me*? Ha!" Her laugh was sharp as a blade. "You think you're so clever, but you're a toddler throwing a tantrum to get his daddy to notice him. You're the boy pulling a girl's braids to get her attention. But too bad for you, neither tactic will work. Your dad will never see past what a shameful, worthless disappointment you are, and my daughter has handbags she cares about more than you." With every word, Cynthia's menace grew until it filled the room. "You're playing with a losing hand, little boy. Go home."

Struggling to keep steady, Tate filled up his water cup a second time. He drained it, crushed the cup, and tossed it into the garbage, all the while looking at Cynthia.

Her phone chimed, and she looked away. Once her eyes left his, her body language shifted. As if he'd never been there in the first place.

He left the room, wishing he could think of something to say. Wishing he knew how to take her down.

CHAPTER TWENTY-FOUR

A furious Tate navigated to the side of the stage Nora's team had staked out. Oscar's arms were folded across his body as he watched the debate. In an attempt to soften her image, Nora was wearing an ivory dress suit instead of her customary bolder colors, and her sharp bob had a soft wave to it. The effect was surprising. She looked more like Tate's mom than ever.

Tate glanced at the seats, where perhaps a hundred concerned citizens were in attendance. The moderator asked a question about consumer protections, and Tate leaned toward Oscar.

"How's Aunt Nora doing?"

Oscar kept his eyes on the candidates. "Really well, actually. She's smiled a few times, and even gotten a laugh or two. Connor almost seems subdued compared to her. I wonder if he's thrown by her performance. Your inner darkness may make the difference in this campaign." Tate didn't respond. Oscar's gaze flitted to Tate. "I was kidding. I know it couldn't have been comfortable for you, but you did a really good thing helping her."

Tate rubbed his eyes. The last thing he wanted right now was approval. "Good, I'm glad."

"How are things going in the field?"

"Nothing to report. Have you seen Alex?"

Oscar looked at Tate. "What's going on?"

"Nothing. I'm just getting a migraine. But have you seen Alex?"

Oscar didn't look convinced, but he answered anyway. "Not since just before the debate started. Can I get you something for your head?"

"No, thanks. I'm just going to look for her. I need to ask her something."

He knew Oscar could see through him, but the man was too kind to press the issue. Tate felt anxious after talking to Cynthia. No, that wasn't entirely true. He'd felt off since he and Alex had spoken earlier. She'd ping-ponged around too quickly, and the way she'd ended things . . . Something didn't feel right.

He walked back toward the series of confusing hallways, this time seeing the pattern easily (as well as the burned-out EXIT sign). He was passing intersecting corridors when he noticed a light still on in the break room. Was Cynthia still there, or had she just left the light on? Before he could decide where to go, he spotted a broad, shadowy figure entering the hall.

Tate slipped into an empty office, leaving the door cracked just enough to peek through. He watched the man turn and walk toward the break room.

It could be nothing, he told himself. But his hammering heart didn't believe him. When the door to the break room opened and closed, Tate waited a moment, listening to the echoes of the debate bounce through the halls. Nora was talking about her plan to prosecute businesses skirting maternity leave laws.

"It is unacceptable that working mothers are forced to return to the workplace so quickly or face losing their jobs," she was saying, projecting real empathy.

He left the office and headed toward the break room, hearing voices over Nora's response. One of them was Cynthia's. Glancing around the hall, he found a light switch a few yards from him. He crept over and flicked it off, counting on them to either not notice or assume the lights were on a timer. He held his breath, but the two kept talking.

He backed up enough that the lights shining through the break room window wouldn't illuminate his face. Yet when he looked into the room, he saw Cynthia glancing out the window. Panic flared in his chest. But a moment later, her eyes snapped back to the man in front of her. Cynthia's arms were folded tightly, but instead of disinterest or disdain on her face, it was fear.

The man had his back to Tate, but it took only a moment to figure out who the short dark hair and wide shoulders belonged to: Sascha Lunov.

Shock rippled through Tate's body, dropping him to the ground. For all his talk of wanting to help Tate, the man was a wild card, at best. Tate couldn't guarantee Lunov wasn't working for Connor, especially now. And Cynthia . . . he'd never seen her look like that before, like she was trying to protect herself. Any other time, it would have been satisfying. Right now, it was unsettling.

Crouching, he sneaked back over to the door and eavesdropped, trying to tune out Connor's voice over the speakers.

"Don't push me, Cynthia," Sascha said, his voice a growl.

"What do you expect me to do? Switch records? Disqualify a child so you can get a second chance at your worthless life?"

"Don't you dare comment on my life."

Cynthia sounded out of breath. "You're an alcoholic! I'm not going to fabricate some reason why you should get bumped to the top of the list when there are children and single mothers and—"

"Yes, your heart aches for those poor children and families, doesn't it?"

"You shut your mouth."

"Get me on the donor list, and this is the last time you'll ever see me."

"I can't just snap my fingers—"

"Enough lying!" Sascha roared. "I know how easy it is for you to change records, Cynthia. Or do you want me to ask the private donor you've been hiding from me?"

Cynthia's response was too low. Tate strained, but he couldn't hear anything, particularly over the sounds of the debate. Connor's voice was more forceful than he'd heard yet. So forceful, Tate couldn't ignore it any longer.

"I've known Nora for years, even before she was married to my brother-in-law. I've tried to honor my brother-in-law's memory, but it's too much to stand here and listen to her talk about working mothers, of all people, when I know for a fact that she considers mothers to be a drain on the economy."

What?

The charge was ridiculous, but something about that line tickled his memory. As much as he wanted to stay and listen to Sascha and Cynthia, something was happening. Tate ran through the halls, around curtains and cords and interns, until he was standing beside a shocked Oscar.

"What is he talking about?" Tate asked Oscar. Oscar shushed him.

"Just before today's debate began, one of my aides showed me a video that was leaked from someone inside the Mallis campaign. In the video, she says some damning things about her plans for our state. I wasn't sure what I was going to do about it when I saw it. Honestly, I wanted to ignore it, but now, after hearing her lie through her teeth . . ." He shook his head, as if overcome by emotion. "I can't let this go. I love Illinois and its people. I love the law. I have spent my career fighting for people who've been taken advantage of by people like her."

"He's a corporate lawyer!" Tate said.

Oscar silenced him with a look.

The blood had drained from Nora's face. She tried to protest, but the moderator cut her off, asking Connor to continue. The audience was growing hostile.

"Nora Mallis claims to care about consumer protections, but what she really plans to do is take down our police force—the men and women who put their lives on the line *every day* to protect our homes and cities! She sees mothers as inferior, and if she was given an ounce of power, I fear for the protections she would take away from working mothers. We can't let her into our government or into our homes, because she will find a way to force her beliefs into every element of our lives. She wants to take away our casinos, our video poker, even our Fantasy Football leagues! Yet the woman's hypocrisy knows no bounds. A high-ranking member of her own staff is a known gambling addict. Too bad for Mallis, the media pays for stories like this." Connor looked right at Nora, triumph burning in his eyes. "It'll be on the news tonight."

The moderator wouldn't let Nora speak until Connor was done. One look at her told Tate she'd been thrown too far off her game. She shook her furious head. "Wolf's accusations of me are so inconsistent, I don't know where to begin to refute them. You call me a puritan, but say I don't support mothers? You claim that I want to attack gambling establishments, yet you accuse me of wanting to take down the very police organizations that would help do this? Connor, if some video really exists, only your sneaking, manipulative campaign could distort the truth so much as to make these allegations appear true."

"So now you're attacking the integrity of Chicago's media? Where does it end, Nora?" Connor demanded. "Is there any part of our state that you don't want to destroy?"

"All right, all right," the moderator said, cutting them both off. "We need to move on—"

"What?" Oscar said, his eyes so wide they looked as if they'd fall out. "How can he cut them off? Nora was hardly even given a chance to respond! It's such an obvious lie!"

Tate grabbed the back of his head. His chest felt tight and his stomach sour. He leaned over, afraid he was going to throw up. "It's not a lie, Oscar."

"What are you talking about?"

"The video . . . everything Connor's claiming. Saying Nora wants to take down the police force? That she's anti-gambling and wants to force her beliefs on people? That mothers are drains on the economy? That was all from the video I took when we were mock interviewing her a few weeks ago."

Tate put his hands on his knees, still leaning forward, but from the corner of his eye he could see Oscar putting the pieces together. "But . . . but, that was all taken out of context! She was saying that's what her body language—"

"You know they'll edit out the rest. All the parts that painted Aunt Nora in a positive light would have been cut before it was even forwarded to any news station. You know that."

"I . . . I know. How could they get that video?" Oscar was squeezing his temples. Abruptly, he dropped his hands and stared at Tate. "What Connor said about a gambling addict, about the media paying for stories like this? Tate, he was talking about *you*."

Tate stiffened. "No! I didn't do this, Oscar! I would never do something like this! She's my aunt!" Oscar didn't answer. "I DIDN'T DO THIS!"

Someone shushed him, and Oscar pulled Tate farther from the stage. "I believe you, Tate, but they're going to spin this! They don't care about the truth; they care about winning an election. They have a smoking gun, and they think you pulled the trigger."

"But I'm not like that! Yes, I gamble! So does Wolf, but no one is out there accusing him of sabotaging a campaign for money! Gambling doesn't make you a monster!"

"No, but you heard how they're painting—"

"I'M NOT AN ADDICT!"

Oscar put a hand on Tate's back. "Listen, Tate, I believe you. We can find a way through this. But right now, I have a job to do, and this conversation will have to wait. Do you understand?"

He wanted to scream again, wanted to march out onto the stage and punch Connor's teeth out. "Yeah. Yeah, I get it."

Tate watched the man walk back to the side of the stage, where the debate had become a runaway train Nora couldn't jump from. Tate pulled out his phone, dialing Alex. After a couple of rings, it went to voice mail. He looked around the backstage area and dialed again. He listened for a buzz or a chime before it went to voice mail again. No luck. Filled with a vengeful purpose, he kept walking and dialing, peeking behind curtains and closed doors and straining to hear any sound. She had to be here. She had to be.

He walked by a bathroom and heard a sniff.

His heart hammering out of his chest, he dialed.

BZZZ—

The buzzing stopped. The call went to voice mail.

Tate threw the door open.

"Alex!" he yelled, walking into the bathroom. There were only two stalls: one was empty, the other showed a pair of expensive heels and long, lean legs under the door. "How the hell could you do this?"

There was a flush, and the door opened. Alex's eyes were red, but she looked otherwise unfazed. She sashayed to the sink, setting down her bag and washing her hands. "I'm not typically in the habit of discussing my bladder, but I guess I have to blame the Diet Coke and bottle of Voss I had earlier." She dried her hands and picked up her bag before meeting his eyes.

"Why?"

The tiny red vessels in her eyes seemed to constrict. "I don't—"

"Yes, you do! Answer me!" he yelled.

She should have yelped or cried or drowned in an ocean of guilt. Instead, her eyes narrowed, and her whole demeanor changed. She looked vicious. "Why do you care, Tate? This entire election is a joke. Do you honestly think the whole thing isn't rigged? This isn't about politics, it's about power and money and making sure powerful people can make more money. Do you think if Nora wins, that will change? It won't. None of this ideological crap matters."

He curled his lip in disgust. "You don't believe that."

"Who cares what I believe? Who cares what I want? No one."

"That's a lie."

She laughed. "Right, because *you* care, don't you, Tate? You *love* me."

"No," he said, not sure if it was the most honest or dishonest thing he'd ever said. "*But our aunt does.* She has loved you your whole life. Who held you and told you to be strong when you were a sad, thirteen-year-old girl whose parents abandoned her night after night? Nora. She gave you a job, Alex! She took you in! She trusted you!" Alex's eyes started to water, and she looked away. "She has always watched out for you, and she refused to fight dirty this entire campaign because she loves you too much to do anything to hurt you, even if it means losing."

"You don't know what you're talking about."

"Stop. Is this what you wanted? Our aunt flailing, publicly humiliated onstage, all so you could get Daddy's approval?"

Her head was shaking, a movement she didn't seem able to control. "It's not that simple. You have no idea—"

"Did they hold a gun to your head, Alex? Did your dad threaten someone you love?" She didn't respond. "You're lying to yourself. About your dad, about Aunt Nora, about everything. You're going to learn the truth soon enough, and you'll realize this is the biggest mistake you've ever made—"

"No," she said, her voice filled with naked self-loathing, "the biggest mistake I ever made was being born. This doesn't even make the top ten."

He stepped back, not wanting her toxic brand of hatred to even touch him. "You are the saddest person I've ever known."

"You have no idea," she said, stepping around him. The door was already closing when he heard her whisper, "Good-bye, Tate."

CHAPTER TWENTY-FIVE

Nora refused to see anyone after the debate and subsequent interviews, so Tate did the only thing he could: he waited for her to get home.

She flicked on the light to the kitchen and let out a small squeal before cursing. "What are you doing in my house?"

"I still have a key," he said, placing it on the marble countertop. "Aunt Nora—"

"No. I don't want to talk to you. I don't even want to see you." Her hair was out of place, and her ivory dress suit looked rumpled. But it was her red-rimmed eyes, more than anything, that showed her distress. "Get out of my house."

"I didn't do this, Aunt Nora. You have to believe me!"

"Then show me what's in your pocket."

His mouth went dry. "What?"

"Show me the totem you keep in your pocket. I've seen you reach for it when you're upset. It's rectangular—just about the right size for a deck of cards. Now show me."

He hadn't even realized his hand was in his pocket, gripping the deck. He released it. "No, it's not what you—"

She sliced a hand through the air. "Enough! Do you expect me to believe you over Oscar? Do you think *he* did this?"

"Of course not!"

"Then are you saying it was Alex? The niece who ran away from home twice when she was growing up—to *my* home—because it was the only place in the world where she felt loved? Do you expect me to believe that *she* betrayed me?"

The way she asked was too desperate, her eyes too searching. She wasn't sure, and that uncertainty was tearing her apart. A sick weight settled on him. Alex had needed Nora for years, and Nora had needed Alex, too. She never had children of her own. She couldn't. He'd seen bills from a fertility clinic that summer he'd stayed with his aunt and uncle. Alex had filled a void in Nora. Feeling important to the girl had given her a different kind of purpose than her work or husband ever could.

Tate bit his tongue, looking around the sterile kitchen. These last few months with Alex and Tate, the house had come alive, and here he was, taking that away from her. Nora was so lonely. Her work and sister and nieces and nephews mattered, but there was an empty recess in her heart. She needed this election, and she needed to believe that Alex loved her as fiercely as she loved Alex. Even if it was a lie.

Slowly, Tate felt the world around him crumble. "I'm sorry, Aunt Nora."

"What do you mean?" she asked, suspicion pulling her eyebrows tight.

"It wasn't Alex."

"You're fired." His eyes slammed shut at the hatred in her voice. "I gave you a chance when *your own father* told me not to, Tate. I believed in you and you did this to me." He shook his head, but he didn't deny anything. "What did they give you? How much was my trust worth? No, I don't want to know. You're sick. I thought I was helping you by giving you a job and a purpose away from your little card games, but I was a fool." Her voice cracked. "I don't even blame you, Tate. I can only blame myself for not having seen it before."

A tear squeezed out of his closed eyes. Her heels clicked against the floor, and he opened his eyes to see her walking across the room toward him. For a moment, he thought she was going to slap him. Instead, she grabbed the house key and glared, her pity and loathing forcing his eyes down. "Get out of my house before I call the police. I never want to see you again."

Tate left the house without any sense of purpose or direction. He just walked, letting his feet lead him wherever they would. If he ended up in a bar with alcohol poisoning, fine. If he ended up in a card game run by the mob, so be it. If he found himself blowing thousands of dollars on scratch-offs or getting beaten down in a dark alley somewhere, he had it coming. He felt too disconnected from the world to care. The hurt inside was too deep.

He'd been set up, and it was no less than he deserved.

He walked past the stone parish he'd found himself in front of all those weeks ago, when Nia came to his rescue. Nothing inside of him stirred to see it now. He was empty. Hollow.

His phone buzzed in his pocket, and habit made him pull it out. His eyes read his brother's name, even as his mind struggled to make meaning of the letters. He didn't have any reason to answer it. He didn't have any reason not to.

He pressed answer but couldn't seem to care enough to speak.

"Tate? Tate, are you there?"

"Yeah." His throat felt dry and sandy, as if it hadn't been used for months instead of . . . however long it had been since leaving Nora's.

"Dude, where are you? Everyone is freaking out. I just went by your apartment. There've been all these calls coming into the house and a couple of reporters have stopped by, and people are trying to say that you leaked that video and they're asking about gambling debts and . . . are you okay?"

"Does it really matter, Ollie?"

"Of course it does. I care about you!"

"I know. But nothing I do is ever going to be good enough, and no one is going to let me be someone else. So I'm done."

Oliver's voice was like an alarm blaring. "What are you talking about, Tate? We love you! Don't do anything—"

He laughed darkly. "I'm not going to kill myself. I'm just done caring about all of this. About anything."

"I know you didn't leak the video—"

"But Dad doesn't, does he?"

"Tate—"

"No, don't bother."

"Tate, stop! Listen to me."

"What?"

"It's Mom. She's . . . she's bad. She was just admitted to the hospital."

His limbs froze to the ground. "When?"

Oliver hesitated. "An hour ago. It's a fibro-flare, but—"

"Mom has never been to the hospital for a flare-up." He put a hand over his face. Her disease meant she was in almost constant pain, and sometimes it was debilitating. For the pain to send her to the hospital for the first time in her life . . . "This is all my fault," he whispered. On the other end of the line, he heard a beeping, followed by a hospital announcement. "You're there with her now, aren't you?"

"Yeah. We, uh, we all are."

We. His dad, Oliver, and Finley, of course. The girl would never let his mom be in the hospital without her.

His mom was in the hospital, and Tate was hunting down a card game.

His voice cracked. "Tell her I'm sorry, Ollie. Tell everyone."

"Tate!"

"Bye." He ended the call and turned off his phone. Because

Oliver would try again, and then it would be Finley calling, and then his mom would call, even if she was hooked up to a morphine drip. They would all say they believed him. They would say it over and over again until he would almost believe that they believed him.

But it wouldn't be true. Something would happen. They'd find money or chips in his pockets. Someone would talk to someone who saw him in a poker room. And the house of cards would tumble to the ground, just as it had with Nora. She'd believed in him once, too. But he'd ruined it.

He ruined every relationship he touched.

Every one.

The question Oliver asked him yesterday—was it really only a day ago?—bounced around forcefully in his head. *When did we lose you?*

Was it the intervention? He'd been around more before then, but what were his relationships with any of them like? He'd flirted with Fin, teased his mom, and joked around with Ollie. He and Juliette had mostly ignored each other. What about his dad? He remembered countless discussions about grades as he grew up, and since he'd been in college, they'd all focused on law school. Or gambling.

Yet the two had spent nearly a month together in close quarters working on Juana's appeal last year. Had they talked about anything that mattered? Anything beyond the trial?

A memory surfaced, and as soon as he thought about it, he wished he could erase it.

Last May, his dad had been interviewed about the case for *60 Minutes*. They'd still had another few days before the Illinois Supreme Court would hear arguments, but the interview had been so positive that his dad was happier and more optimistic than he typically let himself get. They decided to walk around Manhattan rather than going straight back to the hotel.

They wandered into a pizza-by-the-slice joint, debating the

merits of thin crust compared with deep dish. His dad lifted his floppy slice from his plate, and the toppings slid off and plopped right onto his lap. It was so unexpected, so funny, seeing his Dad in a $4,000 Armani-and-mushroom suit that he couldn't help but laugh. What surprised him, though, was his dad's reaction. He snorted, and Pepsi exploded out of his nose. Tate's laughter shook the table, but it was nothing compared with his dad's. The refined, controlled man was laughing so hard, tears were streaming from his eyes, and soda was still dripping from his nose. He dropped the now-bare slice on his plate.

"Thomas Bertram, Esquire, ladies and gentlemen," Tate said, clapping.

His dad wiped his eyes before blowing his nose into a napkin. "It burns!" He winced, causing them both to laugh again.

"You should sue for the cost of the dry-cleaning."

"Or nasal passage reconstruction surgery." His dad smiled before taking a deep breath. "I'm glad you're here with me, Tate."

Tate's heart swelled up like a balloon. He knew it was stupid to be in college and still crave his dad's approval, but he did. He always had. His phone buzzed, and he ignored it.

"Thanks, Dad. It means a lot to me that you let me come. I know you could have picked another intern or a junior partner—"

His dad waved his hand. "I know I could have, but I didn't want more time with any of them. I wanted more time with my son."

Ignoring his phone when it buzzed again, he bit back a goofy, kid-like smile. "That means a lot to me."

"Now why don't you tell me how things are going for you? Are you dating anyone?" His dad reached for his pizza when he saw the naked slice and snorted. He glanced down at his suit. "Actually, maybe I should go to the restroom first to wipe the humiliation off." Tate chuckled. "Hold that thought."

He smiled, watching his dad walk to the back of the run-down restaurant. He couldn't remember the last time they'd laughed

together like that. It felt good. It felt as if they were on the verge of
the first real conversation they'd had in years, and the happiness
surging through him was exhilarating. Tate was halfway through a
slice when his phone buzzed again. He saw three messages, and the
thumping of his heart shifted.

Got 411 on a private game. Starts in an hour. U in?

Hello?

Answer in 5 or they give up ur seat

Tate flexed his fingers, already anticipating the feel of the cards.
The text was from a guy Tate had met last quarter. He'd run a game
every Friday and Saturday night out of his dorm room, and now, he
was working for his aunt in Manhattan over the summer. Tate had
texted him earlier that day, not looking forward to another night in
the hotel suite quizzing his dad about the case. His dad probably
wouldn't even notice he was gone.

His fingers hovered over the keyboard, and before he knew it,
he was typing out a message:

I'm in. Text me the address.

When his dad came back, he had wet patches all over his shirt
and pants. Tate grinned. "Good look for you, Counselor."

"Why, thank you," his dad said, sitting and putting a napkin over
his lap. He mumbled, "Why am I bothering," to himself. Tate snickered, but the sound of his phone pulled his attention away. His buddy
had sent him the address. He'd need to leave in twenty minutes to
make it.

"So, tell me about your life," his dad prompted, cutting his pizza
with a knife and fork now. Tate almost teased him, and the look on
his dad's face told him he was expecting it, inviting it, even. But Tate
had an address and a thousand bucks burning a hole in his pocket.
He'd give his dad twenty minutes and then he'd run.

"You know, it's kind of the same old thing. I'll be taking an extra class for the next couple of quarters to make up for taking this quarter off."

"Sure," his dad said. "But how about life, son? You're in college! Have you liked your roommates? Found any girls that you like? I ran into the O'Briens at a charity auction, and—"

"You're not setting me up with Chloe O'Brien, Dad."

"Is it because of her Harry Potter obsession?" Tate snorted. "Though you loved Harry Potter when you were younger. I remember coming into your room night after night to find you reading with a flashlight under your covers. Your mother said we should cut you off at midnight, but I told her you wouldn't be able to rest until you knew what happened. So we let you read. When you finished the series a week later, I think you slept for fourteen hours straight." His dad laughed.

Tate put down his pizza. It was cold, anyway. "You remember that?"

"Of course I do. Who do you think turned your light off every night when you finally passed out from exhaustion?" his dad asked with a smile. He cleared his throat, and his eyes watered. "Son, seeing how Juana fought for Mateo's every breath has made me realize how important family is." Tate's phone buzzed, and he itched to take it out. "I never want to take for granted just how blessed I am to have each of you kids, how blessed I am to have *you*."

Tate smiled, but inside, he was fighting not to check his phone. He knew they had a few more minutes, but what if there was a problem with the subway or something? He couldn't be late, or they'd give away his seat.

Tate reached across the table. "Thanks, Dad. And, um, you know how you've been asking if I have a girlfriend?" His dad's eyes lit up. "And all these texts I've been getting? Well, that's actually her. She's in Manhattan visiting her aunt and uncle for the summer, and, um . . ."

"You were hoping to see her tonight before we head back to Illinois," he said. He was still smiling, but a hint of disappointment dimmed the light in his eyes. "Of course, son. When do you need to go?"

"Um . . ."

"Now, of course. Do you need money for the subway?"

"No, I'm okay. I promise to tell you all about her tomorrow, okay?" He was already standing, dropping his napkin, grabbing his dad's shoulder. "Thanks, Dad."

His dad gave him a small, heartfelt smile. "I love you, son."

"You too, Dad," he'd answered. At the door, he'd caught a glimpse of his dad in the reflection of the window. Wiping his eyes.

The memory was like a punch to Tate's gut, the pain making his own eyes water.

His whole life, he'd said he wanted his dad's love and attention, but he'd thrown it away when it had been offered so freely. He'd thrown it away, along with six hundred and twelve dollars on a Doyle Brunson—

Stop it, he told himself. *Stop thinking about the hand! You didn't lose six hundred bucks, you lost your* Dad*. Doesn't that mean anything to you?*

It did, but not as much as it should have. Because even now, he could so easily lose himself in the memory of that game. He was already thinking about where he went wrong, how he'd misread the—

Stop!

He had to stop thinking. He looked around, instead trying to figure out where his feet had taken him. Cars and pedestrians were everywhere. Streetlights and tall buildings. He almost dreaded the moment of discovery, seeing where the depths of his depravity had led him. Still, he reached out a hand and grabbed the handle of a heavy door to a building he hadn't even looked at yet. As the door swung open, he saw a handwritten sign in the window:

AA Meeting: Room 412, 6:00-7:00 p.m.

NA Meeting: Room 416, 7:00-8:00 p.m.

GA Meeting: Room 420, 8:00-9:00 p.m.

His eyes jumped to a metal sign next to the door that read "Chicago Temple."

His subconscious hadn't taken him to a game. It had taken him to get help. It was begging him to stop while he still could.

The realization almost destroyed him.

He glanced at his watch: 9:09 p.m. He'd missed the meeting, but he suspected that wasn't the only reason he'd been led here. Too weak to protest against his own mind, he pulled open the door and let his feet continue to guide him. They propelled him forward to the one room he'd done his best to avoid since the moment he'd first stepped into the building last December, when his dad and Oliver had insisted he attend Gambler's Anonymous.

The chapel.

The four-story sanctuary was serene and dim. Tate saw a clergyman speaking to a woman on the front pew, so he slipped into a pew near the back. He took in the stained-glass windows and statues. There were no candles, and Tate found himself missing them, imagining just how many candles his dad had lit for him since Tate's accident. A soft, pretty hum in the background made his eyes close. He wanted to hear it, to open himself up to it. But along with it came all the emotion he'd been pushing back for years. It crashed into him like a tidal wave, dragging him out to sea.

Soon, he was consumed with pain, suffocating on his shame even as a part of his mind argued that he hadn't done anything wrong, that he wasn't an addict. But the memory of his dad's face in the reflection of that restaurant window flashed before his eyes, and he saw the lie for what it was. He wanted to play poker right now more than he'd ever wanted anything in his life. His body was trembling with the need. He put his clasped hands on the pew in front of him and rested his head on his hands.

"Please, help me," he whispered. "I don't know how to stop.

I've lost almost everyone who matters to me, and I still can't stop." Tears coursed down his face. "Please," he cried, still whispering to himself. "I can't do this by myself. I need help." Sobs tore through him. "Please."

He sat there, crying and shaking until a voice whispered, "I thought you'd never ask."

CHAPTER TWENTY-SIX

Tate looked behind him. "Nia? What are you doing here?" He dashed a hand across his face.

She was smiling, but it wasn't a gloating or knowing smile. It was real. He'd never seen a real smile from her before. Of course, she'd never seen one from him, either.

She wrinkled her nose. "I had a tough week, and I wanted to gamble more than I have in months. So I caught the meeting tonight. I always stop here afterward."

"I didn't know you were religious," he said, blinking away more tears.

"Don't tell my parents, but I'm not. It just feels nice in here. Peaceful." She breathed in and sighed. "I didn't know you were religious, though."

"I don't know what I am," he admitted.

"Either way, that was a pretty impressive prayer." Another real smile. No judgment. "Want to talk?"

"Yeah, actually, I really do."

A half hour later, Nia and Tate were sitting in the same pew, and the reverend was the only other person in the cavernous room. Their voices echoed softly, rising in the air to bounce around in the rafters above.

"So what's the answer?" Nia asked when he'd finished telling her everything.

"Huh?"

"To your brother's question. When did they lose you?"

"I honestly believed what I told him at the time: that they kicked me out. But now, I'm not so sure." He paused, letting his thoughts wander into the darkest corners of his mind, back to the first time he could remember wanting something he didn't have; the first time he realized he could use what he observed against people. He swallowed hard. "I think it might have been years before. That summer with Alex."

"What happened?"

"I know I've mentioned this before, but when we first met, she was . . . awful. She made fun of me for everything, harping on every little weakness, my weight, my naïveté. And anything I was better at than her became too stupid for her to like. She was a monster. But she was so beautiful and imperious that the meaner she got, the more I craved her approval. That night, her parents were supposed to pick her up at seven, after dinner. I found her around 9:30 staring out the window, shuffling a deck of cards. I asked her if she was crying, and she snapped at me, saying how she was just trying to get some peace from me for a change, because I was the most pathetic loser she'd ever met. It was so cruel, but I'd seen her wiping her eyes in the reflection of the window. I *knew* she was lying. I didn't even respond. I just turned around, and the second I did, she challenged me to a game of hearts. I didn't know any card games beyond war or blackjack, so I told her I didn't want to play, because I knew she'd just make fun of me for sucking at a game I'd never played."

Tate rubbed his eyes, and he could still see the fear written in Alex's every feature as she realized he was going to say no.

"Her eyes widened and she sat up straighter, and I just knew."

"Knew what?"

"That I had her. She had been messing with me all day, but in that moment, I knew I could play her, too, if I wanted."

"So what happened?"

"She said she'd give me a kiss if I could beat her. I wanted the kiss more than I cared about my self-respect, as it turns out. So I played."

"And you beat her?"

"Not even close. But by the end of that game, I'd picked up on some things. For the next six weeks, we played card games at least a few times a week, but as soon as she could sense that I was really improving, she would say how bored she was of that 'stupid game' and teach me a new one. It was her way of keeping me dangling on the edge of her hook. She taught me at least a dozen different card games, including poker. And every night, I stayed up late learning everything I could about each one. I became obsessed. I had dreams about calculating pot odds."

Nia nodded. "I've had those dreams."

"But here's the thing she never realized: after the first couple of weeks, I could have beaten her at any of those games. She was good, but I was just better. It was so easy for me, and I picked up on her tells fast. I never let her know that, though. While we were playing cards, I was having fun. She was still ruthless and made fun of me, but . . . I don't know how to explain it. It was like I learned her language, and I knew how to keep her winning just enough so that she was having fun, too. She was even nice sometimes."

"That's kind of sweet of you."

"If I hadn't been playing her, you mean?" Nia nodded. "I wanted that kiss, Nia. I knew that as soon as I beat her and she kissed me, she wouldn't talk to me again for the rest of the summer."

"So?"

"So I waited until the last night. We were playing hearts again— you know it? Heart cards are worth a point each, Queen of Spades is worth thirteen, and the person with the lowest score wins the game?"

"Unless someone manages to amass all the points in a hand, and then the other players get stuck with them. Yeah," Nia said, giving him a *move along* nod.

"Well, I knew exactly what I wanted to do. I kept our points close throughout the night so that by the final hand, she'd get more aggressive. And she did. She got rid of her high point cards as quickly as possible, and by the time she realized that she'd given me all of her point cards, it was too late. I dropped the queen of spades on the very last hand . . ."

"And you shot the moon, sticking her with all the points and stealing the win from her," Nia finished.

He nodded. "She was so mad. She accused me of bluffing and lying to make a fool of her."

"Did she still kiss you?"

"Yeah, she did. And it was everything I could have wanted. I even told her that, thinking it would soften the blow. Instead, she slapped me." Tate breathed in slowly. "That was the beginning of the end. Or maybe the end of the beginning. I don't know. But that summer with her . . . it changed me."

"She was a sad, hurt thirteen-year-old, Tate. She didn't know what she was doing."

"No, and neither did I. She couldn't have known how impressionable or obsessive I was or how much I would care about her opinion."

"But she does now."

"Yeah. She does."

"I'm sorry about everything," Nia said. "Including Alex."

His mouth went dry. "Me too. But I think I'm more upset about my aunt."

"That she didn't believe you or that Alex betrayed her like that?"

He looked at the wood grain of the pew in front of him, trying to process her question. "It hurts that she didn't believe me. But Nora will be devastated if she finds out about Alex."

"So you're going to keep taking the fall?"

"I almost have to, don't I?"

"I don't know, Tate. You're saying that Nora has a literal spy in her campaign. I know you don't want to hurt her any further. I'm proud of you for that. But in the long run, how much worse will it be for her when she realizes that Alex was never on her side *and* she wrongly accused you?"

He exhaled loudly. "You're right. But what am I supposed to say? 'Oh, hey, Aunt Nora. Remember how I sort of told you Alex was innocent? Well, I lied. I didn't do anything wrong and she did, so will you hire me back?"

"No." Nia frowned. "But what if I knew a way to right the wrong so none of this matters anymore? Would you be in?"

"Yes, obviously. Why wouldn't you lead with that?"

"Because I don't know if it'll work. But you've managed to get under Wolf's skin, and I think we can use that to our advantage."

"How?"

"I'm not sure yet, but it would probably involve you keeping Wolf occupied."

"I'm not a prostitute, if that's what you're getting at."

She shook her head, but a smile played on her lips. "Well, shoot. On to Plan B."

"Which is?"

"You can't mention this to anyone, Tate. If another soul finds out, I won't be able to keep you from suffering the ramifications, including possible prison time. Do you get that?"

"Yeah, I get that."

"Okay." She dropped her voice so low, not even the angels could hear. "I think we have enough for a search warrant on Wolf."

He wanted to punch the air in triumph. "What do you have on him?"

"Did you know that, until recently, his firm represented the National Gaming Corporation?" she asked. Tate looked blankly at her. "They're the largest operator of racetracks and video gaming machines in the country. They were the firm's biggest client for years. When the first rumors circulated about Wolf having mob ties, we laughed it off. The Outfit owns casinos, and nothing has impacted casino business more than video gaming. Why would Wolf harm his own interests so materially by involving himself with the Outfit? Then we found out that NGC recently chose to retain a new firm, just after they released dismal quarterly earnings."

"Why would Wolf sabotage NGC operations? Did he get in too deep at a mob casino?"

"Not that we can tell. He has a reputation for being ultra-disciplined. The guy won't even have more than a glass of wine at a function."

"So what happened? How did he get in their pocket?"

"That's what we're hoping the warrant will show. The Outfit has their hands in all sorts of businesses, from real estate to hospitals and private clinics to restaurants. Somewhere, Connor made a misstep. We just have to find out where."

"If you don't know yet, how did you get enough for a warrant?"

"A confidential informant pointed us in the direction of a restaurant owner out in Irving Park who had information on Wolf."

Tate sat up. "The owner of Misha's Restaurant? Misha Starkovich?"

"Yes. How did you know that?"

He told her how his campaign spying had led him to Irving Park and beyond, as well as his suspicions tying Landolfo and the liquor licensing to Wolf supporting the new casino proposal.

Nia's eyebrows raised. "Wow. That's some clever detective work there, Nancy Drew."

"It's Veronica Mars, thank you very much."

"Well, Veronica, you're right. That's exactly what we suspect. Unfortunately for Connor, he made a personal visit to Mrs. Starkovich, on account of her connection to the Bratva."

"Which is?"

"She was the leader of the Chicago arm of the Uzhhorod Bratva until she passed the reins down to her nephew last year."

"No shi—sorry," he said, crossing himself and looking heavenward. "This is a Methodist Church."

"Well, I'm Catholic-ish."

Nia gave him an almost indulgent eye roll. "Anyway, Connor went under the guise of representing the NGC, but it's obvious now that he was really there on behalf of the Outfit. He made some veiled threats, gave her some fraudulent paperwork about liquor licensing that Landolfo must have given him, and the muscle Connor had with him removed the machines from nearly all the restaurants and bars she owns all along the North Side."

"So by Wolf pretending to be there on legitimate business, the Bratva didn't suspect the Chicago Outfit was targeting them."

"Exactly," Nia said. "And a half dozen bars and restaurants owned by smaller gangs throughout the city received the same visit from Connor directly. Hundreds of video machines were taken."

The pieces kept connecting in his head like a jigsaw puzzle taking shape. "He couldn't have anyone else in the firm do it, because they'd know this wasn't official NGC business."

"Right again, Ms. Mars."

Tate laughed into his hands. "I can't believe it. I can't believe Connor's doing the mob's dirty work."

"You clearly know nothing about organized crime if you think *this* is dirty work."

"Touché." He looked around the quiet chapel. "But wouldn't Connor have gotten rid of any evidence that implicates him?"

"Nah. The guy's a weasel, but he's smart. He'll have kept records. He probably has specific instructions for the contents of his personal safe to be sent to the police if anything ever happens to him, or something like that."

"And that's what you're hoping the raid will show?"

"You got it."

"Where do I come in?"

Nia smiled, the corners of her eyes crinkling with more menace than joy. "You're going to do what you do best: annoy the shit out of him." She winced and glanced up, crossing herself as Tate had. "Sorry about that."

When they made their way outside, they were both yawning, although Tate was too wired to sleep. He walked with her to her car, where she looked him over. "You need to rest."

"Yeah," he said.

"No, I mean it. I know that look in your eye. Your day has been a train wreck, and you're itching for something to take your mind off it." All traces of humor vanished from her face. "You can't gamble again, Tate. Tell me you feel that."

He put his hand in his pocket, glancing at a passing car. "Yeah, I do."

She grabbed his face and made him meet her eyes. "Tell me."

He wanted to shake off her hand. "I'm not gonna gamble again."

"No. Tell me."

His stomach churned as he clutched his deck tightly. His pulse hammered in his chest and adrenaline surged through his veins. The frustration and exhaustion of trying to prove himself for years bubbled up inside of him. He felt as if his veins were exposed, as if he was a wounded animal offering up his jugular to the stronger, superior animal in front of him. He didn't want to do this.

He had to do this.

He took his hand out of his pocket and held the deck out to Nia. The words stuck in the back of his throat, but he forced them out. "I'm an addict."

And then, without warning, without any ability to stop himself or contain his emotions, Tate began to weep.

And weep.

And weep.

Nia let him cry against her, hugging him tightly and crying herself. After a few minutes, he wiped his eyes. "You suck, Nia. But, man, you're a good sponsor."

"I'm not that good. I was just hoping you'd admit how stupid you are," she said, grinning and blinking away tears.

"Never." He wiped his face one more time. "Thanks."

She unlocked her car door to get in. "Can I drop you off at your apartment?"

"No, I need to go somewhere first."

"Tate—"

The warning in her voice hurt, mostly because it was so warranted. "I'm not going to gamble, Nia. I promise. I'd appreciate a ride, though."

Fifteen minutes later, Tate was asking a receptionist for the directions to Mariah Bertram's room. His feet fell softly on the blindingly white floor. An undercurrent of panic rippled beneath his skin with every step, and he found himself holding his side. Last year, he'd been admitted into this very ER with a curtain rod stuck through him. It had nicked an organ, but his recovery had been so much easier than it could have been. He'd gotten lucky. The doctor had told him that over and over again. He'd gotten lucky.

His parents had said that during the intervention not two weeks later. Maybe fate or the universe or God was giving him a second chance, they'd said. Maybe this was the wake-up call he'd needed to realize he had a problem.

It hadn't been.

Still holding his side, Tate approached his mom's private room. His palms were sweating as he reached for the handle. He paused, trying to calm his breathing, trying to keep from tearing apart at the seams.

He opened the door to find her alone, hooked up to an IV, and mercifully asleep. Crossing to her bedside, he sat in a chair that was still warm. He wondered who'd been sitting here and for how long. He pushed the thoughts aside, taking his mom's hand in his. It was chilly and lifeless, and a spasm of fear struck him.

He kissed her hand, then held it tightly. "I'm so sorry, Mom. I didn't mean for any of this to happen." The words spilled out in a quiet rush. "I didn't know how bad things had gotten, for you or for me. I should have been around to help you and to make chocolate milkshakes so we could sit around late at night watching Cops reruns like we used to do. Do you remember that? Every Saturday night until I was almost fourteen." His voice caught. "I loved that, Mom. I really did."

The veins in her thin, pale hand stood out, making her look too fragile. "I don't know how this all started. I don't know why I let my-self care so much about something that doesn't matter. I don't know what I'm even chasing anymore. I just wanted you guys to love me and to be proud of me, but somewhere along the way, I lost myself." He started crying. "I don't know what's wrong with me, Mom. I don't know why I can't stop."

A large hand gripped Tate's shoulder. He looked behind him to see his dad, the door to the en suite restroom open only a few feet away. Tears were in the man's eyes.

Tate jumped up. "I didn't do it. I didn't betray Aunt Nora."

His dad's face crumpled. "I know you didn't, son." He pulled Tate into a tight hug. "I know you didn't."

"I'm so sorry, Dad. I need help," Tate cried into his dad's shoulder.

"Whatever you need. I'll do anything for you." He leaned back and looked at Tate's eyes. "You've made me proud a thousand times over in your life. I should have told you that every day as you were growing up." A tear rolled down his dad's cheek. "So I'm telling you this now: I'm proud of you. I'm proud of you and I love you, Tate. Nothing will ever change that."

He pulled Tate back into a hug, and together, they cried.

Two hours later, Tate's dad was sitting in the chair next to the hospital bed. Finley, Oliver, and Tate were sitting on a couch against the wall, vending machine snacks scattered at their feet. Oliver and their dad had fallen asleep, leaving Finley and Tate awake, watching an infomercial about Timeless Love Songs for Lovers.

"As opposed to Timeless Love Songs for Apathetic Strangers," Finley said in a low voice, yawning on the couch next to him. Oliver was on her other side, drooling slightly.

"Or Dated Jock Rock for Grandmothers," Tate said.

Finley held a thumb down. "You weren't even trying on that one," she said, yawning again. She rested her head on the back of the couch. Her hair was up in a sloppy bun, and wisps of it framed her face. She was beautiful.

"I'm really sorry, Fin."

She swatted his leg. "Oh, come on, it wasn't *that* bad."

"No, not about the bad joke. I mean about us. *Me.* I screwed up. I don't know how to forgive myself for hurting you, of all people."

She turned her dark eyes to him. Her voice was so soft, he had to strain to hear it. "I know you, Tate—the good and the bad. Even the night of the charity event, I knew you must have been in a bad place to say what you did. You've shown me a million times over how much you care about me. A single stupid comment didn't erase that."

"But I hurt you."

She scrunched her nose up. "Yeah, you did. Part of that is because it was a really douchey thing to say, especially after blowing me off. But another part is that I still struggle to feel worthy of having people love me. As much as I've been working on the relationship with my mom, we'll never really be okay. Realizing that has been brutal. Then everything last year happened, and things with Oliver haven't been perfect." She rubbed her shoulder. "And, like I told you, I've had a crush on you my whole life. The idea that you could like me, too, felt kind of like a dream."

On the other side of the couch, Oliver snored.

"But we both know I'm not good enough for you," he said in a low, sad voice.

She rested her head on his shoulder. "It's not that. I think we're just better as a dream. I don't think we could challenge and push each other to be our best selves if we were together. You know?"

He didn't know. Yeah, he thought she walked on water, and she was undoubtedly too accepting and too forgiving of his flaws. Maybe that was the crush, maybe not. Maybe everything would have changed if they'd gotten together. But they'd never know. Because while she was probably right, she'd also left out one vital detail.

"That's a decent reason, but it's not the only one," he said, prodding her. She didn't say anything. Meanwhile, Oliver breathed heavily and shifted on the couch, eyes still closed. Mouth still open. Tate nudged her again.

"Fine. I still love Oliver, okay? Even if he does suck sometimes."

Tate smiled, if a little sadly. "And even if he pretends to be asleep when you and I are talking?"

"Even then." She pushed Oliver's leg with her foot. "We know you're awake," she said in a loud whisper.

Oliver pretended to stir. "Huh? Why did you kick me?"

She was still lying on Tate's shoulder, and he couldn't pretend it wouldn't hurt when she pushed off him to lean against Oliver, instead. "Ollie," she said, "next time you fake sleep, remember not to swallow. No one swallows when they're asleep."

"I was drooling . . ."

"Only because you're a terrible actor." She moved away from Tate to push Oliver's arm.

"But you love me for it," Oliver said, grabbing the hand that pushed him. His eyes were shining and his smile was blinding.

"In spite of it, really," Fin said.

A hard lump lodged in Tate's throat. Before the ache could settle, a small voice cleared.

"Could one of you get me a milkshake?"

CHAPTER TWENTY-SEVEN

Around four in the morning, everyone was hopped up on milk-shakes and goodwill, watching infomercials while waiting for the doctor to check Tate's mom out. Tate watched his parents sing along to "Islands in the Stream" and Oliver serenade them all to "Can You Feel the Love Tonight." It was painful and silly and would have been perfect if an idle part of his mind wasn't wondering when he could leave, if he could stop calculating the time until all the games he knew of ended.

He reached for his pocket at least a hundred different times, craving the comfort of his worn-out deck of cards. He still couldn't believe he'd just given them to Nia like that. What a stupid thing to have done.

Stop stop stop stop stop.

He was about to jump up from the seat beside his mom's bed when her delicate hand fell on his shoulder. He glanced over to see compassion written in the lines of her face.

"You okay?" she asked softly enough that the others couldn't hear from the couch.

It would be so easy to lie. He could say he was tired or had a headache. It would be for her good. The last thing she needed was stress, after all.

"Do you know why I've never come to the hospital for a fibro-flare before?" she asked before he could respond. He shook his head, watching her wring her blanket. "Because of how much I want to."

"What do you mean? If you want to go, why don't you go?"

She grabbed his hand. "You remember that I studied philosophy in college, don't you?"

"I remember." He smiled. They'd always had that love of thought and debate in common.

"Shortly after I was diagnosed with fibromyalgia, I had occasion to think a lot about Epicureanism. It's such a misunderstood philosophy. People want to confuse it with hedonism, when it's anything but. Epicurus said that happiness stemmed from two things: *ataraxia*, which is like peace and tranquility, and *aponia*."

"The absence of pain," he said quietly.

"I'm on morphine right now, and this may be the first time in seven years that no part of me hurts. Nothing." A tear rolled down her cheek. "As good as I feel right now, though, I'm scared of how awful I'll feel when the morphine wears off and I have to feel *everything* again: burning pain in my joints; a throbbing headache that makes me want to throw up; stiffness and aches that keep me from moving or sleeping. I'll feel every draft and every slight change in humidity in my bones. I will just *hurt*." More tears spilled. "And I don't want to. I don't want to feel like that anymore."

"Mom—"

"I've never come to the hospital, because I'm afraid of how much I would like this feeling. This *aponia*." She squeezed his hand rather than wiping the tears pouring down her cheeks. "Is that what it's like? For you? Does it just . . . numb all the pain?"

Tate bent over his mom's hand and shook with unsuppressed sobs. It wasn't exactly what he felt—the thrill alone was something he couldn't describe—but there was a profound truth to what she was saying. When he was gambling, he didn't feel anything outside of the table. No guilt or shame, no grief or remorse. He wasn't worried about how he measured up to anyone's expectations. He felt unstoppable. And right now, he imagined his mom felt just like that.

The idea that it would all crash down around her in a few hours made him ache.

"Yeah, Mom. That's what it's like."

"Oh, baby," she cried. "I'm so, so sorry."

He got up onto her bed and hugged her. A moment later, he felt several other arms wrapping around them: Oliver's, Finley's, his dad's.

"Promise me we'll get through this together, okay?" his mom whispered in his ear. "Promise me."

"I promise."

Tate's mom was released a little over an hour later. His parents and Finley waited in the lobby while Tate and Oliver went to get the car. The morning was already warm as the two got into their dad's Audi. Tate glanced at the dashboard clock, relieved to know that the card rooms were all closed and he couldn't give in to temptation if he wanted to. One less thing to worry about. He could just buy some scratch-offs—

No scratch-offs. No gambling. Remember?

Of course he remembered. He rubbed his forehead. He could do this. He could.

"You okay?" Oliver asked.

"Yeah, just worried about finals," Tate lied easily. Then he frowned. "No, you know what? I'm not worried about finals. I'm trying to talk myself out of buying scratch-offs."

"You mean the lottery tickets?"

They were almost to the entrance, where the others were waiting. "Yeah. It's like . . . a replacement fix, you could say. Up until the casino fund-raiser, I hadn't played poker in months. But I was buying lottery scratch-offs, so I guess my restraint wasn't quite as impressive as I thought at the time."

Oliver pulled the car up to the curb. "I'm sure it still took strength."

"Maybe." Tate rapped his knuckles on his window. "But isn't the first step admitting I have a problem?"

A ghost of a smile found its way to Oliver's face. He and Tate both got out of the car and helped their mom into the front seat. Once she was in, they climbed into the back with Finley.

"Uh, Tate, would you mind if Dad dropped me off at your apartment?" Oliver asked over Finley. "Maybe I could finish cramming there and then go to campus?"

He knew what Oliver was doing, and resentment and gratitude warred inside him. He wanted to tell Oliver no, to send him packing as soon as possible. But he had to fight that instinct. The same one that kept him obsessively checking his pocket for his deck of cards. "Sure, Ollie."

Fifteen minutes later, Oliver was saying good-bye to Finley while Tate opened his mom's door to give her a hug.

"Come home soon," his mom said in his ear while he crouched at her door. The morphine had started wearing off a few minutes earlier, and she looked as if she was trying hard not to break.

"I'll come home tonight, Mom. I promise."

He wished her smile weren't so grateful. He wished she didn't look so excited about seeing him again. But what was done was done. Hopefully he could make it up to her.

His dad stepped out of the car and clapped Tate's shoulder. "What can I do, son?"

Tate struggled to keep his guard down and let his concern show. "I . . . I don't know, Dad. I'll talk to my sponsor later today. Maybe we can talk tonight when I get home?"

The corner of his dad's lips twitched up. "You're coming home later, then?"

For his mom to be excited to see him was one thing. But the hope in his dad's eyes made his throat ache. "I'll need to study for a few hours, but yeah, you'll see me later."

His dad gave him a quick, tight hug. His throat sounded scratchy as he said, "I can't wait."

Several hours later, Oliver was waiting outside Tate's classroom reading the news on his phone when Tate finished his exam. He stuffed down his annoyance.

"Fancy meeting you here," Tate said.

Oliver's cheeks reddened. He quickly stowed his phone and jumped up. "Hey, I just finished studying and thought we could—"

"Ollie, I know why you're here. You don't have to put on the act."

"Right, yeah," Oliver said, still talking too fast. "Sorry. I just don't know if we're really talking about stuff, you know?"

Tate stopped, looking at his brother more closely. Students pushed to get past them. "You're still being weird. Why?"

"It's just . . . Aunt Nora took a huge hit in the polls this weekend."

Tate cursed and started walking again. "I don't understand why Oscar hasn't sent the full video to the media. It paints her in a *good* light, and it would clear up everything."

"Um, yeah, so it turns out they sent it in this morning. The problem is that retractions are a footnote. Most people either don't care enough or don't want to work hard enough to understand the full story on anything, least of all politics."

They stepped outside, and Tate put on his sunglasses. "I know you're right. This just sucks."

"I wish there was something we could do," Oliver said, but Tate was already in his head, thinking about his conversation with Nia. The warrant.

The sound of a high laugh broke Tate's concentration. He knew that laugh. He looked around and spotted the source, surrounded by a big group of rich kids who all looked as if they were competing for "First to Die" in a horror movie. And in the middle was their queen: Alex Wolf.

The glint from her diamond ring almost blinded him to the fact that her tool of a fiancé was dangling from her arm. And talking about their engagement party.

"I can't believe you were able to book La Piazza on such short notice!" one of Alex's cronies was saying.

"Can I let you in on a secret?" Alex's fiancé, Brooks, said conspiratorially to the girl. Tate wondered if the guy even remembered Alex was beside him. "Mrs. Wolf and my mom planned this months ago, when I told them I was going to propose at the end of the quarter. We had to do it tomorrow night, before my parents leave for *la Côte d'Azur* for the summer. Otherwise, I'd probably have let Alex decide where she wanted it."

Tate's jaw ached from clenching it. Everything this bastard was saying was despicable. How he could presume ownership over the fiercest woman Tate knew was incomprehensible. Yet Alex just stood there, her smile even more dazzling than her ring. Her friends said how romantic Brooks was and took turns guessing where he would take her for their honeymoon.

Tate felt a tugging on his arm, but he shook it off, compelled to stay, to listen, to torture himself with every word.

"You should go on like an Eastern Bloc tour!" one of the girls said.

Brooks gave her a funny look. "Why would we do that?"

"I don't know," the girl teased, "maybe because it could be fun for Alex to get in touch with her roots. You know she's Bulgarian, right?"

"Sure, technically," Brooks said. "But why would she want to go there when she could go to Monaco or Sardinia? It's not like she speaks the language."

"In fairness, neither of you speaks Italian," one of Brooks's friends countered.

Brooks rolled his eyes. "That's different."

The urge for Tate to do violence swelled up in him so forcefully he grabbed Oliver's shoulder. "Talk me down from the ledge. Now."

"Tate, you're better than this," Oliver said, his voice smooth as he pulled Tate away from the group. "And she's not worth it. She knows exactly what she's doing. If you want to feel bad for anyone, feel bad for the small-minded loser who's marrying her."

"Why would I feel bad for him? He doesn't even know her."

"Exactly my point. She's manipulating him, just like she did you. She hates the guy, yet not only has she kept dating him while she's strung you along, but now she's marrying him? I'm not saying he deserves someone great, because he's clearly a xenophobic douche-nozzle, but he doesn't deserve that. Neither do you."

Tate glanced back at the group, searching her face before turning back to Oliver. "You're right."

They started walking again. "I'm sorry, Tate," Oliver said.

"It's fine. Let's talk about something else, okay?"

"Yeah, of course." After a moment of silence, Oliver cleared his throat. "So, uh, do you know how most college guys treat foot fungus?"

"Huh?"

"I don't have it, or anything. I just read about it earlier in some clickbait article. So, do you want to know how most guys in college treat foot fungus, or what?"

They were far enough away that Alex and her friends were lost in the crowd. "Yeah, sure."

"They pee on their feet."

"Come again?"

"Yeah, they pee on their feet in the shower. Can you believe that? I guess the urea helps kill the fungus, or something. I didn't read the whole thing. But man, dudes are gross."

"You're a dude," Tate said.

"Not like that. What kind of degenerate pees on his own feet?"

"The kind that doesn't want athlete's foot, I guess."

That night, after dinner, Tate found himself in the library with his family, where Finley was telling them about the summer play she was directing. Meanwhile, Tate's mind kept wandering to the last card game he'd played, just a couple of days ago.

He forcibly stopped himself.

This is what people do—they talk about their lives with their families instead of replaying games in their heads. They listen instead of running the odds of different hands. They pay attention to things people say, even when it's not about them.

He pushed thoughts of cards out of his mind (over and over again) and tried to follow along with the conversation until a chime sounded on his phone.

"Excuse me, I have to get this." The chime tone was reserved for only one contact—at that contact's insistence. With a frown, he left the room to read the message from Nia.

NEED TO TALK. COME TO GA MTG. 8PM.

He hadn't even typed his reply when his dad came out to the hall. "Everything okay?"

"My sponsor," Tate said. Knowing he wouldn't be able to handle the look of suspicion on his dad's face, Tate showed him the message. "Looks like there's a meeting tonight with my name on it. I think I'll go for a quick run before."

"Okay. Do you need a ride back home tonight?"

He wanted to say no. He didn't want to go at all, but Tate forced a nod. "Sure, Dad. I'll text you when I'm done."

CHAPTER TWENTY-EIGHT

Running was Tate's least preferred form of exercise. For as much as he worked out, he'd yet to experience a runner's high. Back in rehab, he'd run for two, three hours a day, and it was always mind-numbing. Now was no exception. Running in the city was even worse than running on a treadmill. While that was simply boring, this was infuriating. Every time he got fast enough to give himself a workout, he ran across a stoplight or a crowd. By the time he reached the Chicago Temple building, the heat and humidity had him sweating, and his frustration had him red in the face.

"You look miserable," Nia said.

"I'm fine," Tate grumbled. "Are we going in, or what?" He looked past her to glance at the schedule, but Nia was already shaking her head.

"There's no meeting here tonight. This was just a convenient spot to meet up. No one eavesdrops in a church."

"You haven't been to church much, have you?" Tate asked, grabbing the door for Nia. But she frowned, not moving.

"That's not a bad point. Feel like going for another run?"

Not even remotely. "You're hardly dressed for it."

"I always hit the gym with my nephews after work, so I keep clothes in the car. I'll change."

She grabbed a gym bag from the back of her SUV, which was

parked conveniently right outside the building. With the police lights on top.

"Did you abuse your police powers to get this spot?"

"Shut up or I'll arrest you."

"Fair enough."

Five minutes later, Nia was changed and the two were running through the busy streets. The nearest park wasn't even a half mile away, but the Loop was a stupidly busy part of town. After ten minutes, they were both annoyed, running in place at a light just across the street from Millennium Park. Nia bent over to stretch, and the sight of her muscled legs and arms made him realize he wasn't the only one using excessive exercise to cope with an addictive personality.

"Light," Tate said.

Nia popped back up, and they ran across the street, weaving around the crowds until they were in the park. Tourists flocked to the area, but as Tate and Nia passed the famed Chicago Bean, the crowds thinned out enough for them to pick up the pace. Tate glanced at their distorted forms in the metal as they rushed by.

Now that they weren't surrounded by people, he expected Nia to say something. But she was silent.

"So, were we going to talk, or did you really just bring me here to run?" Tate huffed.

She took in a deep breath. "We'll talk. I just love this feeling," she said, her exhale only a little choppy. "Feet pounding on the pavement, breeze in your face . . ."

"Exhaust in your lungs, bugs in your teeth, yeah, I get it. What's up?"

The serenity dripped off her face like perspiration. "We need to make a plan for you to distract Connor."

"Okay, when?"

"Rumor has it, his daughter's engagement party is tomorrow night."

"You're kidding."

"It's the perfect opportunity. We know exactly where he and Cynthia will be, and we know they'll be gone for a long time."

Tate's feet hit the ground a little harder than necessary. "Right, so why on earth would you need me there? You'll have hours to search the house."

"It'll *take* hours to search a house that size, not to mention Connor's office and safe deposit boxes. We need to know if he changes plans or gets a suspicious phone call or gets tipped off somehow. He could have ways to destroy evidence that we can't control. And before you say we should just put someone undercover on the catering staff, Cynthia personally approved the entire staff—they've had background checks and have all worked together before. If something is fishy, they'll smell it."

Beads of sweat streamed down his face. "If you don't think Connor will just have security kick me out on sight, you've lost your mind."

Her eyes tightened. "I know. That's where we're counting on your charms."

"Again, I'm not a prostitute."

"No, but you are a silver-tongued devil. You can talk your way out of anything, if you want to."

He pumped his arms harder, picking up the pace until it felt harried. "Nia, I couldn't even get Alex to break up with her boyfriend when the guy was cheating on her *and* she hates him. How can I talk Connor into letting me stay at his daughter's engagement party? Or Cynthia, for that matter? If you think Connor hates me, you haven't seen anything yet."

Abruptly, Nia stopped. He stopped a couple of paces beyond her and turned back around. She was panting, and her black hair was starting to curl at the temples.

"What's really going on? Why are you so reluctant all of a sudden?" she asked, breathing heavily.

He swiped the back of his hand across his forehead, flinging sweat onto the path. "There's just a lot on my plate right now, okay? Exams, things with my mom's health. The, you know," he hesitated, "addict thing."

"Those are legitimate concerns, Tate, but you're thinking too small. A year from now, will your mom's health be any different if you help me?"

"No," he admitted.

"Will you be any less an addict?"

"I hope—"

"No. The answer is no. That's not something that goes away, even after you stop the behavior, okay? Now, will your grades have materially suffered?"

"Maybe—"

"Of course not. It's one night, and we both know you could ace your finals in your sleep. If anything, it'll do you good to stop obsessing about school for a few hours."

He ran a hand over his sweat-slicked hair. "Yeah, you're probably right," he said.

He didn't mean it.

The truth he wanted badly to suppress, to bury so deep down inside it couldn't be seen, let alone acknowledged, was that since he'd started being honest with himself, he hadn't *felt* like himself. For years, he'd felt smarter and mentally tougher than everyone in the room. He could spot weaknesses in people and know how to exploit them almost instantly without revealing anything of consequence in return. He had *lived* poker, even when he wasn't at the tables. He'd thought he was invincible. Learning that he wasn't, but rather, that he was as weak as anyone he'd ever taken advantage of—it changed everything. He felt exposed and broken, and not even his overwhelming desire to take Connor down could change that. Old Tate would have been all over this job, and he would have executed it flawlessly. Post-Epiphany Tate was a major friggin' buzzkill.

Nia slapped his shoulder, and they returned to running.

"A year from now, you helping me keep a corrupt man out of politics will matter. Twenty years from now, it will still matter. You have to see that."

He was already panting. "Yeah, I see that."

"You can do this," she said.

He hoped she was right.

When Tate got back home to his parents' that night, he went straight to his old room. He tried to study, but his eyes kept sliding off the page, and his hands kept fumbling, searching for a deck of cards, for a comfort that wasn't there.

The following morning, Tate was heading out the door early when his dad waved at him from his office. The older man opened the French doors and smiled. "How are you feeling about today's exams?"

Tate adjusted the shoulder strap of his bag. "Nervous, but I should do well enough."

"I'm sure you'll do great," his dad said. And just like that, they were shifting back into safe territory, as they always had. "And how was the meeting last night?"

Or maybe not.

"It was fine. Thanks for asking, Dad," he said, wishing the lie didn't taste so bitter in his mouth. He'd lied to his dad a thousand times in his life. Why did this one bother him? Particularly when he was only following Nia's orders? He couldn't tell his dad. It could compromise everything if Tate opened his mouth. It could put him in prison.

"I'm glad the meeting was good. I'm sorry I didn't have the chance to bring you home afterward," his dad said, his eyes looking a little too tight.

He knows there was no meeting. "Yeah, it wasn't at the regular spot, so I thought it'd be easier to have Nia take me home. But they still had cookies and juice at the end, so I'm not complaining," he said, trying to make his smile look genuine. The wrinkles in his dad's eyes eased up. Mostly.

What is wrong with you? Only days ago, you could have sold that lie in your sleep. Keep it together!

He removed his bag from one shoulder and swung it on to the other. "I'll be studying late with a couple of friends from class, but I'll be home tomorrow when finals are officially over. Maybe we—do you think we could talk then? About everything?"

His dad's face relaxed the rest of the way. "I'd like that. Good luck with your exams, son. No matter what, I'm proud of you."

Those four words. He wanted them to sink in to the dark corners of his mind, into his every subconscious thought. He wanted to accept them, to revel in them. But right now, they felt hollow. Weighty, too. As if he was being entrusted with something so big and important he could never live up to the expectations attached to it. He swallowed. "Thanks, Dad."

Several hours later, he was in his apartment with Nia and a surveillance guy, getting wired up. For the life of him, he couldn't remember a single question on his finals earlier. He couldn't remember if they'd been essays or multiple choice or true and false.

All he knew was that a couple dozen scratch-offs would hit the spot right now.

"You clean up nicely, for a frat boy," Nia said.

Tate adjusted the cuffs of his suit. It was a nervous tic. His dad's nervous tic, to be precise.

When had he adopted a nervous tic?

He shook out his hands. "Yeah, it's a nice suit."

Nia asked the surveillance guy to take a break, and she pulled

Tate aside. "You've been off since yesterday. Want to tell me what this is really all about?"

He did. He wanted to tell her that he was afraid of everything—that he was afraid of himself—because she was the one person who would be able to understand. But now wasn't the time. Nia needed him. She was counting on him in a way that no one ever had, which meant he needed to stuff down his insecurities and keep them there. He'd have plenty of opportunity to break down in twenty-four hours, after Connor was busted and his finals were over. For now, he could keep from cracking under the pressure. Of course he could.

With a deep breath, he looked her in the eye. "I was distracted, but I'll be fine, Nia. And you should really talk to someone about your obsession with frat boys. It's unseemly."

She patted his face a bit too hard. "There's my boy."

Nia called the tech guy, Stew, back over to finish the job. Twenty minutes later, Tate was straightening his tie in the mirror as Nia reminded him of protocols and code words for an emergency. Then she reminded him again.

"And don't forget," Nia was saying for the third time, "the recording device is in the tie clip, so as long as you don't drop it in a wine glass, we'll easily be able to pick up anyone within fifteen yards."

"Got it."

"And don't get your head wet, or it'll kill your earpiece."

"Is that likely?"

"It is if someone throws her drink in your face."

"Got it."

"And remember that Connor needs to stay occupied until I give you the signal."

"Nia, I got it," he said firmly. "Can we do this already?"

Her eyebrows shot up. "Look who's ready to go now."

"I'm mostly ready for you to chill. We've been over this plenty, and my job is a cakewalk. I just have to keep Connor occupied, which amounts to little more than watching him schmooze Alex's party guests."

"You're right. You're right." Nia squeezed her temples before dropping her hand and looking at him. "Okay, I'm going to set up with the rest of the team. The party starts in two hours. We'll be tracking him as he leaves his mansion and gets to the hotel, but you need to tell me the second he enters the reception, okay?"

"Okay. Got it. Now go! You'll hear from me soon enough, okay?"

She nodded and walked toward his door. As she pulled it open, she gave him a tight smile. "I know it doesn't feel like it, but what you're doing is big, Tate. I'm proud of you."

The weight of Nia's words heaped onto the weight of his dad's earlier that day. So much was riding on this. So many people were looking to him to succeed.

He'd never been so afraid he'd fail.

CHAPTER TWENTY-NINE

Tate arrived at La Piazza hotel an hour early to give himself time to watch for Connor. The earpiece Nia had given him sat deep in his ear so as to be undetectable. She'd said it was so small he would barely be able to feel it. Still, Tate found himself wanting to tug on his earlobe as he waited on the seventh floor of the hotel, wandering the halls outside of the Lakeview reception room. He had his phone out to give himself the appearance of being occupied.

"Movement on Wolf," someone on Nia's team said. Despite the fact that Connor was miles away, Tate's pulse tripled.

"What in the world do you think you're doing here?" a woman's voice said.

It took Tate a moment to realize that the voice wasn't coming from the earpiece. He turned around to see Cynthia Wolf.

"Mrs. Wolf, what a surprise to see you," he said, his thoughts scattering in his head like a deck of cards.

She looked impeccable, as always, in a gold dress fitted perfectly to her. Anyone else, he would have complimented. But the fire raging in her eyes told him how unwelcome that would be, even if he'd had the inclination to flatter her. Which he didn't.

"Mr. Bertram, if you came here to try to talk Alex out of her engagement, you will find yourself painfully disappointed."

He almost laughed. "I didn't come here for your daughter."

"I don't believe you, and I am seconds from calling the police to tell them about the pathetic jilted boy stalking my family."

"I'm not stalking anyone—"

Her glare was molten. "Then why are you here?"

Tate scrambled to collect his thoughts, picking one almost at random. "Because I have nowhere else to turn, and I need your help," he blurted.

"My help? You have to be kidding."

"Yours and your husband's," he said, and Cynthia's eyes went wider, the slight lift in her eyebrows telling him to go on. "My mom was in the hospital this weekend with a bad fibro-flare. You don't know my mom very well, but this is the first time she's ever been hospitalized. I . . . I don't think her doctors are treating her appropriately, but when I tried to tell my dad this, he threatened to throw me out of the hospital."

"Why would he do that?"

Tate swallowed big and hard. "Because of what happened with Nora's campaign this weekend."

"Are you admitting that you're responsible for the leak?" Cynthia asked. Nothing about her expression changed, yet the energy in her body seemed to shift, as if she was getting ready to pounce. She didn't realize that they both knew Alex was responsible.

He cleared his throat. "No, not directly. But I took that video of Nora, and I don't always keep the best company. So I have to assume someone hacked my phone." He tugged the corner of his mouth up in a small, self-deprecating sneer.

"So you decided to crash an engagement party to ask for my help finding your mother a new specialist? Did you honestly think that would work?"

"Did I honestly have another choice?" Tate asked. "You hate me. If I'd called your home or left a message with your assistant, would you have responded?"

"No."

"And it's not like I'm crashing the party itself. I came early to talk to you so I wouldn't make a scene." A memory from the night of the debate came to mind. Sascha growling at Cynthia. The vocal markers of emotion in her voice. "I had a feeling that ambushing you in the middle of an event to request a medical favor wouldn't have the intended effect."

It was the right touch. Her demeanor flipped like a switch, and she shook her head, smiling patiently. "No, it certainly wouldn't have. I suppose I should thank you for your discretion. I'm happy to help your mother, Tate. I'll have my assistant research specialists and she'll be in touch with you tomorrow. Now, please excuse me—"

Before she could take a step, Tate pressed his advantage. "While I'm here, Mrs. Wolf, do you think there's any chance I could speak to your husband tonight?"

"Of course," she assured him. "In fact, now that we're clear that you're not here in a disruptive capacity, why don't I add your name to the guest list? A few guests canceled this morning, anyway, so we would love to have you for the evening."

"Wow, thank you. It'll be nice to congratulate Alex. I hope we can put everything else behind us."

"As do I." Her smile would have looked more natural on a snake. "Now, if you'll excuse me, I need to go make sure everything is set up for the party. I'll see you soon."

She squeezed his arm as she passed him on her way to the ban-quet hall.

Tate hadn't realized how fast his heart was pounding or how tightly he'd been wound until Cynthia was out of sight. He exhaled loudly, almost jumping when Nia's voice sounded in his ear. *"What the hell just happened?"*

"You got me," he muttered quietly, watching the door she'd just walked through.

"I'm starting to think that prostitution idea of yours may have teeth."

"Not as many teeth as her smile."

"You said you didn't want to ambush her at an event—why would that prompt a 180?"

"Sascha."

"Sascha?"

"Sascha Lunov. He's a . . . I don't know what he is. A guy I know. I overheard Sascha hitting up Cynthia at the debate for medical help. She must suspect that I overheard and now she thinks I'm threatening her." Nia didn't respond. "Everything okay on your end?" he mumbled.

"I switched over to private comms. Tate, I don't have time to get into this, but you knowing Sascha Lunov . . . it's freaking me out. He's my informant. I think there's more to this whole thing than he's telling me. Keep your eyes open tonight, okay?" She paused. *"We just got word that Connor left. He's on his way. We'll wait until you confirm that he's there before we start our search. Let me know the minute you have eyes on him."*

A little while later, the banquet hall was starting to fill, and Alex and Brooks had walked through the doors arm in arm. Tate waited until most of the guests had arrived before walking past the guest book and into the stunning banquet hall.

True to its name, the Lakeview room boasted breathtaking views of Lake Michigan through the windows that lined the walls. The room was done up in ivory and gold and was lit by hundreds of candles. The atmosphere was too muted for the occasion, though. Funereal rather than celebratory. And the faces all around him were too false, too made up. Just being in the room made him want to take a shower.

That feeling intensified when Tate saw Connor walk in, right at seven.

"Bark at the moon," Tate said under his breath. "I have eyes on Wolf."

"Was that an Ozzy Osbourne reference?" the tech guy asked appreciatively.

"Stay focused," Nia cut in before Tate could respond. She yelled out orders to her team, and Tate pulled on his earlobe, wishing for a volume knob.

That was when Connor spotted him through the crowd of mingling guests. He looked furious, like a volcano already spewing ash. He said something to Cynthia, who put her hand softly on his arm. Her face changed, becoming entreating and seductive. She had so much more expression than he'd ever seen before, and Connor ate up every word, wearing his devotion to her like a badge. Connor loved her. Tate didn't know how he'd missed it all this time, but Connor genuinely loved his wife.

That knowledge must have made Alex's neglect all the more poignant. Tate had wondered if Connor was too blinded by ambition to even feel love, but that wasn't the case. Tate glanced at Alex, who was standing with her vapid fiancé, sneaking jealous glances at her parents while guests tried to get her attention. She returned to them, flashing her charm, but Tate could see the plain, painful truth: Alex knew her father could love. And she knew he didn't love her.

Tate wished he could summon up anger or righteous indignation for Alex. It wasn't that he'd stopped caring for her—far from it—but the cracks that had worked their way through him had let too much emotion through. He was awash in sorrow. He was disgusted with her. He was heartbroken for her.

No. He had to stop thinking about Alex. It was time to harness the cold fury that would carry him through the night. Because Connor was already walking over, and he could not mess this up.

"I'm sorry to hear about your mother's condition," Connor said.

"Thank you, Mr. Wolf."

"But let me be clear," Connor continued over him. "Whatever you've said to convince my wife that you're actually a decent guy, let alone someone who should be at Alex's engagement party, I don't buy it."

His heart jumped into his throat. "I don't blame you."

A wry chuckle escaped Connor's lips. "Points to you for honesty, I suppose. Now why did you want to speak with me?"

"Because, thanks to you, I'm out of a job."

"Thanks to me?"

"Yes. I don't know if you ordered your staff to hack my phone and get that video of Nora, but we both know I didn't plant it, and I didn't get a penny out of it. So the way I see it, the least you can do is give me the job you offered me a couple of months ago at your house."

Another, bigger laugh this time. "Why are you so sure your phone got hacked? How do you know that someone else didn't leak it?" he taunted, dangling Alex's betrayal in front of his face.

"Oscar's loyalty is as much morality as self-preservation. He's ultrareligious and has a big family. He'd never risk something so stupid."

"And no one else had the video?"

"Only your daughter. And why would she betray the aunt who loves her more than her own parents do?" Tate asked with a healthy dose of venom.

"You have the world all figured out, don't you?"

"Everything but you. Why don't you care about her, Wolf? Why isn't she enough for you?"

"You know *nothing*, you naive little prick. I have given her a life that people only dream of. What is that, if not love?"

"Convenience. You're rich. It's not like buying her things is hard. But spending time with her? Talking to her? *Listening* to her? That takes effort. And she's not worth that to you, is she?"

Nia's voice exploded in Tate's ear. *"WHAT ARE YOU DOING?"*

Tate winced. "Never mind. I'm projecting my own daddy issues, and that's not what I came here for."

Connor looked sharply at Tate. "You came here for a job. Did you think insulting me would help you succeed?"

Tate rubbed his forehead. How had he let himself get so carried away? He wasn't here for Alex. He had to remember that. "Listen, it's been a hard week, and I'm a hothead sometimes. But I could be valuable to you, if you give me the chance."

"As what?"

"An intern, a gopher, anything. Nora fired me and my dad won't take a chance on me again. I need a job and I need the experience if I'm going to get into any law school worth my time."

"I'm supposed to believe that a delinquent punk like you cares that much about his future?"

"My future is the only thing I have left."

Connor shook his head. "What good would you be to me? Look at you: you're a joke. You're hot and cold, you're a mess of tells. I need people on my staff who can be professional, even when they're desperate."

"Mr. Wolf, please—" he begged.

"No. I'm done talking to you. I'm here for Alex, and I've wasted too much of my time talking to you already." He looked around the room. "My wife already said you could stay for the party, so I won't kick you out. But if I see you after tonight, you'll be wishing this had ended in that alley."

CHAPTER THIRTY

Tate left the banquet hall and strode down a long corridor, looking for a restroom or closet or stairwell, somewhere—*anywhere*—he could hole himself up and figure out what the hell he was supposed to do now. Nia's constant stream of obscenities wasn't helping.

"How could you do that, Tate? He just threatened to finish the job, you reckless—"

Tate pulled on his earlobe, wanting to rip the stupid earpiece out and smash it to pieces. "I messed up, but I can fix this."

"How can you fix this? You gave him absolutely no reason to believe you, let alone listen to you! You were a train wreck!"

"I had a plan! I thought it would work!"

"No, you were pouting like some spoiled, desperate little frat boy, and he saw right through it. He's on to you, and we're screwed. I'm screwed. This is a joint task force with the FBI, Tate! I went out on a serious limb vouching for you!"

Disappointment dripped from her words like acid. He pushed open a door into a stairwell and dropped onto the concrete, holding his head.

Nia's breathing was ragged, as if she was trying to get ahold of herself. *"We've searched a fraction of the house. This place is enormous, and there are literally thousands of places he could be hiding the evidence."*

"I know. I get it, okay? I get it!" He hated how small he sounded in his own ears. He hardly recognized the voice as his own.

Evidently, Nia didn't either. Abruptly, her tone shifted. *"Are . . . are you okay?"*

"No."

She breathed again. *"Is it just this? Your conversation with Connor, or—?"*

"What do you think?"

She cursed. *"I can't believe I forgot. That feeling, the first time I knew I was an addict. I can't believe I forgot how terrified I was. How out of control. How pathetic."*

"Gee, thanks," he said, rubbing his nose.

"Everything you're feeling right now is a lie, Tate. I'm sorry I forgot all of this. And tomorrow, I will gladly talk to you for hours about it. But we don't have that luxury right now, because we still have nine thousand square feet of this creepy mansion to go over and only a couple of hours to do that. So I need you to squelch every emotion in your body and think of something that could help."

Squelch every emotion? He kept thinking about what Connor had said to him—worse even than Nia calling him a spoiled, desperate train wreck, worse than Connor threatening his life.

Connor had called him a joke. Hot and cold. A mess of tells.

And wasn't that exactly how he was acting? He was adjusting cuff links and rubbing his head and trying to rip that earpiece out of his head. What had he missed in trying to hide his exposed veins? Tate slammed his eyes shut and focused, trying to remember everything Connor had said, everything the man had done.

"I don't know, Nia. You were listening. He tried to bait me by hinting that Alex released the video. He doesn't care about her."

"I heard all that. What did you see, *Tate?"*

"Um—"

"I can't believe what I'm about to say: I need you to think like a poker player."

Tate frowned. "Nia, are you sure—"

"I'm not asking you to enter a tournament, I'm asking you to bury your emotions and listen to your instincts. Can you do that for me? Can you just breathe for a minute and use your head?"

Tate closed his eyes and inhaled, counting to ten before allowing himself to exhale just as slowly. It barely made a dent in his nerves.

Think like a poker player, he repeated.

Okay. He could do that. He inhaled, remembering the smell of his old card room and holding it in his lungs for a long moment. He imagined sitting at a table, that excited, unstoppable feeling he always had when he sat across from his opponents. When the cards were dealt, though, a stillness always fell on him. The noise of the night faded away, and his concentration deepened.

The despair he'd been steeped in lessened, and it was as if a haze was lifting in his mind. "Connor thinks he's the smartest person in the room, always. His confidence makes him more aggressive than I think he realizes. He's crafty, but inflexible. He loves control and power. He's obviously good at holding back, and his reputation is intimidating. But he can't hide every emotion," Tate said, remembering Connor's face when Cynthia spoke to him. "And he's obsessed with his wife."

"How is that relevant?"

"I don't know. But he's seriously devoted to her. I don't know why Alex doesn't warrant that same love or if he just doesn't know how to spare love for anyone else."

"Huh. Okay. So he's overconfident, loves his wife, but not his daughter."

The image of Vivienne's nursery came to mind, and the outline of Connor's footprints on the plush carpet. "He takes losses hard.

Cynthia was pregnant and they lost the baby at birth. They still have the nursery set up, and Connor goes in there sometimes. I don't think he's gotten over that loss, and I bet that translates to everything in his life. Poker, cases, elections, everything."

"Okay," Nia said. *"Okay, that's good. I'll tell our profiler and see if he can use any of that."* He could hear the sound of papers shuffling on Nia's end. *"You can stay at the party, but steer clear of Wolf. All you have left to do is tell me when he leaves, okay?"*

"Okay," he said, but his mind was whirring, and Tate was left with a different feeling than he'd had all night: determination.

Nia had said it herself: he needed to think like a poker player. And to think like a poker player, he needed to start acting like one.

When Tate returned to the engagement party, he shut off all emotion. He was done letting the sight of Alex or Cynthia or Connor faze him. This was no different than his thirteenth time watching *Lights Out.* This was nothing compared with the time he dislocated his shoulder after he and Yates fell out a window freshman year when campus security busted up their buddy's game. Tate hadn't blinked, let alone cried out in pain, when an officer stopped them only fifty yards from the window. He hadn't broken a sweat at any point during the officer's ten-minute rant about the Cubs' chances that year. And when Tate convinced Yates to pop his shoulder back in later that night, he'd barely made a sound.

He was steady. In control. Imperturbable.

And he was glad of that when he saw a familiar face up ahead, serving appetizers. He moseyed over to the attractive server.

"Excuse me," he said, taking a prosciutto and melon skewer.

Karla turned politely to him, tensing when they made eye contact. She gave him a strained smile, looking around to see if anyone else was within hearing distance. An older gentleman took a skewer from her tray and started eating it beside them. Tate took a bite, eating slowly enough for the older man to finish first. Karla smiled at the man. "Can I get you anything else, sir?"

He took another, smiling back.

Karla's feet shuffled nervously.

"I'll have another, too," Tate said to her, pointing to a mouth that wasn't as full as he was making it sound. "Just a minute."

The man patted Karla and returned to his table. When he was out of earshot, Karla adopted a polite smile, still darting her eyes back and forth. "What are you doing here?"

"Just came for the appetizers," he said, taking another skewer. "But if you have anything more substantial, I wouldn't say no."

She dropped her voice even lower. "I believe the main course will be served later in the Astor room," she said, looking pointedly at the far end of the banquet hall. "They're serving your favorite." Tate noticed an unassuming door against the wall that must have connected to a smaller side room. Overflow for events, probably, but tonight, it was being put to considerably more interesting use. "You'd be surprised by some of the guests who share your tastes," Karla said.

He felt a kick of emotion but ignored it just as another server walked by, shooting Karla a dirty look.

"Looks like I've taken up enough of your time," Tate said. "Thanks for the brain fuel." He held up his empty skewer.

Her smile was tense. "Be careful."

"I think you mean *bon appétit.*"

"That too," she said, walking quickly past him.

Tate surveyed the room, happy to see that none of the Wolfs were watching him. Alex was standing in an informal receiving line with her loser fiancé. His parents stood on one side and her parents on the other. She and her mother wore identical plastic smiles, down to the hint of a sneer that tugged the left side of their mouths up a bit too much. For whatever Alex's issues were with her mother, she'd learned from her well. Too well. But that was Brooks's problem now.

Connor was shaking the hand of a short, stout man with a pelt of thick dark hair. The man laughed at something and Tate caught a glimpse of Michael Landolfo. That was to be expected. So who were the surprise players? The low lighting made it tough to see faces, and while some people congregated around cocktail tables, others didn't. Tate was going to have to walk around the room and hope that didn't arouse suspicion.

No, not hope. Ensure. Nothing was stopping him tonight.

He smilingly made his way around tables, weaving in and out of groups with a polite word or joke. He took note of everyone who looked particularly rich or more powerful than the others. But that was next to impossible. Everyone here was wealthy, but they weren't wearing name badges. He wouldn't know the CFO of a major corporation from Alex's first-grade teacher. And while he spotted Mayor Salter's telltale gray pearls before he could clearly see her face, her presence could be a coincidence; her husband was a surgeon at Mercy General, where Cynthia served on the board. And the appellate court judge Tate recognized as a friend of his father's could just as easily be a friend of the Wolfs.

"Nia, are you listening?" he mumbled.

A moment later, a man's voice popped into his ear. It was Stew, the tech guy from earlier. *"She's talking to the captain. What's up?"*

"Nothing. I was just thinking it would be nice if we could get a look at the guest list."

"Good idea," Stew said.

Tate paused. "Cool, so are you hacking that, or something?"

Stew laughed. *"This isn't TV, buddy. Hacking into a database for La Piazza, the catering company, or the wedding planner would require a warrant, which I don't have. And it would probably take hours even if I had it. You want that list, you're on your own."*

Tate bit his tongue. Nothing good would come out of getting frustrated. "Thanks, Stew."

He resumed his walk around the room, but now he was looking for Karla. He spotted her serving a woman that . . .

No. No, no, no.

Nora was here.

A grenade of expletives exploded in his mind.

It doesn't matter, he told himself. *You're here to keep Wolf occupied. She couldn't think less of you than she does, so whether she sees you or not, nothing changes.*

But it could hurt her.

Yeah. Suck it up.

That's right. He had to keep cool. Stay in the game.

He waited until Karla's tray was empty and wended around the room to intersect her path before she left the room for a new tray. She gave him the same smile she gave everyone else when she saw him.

"Any more of those prosciutto and melon skewers?" he asked.

The other servers were rushing by too quickly to take note of them, but Karla was quiet, all the same, hissing through her smile. "Are you trying to get me fired?"

Tate took a small step closer to her, speaking softly. "Where can I find the guest list?"

"I'll take a picture of it and text it to you, but you have to stop pulling me aside, Tate. We're being watched like hawks here." Her eyes jumped around the room before stopping somewhere behind Tate. He made a point of not turning around, of keeping his eyes on her as he shifted the conversation. Someone was coming.

He held his hands up and took a step back. "Hey, I clearly misread the situation," he said more loudly. "I thought you were flirting, but looks like you weren't. I'm sorry to bother you."

Her eyes snapped back to his. "Thanks for understanding. Now I need to get back to my job, okay?"

A hand fell on Tate's shoulder. "I'm sorry my guest was harassing you," Alex said. "He won't do it again. I promise."

Karla flashed a desperate smile and disappeared. Meanwhile, Alex spun Tate around to face her. "Why are you here?" she asked, her eyes desperate and her breath laced with alcohol. She had a drink in her free hand. He wondered how much she'd have to drink to get through this night.

"I'm not here for you, Alex. I'm not going to make some grand gesture to try to break you two up. You clearly want a life with him, and I'm not going to stop you."

Her reaction wasn't at all what he expected. Instead of nodding or throwing him out, she blinked her glassy eyes, and he could see the hope in them dim. "I didn't think you were here for me," she said softly. "Are—are you going to tell Nora?"

If he'd allowed himself to feel anything, the crack in her voice would have pierced his defenses. But his heart was steel.

He spoke as bluntly as possible to hammer in every point. "I'm here for a job, okay? You alienated me from my family so that you could ingratiate yourself with yours. I think the least you can do is let me beg your dad for a job now that I'm cut off."

This seemed to hurt her more than him admitting he wasn't going to break up her wedding. She rocked back on her heels. "You're asking my dad *for a job*? Why would you do that?"

"Because something tells me there won't be questions about ethics in the interview." He leaned in. "You owe me, Alex. I'm not going to let you ruin my life."

She pressed her hand to the side of her face, not making eye contact with him. Not looking at anything, really. "You know, for a minute, I really wanted it to be you."

"Excuse me?"

"I tried so hard! I thought if my parents got to know you, they'd like you, and you and I could just . . ." A sob escaped her. "But you wouldn't play along, Tate! You sabotaged every plan—"

"No, Alex," he said, his voice sharp with warning. "You don't get to drop that bomb on me. Not here. Not now."

The hand holding her drink trembled. "I just want this to be over."

Tate's laugh punched the air between them. "You're kidding, right? This will *never* end, because you chose this. Everything you did to me, to her—you brought this on yourself."

Her eyes squeezed shut, and he knew without question that her reaction was real.

He didn't care.

Before she had time to open her eyes, Brooks was on his way to them. "Hey, if it isn't the star of your dad's campaign," Brooks said, putting his arm around Alex's waist.

"That's funny. You're a funny guy, Brooks," Tate said, already weary of his presence.

Alex swatted Brooks's chest, looking bright and teasing and as if she wasn't on the verge of a nervous breakdown. "Oh, don't say that. Tate's here to congratulate us."

"Could've fooled me," Brooks said. "The Rushworths just showed up. Let's go," Brooks said, looking at the entrance.

"Brooks—"

"You're really going to stay here and talk to him?" Brooks asked. "Fine. Come find me when you're done." And he was gone.

A million thoughts sprang to mind. A thousand nasty words were on the tip of his tongue. He swallowed them down. "Looks like you're needed elsewhere." He hesitated for a moment before giving her a hug. "Good luck, Alex."

She held on to him a bit too long, and when he released her, she turned without saying anything. He didn't watch her go.

♠

When the party was winding down, Tate finally got a text from Karla.

IF U GET ME FIRED, I END U

Beneath that was the guest list. He saved the photo, sent her a GIF of a tackle hug, and deleted her text. Then he sent the photo to Nia and Stew. "Nia? Stew? You guys seeing this?"

"Looking at it now," Nia said over a clamor in the background. *"This is a who's who of powerful people in Chicago. Mayor Salter, Senator Rushworth, Virginia Gallo—"*

"Who's that?"

"She's the CEO of Gallo Construction. It's an impressive list. But I don't know what you want me to do with it."

Tate held his phone up to his ear, as if he was just taking a call instead of speaking into his tie clip. "You missed it earlier, but Connor's hosting a little private game in the hotel tonight."

"You're kidding."

"Nope."

"This is perfect! We'll have hours to search without having to worry about him showing up on us." She exhaled loudly, and it seemed to echo all the way into his ear canal. *"You're a genius, Tate. You're off the hook."*

"2002 called. It wants its slang back."

"No, literally. As soon as the party's over and you can verify that Connor and his little crew are playing poker, you can head home. I'll keep a couple of plainclothes around the hotel, and they can let me know whenever he leaves. We can even have them detain Connor and the others on suspicion of gambling, or something."

"That's not so easy when that game could include a lawyer, a senator, an appellate judge, and the mayor, among others." Tate leaned up against a wall, glancing around the room and still talking into the phone for show. When Nia didn't answer right away, he continued. "Maybe they won't be playing, but don't we have to assume that at least some of these powerful people are staying for Wolf's game?"

Her answer was curt. Suspicious. *"Yes."*

"Then you need me to stay."

"No."

"If I can get into that room, Nia—"

"No."

"—then I can find out firsthand what's going on. What if we find more corruption, more politicians for sale? Isn't that something you *need* to know? I'm already wearing a wire!"

"Leaving aside the fact that Connor threatened you, we don't have a warrant! If there are judges in the room and you record them without their knowledge, that's a Class 3 felony!"

"Fine, don't record it. I can still inform on everything, right? Aren't I your CI?" More labored breathing on her end. "Come on. Think this through: you need me. I can help."

"You can't gamble," she said, her voice cracking. She wasn't forbidding, she was begging. *"Please, don't do this, Tate."*

"I don't see what other choice I have."

She sounded as if she wanted to cry. If he hadn't erected a fortress around his heart, he might have felt the same way. But he wasn't Tate the Addict right now. He felt more like himself than he had in days, maybe months. Because he knew who he was. Yes, he was an addict, but he was also a damn good poker player. And tonight, he was going to win the biggest hand of his life.

"I'm doing this, Nia. We can talk about the rest later."

"Please don't. The information isn't worth this."

"Yeah, it is. You said it yourself: this is a lot bigger than me."

There was a pause, and then: *"Don't you step near that game until I give you the okay. I'm getting that damn warrant."*

Nia went silent. Tate wasn't sure if she was still listening or if it was just Stew. Either way, though, he didn't need either of them for his next order of business. He pulled out his phone and texted Sascha.

CHAPTER THIRTY-ONE

When the party was all but over, Tate had counted six people who had slipped into the Astor Room instead of leaving with the rest of the guests, and he'd sent pictures of each of them to Nia to help with the warrant. Nora had left without making eye contact with him, which was a relief, given what he still needed to do. Alex and Brooks were saying good-bye to the last stragglers. He'd over-heard Cynthia talking about staying the night in the hotel, which he instantly passed on to Nia. If Cynthia wasn't going home, either, the coast really was clear.

But that wasn't remotely the point anymore.

Nia's job was finding the evidence of Connor's misdeeds. Tate's was taking the man down.

He'd never looked forward to a job more.

A few minutes later, Alex and Brooks made their way out, leaving only Connor, Cynthia, and Senator Rushworth, who looked as if he'd recently lost weight. Tate knew the Rushworths—they were friends of his parents. Their son had dated his sister, before she was caught in a tabloid scandal with a huge star. Too bad for her, her ex, Raleigh Rushworth, was the Rookie of the Year last year and was the new face of Calvin Klein's performance wear line. Of course, Juliette had evidently reformed and was spending the summer in a yurt in Flagstaff, Arizona, with a boarding school friend.

Regardless, Tate knew the family. Raleigh was an oaf, but he wasn't a bad guy. Tate hoped the same could be said of the senator. A moment later, the senator shook Connor's hand and put his arm around his wife, leading her from the room. Connor kissed Cynthia's cheek before she followed the Rushworths out.

Connor turned around and started for the private room, where his poker game was being held. Tate waited until the door had closed before moving from his table. A few heartbeats later, he was holding on to the lever, letting the adrenaline rush through his veins and make him heady with excitement. It was always like this right before a game. The nerves, the thrill would build so much he'd want to bounce. But the second he was at that table, his hands would be steadier than a surgeon's.

Taking a slow breath, Tate pulled on the handle and walked inside.

He was met by stares.

Seven people were seated around a large table, including a slight man in a dealer's vest. He didn't need the vest. The polyester blend of his shirt marked him as the odd man out here.

With fire in his eyes, Connor turned to a brawny man. "What am I paying you for?"

The man frowned and stalked toward Tate. Tate held out a hand, looking at Connor. "Just hear me out. You said you wouldn't hire me because I was a mess earlier, right?" Connor nodded. "How about you consider this my interview?"

Nia's voice popped in Tate's ear. *"You're already in? Stall! We're still waiting on that warrant!"*

Reflexively, Tate tilted his head against the sound of Nia's voice bouncing around in his eardrum. He instantly wanted to kick himself, reacting like that. Was he trying to get caught? A jolt of nerves set his pulse racing, but Tate hardened himself, squashing the nerves like a bug. He had to stay cool. He refused to give himself away.

Connor was studying Tate when the appellate judge rubbed his bald, black head. "What's this all about, Connor?" Then to Tate: "You're Thomas Bertram's son, aren't you?"

Tate let a trace of pleading into his voice. "Yes, I'm Tate Bertram. I'm not here to disturb any of you, Judge Banks. I'm just here for a job."

"You'd accept a job against your own aunt's opponent?" the judge asked. He looked at Connor. "He and your daughter are two of a kind, aren't they? Putting political ideology over family?"

So the judge didn't know Alex was a campaign spy any more than he knew Tate was their scapegoat. Did that mean not everyone at the table was crooked? Or were they just not privy to all of the details of Connor's campaign?

A quick glance showed a table of neutral expressions. Of course. He was in a room full of politicians, lawyers, and titans of industry. And worse, they were all poker players. He couldn't expect to read them like a takeout menu.

Connor wasn't giving anything away, pasting the appropriate look of disappointment and vexation on his face. "Tate, again, I don't think Alex's engagement party is the right time for this discussion. If you'd like to come visit me in the office tomorrow, maybe we can talk."

The Muscle started for Tate again, but Tate took a step back. "Or . . . you could let me play you for it."

The others at the table—the mayor and Landolfo among them— narrowed their eyes, looking back and forth between Tate and Connor. "Are you suggesting a wager?" Connor gestured to the table, the enormous stacks of chips in front of each player. "Somehow I doubt you can afford the buy-in."

Tate thought fast. "Come on. There isn't a buy-in here."

"Why do you say that?"

"Because, by my count, we have the mayor, a judge, the chairman of the liquor control commission, and a lawyer, among other prominent citizens of our fine city, none of whom would ever indulge in illegal activities."

That earned him a few chuckles and just as many glares. But the mayor kept her eyes low. Despite her blank expression and perfect posture, she looked decidedly uncomfortable.

He could have smiled; he already knew her tell.

Judge Banks was one of those chuckling. "Why would you think a simple, social card game is illegal?"

"You and I both know that for this to fall under the category of a 'social game,' it would have to be in a private home, not a public place. That is, if social games were legal in Illinois. Unfortunately for all of us, they aren't."

Judge Banks's smile widened. "Yet you just expressed your confidence that we would never indulge in illegal activities. Are you changing your mind, Counselor?"

Next to him, a man Tate didn't recognize was fiddling with his stack of chips as he followed the conversation. A chip popped out of his stack, and his nostrils flared as he snatched it back up. Tate almost rolled his eyes. That guy would be too easy.

Tate looked at the judge. "No, I stand by what I said."

Nia spoke in Tate's ear, just as Judge Banks was saying something. *"We have the warrant! Now make those bastards sing."*

The judge smiled expectantly.

"It all goes back to what I told Mr. Wolf about the buy-in. Clearly, with so many law-abiding citizens in the room, there couldn't be a buy-in. Because," Tate smiled, looking at everyone before settling back on the judge, "as I don't have to tell any of you, the only time it's legal to play a game of skill or chance outside of a licensed gaming establishment in Illinois is when money can be won without a required upfront payment. Like, oh, McDonalds Monopoly."

"McDonalds Monopoly!" The judge slapped his knee, laughing. "I look forward to seeing you in my courtroom one day, Mr. Bertram."

Connor was grinning as widely as anyone in the room. "Well done, Tate," he said, sounding genuinely impressed. He snapped toward his security guard, then pointed toward a stack of chairs against the wall. "Pull up another chair for our young guest." He looked at Tate. "Are you ready for your interview?"

"I'd say he already passed," Landolfo said from the opposite side of the table. The well-dressed man was perfectly pleasant looking—late forties, stocky, thick dark hair and eyebrows—yet something about him set Tate's teeth on edge. "I suppose this means we're getting our money back?"

Tate covered his ears. "La la la," he said.

Even the mayor smirked at that.

"I'm happy to bankroll the fun for the evening," Connor said. "Next week you can buy me lunch."

"Yeah, I'll just have to wrap it in a Lamborghini," Landolfo said in that same grumbling tone. "Connor, you can't actually expect us to have a real game with this kid in the room."

Douchebag.

"I would have expected a little more appreciation for competition from the guy who's going to run the city's new casino," Tate said.

Connor looked at Tate, not Landolfo. "Believe me, Tate here has enough experience with gambling that you won't need to worry about him."

The subtext was clear: Connor had enough dirt on Tate to keep him quiet. Tate took his seat and watched the dealer work.

Landolfo frowned. "Well, you two are just cute as can be. The kid's been doing his homework on you to impress you, Wolf. And lucky for him it's working."

Tate peeked at his cards—two nines—before putting them down. "I actually tried to find a copy of the casino proposal to see if I could find any problems with it, make suggestions, you know, prove my worth. But I couldn't find anything."

"It's an election year, sweetie," the woman who was sitting to the left of the dealer said. She was in her fifties, maybe, wearing a flattering gray dress and a shrewd air. "Now's the time for big dreams and vague promises." She picked up the two cards in front of her, looking at her hand before putting them back down on the table. She looked at Tate. "The details come later. When it's time to break all those promises."

Connor laughed as sharply as the moment called for. He was glancing at his cards. "Really, Virginia. Are you trying to scare the boy off before the interview is over?"

"Wait, are you Virginia Gallo?" Tate asked.

A pleased smile curled the corner of her lips. "You are a very informed young man."

"I'd have to be a moron not to recognize the CEO of one of the city's biggest construction companies."

"We're hardly one of the biggest."

"With you leading it, I'm sure that'll change," Tate said.

"Enough with the flattery. Are we playing cards or kissing asses?" Landolfo said.

"It's too bad you've never learned how to do both," Virginia said, winking at Tate.

Nia groaned through the earpiece too loudly. *"Please don't tell me she's flirting with you."*

Tate held back a wince at the noise. He looked up to see Connor studying him again. Tate glanced back at his nines. It was a good enough hand to enter betting, but he wanted to observe, and as Virginia and Banks were in the blinds, it wouldn't cost him anything to watch at this point.

He and the guy fidgeting with his chips were the only ones to fold. They both threw their cards into the muck.

Connor raised, throwing chips into the pot. "You all should know that Tate here has a reputation: he never bluffs."

"Never?" The skepticism in Virginia's voice was as deep as her lipstick.

Tate shrugged. "That's what they tell me."

The betting round finished, and the dealer tossed the burn card next to the muck before dealing the flop: seven hearts, three spades, and five spades.

"Then you'll never win," Virginia said as betting continued.

Tate laughed, watching the action. "They tell me that, too."

Judge Banks bet, a strong draw. He didn't have the nut hand, but with two spades in the hole (Tate didn't feel bad peeking—he wasn't playing the hand, anyway), Banks was counting on a flush on the turn or river. "In the interest of fairness," Judge Banks said, nodding toward the fidgeting man, "Taylor's play is tighter than his wife in spandex."

The fidgeting man gave Banks a tired glare. "That's mature, Terry."

Banks continued as if the man hadn't said anything. "He's the state comptroller, yet you've never seen a man worse with money than he is."

Tate smiled. Reading Taylor was as easy as reading a kindergarten teacher's writing on a chalkboard. But Banks was easy, too. The smiling man didn't just talk when he bluffed, he taunted. Pointed, but playful. He was probably a happy drunk.

Tate hoped the man was just here for the poker.

Pushing the thought from his mind, Tate watched the others. Mayor Salter was looking around impassively as she raised. She had a strong hand then, probably a four and six in the hole, and she flopped a straight.

Connor must have agreed. He folded.

"Oh, ho, ho," Landolfo said. "Someone's taking his ball and going home?"

With a patient smile, Connor said, "I'd feel a lot more comfortable if you weren't so interested in my balls, Mikey."

Landolfo scowled, but Connor's words had the desired affect: Landolfo reraised.

Salter met the raise and called.

Virginia and Banks folded. Landolfo reraised.

They weren't even to the river, Salter obviously had the nut hand, and Landolfo was already on tilt.

What an amateur.

Salter met the raise and called again.

This time, Landolfo seemed to wise up. He looked at his cards, growled, and then mucked them, folding.

Salter smiled and claimed her pot.

Tate hadn't gotten a read on Virginia during the hand, but that would come. In a couple of hours, Landolfo and Taylor would be out, Salter a bit later. Banks and Virginia would fall somewhere around early morning.

That would leave just him and Connor.

The way Connor was looking at Tate, he knew it, too.

Game on.

CHAPTER THIRTY-TWO

Three hours later, Landolfo was on full tilt, but after winning a few big hands, he'd managed to stay in the game. The guy played like a maniac, but fortunately for Tate, he'd had a few drinks, too. And with each new drink and winning hand, his lips got a little looser.

While the others small-talked, trash-talked, bet, and called, Landolfo was like a leaky faucet, dripping tantalizing bits of information. Nia gave running commentary.

Landolfo: "Salter, you've gotten too cocky since Wheeler solved your little financing problem after that teacher scandal."

Nia: *"Tony Wheeler of Wheelz Trucks. He's been a big contributor to her reelection campaign. Rumor has it she's planning to outsource some city jobs to his company."*

Landolfo (to Comptroller Taylor, after the nervous man folded with three queens): "How are you going to fill a senate seat when you piss your pants with three ladies on the river?"

Nia: *"Wait, Taylor's planning to run for senate? Rushworth's term ends next, but he's wildly popular. No way Taylor would beat him."*

Landolfo: "That's it, Banks. Just keep being an easy mark. That'll get you elected to the Supreme Court."

Nia: *"Meh. Landolfo's just given up at this point, hasn't he? He's just saying anything that comes to his useless peabrain."*

Tate had to choke down a laugh. As much as he prided himself on his composure, having Nia in his head wasn't making this easy.

But, of course, Connor was watching, looking for Tate's tells. Connor himself was unflappable, as unflappable as Tate had always considered himself. His demeanor, his posture, his chatter—all the same whether he folded, slow-played, or went all-in. Connor wasn't as aggressive as Tate had expected, but he was relentless. Relentless and unreadable.

Just like Tate.

It was exhilarating, matching wits with someone, winning a hand against his equal. He'd never had this before. He'd lost his share of games, but that had been the hands, the circumstances, Tate being in his own head.

None of that was the case tonight. Tate was here, and he was on his game. He had a read on the room as strong as any he'd ever had. He could run the hand odds and pot odds while processing the tells of the other players in a split second. He could feel—almost like a sixth sense—when the pot was going to be his, and he was right. Every time, he was right.

And so was Connor.

The stakes were the highest of any Tate had ever played. It didn't matter that he wasn't playing with his own money. It had never been about money, but about the win. And winning against Connor would be the greatest win of his life.

"You look satisfied with your hand, Tate," Connor said.

"I'm more satisfied with that cheese plate. The aged cheddar with the candied walnuts? Mmm."

Connor chuckled, as if he believed Tate. As if everything that had happened between them was all water under the bridge and this was really just a poker game. A job interview.

What a load of crap.

A half hour later, Mayor Salter and the comptroller cashed out, so Connor called a twenty-minute break. He said good-bye to his—friends? Partners in crime?—before pulling Landolfo toward the corner of the room. They were just far enough away for Tate to hear angry hisses, but no specific words.

Nia didn't have the same problem, thanks to the wire.

"Wolf is piiiiissed," she said while Tate grabbed water from a nearby table. *"They're just about out of range, but I'm getting snippets. Connor's angry that Landolfo's running off at the mouth. Landolfo is complaining about something with the governor. I don't have the context to understand any of that, but these two do not get along."*

Tate wanted to mumble an agreement, but Judge Banks was heading his way. He stopped next to Tate, reaching for a drink.

"You're one hell of a poker player, aren't you?"

"You could say that," Tate said.

"Do I want to know how, considering you barely look old enough to enter a casino?"

"I'm not. I'll be twenty next week, actually."

The judge shook his head, a chuckle dying on his lips. "You shouldn't be here, kid."

"But poker free rolls are legal—"

"That's not what I mean. I mean if you want a job, you should look elsewhere."

"Are you offering?"

"No, you shouldn't be there, either." The judge looked around him casually. "You're smart enough to know what's going on here."

"I'm not leaving. I know why I'm here."

The judge looked at him more closely. The set of his eyes showed his disappointment. "Then when you beat me in the next hand, I expect you to make it count."

With that, Judge Banks took a drink from his water bottle and headed back to the table.

"What was that?" Nia asked in his ear.

"We'll see," he mumbled.

A few minutes later, the break was over, and everyone was back at the table watching their hands get dealt. With the mayor and comptroller both gone, the mood had shifted. If it had ever been a friendly game, it didn't feel that way now.

Virginia was acting bored, feigning a yawn. She was debating a bluff, but she had nothing. Connor was a stone wall, as always. The break hadn't done Landolfo any good. He was reckless, and he was bent on winning, no matter how mediocre his hand was. And it *was* mediocre. Tate knew from the way Landolfo was slouched back in his chair, mouthing off. When he had a good hand, he stayed upright. Still mouthing off.

What a frickin' amateur.

Banks was already teasing everyone. "Mikey, it's really too bad Governor Dalton isn't here to see what a terrible loser you are. Maybe that would convince him you can't run the casino," Banks said. He and Tate were sitting in the blinds, and they both threw their chips in.

Virginia moaned, tossing her cards into the muck. "Watching you guys measure your tiny junk is enough to make a girl want to hang herself. You know that?"

Landolfo sneered and raised. "Maybe you wouldn't have to bribe politicians to accept your bids if you weren't such a raging b—."

"Mikey, Mikey, Mikey," Banks said. "Don't tell me you think you can cast the first stone. You've been in bed with the Outfit longer than your mother. But at least she's getting paid."

The sound of Nia snorting on the other end of the wire set Tate off. He could have helped the wave of laughter that struck him. He didn't.

"Isn't this precious," Landolfo said. "Banks has a new boyfriend. You think you can keep this one from the press, too? Or from your wife?"

"You're cute when you're jealous," Banks said as the flop was dealt. He looked down at the cards and his smile widened. "Now why don't you run along, Mike. There's nothing for you here."

Landolfo told Banks exactly where to stick his advice. Betting continued, with Tate reraising when the time came.

"What do you have, kid?" Landolfo asked. "You've been slow-playing all night—"

"No, he hasn't," Virginia argued. "You just haven't noticed because you can't shut up."

"Stay out of it," Landolfo told her. His hand hovered over his last stack of chips, and Tate knew the man was trying to intimidate him by threatening to go all-in. If it wasn't so pathetic, Tate might have laughed. He hadn't paid much attention to the hand. Banks had already told him how this hand was going to go down, but even if he hadn't, this pot was Tate's.

Landolfo repeated his question. "What do you have?"

Tate glanced down at the flop. Ace diamonds, three spades, ten hearts.

"This is why you're such a terrible poker player," Tate said. "You're so concerned with what I have that you've forgotten what you have. Or don't, more accurately. Because right now, you think that ace on the table means something. Like it materially improves upon the High Five you had in the hole. Maybe you think you're strong-drawing, that you'll have another ace on the turn or the river. But that's because you're too stupid to realize that Virginia mucked an ace already, making the chances of another ace really, really low."

Virginia raised her eyebrows.

"Shut up already," Landolfo said, to no one in particular. He looked at the dealer, throwing more chips into the pot. His stack had been dangerously low before this. Now, it was laughable.

Banks called. He was down to his last few chips, too.

Tate reraised.

Landolfo cursed. "You think you're hot stuff, huh, kid?"

Tate shook his head. "No, I'm just not a donkey. You really think bluffing is going to help you right now? You have a pair of aces post-flop, but what you don't realize is that Banks and I walked into this with a pair. We both have a set, now. And mine just happens to be higher than his."

Banks looked at him sharply. Tate wasn't sure if he was hamming it up or not, but it didn't matter. "You're kidding."

Tate shrugged. "Think that if you want. You're sitting pretty with all those threes. But with my tens, I'm sitting a hell of a lot prettier."

Banks swore. "Well, that sucks," he said before mucking his cards.

Landolfo pounded his hand on the table, causing Virginia to jump. "Are you really that stupid, Banks?" Landolfo yelled. "The kid's bluffing and you fell for it!"

Tate stole a glance at Connor, who was following the action like a coyote watching sheep. Banks stood. "If he is, he's a helluva lot better at it than you are."

Landolfo shook his head. "All-in," he said, pushing his remaining chips into the pot. He flipped his cards over, revealing an ace of diamonds and a four of clubs.

"And here you thought he had an ace and a five," Banks teased. Tate smiled at the man.

At the same time, Virginia was telling Landolfo how stupid he was. "He has you covered!" Virginia said. "He has more than double your chips. You going all-in doesn't prove anything when he stays in the game regardless of who wins this hand."

"It doesn't matter," Connor said, his voice as calm as a pond on a quiet day. "He's already made his bet."

Tate called, matching the bet. But he didn't show his hand.

The dealer flipped over the turn and river next to the ten of hearts.

Five of diamonds.

Queen of clubs.

Everyone around the table looked to Tate, waiting. Even Connor seemed to be holding his breath.

Tate flipped his cards over: a pair of tens, just as he'd said.

Landolfo jumped up, cursing and knocking over his chair.

"Calm down." Virginia's tone reeked of disgust.

"I want to see the hand," Connor said, in that same mild voice.

Tate cocked his head, pointing at the table. "You're looking at it."

"Not yours," Connor said. He looked at Banks. "Yours.

Banks frowned. "I mucked my hand."

Connor looked at the dealer. "Do you know which cards were his?" The dealer nodded. "Then show me."

Banks's frown deepened. "We haven't been showing hands when we fold. What are you getting at?"

"I think you two colluded."

Banks's laugh was dark. "You saw the kid's hand. He won."

"Oh, I know he won. But I think you were bluffing to drive Mike out of the game."

Virginia's eyes narrowed. "Mike's been a maniac all night. If anything drove him out of the game, it was his own stupidity. The kid here had a read on us all."

"He had a read on you and Mike. What I want to know is if he actually had a read on Terry."

Virginia shifted in her chair, putting her arm up on the back and facing Connor. "Hang on. You claim to be a master poker player. You tell us if Terry had threes in the hole."

"I did," Banks said.

"He's not that good of an actor," Tate agreed.

"Then let's prove it." Connor looked at the dealer, nodding his head.

The dealer grabbed Terry's discarded hand and flipped the first card over: three of clubs.

"See?" Virginia said.

"He's not done," Connor said.

The dealer grabbed the second card. Virginia took in a sharp breath as the dealer flipped the card over.

Three of diamonds.

With a string of curses, Landolfo grabbed his suit coat and stormed out of the room.

Virginia blew air through her lips. "Told you," she said. "I'm cashing out."

Connor turned to her. "But you're still in the game."

"The kid's too good. With Mike out and Terry next, it's only a matter of time." She glanced back at the cashier, who was doubling as their waitress. "Cash me out?"

The woman nodded.

"I'm cashing out, too," Banks said. He looked deliberately at Connor. "I don't imagine you're surprised by this."

For the first time since Tate sat at the table, an emotion was peeking through a fracture in Connor's stone wall. He was flustered. He'd known Banks was overacting, but he hadn't known why, and he'd misread the situation because of it.

Connor patched the metaphorical crack and looked at Tate. "Why don't we take fifteen?"

"Sure," Tate said. He stood and made his way to Banks, who was putting on his suit jacket. "It was good to meet you, Judge Banks."

"You, too." The judge shook his hand. "You're smart, kid. You know what's happening here. I hope this win is worth it."

Tate put his hands in his pockets, empty except for his keys and wallet. "It always is."

Banks was walking away when he stopped and turned. "How did you know?"

"About your cards?"

"About my cards."

"I was telling the truth. You're not that good an actor. And I am that good at poker."

Banks laughed. "Yeah, I can tell by all the money I lost to you tonight."

"Wait, so Wolf didn't really 'bankroll the fun for the evening'?"

"Ha! Not hardly. The only fun he bankrolled was yours," Banks said before walking away.

"I heard that," Nia said.

Tate watched Banks and Virginia say their good-byes, watched Connor follow them out of the room. When they were gone, Tate exited through the large banquet room and out to the hall, where he went to the restroom. He walked straight into a stall, pulled out his phone, and texted Sascha.

DIDN'T NEED THE MONEY AFTER ALL. THANKS FOR OFFERING TO BANKROLL.

He pressed send, and a moment later, he heard the soft buzz of a phone. Tate flushed the toilet and stepped out of the stall to see the man himself.

"Hello, Tate."

CHAPTER THIRTY-THREE

Tate gave Sascha a once-over. "Are you okay?"

Sascha looked drawn, the area beneath his eyes sunken and almost blue. Tiny red spots dotted his face. He was wearing a tailored suit, but a black robe and reaper's scythe would have looked more appropriate. He looked like he had come to collect a soul. Or to trade his in. "I'm dying. So, no. I am not okay."

"Why are you here?"

"I heard about a poker game I didn't want to miss."

"You're an alcoholic, not a gambler."

"Are the two mutually exclusive?"

Tate frowned. "Sascha, of all the places in the city to show up, why are you here, right now? Why were you at the debate the other night talking to Cynthia?"

Sascha turned toward the sink and washed his hands. "You saw that?"

"Yes. And, believe me, I want to help you. But showing up in the middle of the night? Are you going to march into Cynthia's hotel room and demand she put you on the donor list? Are you going to hold Connor hostage? What do you think is going to happen?"

Sascha shook out his hands before putting them beneath an automatic dryer. When the air stopped, he looked at Tate. "I'm here to play poker."

"If Connor knows you and I—"

"Let me deal with Connor."

Sascha left the bathroom.

"I don't like this," Tate said. He crossed to the sink and splashed water on his face. He dried his face with a paper towel and glanced at himself in the mirror. "Nia? Stew?"

No answer.

"Nia?" He tapped on his tiepin just before fear gripped him: the water. Had he killed his mic?

No. It couldn't be that sensitive. It couldn't be. They had to still be there.

"Can you hear me? Nia?" When she still didn't answer, he squeezed the paper towel tightly in his hand—the only expression of panic he'd allow beyond the frantic clamoring of his heart. He took a deep breath, willing his heart rate to slow, before he threw the paper towel into the garbage.

He hoped he wasn't on his own.

Yelling reached his ears before he'd made it halfway through the banquet hall, but it wasn't Nia. The security guard stopped him.

"I don't think you should go in there."

"Did Mr. Wolf ask you to keep me out?"

"Not exactly."

"Then I'm going in. The break's about up, and I'm not letting Wolf screw me out of that pot."

The guard wore a heavy frown but let Tate in.

He was just in time, because Connor looked ready to take a swing at Sascha.

"Whoa, whoa, whoa!" Tate yelled, rushing between the two men. Connor strained against him, but Tate pushed him back. "Who is this guy?" Tate said, looking back and forth at them. "Don't tell me you're bringing someone else into the game now."

Connor backed up, straightening his shirt. "He isn't staying."

"He'd better not," Tate said, glaring at Connor. Then to Sascha, he said, "How did you get in here, anyway, man? You look like you should be in a hospital."

"Or a drunk tank," Connor spat.

Sascha bared his teeth. Despite his sunken eyes—or maybe in part because of them—the look was menacing. "You know she'll hate you when she finds out."

"Don't be naive, Sascha. She'll never find out, and you'll be dead before you can prove anything."

"What is going on here?" Tate asked.

"Your friend sent me to prison," Sascha said.

Tate reeled. "What?"

Connor tutted. "You fool. You sent yourself to prison."

"I did everything you asked me to do."

"Except you left a paper trail."

"You put the account in my name! I could never have known—"

"That you shouldn't touch what belongs to other people?" Connor snarled.

"You haven't had a problem claiming things that aren't yours," Sascha growled. He flexed his fist, but he was also panting. Winded. His lips stretched across his teeth in a gruesome smile. "The difference is, I never took anything that didn't want—"

"You shut your mouth!" Connor yelled, marching on Sascha again. Tate stopped him before he could do irreparable damage. Sascha looked like a strong wind could push him over.

"Enough!" Tate roared. Where was Nia? How could she have given him such a shitty mic that a tiny splash of water could break the damn thing? What was he supposed to do? She had told him to be wary around Sascha. There was more to his story, she'd said.

A lot more, obviously. But he had to rein things back in. Even if the mic was broken, he could still inform on everything, right? As much as he wanted to watch these two hash it out, he didn't know what the result would be. He couldn't control the outcome, and Nia would kill him if he screwed this up.

"Guy—Sascha, was it?" Tate asked, wanting to bite his own tongue. "I think you need to leave."

Sascha's gaze was hot enough to melt iron. "And I think you should stay out of this."

Tate looked at Connor. "What do you want me to do. Should I call the cops?"

Connor's eyes flitted to the poker table. "No. Go get that worthless security guard I hired to escort this man out of the hotel."

"Don't bother," Sascha said. "I'm leaving."

Tate stood near Connor, hands in his pockets, and watched Sascha exit.

"So, uh, that was messed up," Tate said.

"That was old news." Connor looked around the room before fixing his eyes on Tate. "How serious are you about wanting a job?"

"Deadly."

"No need to be melodramatic," Connor said. "You're a different sort, you know that? You're annoying as hell, but you're dogged and resourceful. I could use someone like you."

"Thank you—"

"The problem, though, is that I don't trust you."

"Like you trust Mike Landolfo? Or Mayor Salter? Or that . . . that milquetoast comptroller, Taylor?" Tate asked. Connor tilted his head, like he was considering. Like he was inviting Tate to continue. "This isn't a matter of trust, but of leverage. Do you want me to tell you all the casinos or private clubs I've walked into so you can pull surveillance feed as proof of my illegal underage activities? Do you want me to send you the link to the security video I kept from my own card room? I only ran it for a few months, but I'm pretty sure it would get me in a few years' worth of trouble."

"I have a better idea."

"Yes?"

"A picture."

"What?"

"I want a picture of you, me, and this poker table."

A sick feeling settled in Tate's stomach. "Why?"

"For my wall of fame. Who cares why I want it? You're offering me all sorts of damning leverage, but all I want is a picture. Isn't that better?"

"Okay . . ."

Connor pulled out his phone and held it in front of them. "Say cheese."

Tate's mouth went bone dry as he held two thumbs up. The flash went off, and Tate felt his throat close. "What are you going to do with that picture?"

Connor was already looking at his phone. His thumbs darted across his keyboard. A quiet *whoosh* sounded from the phone, and Connor smiled.

"There."

"What did you do?"

"I sent it to your parents. Told them how happy I am about my newest intern."

"Why would you do that?" Tate demanded. "I told you I'd give you all the leverage you need!"

"Yes, you did. And I've used the most important one already. Tate, you're a good poker player, but you rely too much on things like odds and even tells. What you lack is a killer instinct. It's the same problem you'll have as a lawyer if you aren't careful. Fortunately, it's a problem I plan to help you solve. This was the first step."

Hatred boiled inside of him, burning his throat, singeing his mouth. He wanted to do violence to this man. He wanted to bloody his fists on Connor's face. Wanted to wear the skin down to the bone.

No. No, no, no.

He had to switch off his emotions.

A moment later, Tate's phone started buzzing. And buzzing. And buzzing. His dad, probably. Maybe his mom. Please, not his mom. Either way, he knew they were devastated. Tears burned the back of his eyes, but no way in hell was he letting them fall. He could drown in a sea of regret tomorrow.

Tomorrow.

He would tell them everything tomorrow. He didn't care about a broken mic or about politics. He cared about repairing his relationship with his parents. He would make Nia corroborate every damn word, and if she refused, he'd . . . he'd . . . he didn't know what he'd do.

His mom was probably staring at that picture right now, every part of her aching. He could feel her betrayal as if it was his own. Years' worth of lying, of broken promises. He'd finally bared the darkest parts of his soul, and for the first time in memory, things had finally felt hopeful between them.

And Connor had taken it all away with a single picture.

It didn't matter that they would know everything tomorrow, assuming Nia let him say anything at all. That knowledge wouldn't erase the profound sense of hurt they felt now. That knowledge wouldn't erase his mother's tears or his father's prayers.

"You're angry at me," Connor said.

"I hate you," Tate admitted.

"Good. That one point needs to remain crystal clear: this relationship isn't about trust, it's about leverage."

The urge to punch Connor's teeth out was overwhelming, and if he let it, his fury would only build. But he wasn't giving in. He was ending this.

"Enough talk, Wolf. Let's finish the game."

Wolf had sent the dealer and cashier home when the others left, so only the two of them remained. Wolf took the dealer button and placed it in front of him. They posted their blinds and Wolf dealt. Keeping his cards on the table, Tate lifted up the corners to see a two of diamonds, nine of spades. When the flop gave him nothing, he folded.

Wolf collected the pot.

The next hand, Tate dealt. He had pretzels—a pair of eights. He bet, Connor called, and the flop came three of clubs, nine hearts, ten diamonds. Connor bet. Tate raised. He picked up a jack on the turn and a seven on the river for a straight, beating Connor's three of a kind.

And so it went.

For an hour, maybe more, they went back and forth, each winning a big hand here and there and losing just as often. They were as equally matched as anyone Tate had ever played against. When Connor had a monster hand, his play was identical to when he folded. He didn't push his chips in harder when he was bluffing than he did when he had the nuts. He was steady.

It wasn't like in movies, where the players talked to each other all the time. There were long periods of silence where the chips and cards did the talking. Tate liked it that way, liked tuning everything out except his opponent and the game. Evidently Connor did, too. Because every time Tate looked up, Connor was watching him. Always watching.

Connor's pot was larger than Tate's, and although the man didn't do anything in particular, he reminded Tate of a spider collecting flies. He had a way of staking a claim on something and assuming it was his. Like the way he always put his hole cards down near the board cards that had given him his win, or the way he kept his stack of chips a little closer to himself than necessary. It was stupid and possibly even in Tate's imagination. But it had given him a theory.

On Fourth Street, Tate had a draw hand. There were two

diamonds and two spades on the board, and another spade would complete his flush. The odds weren't great, but he needed a win to shift the pot back in his favor again. More important, he needed to test his theory. Connor had been running good the last hour, and Tate was pretty sure he had three of a kind now, with how the man's eyes had lingered maybe a fraction of a second longer on the jack Tate had dealt on the turn. Time to see if he was right.

Connor raised. Tate reraised.

"So now that you have me by the balls, don't you think it's time to be straight with me?" He dealt the river, keeping his gaze on Connor.

Connor glanced at the river card—the diamond Tate had just dealt—before returning to Tate. He bet. "What do you think you know?"

He was about to answer when Nia's voice popped in his ear. *"WE GOT IT! He kept a ledger, Tate, and we got it!"*

It was everything Tate could do to stay in his chair. The mic was working. Nia had the ledger. He felt as if a balloon was tied to each of his limbs, like the sun was rising in his chest, like . . . hell, he felt like standing on the table and dancing a jig. Tate looked at the table, at the third diamond, and he pushed a stack of chips in, anyway.

Connor was still looking at him, wearing a knowing smile.

Then the man folded.

He folded?

He hadn't deliberated for a moment, and even at his most aggressive, Connor deliberated. This was too abrupt. What had changed?

Nia was talking again, and she sounded like she was bouncing. Or high. *"I can't believe it, but we finally found it. It was in the nursery you told us about in a false bottom of the storage ottoman, of all places! I forgot to turn my comms back on, and Stew's been occupied, but we're already en route to you, and we're gonna bust this bastard tonight. We're maybe ten minutes out. Keep him occupied. I'll signal when we're getting close."*

Tate pulled his attention from Nia's words—those lovely, lovely words—to focus. He rethought the hand as he added the pot to his growing stack of chips.

Tate had been holding rags, but there were three diamonds on the table. Connor could have suspected Tate was holding a flush, but to fold fast like that on Fifth Street with a good hand? Why had he believed Tate now? What had been different about Tate's play?

Nia was still talking. *"I know you can't answer me, but I just can't keep it in, Tate! I'm freaking out!"*

He wanted to smile, but he . . .

He wanted to smile.

Holy hell.

He must have responded in some way to Nia. A tilt of his head, a light in his eyes, a quicker breath, something. That was why the man had been watching Tate so closely. Nia had been in his head all night. Tate knew he'd tugged on his ear at least once when she was yelling at him, right when he'd been begging Connor for a job.

The man had suspected it then, and he knew it now.

Tate had a tell.

It had nothing to do with cards but with the continued assault on his auditory canal, but Connor didn't know that. And that meant Tate could use it against him.

Connor pulled the dealer button in front of him, all the while watching Tate collect his chips. He repeated himself: "What do you think you know?"

Tate smiled. "I know Landolfo needs to learn to shut his mouth."

"Everyone knows that."

"And that guy—Sascha, was it? You and he have a sordid history."

"He showed up in the middle of the night. Not a tough guess."

"Well, then. Let's break it down by table position, shall we?" Tate said. They both tossed their blinds into the pot, and Connor dealt.

After a glance at his cards, Tate doubled the blinds. Connor was steeped in thought for a long moment—or at least he pretended to be.

"Mikey Landolfo, your good friend, is practically married to the mob. We both know it. It seems a large number of bars and clubs owned by rival gangs throughout the city have lost their liquor licenses of late."

"Have they?" Wolf asked, still deliberating.

"Yes," Tate said. "And, as everyone knows, having a liquor license is a requirement for operating a video gaming machine in any establishment. So, unfortunately, a lot of gangs have been negatively impacted by this very sudden and drastic loss of income."

Connor called. "I can imagine."

Connor dealt the flop, and Tate kept a watch on the man's eyes rather than the cards themselves. When Connor glanced for a heartbeat longer on one card than the others, Tate followed the man's gaze down to an ace of hearts. Next to it were the ten and jack of hearts.

Interesting.

With Connor's eyes on that ace, Tate could only assume he'd flopped a set. Tate drew on his memory of Nia's excitement and let himself feel a hint of a reaction to the board. He hoped it was the right reaction.

Tate bet.

Connor raised.

"Tony Wheeler has been a big contributor to Mayor Salter's reelection campaign, and I bet you dollars to doughnuts we're going to see Wheelz Trucks winning a very lucrative bid in the next couple of weeks." Tate tapped out an old piano piece he'd learned as a kid on the table. "Something tells me Virginia Gallo is in the same spot. If the casino proposal goes through, she's going to find more work for her little construction company than they've ever had, and the governor will be able to claim he's supporting local small businesses. That'll win him huge points."

Tate reraised, setting a large stack of chips in the pot.

"You think the governor is involved with this whole scandal you've imagined?"

"Of course I do," Tate said. "And as disappointing as it is, it looks like Judge Banks had a little help covering up a scandal that would have negatively impacted his chances of being elected to the state supreme court."

Connor smiled. "Can you imagine if someone had actually set Terry up, too? If they'd planted just the right—or wrong, as the case may be—intern as a honeypot before providing him with the means to cover it up, provided he give a favorable ruling here and there?"

The implications made Tate want to shiver. Connor returned to his study of the table—eyes flickering once more to that ace—and then he started shuffling two stacks of chips.

"Taylor's an interesting case, though," Tate said. "He's planning to make a run for senator, so he's, what, getting in good with the governor and all that implies? How does he hope to beat Rushworth?"

"Senator Rushworth will get some distressing health news soon and will, unfortunately, be unable to continue in office."

Nia was back in Tate's ear. *"What in the world is that supposed to mean?"*

"Wait, how do you—Cynthia," Tate said, answering his own question. "She found out the results of Rushworth's tests and gave them to you before he found out himself? That's despicable." When Connor didn't answer, Tate continued. "So the governor is planning to appoint Taylor? I've seen Chihuahuas with more composure."

Still no answer, which was hardly a surprise. The only real surprise was Connor giving him anything at all. Didn't the man have an iota of self-preservation? Did he really not care about what Tate could do with this information? Or did he simply not believe that Tate would—or could—do anything with it?

Yes, that was it. Connor wasn't stupid; he was proud. Too proud. And too used to winning in all aspects of life. His wealth and success meant that he couldn't imagine that anyone, let alone someone like Tate, was smart enough to take him down. He probably saw his relationship with the mob as purely tactical.

Connor called. He had less than half of his remaining stack in front of him now.

Whether the man knew it or not, the whole thing would be in the pot soon.

Connor dealt the turn: nine of hearts. In all his years of playing poker, Tate had never seen the board set up a straight flush so easily: the ace, jack, ten, and nine of hearts lay there for the taking.

Now to make sure Connor knew exactly who'd be taking it.

"That's quite an impressive list of sins," Connor said. "But everyone has a price, isn't that right?"

"Absolutely." Tate pretended to pause, to think, before making an aggressive bet. "Let's talk about yours."

"Go on," Connor said, looking at Tate's bet. He grabbed enough chips to match it.

"That man, Sascha. You and he worked together twenty-something years ago, huh? Was he your accountant?"

Connor's hand tensed around his chips, but he gave no other sign of being upset. "Yes."

"That must have sucked when he slept with your wife."

"He what?" Nia hissed in Tate's head. *"Fill me in later. We're two minutes out. Get ready."*

Connor clutched the stack till his knuckles went white. He pushed it into the pot, then another. He had only two small towers of chips left. Tate felt as if he was on a roller coaster, and his car was climbing, not quite to the top, but still mounting. Anticipation and excitement bubbled in his chest.

He couldn't wait.

"What would she do if she knew you set him up, that you were the reason he went to prison?" No answer. Tate pushed another stack of chips in. "Maybe I'll have the chance to tell her later, you know, now that you and I are going to be working together."

"You arrogant prick," Connor said, calling Tate's raise. "Do you really think I would ever let you come work for me?"

Tate put a hand over his heart. "Ouch, Connor. And I haven't even gotten to the good stuff yet, like you helping Landolfo screw NGC over, or how the mob made sure you're running so Nora doesn't prosecute the governor—"

"Shut up." Connor said.

Nia: *"We just entered the building."*

Connor picked up the deck and dealt the river.

Tate looked down at the table—at the river card that had sealed his fate—and laughed. He pushed his entire stack into the pot and locked eyes with Connor. "All-in."

"I don't think you have it," Connor said.

"Then find out."

Connor stared at the board, at those five cards, obviously trying to calculate the odds that Tate had the absolute, unbeatable, stone cold nuts.

His eyes flitted again to the ace. "All-in." Connor pushed his remaining stacks into the pot. He flipped over his hand to reveal what Tate already knew. Connor was holding aces. "Show me."

Nia: *"On our way up."*

"Tell me one thing first," Tate said.

Connor's stare hardened. "What?"

"Why do you hate your daughter?"

"I don't hate her—"

"She betrayed Nora, a woman who loves her more than anything in the world, just to get your approval. And it didn't work. Why?"

"You don't know what you're talking about."

"Yes, I do. You hate her. Yet you love your wife, and I know how badly you wanted Vivienne. Why?"

"Enough."

"Admit it, Wolf. Why do you still go into Vivienne's nursery when you can't even give an ounce of love to your own daughter?"

Connor pounded a hand on the table. "Because she's not mine!

She should have been Vivienne, but she's not! Now show me your damn cards!"

He'd known it was coming, but still, Tate felt like the room was spinning. He grabbed the sides of the table. Steady . . .

Nia: *"Just reached the seventh floor."*

Tate picked up his cards and stared a bit numbly at them before flipping them over: two of clubs, seven of diamonds.

His rags landed right next to the river card: the queen of spades.

Connor planted both hands on the table and sprang up. "I knew it! I knew you didn't have it!" He let out a low, mean chuckle. "You lying piece of shit. And here you tell everyone that you never bluff."

"I've never told anyone that, but I don't mind if other people do." Tate winked at him, leaning back in his chair and putting his feet up on the table. "For the record, though, I wasn't bluffing."

Nia: *"Outside the banquet hall. Waiting on your signal."*

Connor was shaking his head, arranging his chips. "You went all-in with the worst hand in poker, *and you lost.*"

"Ah, I think I see where the misunderstanding is coming from," Tate said. "Are you familiar with the game hearts?"

Wolf stopped stacking long enough to look up. "Yes."

"Then you should know I didn't lose. I shot the damn moon."

The doors to the private room burst open, and in poured the cavalry.

CHAPTER THIRTY-FOUR

N ia, her partner, and a half dozen officers had them surrounded. "What is this?" Connor yelled as Nia's partner cuffed him. "You can't be serious. Do you know who I am?"

"We do. You're Connor Wolf," the detective said. "And you're under arrest."

Nia grabbed Tate a little rougher than necessary, pinning his hands behind him while her partner read Connor his rights.

"Got to make this look good," she mumbled. "No one can know you were helping us."

With his hands behind him and Nia gripping his shoulder tightly, Tate smiled. He waited for a pause amid all the talk of fraud, extortion, and conspiracy to catch Connor's eye.

"See you in county, Wolf."

The detective and officers took Connor and his security guard downstairs, with Tate and Nia following. They marched them out through the main lobby where the only people awake were the hotel staff. Outside, the street and building lights illuminated the muggy predawn morning.

Connor and his security guard were both put in squad cars while Nia put Tate into the back of her SUV.

Sascha was already there. He looked exhausted, but his deep-set eyes were almost glowing. A few seconds later, Nia climbed in, and they were driving toward her precinct.

"I didn't think you'd mind company," Nia said, looking at Tate in her rearview mirror.

Tate was still looking at Sascha, studying his face. "You know, most people don't realize that Sascha is a Russian nickname. My buddy Yuri explained to me once that it's short for Alexander," Tate said. Sascha nodded. "Connor said he never loved Alex because she wasn't his. He said 'she should have been Vivienne.' But he wasn't talking about adoption, was he? You're Alex's dad. Alex *was* Vivienne."

"Yes."

"How?"

"About twenty-one years ago, I was his firm's accountant."

"And he set you up."

"Not immediately. He wasn't doing anything illegal then, but he worked eighty hours a week and had a lonely wife. She would come around the office at nights to see him, and he never had time for her. I thought she was the most beautiful person I'd ever seen. After a few months, we started an affair. She fell in love with me and wanted to leave him. I was poor, but she claimed not to care. She said she had enough money for both of us and we could start a new life together."

"Cynthia said that? Cynthia Wolf, the woman who cares more about money and reputation than her own child?"

"That is not the woman I knew. She was brimming with passion and love, and she gave it freely. Her parents never would have approved of her being with a poor immigrant, but that didn't stop her. She was willing to risk everything for love once."

"So what happened?"

"We had planned that she would talk to Connor, or at least leave him a note. She had leased an apartment for us, and we were supposed to meet there one night. She never showed up, but the police did. I don't know how long Connor had known about us, and for years, I thought Cynthia had been in on the setup. Connor made it look as if I was embezzling funds from the firm, and he put me away for fifteen years. Cynthia didn't show up in court, and I haven't heard from her since that day. I've hated her for twenty years. And she has hated me, too, so much that she never told me about our daughter."

"So is that why he got in with the mob? To frame you?"

Nia was shaking her head, but she didn't say anything.

"No," Sascha said. "Several months later, Cynthia delivered a beautiful, olive-skinned, black-haired, dark-eyed Russian daughter. I can imagine the magnitude of Connor's fury. He hired someone to change records and pay off staff to say that Cynthia's baby had died in childbirth. They sequestered themselves at home, as if in grief. Then a few months later, he hired someone again to make it look like they'd adopted a three-month-old baby from Bulgaria."

"So the mob has owned him for twenty plus years?"

"Actually, it might only be a year," Nia said. It had started to rain, and her wipers swiped across the windshield every few seconds. "My unit keeps close tabs on the Outfit, obviously, and last year, we saw them making moves into Cynthia's hospital, the same hospital where she delivered Alex. A handful of nurses, a board member, and the CEO all have mob ties. We still don't know if they learned about Connor and Cynthia's cover-up by going through records or if Connor had used someone on the mob payroll to cover up everything with Alex. Either way, though, by the time Connor had announced he was running for office, the mob owned him."

Tate held his head in his hands. "This is unbelievable."

"I know. It's like a soap opera," Nia said.

"No." Tate rubbed his forehead. "Imprisoning an innocent man? Pretending a baby died? A faked adoption? That's straight Dickens right there."

♠

Tate was at the precinct for hours, holed up in an interviewing room while Nia took his official statement. When he came out, he saw Cynthia and Alex waiting at Nia's partner's desk. The women had their arms folded and their legs crossed in identical fashion. It was strange to think that the resemblances between them were inherited, not simply learned.

"Does she know yet?" Tate asked.

Nia followed his gaze. "Which one?"

"Both, I guess."

"Not yet."

"Alex needs to talk to Sascha. She deserves to know."

"She'll find out soon enough. Cynthia altered medical records and falsified documents, or she was complicit, at the very least. The statute of limitations has probably expired, but it's all going to come out when Connor is charged. Cynthia will be removed from the Board at Mercy Hospital and ousted from every charity. He's going to prison, and she's going to be blacklisted."

Tate nodded, his eyes heavy and his head full of cards and chips. He wanted to close his eyes and dream of every hand he'd played against Connor. It was the best Tate had ever played, and thinking about it kicked his heart into a higher gear. The only thing he wanted to do more than savor the memory of that game was play another.

"You going to a meeting later?" she asked, stealing his attention.

He was annoyed, but he knew he shouldn't be. He *needed* to go to a meeting, even if he didn't want to. "Will you go with me?"

"Of course."

"Then I'll go. But I need something from you today, and you cannot say no, Nia."

"If you say money—"

"I need you to tell my parents that I was part of this investigation." He told her about Wolf taking a picture of them and sending it to his parents. Remembering that made him feel panicky, as if he was fraying at the edges. He didn't have the nerve to even check his phone, although he knew he deserved to engrave their pained messages on his heart. "My dad said he was proud of me for admitting I need help. After Connor's message, I don't know how he'll ever trust me again, but maybe if you talk to him—"

"Of course I will. I'll drive you home and we can tell them soon, okay?"

Emotion surged through him, making his eyes well. "Thank you."

"Go have a seat at my desk and I'll grab you in a few."

"Actually, do you mind if I'm the one to tell Alex?"

"About who she really is?" He nodded. "You can tell her anything that doesn't involve the case, but . . . be careful with her, Tate."

"I won't hurt her."

"She's not the one I'm worried about."

Tate walked around Nia's desk to get to where Alex and her mom were sitting. They were both facing the wall opposite him, so they didn't see him approach. "Can I talk to you?" he asked Alex.

"No," Cynthia said, looking at Alex in that same, imperious way she always used with her daughter. Yet Tate saw the facade for what it was. "He was brought in here along with your father. He's probably the reason your father is here in the first place."

Tate looked at Cynthia as he said, "Actually, her *father* is exactly the reason I want to talk to her." Alex looked up at him, the endless depths of her dark eyes drawing him in. "Please, Alex. I just want five minutes." He offered her his hand.

She glanced at her mother and then at Tate. After a pause, she took his hand. "Okay."

He pulled her to a stand, and as the two began walking, Cynthia said, "Please. Please don't."

Tate turned back to look at her, and for the first time since he'd known Cynthia Wolf, she looked her age. She was standing and wringing her hands. Her eyes were saucers. Her forehead was wrinkling and her brows were tugging together. The force of her regret and worry was making a final stand on her face. It was the most beautiful she'd ever looked.

"I'm sorry," Tate said.

He turned away from her, put his hand on Alex's back, and led her to the interview room.

For half an hour, they talked. For half an hour, Alex screamed and swore and denied everything before going practically catatonic. And for half an hour, Tate fought the urge to hold her and smooth her hair, to kiss her forehead and tell her everything would be okay.

It wouldn't be okay. Her life was crap. Despite her suffering, he didn't trust himself to comfort her. He didn't trust her with his heart.

So as she curled into a ball, rocking and hugging herself, he stood there and just watched. For what felt like ages, he watched and waited in silence.

Alex looked like a husk. A shell of herself. She sat on a chair hugging her legs tightly to her chest so only her eyes were visible behind her knees. When she finally spoke, her voice sounded as if someone had taken a cheese grater to it. "When I was twelve, I asked for one of those ancestry tests for Christmas. I was told I was adopted from Bulgaria, but I didn't know if I was Turkic or Romani or Slavic or what. So I wanted the DNA test that pinpoints exactly what your ancestry is and where you come from. I thought it would be cool to know. When I asked my parents, they acted so hurt and made this big show about how they weren't enough for me and how they'd failed me. I fell all over myself to prove to them that they were enough. I told them I didn't need a DNA test to know we were family and promised I'd never talk about it again. Then I asked them if, instead, we could go somewhere for Christmas, just the three of us. Do you know what they said? They said they thought it was too soon, that they were still *too hurt to go*. Like I'd mortally wounded them by simply asking to know where I came from. They kept that shit up for a month straight. I felt so guilty, I stopped eating, stopped showering. I didn't want to get out of bed. And then one morning, out of the blue, they whisked me away on a family vacation to Aspen for a weekend, just the three of us. They said they forgave me for hurting them and that they loved me, and they showered me with attention. I was so relieved that they loved me again. It was the happiest I've ever been. *And it was a lie.* They knew they'd manipulated me to the point that I'd never ask about my biological—" Alex hiccupped a sob, putting a hand over her mouth. "She's my *biological mom.*"

"I'm sorry, Alex," he said, wanting to say so much more, wanting to hold her and tell her he understood precisely why that realization was so painful.

His resolve was crumbling when she waved off his sympathy, tensing her jaw. "So, what now? Am I supposed to meet this man, start calling him 'Daddy' and then watch him die?"

"I think he'd want you to call him Sascha."

"You know what I mean. Why do you have to be such a dick?"

For her to act like this now, after everything, was too much. "I told you because I thought you needed to know. What you do now is up to you."

"Wait, where are you going?" she demanded.

He breathed out a weary laugh. "Why do you always do this? The second you let a glimpse of your humanity show, you turn around and go full ice queen on me. I know you're hurting. Anyone would be! You just found out your entire life is a lie, and I get why you would want to lash out and close yourself off to everyone, but I can't take it anymore! You know how much I care about you. Too much, frankly. I can't do this. I can't be a part of your life."

"I NEVER WANTED YOU IN MY LIFE!" she screamed. "You're like a . . . a black cat! You show up, and the worst possible things happen to me. You're my personal bad luck charm!"

"You are such a liar," he said, stabbing the air. "You can't handle seeing me because I'm the only person you know you could actually care about, and that goes against all of Mommie Dearest's programming! You're scared to death of feeling anything, especially with me. You think I'm a loser? At least I make my own choices! You're not even a person anymore, Alex! You're a puppet!"

"I hate you. I never want to see you again."

"That makes two of us."

Nia found him twenty minutes later sitting in the aisle of a nearby convenience store surrounded by three hundred dollars in scratch-offs.

Her hand fell heavily on his arm. "Come on. I'm taking you home."

When they arrived at his house, Aunt Nora answered the door. Her mouth fell.

"Still can't control those reactions, huh, Aunt Nora?" Tate said. Nia gripped his arm.

"What are you doing here?" she asked. She looked at Nia, who, in her dark pantsuit and slick ponytail, looked exactly like any detective on any TV show ever. "Did the police bring you home? What have you gotten yourself into now?"

Nia stepped in front of Tate. "Mrs. Mallis, can we come in? I need to speak to Mr. and Mrs. Bertram."

"Absolutely not," Nora said, glaring at Tate. "My sister got some *very* disturbing news last night, and she's not in a mood to see anyone."

"This is my house, Aunt Nora, and you don't know sh—"

"Stop arguing and get in the house," Tate's mother said. He looked past Nora to see his mom standing at the foot of the stairs in yoga pants and a sweatshirt that were loose on her. She looked worse than she had in the hospital, even, her face pale and gaunt and her eyes sunken.

Nora was clutching the door handle. "Mariah, I don't think—"

His mom's voice was quiet, but firm. "If my son wants to talk to me, I'm going to listen."

Nora muttered a curse but stepped aside for Tate and Nia.

"I'm sorry, Aunt Nora. I hope you'll let me explain," he said. She didn't answer.

Tate's mother invited them to come upstairs to the library, where Tate's dad was waiting. Tate helped her up every step, and when she put her arm around him, she gave his shoulder a small squeeze that made him want to cry. They reached the library and Tate saw his dad pacing. His eyes were puffy from crying, a look Tate remembered from the hospital last year.

Tate's voice broke. "Mom, Dad, this is Detective Nia Tafolo, from the Chicago PD. She's also my sponsor."

Nia shook both of their hands before they all sat.

"Mr. and Mrs. Bertram, thank you for your time. I want to assure you that your son's not in any kind of trouble," Nia said, though the words seemed to have little impact on his parents. They looked as if they were waiting for the other shoe to drop. "In fact, your son has been instrumental in helping us with a criminal investigation. I can't tell you the details, but I know you got a text last night with a picture that doesn't paint your son in a very good light. I want you to know that the picture was taken entirely out of context."

Tate's dad narrowed his eyes. "Was he or was he not gambling?"

Nia looked at Tate. He swallowed a heavy lump. "Yes, I was, Dad. I could tell you that I didn't have a choice, but I'd be lying. I did it to help Nia's case, and I was wearing a wire. But if she'd been there, there's no way she would have let me do it."

Nia nodded.

"It helped, though?" his mom asked.

"With the case? Immensely," Nia said. "Without going into detail, I can tell you that if everything works out the way I'm hoping, this will be one of the biggest cases in decades, and we couldn't have done it without Tate. But I worry that this will be a real setback with his addiction recovery."

"Why?" his mom asked.

Nia looked at Tate. "Because it's the last hand he's ever going to play. *Ever*. And he lost."

Tate smiled. "I won."

"Semantics." Nia's smile was more patient than it would have been in any other scenario. He was grateful for that. He was grateful for her.

His dad was fidgeting with the cuffs of his suit, and his brows were pulled tightly together. "Do you think the end justifies the means?"

Tate let his own brow wrinkle. "I don't know, Dad. But I hope rehab will give me some more clarity on this."

Surprise circled the room like a wave at a Cubs game.

"You're going to rehab?" his dad asked.

Tate tried to swallow again, to clear his throat. But something was lodged there. Years of regret didn't go down easily, it seemed. "I didn't believe I had a problem before, so I didn't give it a real chance. Things will be different this time."

"Do you still want to gamble?"

"More than anything," he admitted.

"When do you want to check in?"

"Tomorrow. I just need time to pack and I still need to take my . . . what time is it?" His eyes flew to the grandfather clock in the corner.

"What's wrong?" his mom asked, looking as if she was expecting a bomb to detonate.

"My last final! It starts in twenty-five minutes!"

"I can call your professor—" Nia started, but Tate cut her off.

"No, just abuse your police privileges and get me to campus, okay? Mom, Dad, I love you and I'm sorry. You can send Oliver to pick me up again after my exam, okay?"

The last glimpse he caught of his dad's face showed concern.

But as Tate dragged Nia downstairs at an ankle-breaking pace, he heard his mom call out, "Give 'em hell, son!"

CHAPTER THIRTY-FIVE

The next morning, Tate's bags were packed and resting by the door as he hugged his dad. His mom was on the phone in the study while Nia was waiting outside in her SUV.

"Are you sure you don't want us to come with you?" his dad said, his hands on Tate's shoulders, bags under his eyes. His parents had spent most of the night talking with him, and while it had been cathartic, there had been an unholy amount of crying. His dad's words.

"You and Mom deserve the rest," he told his dad, which was true. What he wasn't allowed to say, though, was that rehab was his cover. There would be talk of him being arrested for underage gambling, a plea deal, blah, blah, blah. The details were Nia's job.

Tate smiled at his dad. "For the first time in a year, you'll know where all your kids are tonight. That has to be worth a good night's sleep."

He cocked an eyebrow. "Do you really believe Juliette is still sleeping in a yurt in Flagstaff?"

"If I'm reforming, anyone can." He took out his phone. "Besides, one of her friends tagged her in a picture yesterday. They were spelunking, and it looks like a bat flew into her hair and got stuck."

His dad chuckled at the picture before giving a sad smile. "Hopefully she comes home soon, too."

"We all find our way back eventually."

The door to the study opened, and Tate's mom came out. "You'll never believe who that was," she said, shuffling over to them. "Cynthia Wolf. She said she's heard that my pain hasn't been managed well, and she gave me the name of a new doctor who specializes in alternative pain management. She's going to e-mail me some studies that back up his methodology. Wasn't that kind of her?"

"Very," Tate said.

"That's great, Mariah," his dad said, kissing the side of her head. She leaned into him with a contented sigh. For everything they'd been through over the last year, they were totally devoted to each other. Tate was glad Alex had never seen his parents together. Looking at how perfectly the two of them fit was almost like looking at the sun. It would have blinded the girl.

"I should really get going," Tate said, glancing at his feet. "And again, I'm sorry. For everything."

His parents wrapped him in a warm hug. "Don't be sorry," his mom said. "Just get better."

"And remember how much we love you," his dad added. "How much we will always love you."

"I love you guys, too."

Tate climbed into the back of the car, still sniffing.

"You ready to go?" Nia asked. She was wearing a loose dress and flip-flops in place of her usual pantsuit. The change felt symbolic, as if she was telling him this was personal, even if she was supposed to be his court-mandated escort. He appreciated the gesture.

"Actually, do you think we can make one more stop?"

"If you think we're stopping for doughnuts—"

"It's not doughnuts. I want to say good-bye to Sascha."

She started the car. "Let's go."

Tate had expected a Powerball winner to live in a mansion, or at least something with its own driveway. Instead, Tate found himself knocking on the door of a twelfth-story apartment in Hyde Park, only a few blocks from Yates's apartment. The building had probably been nice enough once, but it was showing its age. Tate looked at the worn carpet and faded walls while he waited for Sascha to answer.

The door swung open.

"What do you need?" Sascha asked.

"Nothing," Tate said. "Don't worry. I'm leaving for rehab and wanted to say good-bye."

Sascha looked him over. "Good for you. Come in."

Tate closed the door and followed Sascha to a sitting room with a nice view of the bay. He sat across from the older man. "So, how are you doing?"

"Still dying."

"Yeah, you've mentioned that once or twice," Tate said with a dark chuckle. "I mean otherwise. Have you talked to Cynthia? Or Alex?"

"Alex called me yesterday. I doubt Cynthia will call."

"Why wouldn't she?"

"I'm a reminder of her greatest mistake. Why else would she have named Alexandra after me?"

"Maybe because she still loved you."

"I can't believe that. It's more likely that she hated Connor so much. She stopped allowing herself to enjoy love or happiness years ago. Knowing her, I imagine she's channeled all of that emotion into her pride. And her pride is a terrifying thing."

"Yeah, so is her daughter's." Tate looked out the window to see geese swimming on the water.

"Alexandra is hurting. She doesn't know who she is. Surely you can sympathize."

"I can and do," Tate said. Sascha rubbed the back of his head, and Tate remembered something. "You said you broke into Nora's house to get something that was yours. What was it?"

"I stole Alexandra's brush," Sascha said. "I'd heard the story about her adoption and confronted Cynthia about it. She fed me the same lie, so I stole the brush and had a DNA test done to prove that Alexandra is my daughter. She thought I only wanted proof for the bone marrow transplant." He shook his head.

"Didn't you?"

"Of course not," Sascha said. "If your 'buddy Yuri' taught you nothing else about Russians, it should have been how important family is to us. As important as God and country. Not raising my daughter is the greatest shame of my life; your friendship with her is what kept me helping you long after I wanted to stop." He looked both broken and stubbornly proud as he said this. Like a crumbling statue. "I want to know my daughter before I die, and I will leave her everything I have. I don't want her taking a cent of Wolf's money. Or Cynthia's."

"I know Alex better than anyone," Tate said, wanting to weep for how painful that truth was. "I know how much she'll appreciate it."

Sascha's smile looked rusty. "I'm glad. Thank you."

Tate's nose tingled. "Anyway, I'd better go. I'll probably be gone for . . . I don't know. However long it takes, but I hope you'll be here when I get back."

"I hope so, too. Good luck, Tate."

"Thanks." They both rose, and Tate gave the man a hug. He was thinner than he had been even a couple of weeks ago, no doubt a result of being terminally ill. "Thanks for looking out for me."

Sascha gripped Tate's shoulder with surprising firmness. "Thank you for caring for my daughter."

With a smile and a wave, Tate left Sascha at the door. He walked out into the hall to find someone pacing.

"Alex?" Tate said. The girl was wearing a White Sox hat, shorts, and one of Tate's t-shirts. He thought he'd left it at Nora's.

She spun around, and he saw that she was biting a fingernail. She dropped her hand, but not before he noticed her engagement ring was missing. "Tate? What are you doing here?"

"I came to say good-bye."

"You're leaving?"

"I'm going to rehab, not that it's any of your business."

She blinked hard. "Oh. Um, is—"

"He's inside. Go easy on him, okay? He's a decent man; he doesn't deserve your wrath." Tate turned from her and walked down the hall.

"Tate?"

He pressed the elevator button, worried about the next words that would come out of her mouth, but unable to keep himself from asking. "What?"

"Do you—do you think he'll like me?"

He closed his eyes, nodding. "He's going to love you, Alex." The elevator dinged, and the doors slid open. "In fact, he already does."

"Oh. Thanks."

He walked into the elevator and stared at his reflection in the metal. The doors had already closed and the elevator had begun its descent when he braved speaking. "You're welcome."

CHAPTER THIRTY-SIX

Tate's hand was in his pocket, playing with a chip, feeling the ridges around the edge in a comforting, if nostalgic, way. He felt a small flutter of nerves in his stomach. Instinct told him to squash them, to wipe his expression perfectly blank. Instead, he let himself blink a bit too quickly and breathe a little faster than normal.

"Hi, everyone." He was met with a couple of waves. "I'm Tate, and I'm an addict."

"Hi, Tate," the group said.

He looked at the twenty-two faces he'd come to know in the last two months. "It's been kind of a rough day. I went to the funeral of someone I didn't know very well but who made a big difference in my life. His name was Sascha, and he had leukemia. His daughter is kind of an ex of mine, and she was there, too. We haven't spoken since I left for rehab, and seeing her today, especially there, was . . . rough. Like a punch to the gut after being stabbed in the gut, feelings I know all too well." A few people laughed. "She and Sascha only met a few months ago, and I've been pretty angry at her, for a lot of reasons. I'm angry that she was able to get to know him while I was stuck in rehab. Don't get me wrong, I'm grateful I went, but I can't ever get that time back. I missed a lot, like getting to know Sascha and going to my friend Juana's wedding and campaigning with my aunt."

He thought of the letters he'd written Nora in rehab, as well as her final response: "I forgive you for lying. And I forgive Alex, too. Just get better and come home."

He was grateful she'd understood and had forgiven him. But he was still hurt that she'd forgiven Alex so easily . . . as easily as she'd written him off.

"I've been home for a couple of months, but I'm . . . I'm still angry at all of them for letting life go on without me," he said, clutching the chip in his pocket. "But I'm more angry with myself for being so weak in the first place. I'm angry that I could let gambling take control of my life like that. The worst part is that even now, I still want to gamble. I miss it. I miss the feel of the cards in my hands and the smell . . ." He shook his head. "Sorry, that can't be helping anyone, can it?"

There were a couple of head shakes and a few laughs.

"I'm really mad at my ex, or whatever she is. Her last name was listed as Sascha's last name in the program. She cut her parents out of her life entirely and changed her name. And she gave a eulogy and cried. You don't know this girl, but she has made it her life's work never to cry, and here she was weeping openly. She was talking about how much Sascha loved her and how she'd never felt such unconditional love from anyone before, and how she wished that her bone marrow transplant could have saved him, and how she wished that she'd have known him sooner so she could have donated sooner, and all I could think was: Who are you? Why wasn't my love enough? You wanted unconditional love, but you rejected mine? It made me feel so worthless, like I must be the stupidest, most pathetic person on the planet." He didn't know when the tears had started, but he let them fall as he shifted from one foot to another. "Deep down, I know that's the addiction talking. I know that I used gambling as a way to cover up my insecurities and as a replacement for the things I didn't feel like I was getting from the people I loved, even though my gambling prevented me from getting those same things in the first place."

He felt his thoughts derailing, so he pulled the chip out of his pocket and held it up for the room to see. "But I also know that it's been four months since I last gambled, and I'm not losing another second to my addiction. So, uh, thanks for listening."

He sat, and Nia leaned over to him. "Well said."

After the meeting, the two of them went down to the chapel. It was their ritual after every meeting now. Although half the time, they didn't say much, today, he could tell Nia had news. She was a little too eager, leaning forward maybe half an inch farther than normal.

As soon as they sat in the pew, he said, "Spill."

She flicked him in the shoulder. "Should you be reading people?" she whispered.

"Come on, it's a life skill, not just a poker skill. Like you don't read people in your job?"

"I'll give you that," she conceded. "How's your mom?"

"Really good. The new specialist has adjusted some of her medications and has her on a paleo diet and even doing strength training. She's the best she's been in years." And he still couldn't believe they had Cynthia Wolf to thank for it.

Nia smiled. "And your dad?"

"Busy, but good. He's been hinting to me that he needs a new intern, but I don't think I'm going to do it. I still care too much what he thinks, and that's not the healthiest dynamic for me."

"You sound like a recovering addict, you know that?"

"I've been called worse. By you, no less." She shrugged. "Besides, I think I want to be a district attorney. Work alongside the police, and all that."

Her lips drew into a big grin. "We'd be lucky to have you."

"Thanks, Nia. Okay, we've gotten the niceties out of the way. Now spill."

"This is totally confidential. If you tell anyone—"

"You'll have me arrested, yeah, yeah. I know. Spill."

"Okay, but only because you're still my informant," she said, as if she wouldn't have told him anyway. "I'm not sure if you want to know this, but your last game with Connor has finally paid off." Tate sat up straighter. "We wouldn't have even known where to investigate without it, Tate. But that gave us enough to get warrants for wire taps, and we've found enough to charge them with corruption, extortion, attempts to sell the senate seat, pay-to-play, you name it. Everyone at that card game and the governor. They'll all be behind bars tomorrow morning. And you were right about Judge Banks—he was willing to testify for a reduced sentence."

"Wow, that's awesome!" He struggled to put the right enthusiasm behind the words.

She wrinkled her nose at him. "Do you wish I hadn't told you?"

"I'm glad you told me. And honestly, I know I can't gamble again—I do—but I'm glad something good came from my playing poker, for a change. That last game, Nia. I went out in a blaze of glory."

She smiled. "Maybe, but I still can't believe you let yourself get that B in your class."

He groaned. "B minus."

"Why'd you take the grade instead of letting me talk to the professor? You could have taken the exam without falling asleep in the middle of it."

"Because it was my choice to play cards, not yours. It's the grade I earned."

She paused before patting his shoulder. "You're pretty smart for a dumb frat boy." He chuckled, shaking his head. "You sticking around?" she asked.

"For a bit, yeah. I'll see you next week?"

"I'll bring the dumplings," she said.

After Nia left, Tate said a prayer for Sascha. He didn't know how prayers worked on the other side, or if they worked at all, for that matter. But he prayed all the same. He couldn't stop thinking of

Sascha's lifeless body in that casket, his lips stretched into an unnatural smile. Or maybe it had been natural to someone else. Like Alex.

The image of her tears was burned into the backs of his eyes. He said a prayer for her, too.

And then he pulled out his books and studied. It was peaceful in the chapel, and watching Fin and Oliver make out at his and Ollie's apartment was more than he could handle tonight.

When he'd finished the last of his homework, he stowed his books in his bag and walked out of the Chicago Temple building into the brisk November evening. Snow crunched beneath his feet, and his breath rose in little clouds in front of his face. He watched one of the clouds until it evaporated.

Which was when he saw her.

It was surreal to go from thinking about her to seeing her now. Almost dreamlike. Tate thrust his hands into his pockets. He gripped the coin but didn't say anything.

"Hey, Tate" she said, her eyes glossy and her nose red from the cold.

"Hey, Alex."

"I, um, I thought you might be here tonight."

"Yup. I was. Good guess."

She nodded, shivering beneath her pea coat. "Actually, I've come the last five nights hoping I'd see you here."

He cocked his head. "Hang on. The meeting ended over two hours ago. How long have you been waiting?"

"I got here just after the meeting started."

"And you've been out here the whole time?"

"Mostly in the lobby. And once I went to the bathroom, and I really hoped I wouldn't miss you, so I asked a custodian to keep an eye out for you. I was worried he missed you, too."

"He didn't miss me."

"I did."

He held his arms out to the sides. "I'm right here."

"That's not what I meant." She sounded choked.

"What did you mean?"

She closed her eyes for a long moment. "You're really going to make me work for this, aren't you?"

"Oh my word, yes."

When her eyes opened, tears clung to her lashes, and the sight sent little pricks of heat straight to his cold heart. "I missed you, Tate. Everything you said was right, about me and my mom and . . . and Connor, and everything. I was too angry and too hurt to admit the truth, and you know what a number my mom did on me for all those years. Imagine being told since you were a little kid that love is a lie and that the only way to keep someone interested in you is to always hold something back. It's been hard to get past. It all has." Her clasped hands were trembling. "But I've been seeing someone—a therapist, not a guy—and I'm working through a lot, and part of what I've realized is how terribly I treated you and why I did it." She took a small step closer to him.

"And why was that?"

"Because you were everything my mother had always warned me against: someone I wanted to have a relationship with because of things like attraction, friendship, and enjoyment instead of things like stability, reputation, and wealth."

"Telling me I'm not stable enough for you isn't winning a lot of points right now."

"No, that's not what I meant!" she cried, waving her hands as if she could erase the words. He liked seeing her scramble more than he should have, and he had no intention of stopping it. "I'm . . . I'm trying to say that I've learned a lot about myself and about life since I met Sascha. He told me how much he regretted not going to see my mom the minute he got out of prison. And at the same time, even though she'd never admit it, I know my mom regrets having believed my fath—Connor when he lied about Sascha using her for access to the company accounts. They both made so many mistakes, and I don't want to make them, too."

"I'm happy for you," he said. Seeing her like this—asking for forgiveness without actually asking anything—warmed him. The ice around his heart was melting, dripping off into a little, swirling pool in his stomach. "But it's cold, Alex, and I kind of need to go, so . . ." He shrugged. "See you around."

She growled. "I'm trying to say sorry, I'm baring my effing soul, and you're shrugging it off? Work with me here, Tate!" Then she winced. "No, this isn't your fault, I'm just—"

"Alex?" he said.

"Yes?"

"Next time you apologize, try using the actual words."

She stepped right in front of him and held his arms, her eyes pleading. "I'm so sorry, Tate! I'm sorry I rejected you and called you all those horrible things and didn't want to listen to you. I'm sorry I was too blinded by my mother's cynicism and Connor's neglect and disdain to recognize something real when it was right in front of my face! I'm sorry about Brooks, and about hurting Nora and framing you and messing everything up, and I don't know how you'll ever forgive me when I still can't even look at myself in the mirror. Okay?" Tears rolled down her cheeks, leaving a frosty trail on her face. "Is that what you want to hear? Do you want to hear that I think I loved you, and I'm terrified I've ruined any chance at you ever loving me back?"

Tate wanted so badly to pull her to his chest, to smooth her hair and kiss her forehead and tell her everything would be okay.

So he did.

She cried against his shoulder, clinging to him as he held her. After her tears dried up, she pulled back and searched his eyes. "I'm sorry, Tate. I'm so sorry."

Tate reached a hand up to her face, letting his fingers graze her cheek as he brushed the single remaining tear from it. She tilted her head up at his touch, and he leaned in, kissing her. Her lips were soft and salty, and the taste thawed him completely.

He bumped his forehead against hers, and their noses were touching.

"So?" Her eyes were so warm and inviting, he wanted to move in. "Can you forgive me?"

"Only if you can beat me at hearts."

She laughed, kissing him again and again until they were both smiling too much to kiss anymore. When they broke apart, she took his hand and guided him to her car. "And here I thought you weren't gambling anymore," she said when they got inside.

"Just on us, Alex Lunov. Just on us."

THE END

ACKNOWLEDGMENTS

Writing acknowledgments once was dreamlike. Writing them a second time, it turns out, is equally surreal. Maybe even more so, because at this point, people I don't know are reading these. Like, actual, honest-to-goodness *readers*. So, if you made it this far, thank you from the bottom of my heart. Ten points to Ravenclaw!

Huge thanks to my agent extraordinaire, Dawn Frederick, for taking me under her wing and for kicking butt and taking names. When things got bumpy there for a bit, I knew I was in good hands. I couldn't be happier to be Team Red Sofa.

I am once again in awe of my editor, Kelsy Thompson. You are a wizard, and I can't imagine this story reaching its potential in anyone else's hands. Thank you. And thanks to the entire incredible team at Flux, including Mari Kesselring, McKelle George, Megan Naidl, and those who've worked tirelessly behind the scenes to bring Tate's story to life.

Thanks to Robert Woolley, who blogs as Poker Grump, for letting me borrow his bad beat story and for introducing me to (and getting me hooked on) bad beats, in general. Thanks for lending your expertise.

I owe a debt of gratitude to my reader, Lisa Thao, for helping me make Tate's world a more beautiful one. Thank you for your thoughtful, caring insight.

To the BYU Philosophy department: Tate should be so lucky as to learn from you. And to my favorite professor, Dr. K. Codell Carter, thank you for changing my mind about Kant and for instilling in me a life-changing, mind-expanding love of philosophy.

I have a tremendously supportive writing community consisting of too many people to name (which is my way of apologizing in advance to whomever I miss). Huge hugs to my fellow debuts, Storymakers, and sassy soul sisters: Katie Nelson, Emily King, Breeana Shields, Rosalyn Eves, Tricia Levenseller, Caitlin Sangster, and Ellie Terry. This adventure has been all the more enjoyable and enriching because of your friendship. Special thanks to the aforementioned Katie and Emily as well as to Anna Priemaza for letting me break down in a safe, nurturing space and for building me up afterward. To the entire Class of 2K17 and AZ YA/MG crew: thanks for all the love, friendship, and support.

I'm beyond grateful for my critique group, Darci Cole, Heather Romito, and Stacey Leybas, and for the continued insight of my writing bestie, Gina Denny. I love your guts. To Eileen Souza, thank you for understanding how painful it was to write Alex's adoption story line and for catching the significance of the milkshakes. To my soulbestie, Aubrie Baird, thanks for genuinely thinking everything I write is genius (even when it isn't) and for just being amazing and you. Ah! FEELINGS!

As always, thanks to my super fab sis Molly Tagge for reading every word I write and for making my career a priority in your already busy life. I owe you a fountain of Diet Coke in which you can bathe your way into glorious immortality, no matter what Ben says. Thanks for coaching me through Tate's addiction and for fleshing Alex out into the tortured little monster she is. To Ben and Cheryl Bikman, my resident Russia experts: spasibo. Or however you say "thank you" in Russian (that's what I use you guys for, let's be real). And my eternal thanks to Joel Bikman for reading this for the poker and loving it for me.

To my entire Bikman/Cooper-Leavitt and White family, I love you. Thank you for going out of your way (in some cases, literally) to continue to support, promote, encourage, and love me. Best. Family. Ever.

Most importantly, again—always—thank you to Jeff, Elsie, and Hugo. You three are my whole heart. Every day with you is a study in love, selflessness, and the joy of sacrifice (i.e., giving up something of value (e.g., sleep) for something of greater value (e.g., every second with you)). And you know I mean business, because I'm doubling up on parentheses, which you know my tangential heart loves greatly. Well, Daddy knows. Elsie and Hugo, you're still super young, and even as bright as you are, I doubt you can grasp . . . wait. I'm doing it now, aren't I? Sorry. Anyway. Point is, I love you three to complete and utter distraction. You are my best, best, best.

ABOUT THE AUTHOR

Kate Watson is a young adult writer, wife, and mother of two and the tenth of thirteen children. Originally from Canada, she attended college in the States and holds a BA in Philosophy from Brigham Young University. A lover of travel, speaking in accents, and experiencing new cultures, she has also lived in Israel, Brazil, and the American South, and she now calls Arizona home. Kate's first novel, *Seeking Mansfield*, debuted in 2017, and she contributed a short story to Eric Smith's *Welcome Home* adoption anthology. *Shoot the Moon* is her second novel.

GLOSSARY OF TERMS
Hearts

Hearts - A card game where the player with the fewest points at the end of the game wins. After each hand, penalty cards are assessed. Players holding heart cards will receive one point for each heart card they hold, while the player holding the queen of spades will be assigned an additional 13 points.

Shoot the moon - Shooting the moon is a strategy whereby a player intentionally gets all 26 penalty (point) cards in a round. If successful, the player who shoots the moon will be assigned zero points for the round and each of the other players will be assigned 26 points.

Texas Hold 'em

Texas Hold 'em - A form of poker in which players are dealt two individual cards (hole cards), and then five community cards are dealt face up on the board in three stages: the *flop*, or first three board cards, the *turn*, or fourth card, and the fifth and final board card, the *river*. Players seek to make the best possible five-card combination using their hole cards and the community cards on the board. Betting occurs before the flop and then again after each subsequent deal. After each deal, players may fold, check, call, or raise.

Poker Hand Rankings

Straight flush - Five cards of the same suit in sequential order, e.g., A, 2, 3, 4, 5 of diamonds.

Four of a kind - Four cards of the same rank, e.g., 2 spades, 2 hearts, 2 diamonds, 2 clubs.

Full house - Three cards of the same rank (three of a kind) and two cards of the same rank (two of a kind), e.g., 10 spades, 10 hearts, 10 diamonds + 3 clubs, 3 spades.

Flush - Five cards of the same suit.

Straight - Five cards in sequential order, offsuit.

Three of a kind - Three cards of the same rank.

Two pair - Two cards of the same rank plus two cards of a different rank, e.g., 4 hearts, 4 spades + Q diamonds, Q clubs.

Pair - Two cards of the same rank, e.g., 7 clubs, 7 spades.

High card - In the absence of any better hand, the player with the highest card will win.

Player Actions

Call - To match a bet.

Check - To pass; to decline opening a betting round while still staying in play.

Fold - To lay down your cards as a way of removing oneself from a hand, thereby forfeiting any money previously bet.

Raise - To increase the previous bet; to increase the stakes.

Terms

Aggressive - A style of play where someone bets aggressively to increase the size of a pot or to pressure other players to fold.

Aggro - An aggressive player.

Aggrodonk - A poor player who consistently plays aggressively.

All-in - To bet all one's chips on a hand.

Backdoor - A draw hand that is made on the turn and river.

Bad beat - A hand that is lost despite the strong odds of winning.

Bet - To wager money on a hand.

Blind - A forced bet made at the beginning of a hand.

Bluff - To bet or raise, despite having a weaker hand than an opponent, with the intention of pressuring opponents to fold.

Board cards - The community cards dealt faceup on the board for the use of all players, comprising the flop, turn, and river.

Brush - A poker room employee who assists in making sure games run smoothly. Often assigned to manage seating and player lists, buy and run chips, and more. In smaller operations, the brush will typically have more responsibility than in larger ones.

Burn card - A card the dealer removes from the top of the deck and discards before dealing the flop, turn, and river, respectively.

Cash Out - To exchange the rest of one's chips for cash when leaving a game.

Cover - To have more chips than another player.

Culling - A form of cheating in which a dealer identifies a card and deals it only to her accomplice.

Dealer button - A marker to identify which player is acting as dealer in a game; in games with a designated dealer, it serves to identify who acts last on a hand.

Donk - A donkey. A derogatory term for a very poor poker player.

Doyle Brunson - One of the most famous modern poker players. When referring to a pocket hand, it means a ten and two of different suits, a hand with which Doyle Brunson famously won two back-to-back World Series of Poker titles in the 70s.

Draw - A weak hand that has the potential to become strong post-flop.

Eagle - One of Phil Hellmuth's poker animals. Refers to only the most elite professionals in the game.

Fifth Street - see *river*.

Flop - The first three community cards dealt faceup on the board after the first betting round is over.

Flop a straight - To have a straight after the flop is dealt, made with the two hole cards a player was dealt and the three cards in the flop.

Flop the nut straight - To have the best possible straight post-flop.

Four Horseman - Four kings.

Fourth Street - See *turn*.

Full of - Three cards with two others; e.g., Aces full of kings would mean a full house consisting of three aces and a pair of kings.

Hand odds - The likelihood of one's cards winning a hand.

High-five - A hand consisting of an ace ("high" card) and a five.

Hit by the deck – A run of very good hands.

Hole - Two private cards dealt to each player.

House – The host, typically the cardroom or casino.

Maniac – A term for someone playing a lot of hands aggressively.

Monster - A very big hand.

Mouse - One of Phil Hellmuth's poker animals. Refers to someone who plays very conservatively and with strict rules for play. A mouse will very rarely bluff.

Muck - To fold your hand; also refers to the discard pile.

Nit - A very tight, risk averse player.

Noob - A new, inexperienced player.

Nut hand (the nuts) - The best possible hand at a given time. Folklore attributes the origins of the term to the Old West, where a player would go all-in by betting his horse and wagon. To do so, he would put the nuts from his wagon's wheels into the pot, demonstrating not only his confidence in his hand, but also that he would make good on the bet, as he would be unable to run if he lost. Thus it was assumed that one would only bet "the nuts" with an unbeatable hand.

Phil Hellmuth - One of the best modern professional poker players.

Plus - Money the house owes to a player.

Pocket - Hole cards.

Poker animals - A system of classifying poker players set forth by Phil Hellmuth.

Pot - All the money that has been bet on a particular hand.

Pot odds - The ratio of the size of the pot to the cost to call.

Pre-flop - The first betting round that occurs based on the hole cards before the community cards are dealt.

Pretzels - A pair of eights.

Quad - Four of a kind.

Rags - Cards of low value.

Rainbow - Cards of different suits; offsuit.

River - The fifth and final community card that is dealt face up on the board. Also called *fifth street.*

Royal Couple - The king and queen of diamonds.

Royal Flush - An ace-high straight flush in any suit; the best possible hand in Hold 'em.

Running bad - Having a run of bad luck.

Running good - Having a run of good cards or good luck.

Set - Three of a kind. Also called a *trip.*

Show your hand – To unintentionally give away details one intended to keep private.

Slow-play - A deceptive play where a player's betting makes it appear as if one has a weak hand when it is, in fact, strong.

Stacked against - Refers to what appears to be an unfairly unfavorable situation; in gambling, if the cards are stacked against someone, it means they are purposefully arranged in a way that will keep the person from winning.

Stacking and racking - Running good.

Steal - To raise during the opening round of betting in order to intimidate players into folding; To reraise.

Steel Wheel - A five-high (A, 2, 3, 4, 5) straight flush.

Strong Draw - A weak hand that has the potential to become a straight or flush post-flop.

Tell - A subconscious behavior that can give hints about an opponent's hand.

Tight - To play fewer hands than normal, whether compared to oneself or to other players.

Tilt - Refers to compromised, reckless play, often as a result of emotional decision-making.

Trip - Three of a kind.

Turn - The fourth community card that is dealt face up on the board. Also called *fourth street*.